The Necklace IV

Brighton – December, 1999

Linda S Rice

ISBN 1517478804
ISBN 13: 9781517478803
Library of Congress Control Number: 12661710045

Acknowledgments

Many thanks to friends, acquaintances and relatives, who encouraged me to move forward with publishing *"The Necklace – The Dusky Club, June 1962,"* the first book in the series, the sequels, *"The Necklace II – Back to Brighton, November 1962,"* and *"The Necklace III – London, 1967,"* and now this fourth book that continues the time-travel adventures of Susan in her quest to be with James, a member of "the most famous band of all time."

Special thanks to my sister-in-law, Nancy Flood, for her editing help and to my numerous Facebook friends, for their encouragement and time spent previewing this work. Also, thanks to Siobhan Deason, who assisted once more in the cover design, and to my cover models, Viki Navardauskaite and Daniel Reyes.

Lastly, and most importantly, I'd like to thank my husband, Michael, for his patience while I wrote, re-wrote, revised and edited over the many months it took me to complete all four of these books.

Stay tuned for the next book of the series, *"The Necklace V – Strawberries & Wine"* which will be available in August 2016. After that… the final book of the series, *"The Necklace VI – Snow on the Mountain."*

To contact the author, e-mail Linda at: LindainMtLaguna@aol.com or visit her website at www.LindaSRice.com. Connect with Linda on Facebook at https://www.facebook.com/TheNecklaceLindaSice or on Twitter at @Lindainmtlaguna.

Prologue

It was March, 1987. James was standing in front of the glass display window of a high-end jewelry store in the Galleria Mall in Costa Mesa, California. As was usual when out in public, he was in disguise, this time with a gray wig, mustache and beard. His attention was focused on a row of diamond watches, and he was wondering which one his wife might like for their eighteenth wedding anniversary. Not that she didn't already have quite a few expensive watches, but he was at a loss at to what else to get since he'd waited until the last minute and felt pressed to get something before he left the mall.

As he glanced to the side, a young girl with long blonde hair came up to stand next to him, also gazing in at the watches. He heard her give a heavy sigh and mutter under her breath, "Too expensive…I guess I shouldn't have waited…"

He looked over at her briefly before saying, "You too then? Here it's my anniversary tomorrow, and I can't figure out what to get my wife."

The girl seemed embarrassed, knowing he'd heard her musings, but turned and looked at him. She appeared to be a young teen, possibly thirteen or fourteen years old with blue-green eyes the color of the ocean, and a very pretty face. She reminded him of someone, but he couldn't quite think of who.

"Yeah, it's my grandma's birthday tomorrow and she just broke her watch. My mom and I were thinking to get her a new one. I guess maybe I need to go to a place like Walmart though…" She looked back at the display window. "These are stupid expensive."

When she tossed her head and some of her hair flew around her shoulder, a sudden jolt hit James as a memory of an older girl with long blonde hair and green eyes flashed into his head. He closed his eyes for a moment, conjuring up the memory, and it wasn't long before a face came into focus in his head…followed by a name…

Susan.

Not Susan, his wife, but another Susan. One he'd tried to erase from his memory, and who he'd been pretty successful at obliterating from his mind since one disastrous day almost twenty years ago.

When he opened his eyes, however, it was impossible for him to take his gaze from the profile of the young girl, and when she turned to look at him again, she started to feel uneasy.

He immediately sensed it. "I'm sorry…I don't mean to be staring at you," he said. "You just remind me of someone else…someone I used to know a long time ago…"

"Oh yeah?" She seemed to relax. "Hey, you have an accent. Are you from England or something?"

"Yeah. I'm just here…visiting…"

In reality, he and his new band, which included his wife, were in Los Angeles recording a new album. He'd slipped away to the mall while she was taking their three children for a second day at Disneyland.

"My mom's always wanted to go to England, but I think it's because she liked this famous band when she was younger. You probably heard of them. They were known as the greatest band of all time…but then they broke up or something…"

James froze, his brain spinning. The young girl continued. "She has like all their records and everything and still plays them all the time… and it's really funny 'cause she goes nuts when she hears this one song. Her face gets all weird and she acts like she was just struck by a lightning bolt or something. It makes my brother and me laugh."

He tried to stop his heart from beating fast. "Yeah, I've heard of that band…So, what song makes her go all nuts and weird?"

"It's called *'All My Kisses.'* You probably haven't heard of it…She gets all funny looking in the face and moans things like, *'Oh, James'* and Steven...that's my brother...we just laugh. Now give me Guns N Roses or Van Halen..."

James had to steady himself and take a deep breath before he could speak. His face had paled. The young girl looked at him quizzically. "Hey...something wrong? You havin' a heart attack or something? One of my grandpas died of a heart attack..."

He shook his head before finding his voice, which was barely a whisper. "Your mother...her name...it wouldn't happen to be Susan, would it?"

She stepped back a few feet, eyeing him suspiciously and started to feel uneasy again.

"Does she, by any chance, wear a silver necklace with ballerina shoes on it?"

"How did you know that!!?" she exclaimed, starting to feel panicked. Then she caught herself, not wanting him to know her mother's name for some reason. "...Maybe that's her name...maybe it isn't... maybe you shouldn't be asking...maybe..."

With those words, she turned on her heel and ran as fast as she could through the throng of people, looking over her shoulder every now and then to see if the creepy old guy was following her.

When she got to the escalator in the middle of the mall where she was to meet up with her mother, she was relieved to see her there.

"Mom! Mom!" she yelled, grabbing her mother's arm. "Let's get out of here. Some creepy old man with gray hair and a beard was asking me questions about you!! And...and, he knew about your necklace...!"

Susan looked in the direction from where, Michelle, her daughter had come running.

"What are you talking about?" she asked, kitting her brows together. "What creepy old man?"

"Come on, Mom!" Michelle cried, pulling her onto the escalator. "It was some guy with an English accent, and he even knew your name and everything..."

Susan glanced up over her shoulder as the escalator moved downwards to the parking level of the mall, trying to see who the old guy was, but she knew her daughter was stressed out, and thought she'd ask her more about it when they got to their car.

But, by the time they got there, they saw that Steven was already inside with the radio blasting a song by Duran Duran. He and Michelle started to argue over the radio channels, and by the time Susan had driven out of the parking lot, the creepy old guy was forgotten.

James had to stop himself from running after the young girl as memories of the distant past flooded his brain and heart. What did it matter if the girl's mother was Susan…his Susan, the history student and ballerina from all those years ago? It didn't matter in the slightest… not one bit. He was beyond happy with his life and the direction it had taken. He was famous to the point of being a legend. He had a wonderful wife, who he loved deeply and devotedly, three delightful children and wealth to startle the imagination. Why would he even waste a moment's thought on someone who had brought him nothing but painful memories?

His curiosity, however, got the better of him and he began walking briskly in the direction the girl had run, quickening his pace as he weaved his way through the crowd. He thought he saw two blonde heads, one taller than another step onto the escalator. He followed and rode down after them to the parking level. When he got to the bottom, he spotted them heading down a parking aisle and made to follow, but stopped dead in his tracks as the taller of the two stopped at a car and opened the driver-side door. She turned to look over her shoulder, and he saw her hand come up to tug on what looked like a chain around her neck, then she got into the car. Moments later, the car backed out of the parking space and pulled away.

Yes, it was definitely Susan, an older but still incredibly beautiful woman, the woman he had once loved so intensely all those years ago. He took a deep breath and shook his head to try and clear thoughts of her out of his mind.

When a horn honked at him impatiently, he realized he was stand-ing in the middle of the exit lane of the parking garage. He walked back to the escalator, stepped on and rode back up into the mall, his mind drifting into the clouds of the past. When he got to the top and stepped off, all he could see was a vision of the blonde, green-eyed girl he'd once loved, and he knew he had to pivot his thoughts in another direction before the vision found its way back into his heart.

Chapter 1

Susan Despondent

"Susan!" exclaimed Donald, saying her name for the fourth time, this time more loudly. "Are you paying attention to me?! I don't know what's been wrong with you lately, but this distracted and melancholy attitude of yours has *got* to stop!"

Susan glanced up from the book she was reading, even though "reading" wouldn't exactly be the term to use for what she was doing with the book. Staring at it blankly would be more accurate.

"What?" she asked disconsolately, looking up at him.

"I asked you if you'd like to go out to dinner. I've asked you three times now..."

"No...no, thank you...I'm not all that hungry..."

"You're hardly ever hungry anymore! In fact, you rarely cook anymore. It used to be your favorite pastime. You'll turn to skin and bones. And, you used to love to go out to eat and try a new restaurant..."

Donald got up and came to stand in front of her. "What's bothering you Susan? You haven't been the same since I got back from Sacramento and D.C. on the Trinco case. Did Steven do or say something to upset you again?"

"No...I haven't talked to him in week. He's always busy."

"Did Michelle say something to upset you?"

"No; I talked to her last night and she's all excited about getting to meet with Gloria Alred on one of her discrimination cases..."

"Then, what is it, Susan? Did I do something wrong? You didn't even seem like yourself on our trip to Europe after I got back from D.C. You certainly don't think I had anything going with Melanie, do you? Aside from the fact that she's gay, you have to know I'd never cheat on you."

Susan cringed, the word, "cheat" stinging her mind and conscience.

"No, Donald; I don't think you had anything going with Melanie…" Her voice trailed off. "I'm sorry…I don't mean to be this way…it's just that…" She closed the book, setting it on the end table next to her and looked out the window, a faraway look on her face.

"What? What is it? Are you feeling ill?"

She shook her head, stood up and walked over to Donald, wrapping her arms around his waist. She pressed her face into the front of his shirt.

"I'm sorry. I don't know what's wrong with me…" she whispered.

He wrapped his arms around her and squeezed gently. "I'm worried about you. I love you so much, but something's changed about you, Susan, and it scares me. Maybe you should go see a doctor…"

She pushed away from him and turned her back. "What do you mean something's changed about me?"

"You look sad all the time…and I notice you have tears in your eyes…and you keep playing with that necklace of yours more and more, especially since you put your grandmother's engagement ring on it. Maybe you should take the thing off if if's making you sad."

"No!!!" she exclaimed, a panicked look coming over her face as she turned to look at him. "It's not the necklace! Or…or grandma's ring…" She swallowed. "It's nothing…really…nothing…"

"You're lying to me and I know it! Something's wrong and you're not telling me! Did something happen when I was gone? Did something happen when you were with your girlfriends on the cruise you went on?"

Susan just shook her head, clutching the ballerina necklace and twisting the chain back and forth between trembling fingers as tears filled her eyes again.

Donald came to stand in front of her and grasped her gently by her shoulders.

"Please, Susan, please tell me what's troubling you. It's been almost two months now, and every day you seem sadder and sadder. It's almost like someone died or something...tell me, please..."

She looked up into his face. "I don't know, Donald...truly I don't," she lied. "I...I had a good time with Alice and Joy...we...we had a lot of fun...and laughs...and I kind of miss them now..."

"You miss your friends? I thought you told me they were annoying and they did something to piss you off, but you never told me what it was."

"It doesn't matter now. I guess I've just been shut up in the house too long and all my friends seem to be too busy for me. Even John, who I used to talk to once a week or so, doesn't call me anymore now that he and Keiko are married. Lynn's pottery business is going so well that she never has time to talk to me...and you're always in court or working late..."

"I know, I know...But I'm always asking you to meet me for lunch, and you never do, and when I have a day or two off, I ask to take walks or hikes with you, but you always want to go by yourself with your headset on listening to that same old music over and over again...you know, that band of yours you obsessed over when you were young. Who was the guy you were all nuts over?"

She sucked in a deep breath, her heart starting to pound in her chest, and walked into the kitchen.

"James," she mumbled. "His name was James..."

"Yeah, well, whatever his name was or is...don't you get sick of listening to the same stuff over and over?"

"No."

"Fine, Susan...so do you want to go out to dinner or not? I haven't had much to eat today and am near starving."

"I told you...I'm not hungry."

"Your attitude is really starting to get on my nerves. I've had just about enough of it!"

"Fine! If that's the way you feel...go out to dinner by yourself! See if I care!!"

"You don't care, do you? That's just it...I don't think you care about me at all anymore!"

"That's not true and you know it!!"

"But I *don't* know it! It doesn't even seem you want me to make love to you anymore! It used to be so good between us, but now you just lay there…like you can't wait to get it over with…"

"I've just been tired…"

"Yeah, tired of me, you mean! You barely do anything all day long but mope around the house. You can't be tired!"

"Just leave me alone, Donald!!" Susan screamed, running past him and out of the room. "Just leave me the fuck alone!"

She ran up the stairs and he heard the bedroom door slam closed.

"Fine with me!!" He yelled at the top of his voice. "That's just fine with me!! I'll be at my office tonight if you need anything! And just maybe I'll stay in the condo downtown until you come to your senses!"

There was no response from Susan. A few minutes later, she heard the front door close and as she looked out the bedroom window, she saw Donald's car head down the driveway to the street. He turned and a moment later, was gone. Her hands were gripping the bottom of the window sill, and she felt her tears dropping down onto them.

James's wife of twenty-eight years had a brain tumor, and the best and most talented doctors and surgeons in the world agreed there was nothing that could be done to reverse the outcome. It was only a matter of time before she would succumb. All that was left was hope, and although everyone, especially James and his oldest child, Carrie, prayed for a miracle and tried to be positive, as the days wore on, the tumor could not be stopped.

On a dark September day in 1997, with only James at her side, the Susan who had been the love of his life since he'd met and married her in 1969, passed to the other side as James laid beside her and held her in his arms.

Carrie, and James's two sons, Robert and Thomas, were outside the bedroom door when they heard James's painful and heart-wrenching cry, knowing that their mother was gone. The three gathered together in a mutual embrace, all of them so steeped in grief that they couldn't speak.

Carrie was the first to break away and go to the bedroom door, where she knocked softly. Receiving no answer, she turned the door handle and entered the room. She saw her father laying on the bed with his arms wrapped around her mother, and for a moment, was at a loss as to what to say or do. But, her dad had relied on her during the past fourteen months as she helped him get through one doctor's appointment and test after another, and she had prepared herself for this moment weeks, even months, ago.

She approached the bed and laid a hand on her father's shoulder. "It's over now, Dad, she said softly. "It's over...she's at peace now..."

James didn't move, only hugging his wife tighter to him. Carrie squeezed his shoulder. "Please, Dad...please come away now..."

But James wouldn't leave. Carrie felt his shoulders heave beneath her hand and loud sobs escaped his throat. "Leave me, Carrie...please leave me for a bit...I just want to hold her a little more...please..."

Carrie lifted her hand off his shoulder, dropping it to her side. "Okay, Dad...I'll leave you a bit longer. I'll be waiting out in the other room with Robert and Thomas. Come out when you're ready, okay?"

She saw him nod as he crushed the body of her mother closer to him and buried his face in her chest then she turned and left the bedroom, closing the door softly behind her.

Susan turned away from the window and reached to the nightstand next to the bed, pulling a tissue from the box that was sitting there. She wiped her eyes and blew her nose before sitting down on the edge of the bed and heaving a heavy sigh.

Shit! That's what her life had turned to...a pile of it! What in the hell was wrong with her?!

Instinctively, she reached up to pull on her necklace. She'd been trying to break the habit, but it hadn't been working very well. When she felt the ring that was hanging on the silver chain along with the ballerina shoes, her heart wrenched again as she thought back to that day in August, 1967…the day she would have married James, the man she had loved since she was twelve years old and who she had traveled back in time to be with…

If she'd been able to remain, would history have been changed? Would she have been able to stay in the past with him and give birth to the child they had created together?

She would never know. Her two friends, Joy and Alice, who had traveled back into the past with her, had betrayed her. As she stood in her wedding dress and was on the brink of walking down the aisle to pledge her life and love to James, Alice had activated the "Return" App on her iPhone and all three girls had been returned to the future.

Memories of that day and finding the engagement ring that James had called the *little sparkler* still on her finger when she returned to the future, sent a crushing pain through her whole body, and she wasn't even sure if she could stand back up.

She shook her head. She had to get herself back together. James had gone on with his life despite her destroying his heart once again by vanishing into thin air, finding true happiness at last with the woman who became the love of his life, and who also had the name of Susan.

She was jolted from her memories as she heard her mobile phone ringing downstairs and rushed down to answer it.

It was her daughter, Michelle. "What in the hell is going on, Mom?!" she exclaimed in an irritated voice. "Dad just got to the office and is mad as a hornet…something about you being off your rocker, all depressed and crazy but refusing to talk. He's been going on about it for weeks now."

"I'm fine, Michelle…"

"Well, you don't sound so fine. Even Steven said last week that you sounded all weird and down about something. So what is it then? I don't have a lot of time. Since Dad and I decided to share an office suite, I've been working my ass off to get all the new furniture ordered and delivered, plus all the other crap that needs done with phones, the computer server and everything else…"

"Just never mind then…"

"Well, I *do* mind. Even though I have my own office separate from Dad's, we're still sharing the same space and I'm tired of his shitty attitude, which appears to be related to you."

"Nothing is wrong…I'm just tired…That trip I went on with Joy and Alice a couple of months ago wore me out…"

"That's bullshit and you know it! Hell, you've been back for over two months now! Dad thinks it's something else."

She gave an exasperated sigh but then suddenly, her voice softened. "Hey, Mom…I'm sorry…I shouldn't be snapping at you. To be honest, this office move combined with my wedding plans and my pending court cases has me running 24/7. Thomas isn't happy that I took on another case so close to our wedding…In fact, he told me to tell Emily to find another attorney, but I can't do it. She's been my friend since elementary school, just like your friend, Lynn. And what her boss did to her at work is just plain wrong! Talk about a clear-cut case of discrimination on top of the sexual harassment…well, anyway…Mom, will you just tell me what's wrong? Is there anything I can do to help?"

"No…no, there's nothing you can do…" Susan reached for her ballerina necklace again, slipping the tip of her little finger in and out of the ring hanging on the end.

"Are you sure?"

"Yeah, I'm sure…"

"Well, hell…I just got a message that I'm needed downstairs in the judge's chambers. I gotta go, Mom. Talk to you later, okay?"

"Sure, that's fine, sweetheart. Later then…"

Michelle disconnected before Susan had a chance to say her usual "I love you" or "goodbye."

"Bye…" she whispered into the dead phone

Christmas, 1997 came and went without James even noticing. He was still so grief-stricken, that his favorite holiday meant nothing to him. Without his Susan, he didn't care if there was ever another Christmas.

His middle child, his son, Thomas, now age twenty-six, had returned to London where he was quickly gaining prominence with the London Philharmonic as one of their concert pianists. Carrie, his first born, at twenty-eight, was still with him in the family's Colorado retreat where Susan had passed away, and doing her best to coax him out of his grief. And, James's and Susan's third child, Robert, now twenty-four, was in Paris at a prestigious chef's school, his dream of becoming a famous chef well on its way.

"Here's your afternoon tea, Dad," Carrie said, setting a steaming mug on the lamp table next to him. "Just the way you like it...two sugars and just a spot of milk."

"You say that every time you bring my tea."

"I know...and you've been reminding me to make it that way ever since I was old enough to hold the tea kettle."

James gave a wan smile, grasping Carrie's arm as she stood at the side of the reclining chair he was sitting in. He'd been sitting there most of the afternoon as he'd been doing for months now. Today it was snowing and he watched the flakes swirl and fall like bits of confetti.

"Stay with me for a bit, will you?" he pleaded softly.

"Sure," she said, lowering herself onto the sofa next to his chair. "You want to talk, Dad?"

"It's time, I think..."

Carrie just nodded, waiting for him to go on. It was rare that he spoke at all, and she didn't want to interrupt his thoughts.

He continued. "I was thinking of closing up the house here...you know...and, and...going back to England." He turned to look at her, eyebrows raised.

"I think that's a great notion, Dad."

He looked down at his hands for a moment before picking up the mug of tea and blowing across the top. "You don't know how much I appreciate your staying here with me all this time…I've taken you away from your travels…and, from your time with David."

"David understands, Dad. Plus, it's not like we're engaged or any-thing…besides, I'd much rather be with you…I want to make sure you're okay…"

"I'm okay…I'm working through it, you see…"

"I can see that. I'm working through it too, you know."

"I do. I know how close you and your mum were. I know you miss her as much as I do."

Tears brimmed in the back of Carrie's eyes, but she blinked them back, wanting to be strong for her dad. "I do…"

"But it's time for us to go on now, isn't it?"

She reached over, putting her hand on his shoulder. "Yes…I think so…"

James stood up, the mug of tea held in both hands, and walked to the window. "Your mum loved watching the snow fall, you remember?"

"I remember…when I was little, she showed me how to catch snow-flakes on my tongue."

James smiled but said nothing else.

"And we made snowballs and rolled them down the hill to see if they'd get bigger…Dad?"

He turned to look at her.

"It's going to be okay, you know. We're going to go on with life, just as…just as she told us to do…remember?"

He nodded sadly. "Yeah…that's what she said…that's what she wanted…"

"So, how about I call the airline and book us a flight out on Thursday? How does that sound? It'll give us a couple of days to close things up here and pack whatever we want to take."

"Thanks, Carrie. That sounds fine. I don't know what I'd do with-out you sometimes…"

Chapter 2

Michelle Learns the Truth

Susan was standing in the kitchen of her and Donald's mountain home. Michelle was sitting at the kitchen table, nervously stirring ice cubes in her glass of iced tea. They rattled around the sides.

"I don't believe any of it, Mom…it's just not possible…there's no way any of that could have happened…time travel??!! It's just plain nuts!"

"Why did you really call Lynn, Michelle? You had no business calling my best friend and telling her I was on the verge of suicide! You know that's not true!"

"And how am I supposed to know that? You won't talk to Dad. You won't talk to Steven, and you haven't answered your phone for the past week when I've called. What are we supposed to think?!"

"That I want to be alone…I like to be alone."

"Yeah, you and the cats…that's what Dad says…you'd rather be with the cats than with him!"

"Maybe I would…Maybe I'm tired of being whined at…Maybe I like peace and solitude…maybe…"

"Damn you and your 'maybes,' Mom!" She stood up and paced into the great room before coming back into the kitchen and planting both hands on the kitchen island. "What Lynn told me is crazy…you and that James guy from the most famous band of all time…things like that only happen in movies, not in real life for Christ sake!"

Susan sat down at the kitchen table and looked out the window. She reached up and started toying with her necklace. Michelle's eyes focused on it immediately.

"So, Lynn told me to call your other friend, John, and he told me an even crazier story...and then he said I should call your friends Joy and Alice..."

"And they told you something even more unbelievable, didn't they?"

Michelle sat back down at the table. "Yeah...they did...None of it makes any sense, Mom...I mean, I remember you telling me about the James guy when I was young...and, and I remember you playing all his music and the music from that band...and I know you were nuts over him when you were like a teenager and everything..."

Susan looked up and stared into Michelle's face, her own face stoic. "It never ended, Michelle...it never ended..." she whispered, twisting the chain of her necklace between trembling fingers. "I thought it had...I thought I'd erased him out of my mind..."

"But then you went to that concert in Texas with Lynn, right? She said you went all crazy like you were a teenager all over again, and that you just kept thinking about him and dredging up old memories of what he meant to you...and then you two went on a cruise. I remember when you went on the cruise. It was last year, 2014...June, wasn't it?"

Susan just nodded.

"Lynn said you met two ladies from Haiti at dinner, and that they had some kind of magical or mystical powers...that they claimed they could send you back in time...to be, to be with your James guy..."

"And that I'd find out something important that I needed to know..."

"Yeah, that he was a no good womanizer and cheater."

"That's what John thought, but that was the second time I went back, not the first."

Michelle sat back in her chair. "Then what was it you needed to know?"

"That he wasn't the paragon I'd made him out to be in my mind... that we would never have gotten along...that what I had here in the present was better than anything I would ever have had with him..."

Susan laid her arms on the table and lowered her head. "But it didn't matter, you know. It didn't matter that he wasn't the paragon I thought him to be. It didn't matter that he was bossy or controlling or, or that he had old fashioned ideas…I made a mistake when I went back the first time…"

"That's what your friend, John, told me…"

"I gave James my necklace…"

"And you had to go back in time again to get it back."

"Yes."

"Well, I don't believe any of it! It sounds more like all of you got together and went on some kind of drug high. I've never known you to take drugs, but there's always a first time for everything, isn't there?"

"We weren't on drugs. It really happened."

Michelle got back up from her chair and began pacing back and forth, her hands behind her back. "So, exactly *how* does this happen? Do you get into a machine of some kind? Do the Haiti ladies put you in a tube or something? …Not that I believe any of this anyway…"

"We explode into sparks, like fragments of confetti on one end and then it all comes back together on the other end."

"And you get to be the age you want and you get to decide what you want to look like and what talents you want to possess, right? But you get to keep your brain from the present."

"That's right."

"The first two times you went back, you only got to stay for seven days, but the last time you got to stay as long as you wanted…"

"Actually, you missed one time. I…uh…didn't exactly succeed in getting the necklace back the second time I went into the past. I kind of got distracted, and I had to make another quick trip to get it back."

'Yeah, well, none of your friends told me about that. In fact, your friend, John, didn't really want to talk about it at all. I could only drag a few bits of information out of him."

"Like I said, you had no right to contact my friends!"

"And as I told you, I *had* to do it to find out what's been going on with you!"

"You've already said you don't believe me…"

"How could anyone believe something so...so...*unbelievable?!!* So impossible and crazy?!"

Michelle stopped pacing. "Are you getting early dementia?"

"No! Of course not! And, do you think my friends who went with me on my trips into the past all suddenly came down with dementia?!"

"I want to talk to the Haiti ladies."

"Grandmere...I mean, Mika, is dead."

"Then I want to talk to the other one."

"Are you going to do an attorney's interrogation on her like you're doing to me now? If that's the case, I won't give you her contact information."

"I just want to ask some questions."

"Are you sure you're not going to grill her like she's on the witness stand or something?"

"I promise. Just give me her contact information."

Susan bit her lower lip, wondering if she should give Michelle Marta's e-mail address or not. Then she thought, *What the heck!*

"Okay, just a minute."

Susan got up from the table and went up the few steps into the room she referred to as "the library." She retrieved her address book from a desk drawer and returned to the kitchen, flipping through pages.

"Here." She handed the book to Michelle, who pulled her iPhone out of her purse then typed the e-mail address into her contact list.

"When was the last time you talked to...to...Marta?"

"A little less than three months ago...right after I got back from being in the past the last time."

"When you went with Joy and Alice?"

"Yes."

"So, did you get in a fight or something with your James guy? Is that why you came back?"

"Joy and Alice didn't tell you??!!"

"No."

"They...they betrayed me...they made us all come back..."

Susan stood up and walked out of the kitchen, where she stared out the windows of the French doors. Michelle saw her shoulders move up and down, and knew she was crying. She moved behind her and put her hand on her mom's arm.

"I hate to see you this way, Mom."

"I'm sorry, Michelle. I don't mean to be this way...or to worry everyone...It's just that what happened on my last trip...well, I just can't put it out of my mind...Um, I'm sorry, dear, but I really don't want to talk about this anymore, okay?"

Michelle squeezed her arm. "Okay, I need to go anyway. Now that the new office is all set up, Dad and I are interviewing paralegals. Dad still hasn't been able to find anyone to replace Melanie."

Susan turned around and gave her daughter a hug and kiss on the cheek. "I'll be fine...really, I will..."

Michelle kissed her back and left, stopping on her way through the great room to pet one of Susan's cats.

Chapter 3

James Overcomes his Loss

Two years had gone by since James's wife, Susan, had passed. It was September, 1999 and James, Carrie and Thomas were in Paris for Robert's graduation from chef's school.

"Your mum would have been so proud of you, Robert," said James, giving him a hug. "And I'm awfully proud of you myself. I'm sure you're on your way to a five-star restaurant!"

"Thanks, Dad," responded Robert. "I've actually been offered the position of head chef at Le Fonda in London. It's not that far from Cherry Studios, where you record your music. The owners are taking a chance on me, allowing the restaurant to be totally vegetarian. You'll have to stop by when you're in town and I'll treat you to a special dish."

"Hey! What about us?!" Carrie exclaimed. "You can't leave Thomas and me out! We expect to enjoy one of your specialties too!"

Robert smiled. "Of course! You're all welcome any time!"

James looked on as his three children began chatting and teasing each other like they usually did when they got together, which wasn't all that frequently anymore. Although Carrie visited him most often at his home outside of London, she spent most of her time traveling the globe, collecting art antiquities or looking for inspiration for her own work, which was mostly sculpting or painting.

And, even though Thomas lived in London in a penthouse that James had bought him after graduation from the prestigious London Music Academy, the only time they got together was when Thomas coaxed him to come into town. Thomas had thrown himself into music with the same passion as his father, only his interest leaned heavily towards classical rather than pop or rock. Knowing this, James had gone out of his genre and written a classical piece, which he felt would emphasize Thomas's piano skills. It was called *"Nature's Concerto,"* and had won great acclaim when performed just a month previous.

"So, Dad," Carrie said, breaking away from her brother's conversation that had turned towards a book they had both recently read. "What are your plans for the end of the year? You said you wrote a few songs when I was in India. Are you going to record them? You think you've got enough for an album?"

"Yeah, I might. I'm starting to find inspiration again…not like it used to be when your mum was here, but I think it's coming back."

"I told you it would, Dad. Mum's still here, you know…in spirit… She always will be…"

James gave her a hug. "I know."

"So, what are the family plans for Christmas this year? I know we didn't do anything last year or the year Mum died, but I think it would be great to get together."

"I haven't thought about it really. I just don't seem to care much about Christmas anymore."

"Well, I'll tell you what…I'll talk to Thomas and Robert and we'll come up with a plan. Sound good?"

"Sure, okay."

"Thomas also told me you're planning on going back to Brighton the beginning of December. He said you were thinking of doing a small concert at the Dusky Club, where it all started for you. Is it true? Are you thinking of performing again?"

"I've been toying around with the idea, yeah. Thought I might do a medley of my best stuff…kind of rejuvenate myself."

"I think that's an awesome idea! I definitely think you should do it. I'll try to be there, but I actually was going to meet David in Rome at the beginning of December. He discovered some villas with unidentified sculptures from the fifteenth century. I've been dying to check them out."

"Don't worry about coming to Brighton. Thomas already said he'd come. Robert has commitments he can't get out of, so it's fine for you to go see your sculptures. By the way, when are you and David going to get married? You've been with him off and on for over three years now. I thought you would have tied the knot by now."

"Naw...lately we've been more off than on. We get along great, but the physical chemistry isn't there. We're more like brother and sister than romantic partners. I'm happy with it that way, and so is he."

"I just was hoping you'd find happiness with a nice fellow, and David seems quite nice to me."

"He is, but like I said, the passion just isn't there..."

"Hey, what's all this about passion?" interrupted Thomas, as Robert left to talk to some fellow graduates. "I could use some passion in my life!"

"You have plenty of passion in your music," Carrie teased him. "A woman would just distract you."

"Doesn't mean I wouldn't mind having a little."

James winked at him. "Maybe you'll find some in Brighton when you're there with me."

"So, Dad, did you find passion when you were in Brighton all those years ago...or do you even remember?" asked Carrie. "I heard you had quite a reputation in those days."

"I might have," James responded quietly.

Carrie and Thomas winked at each other, then Thomas excused himself to go help Robert pack his things for the trip back to London. Carrie said she needed to use the ladies facilities then was going to head to her hotel since it had been a long day. James gave her a hug and decided he'd also go back to his own hotel suite.

When he got there, he called room service and ordered a bottle of white wine along with a cheese and vegetable platter. He and his Susan had become staunch vegetarians shortly after being married, and he had lived that lifestyle ever since.

He poured himself a glass of wine and sat in front of the window looking out at the lights of Paris...and he thought about the question

Carrie had asked him...about whether he had ever found passion when he was in Brighton all those years ago...

The answer was, "yes," a definite "yes." And as his mind wandered back into the faraway past, a vision of a blonde, green-eyed girl passed through his head. He closed his eyes, and could almost see her before him, her perfectly molded face and kissable lips, her soft and shapely body that had fit so well with his...

Oh yes! He had definitely found passion with the American history student, who had captivated him the moment he first laid eyes on her, and who had unashamedly surrendered her virginity to him. Their passion had been like fire, just like their relationship.

And, just like a fire that burned too intensely, it had been extinguished just as quickly. The pain of how it had been extinguished had smoldered in his heart for months after she mysteriously vanished on the day they were to be married, and he never thought he'd get over it.

But that was all so, so long ago. And the girl who had caused him so much anguish was just a dim memory.

"I don't believe you!" Michelle said to the dark-skinned woman on the other end of Skype. "Things like time traveling aren't real...it's just not possible!"

"But it is," said Marta calmly from her home in Haiti. "And your mother experienced it not just once, but on four occasions."

"So she could be with that James guy, right?"

"Yes. She was supposed to learn something from the first trip... which she did...but because her necklace stayed in the past with him, it all went wrong. My Grandmere said it was impossible for something to stay in the past. Even with all her powers and knowledge, she could not figure it out."

"Which is why Mom had to go back again, right?'

"Exactly. But even though she did retrieve her necklace, the link between her and James still could not be broken. Grandmere was greatly puzzled. She even consulted with one of greater powers than her own, and it was unheard of. She thinks maybe they have another connection of some kind...like maybe a previous incarnation, and that there might be some "past life residue," as she called it, that needs to be resolved."

"Well, that makes no sense to me either. I'm not much into rein-carnation or any of that stuff. So, you're saying her two friends, Joy and Alice went back with her the last time?"

"Yes. Grandmere felt sorry for her because she said her husband... excuse me; that would be your father...was having an extramarital affair."

"Well, he wasn't."

"That may be true, but Grandmere sent her back. She was forced to return, however."

"Forced how?"

"Her friends used an App we installed on her iPhone to return all three of them together without your mother knowing it was going to happen. She was very distraught over it. She begged me to send her back again within moments of her return, but I could not. Grandmere passed to the other side while your mother was gone, and I needed to do things before I inherited her powers. I haven't heard from your mother since."

"Do you know why she was so upset about coming back? Her friends wouldn't tell me."

"I don't know if I should tell you either..."

"Please...I need to know...She's even more distraught, as you call it, now. She won't eat...She can't sleep...She won't talk to anyone. We're worried about her. It's been what then...almost three months since she did this...this...Oh my God! I can't even believe I'm talking to you about this...she time-traveled?!!"

"She wanted to stay in the past with James. She didn't want to come back the last time. She was pregnant with his child and she was going to marry him. In fact, it was their wedding day when Alice used the iPhone to bring them all back...And, even though she had the necklace back again, she brought back something else…the engagement ring James had given her…"

Michelle was speechless and her face paled. After a full minute, she gathered herself together, swallowed, and said, "You're making all this up aren't you? Just like Mom's friends are making all this up…"

Her voice faded to a whisper, as she suddenly thought of the ring that was now on her mom's necklace along with the silver ballet slippers. Oh my God! It wasn't Grandma's then…it was…James's??!

"I know what you're thinking," said Marta, interrupting Michelle's thoughts. "It is true."

"I don't know what to say about all this."

"Perhaps if you want to help your mother, you should go with her back into the past and help her get the ring back to James. I'm thinking if he has it back, the link, or whatever holds your mother and he together, will be broken for good. At least, that's what I would hope for."

"Go back with her??!"

"Yes. I can arrange for it."

Michelle blinked a few times.

"Well?"

"When? How? Where?"

"I will think on it and let you know. In the meantime, you also think about it. Tell me by this weekend and I will begin to make arrangements."

"What I really think is that I must have a screw loose to even be contemplating such a thing."

"Just let me know…I need to go now. I hope you decide to do what may help your mother finally overcome this. Goodbye."

With that, Marta disappeared from the screen of Michelle's laptop. Michelle laid her head down on her desk and closed her eyes. She must be insane to even think about going into the past with her mom. This was all too unreal.

James checked into the Claridon Hotel in Brighton on December 1st, 1999. Thomas wasn't due in until the 4th, and the mini concert at the Dusky Club wasn't until the 5th. James thought he'd spend the extra few days alone exploring old haunts as well as make sure all was set to go at the Dusky. The sound system needed checked and he wanted to do a bit of rehearsing in advance of the actual performance, which would be taped then released on video.

As he rode up to the penthouse suite in the elevator, a wave of nostalgia wafted over him and he had to steady himself as memories suddenly flooded his brain. He'd never actually stayed at the Claridon before. There were now several other newer and more prestigious hotels in Brighton, but he'd picked this one because of its proximity to the Club.

At least that's what he told himself when he had one of his team make the arrangements…

It wasn't actually the truth, however. The truth had to do with something else. It had to do with memories of a girl he once loved, and who he thought had loved him in return.

Susan.

He didn't know why, but he'd been thinking of her off and on for the past few weeks, in fact ever since he'd been in Paris for Robert's graduation from chef school. It was Carrie who'd planted the seed in his mind when she asked him if he'd found passion in Brighton all those years ago…before the most famous band of all time, of which he was a member, had become famous.

And he had…he most definitely had…and the more he dwelled on it, the clearer the memory of the blonde, green-eyed American girl became. He was anxious to see the Dusky Club again, to re-live the moments when he'd first seen her and when he and the boys had made a wager as to whether and how quickly he'd be able to seduce her. It had, in fact, taken him longer than he thought it would, but in the end she had surrendered, but not only surrendered; she'd made him a gift of her virginity, and that's when she had truly captured his heart.

23

As the bellman opened the door to the suite on the uppermost floor of the hotel, he continued to think about Susan. Being with her had most certainly been filled with ups and downs. While he thrilled at their passion and sexual chemistry, she'd upset and tormented him no end with her independent nature and refusal to conform to the standards of the day. She'd driven him to states of emotion he'd never experienced before, one moment feeling tender love for her, and the next feeling outraged and frustrated at her rebelliousness.

That was all so far in the past, however…so, so long ago…and he didn't even understand why his mind was so full of her memory other than Brighton itself stirring up something inside him that had laid dormant for over thirty years now.

Absentmindedly, he handed the bellman a tip, and when asked if there was anything else he needed, he shook his head. As the door closed behind him, he walked to the window and looked out into the late afternoon. The sun was shining, but he could see clouds moving in from the distance and knew a chilling winter rain would soon envelop the city. He turned his thoughts to the upcoming concert, doing his best to block more thoughts of Susan from invading his brain.

It was a futile effort however…She just wouldn't go away…

Susan was baking a blackberry cheesecake for her neighbors when she heard a knock on the door. The door opened a few seconds later before Susan could get to it. It was Michelle.

"Mom!" she yelled. "Are you here?"

"Of course I'm here!" Susan replied. "If I wasn't, the door wouldn't have been unlocked."

"Well, you could have forgot, you know."

"I never forget."

"I didn't come here to argue with you, Mom." Michelle flung her purse and sun glasses onto the coffee table in the great room and came into the kitchen. "I wanted to tell you that I talked to that Haiti lady."

Susan said nothing.

"And...I can't believe I'm actually saying this...but...I'm half convinced this time travel thing you did might even be true."

Susan raised her eyebrows and crossed her arms over her chest with an almost smug look on her face. "Go on."

"Anyway, she told me something that happened on your last trip, if that's what you call it, that I find disturbing."

Michelle sat down at the kitchen table. "So, did you really get pregnant by your James guy and were you going to marry him and try to stay in the past? Is that ring you wear on your necklace now the engagement ring he gave you...and not...not great grandma's ring?"

She looked at her mother with a pleading look in her eyes as if she wanted her to deny everything and say it was all made up after all.

"Yes...to all your questions."

Susan came and sat down at the table across from her daughter.

"I have to ask this then, Mom...How could you do such a thing to Dad? Don't you love him anymore? What you did was cheating...big time cheating!"

Susan hung her head for a moment before looking back up at Michelle.

"Yes, it was cheating...I know that...and...and, I felt guilty, especially the last time when I thought your dad was having an affair with Melanie. I knew it probably wasn't true, but I convinced myself it was...just so I could be with James again."

"Why, Mom?"

Susan stood up and began pacing around the kitchen. "Everyone thinks things are so wonderful between your dad and me...that we have a marriage made in heaven...that I'm the luckiest wife on the planet...but, it's not that way...not really..."

"Then why?"

"For the past ten years, ever since your dad started representing people in high positions, especially well-known politicians, he began to change. He started working longer and longer hours, even lots of nights until midnight or later and on weekends too."

"That's when he bought the condo downtown near his office, isn't it?"

"Yeah…so he could work even more hours and not have to come home…And then he started to take on higher profile cases that took months of preparation and he had to be out of town a lot, mostly in Sacramento, but then more and more in D.C. It seemed like I barely saw him at all for months on end…"

"But he takes you on long, fabulous trips after his long, important cases. You've even said how wonderful it is…just like being on a honeymoon again. Steven and I used to laugh, thinking there weren't any other parents we knew that kept going on honeymoons."

"And, the trips *are* like honeymoons, but it's not enough, Michelle. Sometimes I feel so lonely…I feel like a book someone puts up on a shelf and only takes down once in a while to read a few enjoyable pages. It wasn't like that before. We used to spend every weekend together, working in the yard or around the house. He was home for dinner almost every night and worked on his case preparation here instead of at the office. I used to help him a lot too, but then he needed paralegals and a secretary and a bigger office…"

Michelle sat back in her chair. "I see…So, you started spending more time with your old friends from school, visiting them…And, then you went to that concert to see James with your friend, Lynn."

"I did…but, I'd been thinking of him a lot even before the concert. I'd never really forgotten him. It was an old habit to think of him whenever things in my life became bad or…when I started to feel lonely. I started to daydream about him again, like I did when I was a teenager. Somehow, it made me feel alive again in a way…and I listened to the music again. It was like a tonic to me."

"Oh, Mom!" Michelle exclaimed, getting up from her chair and giving her mother a hug. "I didn't know…I never guessed. I don't know what to say. I love Dad, but I love you too. I hate to see you unhappy like this."

Susan backed out of the embrace. "I know, Michelle…I know." She reached up for her necklace and began twisting the silver chain between her fingers. Michelle instantly noticed it and reached her own hand forward to touch the ring that hung on the necklace along with the tiny ballerina shoes.

"So, he gave you this ring, did he? Doesn't look like much for someone so rich and famous."

"Well, there's a story behind the ring."

"Will you tell me, Mom? Let's go into the other room and sit down and you can tell me all about it. I want to know everything…"

Susan and Michelle moved into the great room, where Michelle sat in the recliner and Susan sat on the sofa. Susan took a deep breath and began to tell her story.

Two hours later, after she and Susan had imbibed a bottle of wine together, Michelle stood up and said she had to leave.

"I've decided to do something for you, Mom," she said, hugging Susan goodbye. It's going to be a surprise, but don't plan on going anywhere or doing anything special next week…I'm taking you on a trip…"

Chapter 4

Michelle Takes Susan Back

James went to the Dusky Club the morning after arriving in Brighton and let himself in with the key he'd been given. The place smelled musty, but it was obvious people had been there cleaning and getting things ready for his mini concert.

He flicked on the lights and gazed around the room. It looked even smaller than he remembered. How were a hundred and twenty people going to fit in here? It didn't look like it could hold more than seventy five or so.

He glanced to the side of the room towards the front by the stage area. It was where Susan had sat when he first noticed her. She'd been sitting on a bar stool at a small table. He recalled the pink dress she was wearing and how she didn't fit in with the rest of the girls who frequented the Dusky. Her golden hair had shone brightly even through the haze of cigarette smoke that permeated the club. He remembered offering her a ciggy and her turning him down with some remark about how it was unhealthy. She'd been right.

He walked up to the stage area and looked out to where the audience had been all those years ago, and where a new audience would be in just a few days. It almost seemed surreal. Then he remembered the practice room upstairs above the stage area, and wondered what it was being used for now. He walked over to the door at the side of the stage and opened it, seeing stairs leading upward into the dark. Finding a light switch, he flicked it on and began climbing up the dusty steps.

When he got to the top, he opened another door and stepped into the space where the band had spent many afternoons working on songs and rehearsing for their gigs at the club.

Flicking on another light switch, he spied a table with a few old chairs around it and a piano set against a wall. He wondered if it was the same one from thirty-seven years ago, the one he'd played so many times. He sat down at the bench in front of it and lifted the lid. Laying his hands on the keys, he began playing a random song, but the piano was terribly out of tune, and it almost hurt to listen to it. He closed the lid back up and turned around on the bench as more memories floated in and out of his brain.

He began thinking of Susan again, and how she'd looked when she'd first come into the practice room the first night he met her. The sight of her had taken his breath away, and he'd been quite certain of his ability to bed her that night. He smiled at the thought, recalling how his young body had hardened and he had to turn away from her, hoping she hadn't noticed the bulge in his trousers.

Ah yes…remembering Susan brought a smile to his eyes, and a smile hadn't reached his eyes in a long time.

He went back downstairs, turning out the lights and locked up the club before heading back down the street to the Claridon. He felt keyed up for some reason, but wasn't sure why. Maybe it was because he hadn't performed in front of an audience for so long and was nervous. Maybe it was because he hadn't been back to Brighton for so long and was feeling nostalgic. Or, maybe it was because memories of Susan were starting to awaken something in his heart once more…

"So, when can you do this thing?" asked Michelle impatiently, staring into the screen of her laptop at Marta. "I have a lot going on and a lot of cases backed up. I need to make plans."

"Whenever you wish, of course," responded Marta.

"Well, you're the one who suggested I go back with my mom! What are your ideas?"

"Your goal would be to make certain your mother gives the engagement ring back to James."

"Yes, yes...You told me that..."

"And, keep this in mind...*She* must be the one to give him the ring. It must pass from her hands into his. I'm hoping that will break the bond between them once and for all..."

"Okay, okay...But, what time would we go back to? I don't know that much about James other than he got married when my mom was in high school and she told me she freaked out about it."

"His wife passed in September of 1997. I think if I sent you back to the year 1999, he would be past his mourning and likely approachable again. That might be a good time to go."

"That sounds fine to me then. But, how old would James be? How old would you make Mom? I'd prefer to stay my own age, if you don't mind."

"James would be 57, and all other times your mother went back, she was three years younger than him, so that would make her 54. I would like to make you the actual age you were in 1999 also. That would be 24, correct? If you went back at your current age, you'd be 39 and that would be rather strange to have a mother who was 54."

"Yeah, I'll be 24 then. Okay, I guess that would work. Where would we go to be able to meet him? I mean, he's incredibly famous, likely near unreachable, with security all around."

"He performed in December, 1999 at the Dusky Club in Brighton, England. I could send you to Brighton and you could go to the concert. In fact, it's the same place where your mother first met him when she was sent back to June, 1962."

"Well, do you think we'd stand a chance of getting to him?"

Marta smiled a small, secret smile. "Oh, I'm quite certain you'll be able to get to him. Don't worry about that. The club is very small; you will have no problem."

"Fine then. I'll check my schedule and confirm with you tomorrow. I think I must be crazy for even talking to you and believing this, let alone agreeing to travel into the past. No one would believe me if I told them."

"I'll wait to hear from you tomorrow."

"Yeah...tomorrow then...Bye..."

The laptop screen went dark.

Michelle immediately picked up the phone and called her fiancé, Thomas. She'd already told her dad she was taking time off. He wasn't on a case at the moment and said he'd do follow-up on her discrimination and abuse cases, making sure to take good care of her client friend, Emily.

Thomas was furious.

"First you put me off for five years before you agree to marry me, then keep taking on cases and don't have time for our wedding plans, and now you're gallivanting off with your mom on a trip??!"

"Yes, Thomas. I told you my mom's been having some serious depression. I need to help her. That's what daughters do! I thought you'd be more understanding."

"What I understand is that our wedding doesn't seem to be important to you!"

"That's not a fair thing to say, and you know it's not true! We still have plenty of time!"

"Not for the kind of wedding you want, Michelle!"

"I'll figure it out when I get back, Thomas. I promise. Believe me, okay?"

Michelle heard a heavy sigh at the other end of the phone.

"Fine," Thomas said, coldly. "You do that...you figure it out then. Call me when you get back."

He hung up without another word, and Michelle sat with a dead phone in her hand for a minute before giving a sigh herself then calling Susan.

⌒⊙

James meant to only drink a glass or two of wine back at the hotel that night, but he was into his second bottle before he knew it.

When he'd come into the hotel lobby after leaving the Dusky, memories hit him in the face like heat from a furnace. He could almost picture himself and Susan standing in the lobby while he tried to coax her to take him up to her room. When he asked to kiss her the first night they'd met, she'd stuck her hand out towards his face, and he smiled as he recalled kissing her fingers one at a time, then her palm and her wrist as he trailed fingers up her arm. He knew full well the effect he had on her, just as he knew the effect he had on all girls.

He smiled again as he got into the elevator and hit the button to take him up to the penthouse floor, also remembering the second night he'd been with Susan, and had pulled her through the lobby, into the elevator then down the hall to her hotel room door. She'd thwarted him once again, but their kiss that night had sent them both over the cliff, and it was then he realized that he wanted more from the beautiful American history student than just her body.

As he got out of the elevator, he realized he nearly had an erection just thinking back to the days and nights he and Susan had spent together locked in each other's arms, and shook his head in disbelief as he opened the door to his suite. How could her memory have such an effect on him all these years later? It seemed crazy. He decided he might just take a cold shower to cool his thoughts.

Instead, he ordered up some wine and sat gazing out the window at the lights of Brighton, and the more wine he drank, the more he thought of Susan.

"Where are we going, Michelle?" Susan asked as she opened the front door. "How long are we going to be gone? I need to know what to pack. When you called me two days ago, you were vague."

"I already told Dad we're going to be gone, but I'm not sure how long yet. We're just going to wing it. The trip is a surprise, and you don't need to pack anything. It's already taken care of."

Susan looked suspiciously at Michelle. "You're not making sense…"

"But I am, Mom…don't you remember…you don't need luggage to time travel…"

Susan sucked in her breath and her face became pale. "What do you mean…time travel?"

"Just what I said. I talked to Marta and it's all arranged. We're going back so you can see James again. I was feeling sorry for you."

Michelle thought, *Best not tell her about giving the ring back yet. We can wait until we get there or she might freak out.*

Susan grabbed the back of the couch with both hands, trying to steady herself. "But the cats…"

"I already talked to Steven about it, and he agreed to bring Kristy and the kids to come stay here while we're gone, and if they need to leave, the neighbors will take care of the cats."

"But…when…where…?"

"All taken care of, Mom! Let's go into your library room and turn on your laptop." Michelle looked at the clock on the wall. "We only have about fifteen minutes before blast off."

"But…"

"No buts…come on…I went to a lot of trouble to arrange this, and Thomas is pissed as hell at me. I want to go so you can be with your James again, and then I need to get back and work on the wedding plans."

She stalked up the short flight of stairs to the library room with Susan trailing behind.

Michelle sat down at Susan's desk and turned on her laptop. Five minutes later, she had Marta on Skype. Both women saw that she was lighting candles.

Then, Marta came up to the screen. "Are you ready?"

Michelle nodded. Susan felt in a daze.

"Very well then. In a few moments, both of you will be transported back in time to December of the year 1999 to the Claridon Hotel in Brighton, England."

Susan gasped and clutched at her ballerina necklace, tightly holding the ring in her hand.

"James will be staying in the same hotel and will be performing in public at the Dusky Club for the first time since his wife passed. You will have tickets to the concert. Susan, you will be in your 54-year-old body. Michelle, you will be in your 24-year-old body. You will both be dressed in the style of the day and you will have keys in your purse to two adjoining rooms in the Claridon Hotel. Susan, you may recall the hotel is just down the street from the Club. You both will have adequate money for whatever you need or want.

You will both be equipped with iPhones that have unlimited battery power, allowing you to communicate with each other or check in with those that are here in the present. As before, there will be a "Return" App, which will be on both of your phones. I made an exception for you this time, Susan, and that is, you do not both need to return together, but should something harmful come to either one of you, both of you will be returned immediately. And should you decide to return together, either of your phones can be used, but then both of you must come back at the same time. You cannot leave the other behind using just one phone. Do you understand? Do you have any questions?"

Susan nodded her head dumbly to the first question, then shook her head to the second. Michelle just shrugged her shoulders.

"Then both of you lay on the floor and close your eyes."

Michelle laid down first, looking up at her mother. "Come on, Mom!"

Susan slowly lowered herself to the floor and laid down. Michelle reached over to grasp her hand and squeeze it.

A moment later, both women began to glow and become transparent, then suddenly exploded into thousands of sparks, resembling confetti, and floated upwards, outwards and away...

Chapter 5

Thomas Meets Michelle

Thomas, James's son, arrived in Brighton the afternoon before James was to perform at the Dusky. He didn't want to stay in the penthouse suite at the Claridon with his dad, so checked into a regular room on the fourth floor. James was out somewhere, so after Thomas unpacked, he wandered down into the hotel lobby where he made himself comfortable in one of the over-stuffed chairs and ordered a cup of tea. After taking a few sips, he decided to get a newspaper from the small gift shop next to the hotel's registration desk.

As he got up from his chair, he saw two women enter the lobby and head towards the desk, suitcases in tow. They were both the same height, one older than the other, both with long blonde hair, one of which was tied back in a ponytail. It was obvious they were mother and daughter from their facial features, which were strikingly beautiful. The younger woman, who appeared to be in her mid to early twenties strode briskly up to the desk, the older one trailing behind with a somewhat awed expression on her face. Her eyes roamed the lobby from side to side, then up and down as if she were in a cathedral rather than just a hotel lobby.

Thomas continued to observe them, trying to be nonchalant about it as he slowly strolled into the gift shop. He'd seen a lot of beautiful woman in his life, but none with quite the arresting loveliness as these two. They had him mesmerized, especially the younger one. He wondered who they were and where they were from.

A few moments later, as he was coming out of the shop, newspaper under his arm, he heard the younger woman tell her mother to go on up to her room, that she wanted to go to the gift shop to see if they might have a local newspaper. As she turned towards the shop, she almost bumped into him as he was coming out. He quickly ducked to the side, but her arm still brushed against his as the entrance to the shop wasn't very wide.

"Oh! Sorry!" she said, looking up at him.

He sucked in his breath. She had the most remarkable eyes he'd ever seen before. They were like fine turquoise and framed with long lashes beneath perfectly arched eyebrows. He almost found it hard to speak.

"Oh, no…Quite all right," he mumbled. "Ummm…I heard you're needing a newspaper. I just took the last one…here you go…you can have it…"

He felt like an idiot, the words stumbling out of his mouth like a nervous teenager.

And she suddenly felt a bit nonplussed herself as she took in his countenance. He looked like…Oh my God! He looked so much like her mom's James! Well, almost… He had blue eyes instead of brown, but they were the most unusual eyes *she'd* ever seen, with what appeared to be flecks of gold sparkling outwards from the iris. They were quite hypnotic.

She smiled nervously, but he didn't seem to notice her discomfiture. To him, it was a brilliant smile that lit up her whole face.

"Why, that's awfully nice of you," she stuttered. "Are you sure you don't want it? I can try to find somewhere else that sells papers…"

"No…really, please take it…I was just getting it to pass the time…" He handed it to her.

"Uh…why, thank you so much! Um…how much do I owe you then?"

"Nothing…nothing…my pleasure…really." He swallowed, wondering if he could be so bold as to ask her name, but before he could say anything else, she bit her lower lip, proffered another thank you and turned away from him, quickly striding towards the elevator. His feet felt stuck in cement as he watched her get into the elevator and the doors swished shut behind her.

⌒⊙

Susan followed the bellman up to her room on the fourth floor, a room which adjoined the one where Michelle would be staying. After giving him a generous tip, she tossed her purse on the bed and sank down on its edge

Was she really here then? Back in the same hotel she'd been in when she first went to the Dusky Club and met James back in June, 1962? This wasn't the exact same room. She recalled that room number had been 4027, which was down the hall in the opposite direction from the elevator and on the other side. She didn't know if she could handle being in the same room again. The memories slamming through her head were bad enough just being in the same hotel let alone in the same room.

This "trip" Michelle suddenly decided to bring her on was so unexpected to Susan that she was in shock. The two woman had "materialized" outside the lobby doors leading into the hotel, but instead of it being midnight as it had been on previous trips, it had been late afternoon. As Susan stood in stunned disbelief, unable to move, Michelle took charge, telling her in hushed whispers to get a grip on herself and go through the doors. When she still didn't move, Michelle shoved at her back, and in they both went.

As Susan took in the lobby, so many memories came flooding back all at once that it left her head spinning. She stumbled, rather than walked, behind Michelle to the registration desk, her eyes large in her face as she scanned the lobby. She looked towards the spot where she had stood and offered her hand to James to kiss the first night she'd met him and gave a heavy sigh. For him, it would have been thirty seven years ago, but for her it had only been a year and a half.

Her thoughts were interrupted when Michelle handed her a room key and told her to go on up, that she'd be up in a few minutes after getting a newspaper from the gift shop.

She was still sitting on the edge of the bed when she heard a knock on the door that joined her room to the one next door. She got up, went to the door, unlocked it, and Michelle came in, a newspaper in hand. Her face looked flushed. Susan raised her eyebrows.

"Was there a problem getting a newspaper?"

Michelle just shook her head. "Uh, no…They actually were sold out, but…uh, I bumped into this guy coming out of the gift shop, and he ended up giving me his. He said he bought the last one."

"He offered you his newspaper?"

'Yeah…it was, ah…really nice of him, don't you think? I even offered to pay for it, but he insisted I take it…But that's not all, Mom…"

"What's not all?"

Michelle went over to the desk under the window and sat down in the chair in front of it. "Well, I must have imagined it…but, he looked just like your James! I mean, after you told me your time travel stuff, I looked up pictures of your James back from the days when he was young, and the guy who gave me the newspaper looked so much like him, that I thought I was seeing things…"

"Well, maybe you were…"

"I guess so…I wish you'd been there. You know what your young James looked like more than me. Oh, but there was a difference. Your James, I know, has brown eyes…this guy had blue eyes, and they were the most unusual eyes I've ever seen. They had like little bits of gold in them…"

Susan started. "Gold in them? Really?" She thought of James's eyes. They were hazelnut brown, but had flecks of amber floating in their depths. She shivered as she recalled how they sparked and became brighter when he became aroused and wanted her. "Sounds as if you found him rather attractive…"

Michelle interrupted. "Well, no…not really…I mean he *was* nice looking…and those eyes kind of drew me in…"

"I know all about how eyes can draw you in, believe me…but you're engaged to Thomas, right? Can't be thinking of other guys…"

"Actually, I'm kind of pissed at Thomas. He was really rude to me when I told him I was going to take you on a trip. He hates

40

that I'm not there planning the wedding and that I've taken on new clients."

"Didn't you hire people to take care of most of the wedding stuff?"

"Yes! And that's why I don't know why he's being all stupid about it. The wedding isn't until June. That's six months away. I think he's more upset about me taking on more clients."

"But he has his own clients, doesn't he?"

"Yeah, but his law firm isn't doing as well, and...sometimes I think he's jealous of my success. He handles mostly drunk driving cases, while I do discrimination and have some mentors who are pretty high and mighty in that field. Plus, Dad is really successful. He has to turn clients down."

"Well, you worked really hard to get where you are, even putting off marriage. You just happened to be in the right place at the right time, and having ties with your dad certainly hasn't hurt. Thomas hasn't had the same advantages you have."

"And I think it really bothers him. When we first met about ten years ago, we were both struggling, but then my practice took off and Thomas's...well, not much happened. And, now that I've moved in with Dad, Thomas seems even more upset."

"I didn't know any of this, Michelle...I'm sorry..."

"If you weren't so caught up in your time travel shit, maybe you would have noticed..."

Susan went across the room and laid her hand on her daughter's shoulder. "I really am sorry...you're right...I've been distracted and... and not paying attention."

Michelle reached up and covered her mother's hand with her own. "It's okay, Mom. Things will either work out between Thomas and me, or they won't. It's just that he seems so different lately. I'm wondering if maybe I'm making a mistake..."

"Well, maybe this crazy trip we're taking will clear your head a bit. Maybe you'll miss him..."

"Maybe..." Michelle smiled then laughed. "But, who knows... maybe I'll run into the guy with the blue and gold eyes again and have a torrid love affair with him like you did with your James..."

Susan laughed back. "You never know, Michelle...you never know...Hey, why don't we unpack, change clothes then go down to the dining room and have some dinner? You might just run into your newspaper guy again..."

⌒◯

When James got back to the hotel the day Thomas arrived, Thomas was waiting for him in the penthouse suite watching the news on t.v.

"You're all over the telly, Dad," he said, turning the volume down. "Looks like a lot of press and media are moving in. I hope they don't invade our hotel."

"They won't," responded James, setting a shopping bag on the coffee table in front of the sofa then kicking his shoes off before sitting down. "Security has this place locked up tight and everything was negotiated with the hotel owner a few months ago. Other than a few stray tourists and people who made reservations before I even thought to come back to Brighton, no other rooms are being rented out. In fact, no one knows I'm staying here."

"Thank God for that! I just hate it when the paparazzi get in your face and chase you down. Are you sure no one recognized you when you've been out the past couple of days?"

"My old man disguise works really well," he said, pointing to the shopping bag. "Especially when I use the cane and limp along mumbling and shaking my head. People avoid me."

Thomas laughed. "I don't doubt it...So, what about the tourists who are staying here? Aren't you worried you'll be recognized and the news will leak out?"

"No. I don't remove the disguise until I get off the elevator on the fifth floor, and I'm the only one on the fifth floor other than security. I don't know why you won't stay up here with me..."

"I just didn't feel like it, no offense meant, Dad. You keep late hours and I keep early hours, plus we can still spend time together like we are now."

"Are you hungry? I haven't had anything to eat since this morning when I had something sent up. I was going to have luncheon in Little Dippington on the way back from my Auntie Annabelle's cottage, but got distracted in one of the shops there then had to get back here to check the sound system again at the Dusky."

"Didn't Auntie close up the cottage a few months ago? Wasn't she going to sell it?"

"Yeah. She moved in with Auntie Gin over in King's Head in June. Both of them are up in their eighties now and thought it a good idea to move in together. The house in King's Head is a single story…no stairs…so they thought that would be the best place for both of them."

"So, what made you go out to the cottage?"

James leaned back into the sofa, laid his head back and closed his eyes for a moment. When he straightened up, he looked thoughtful. "Oh, just thinking of old memories of when the band began here in Brighton…there seem to be a lot of memories popping in my head lately…I went out to the cottage a few times with…with someone… but that's all in the far past…I'm ready to concentrate on music again now."

"Well, Dad, I'm glad you're feeling a bit more yourself again and doing this concert. I think it'll jump start you again…get you back out there."

"Yes, I actually believe it will…So, when did you get here today? Do anything special this afternoon?"

"I think I got in around 4:00 or so, unpacked my bag then went down to the lobby for a cup of tea. Two Americans walked in while I was there, two women actually. I ended up giving one of them the newspaper I bought; it was the last one."

"Americans?"

"Yes. They were obviously mother and daughter; you could tell by looking at them. Probably tourists. Both blondes, and both quite beautiful. It was the younger one I gave the newspaper to. She had the most gorgeous greenish eyes…I almost became tongue-tied."

James started. "Greenish eyes? What color was the mother's?"

"Well, I didn't see the mother's eyes. The daughter checked them both in, handed her mum a key and told her to go up to her room while she went to buy a paper. But, the younger had eyes the color of aquamarines...blueish green they were. Quite remarkable!"

When James didn't respond, Thomas looked at him closely. "Something wrong, Dad?"

"No, no...nothing at all...I was just remembering a blonde American girl I met during my days at the Dusky. She had green eyes, and I've never seen the likes of them since...just reminded me is all."

"Well, I'm surprised you'd remember...I heard all about you and the hundreds of girls you had climbing all over you back in those days... as a matter of fact, now that you're coming back out in public, I venture that you'll have hundreds, even thousands of them falling at your feet again, especially now that you're what they'll consider available."

"Well, I'm not available. Not even thinking of it."

"Not thinking of it *yet*, you mean."

"No...I think forever...No one can ever replace your mum..."

I know, Dad, but I hate to see you lonely. You never know...maybe the mum of girl I gave the newspaper to will have green eyes, and..."

James interrupted him. "Enough, Thomas! Remember, I said I'm hungry. Let's order up something good from room service and see if the hotel has any movies on their in-house channels."

"Sounds good to me...where's the hotel menu?"

James retrieved it from a desk and tossed it on the coffee table in front of Thomas.

"Order me French toast and see if they have strawberries to go with it."

"French toast for dinner?"

"Yeah...I'm just feeling in the mood for French toast...with strawberries..."

James moved towards the window and peered out at the lights of Brighton then he turned his head and added, "Have them send up a bottle of wine too...Chardonnay, please..."

Then he turned back to the window and looked out at the lights once again.

Chapter 6

The Mini Concert at the Dusky Club

"We actually have tickets to this concert?" Susan asked Michelle for what seemed like the fifth or sixth time.

"Yes, Mom...we have tickets. Remember Marta told us we'd have tickets? Quit being so anxious."

Michelle was stretched out on the bed in Susan's room touching up her nail polish. Susan was trying on a green dress for the third time after deciding against the black one or the blue one that Michelle said she liked best.

"Are you *sure* the blue dress would look better than this one?"

"Mom! Stop it! We have two hours before we need to leave. Would you just relax! Why don't you finish off that bottle of wine we brought up from dinner last night? You're getting on my nerves!"

Susan went over to the mini refrigerator at the side of the room. "Good idea...I'm getting on my *own* nerves."

She grabbed a water glass sitting next to an empty ice bucket on the dresser, retrieved the bottle of wine from the mini fridge and poured the rest of the bottle into the glass. She took a sip and then sat on the side of the bed.

"I don't think we should have come here, Michelle. I think this is a mistake. After what happened all those years ago, I don't think he'll *ever* want to see my face again!"

"It's been over 30 years. He won't even remember you...men aren't good at remembering..."

"But what if he does? What if he sees me and recognizes the necklace? Oh! And, now I have the engagement ring on it!"

"Then take off the damn necklace and don't wear it."

"Not wear it?! I've never, ever taken it off other than when I gave it to James or he took it from me."

"Then wear it and take the risk. I still think he won't remember you...didn't he sleep with like a thousand women or something? Then he was married for almost thirty years..."

Susan took a few more sips of wine. "Maybe we should just go back to the future..."

Michelle screwed the top back onto the bottle of nail polish and slammed it down on the night stand next to the bed. "No! We're here and we're staying here! And, we're going to the concert!"

"Why did you really bring me here Michelle? Why are we here at this particular time and place? You never told me...you just swept me away here without saying why..."

"Drink the rest of the wine."

"Why?"

"Because I asked you to...because I have something to tell you."

Susan tipped the glass and the last of the wine slid down her throat.

Michelle began pacing the room in her lawyer-like stance, waving her hands in the air to dry the nail polish.

"Okay, so when I talked to Marta, your Haiti lady, it was her opinion that you still have this link or whatever it is with James because last time you came back with the engagement ring. She said that wasn't supposed to happen, just like your leaving the necklace in the past with him on your first trip wasn't supposed to happen."

Susan said nothing, just staring at her daughter as she paced.

"So...when I told her how depressed and near crazy you were, she recommended I take you back here so you could give the ring back to James, and then maybe you'll be released from whatever bond there is between you...at least that's what she thinks..."

Susan felt stunned. "Give him my engagement ring back?" she muttered. "And just how would I go about doing that? I mean, even if I *wanted* to do that?! ...which I don't!"

"You don't need it, Mom! It shouldn't even have come back with you...maybe you could tell him you found it on the floor..."

"No! I don't want to give it back! It's all I have to remember him by!"

Michelle stopped in the middle of the room, put her hands on her hips and stared her mother down.

"You don't *need* to remember him! You don't need him in your life at all! Didn't you say he's been a curse to you for over fifty years? Don't you want to be happy...live life like a, like a *normal* person?"

Susan set the empty glass on the bed, folded her hands in her lap and looked down at them.

"It's too late, you know. I know what it's like to be with him...I'll never be able to forget him for as long as I live...Never..." She looked up at Michelle with a pleading look in her eyes. "Do you think I could be with him again? I know you probably think it's a horrible thing to say considering your dad and all, but it's almost as if I've had a dual existence ever since I went back in time with Lynn and met him in person...and got to spend time with him..."

Michelle tilted her head back and closed her eyes. She inhaled then exhaled loudly before looking back at her mother.

"Mom, I just don't know what to say to you. You even have *me* confused now. Why don't we just go to the concert and see what happens. If you hook up with him again, maybe you'll discover he's changed in the thirty-two years since you were with him. Maybe *this* time you'll discover he's not what you need or want in your life and it'll be over and done with...chapter ended...book closed..."

A stray tear rolled down Susan's face.

"Even better, though," continued Michelle, "would be if he doesn't recognize you after all these years, and you could say you found the ring on the floor and shove it in his hand after he gives you his autograph or something..."

"I know you're right, Michelle...I really don't need him in my life, do I? Okay, I'll go to the concert...and, and I'll figure a way to give him the ring...and then maybe we can go back to the future and I can get myself together..."

She stood up. Michelle came over and hugged her. "It'll all work out, Mom…don't worry…go on and finish getting dressed then we can stop in the hotel bar on our way to the concert and have a glass of wine to calm your nerves…"

⌒♋

"Dad! You look ridiculous in that disguise! Like a disgusting old man!" Thomas laughed as James opened the door to the penthouse suite. It was a little after 5:00 in the afternoon on the day of the mini concert at the Dusky Club.

"Of course I look like a disgusting old man! Nobody notices me this way, and if they do, they move away…especially if I start mumbling incoherently. I can go just about anywhere I want dressed up like this."

"But do you have to have those food stains on the front of your shirt like that? Ugh…sickening…"

"Adds character, it does! So, are you ready to leave then? I need to check the sound system one more time, make sure all my guitars and the piano is in the right place, the lighting is right, and I need to talk to the technicians who'll be doing the recording."

"How many songs are you going to do?"

"I'm thinking twenty-five but I might add a few more depending on how I feel. I've already talked it over with the other guys. Phil is going to be on drums tonight. He's the only one who doesn't know all my tunes, but he knows all the ones on the set list."

"Where is your set list? Can I take a look at it?"

James pulled a folded paper out of the sagging jacket pocket and handed it to Thomas.

"You're playing your favorite song you wrote for mum? Are you sure you can do it without falling apart?"

"I'm sure. I've played it about ten times at the Club since I've been here. I can handle it."

"Mum would be so proud of you, you know? I am too. And so are Robert and Carrie. We're all happy to see you out there again."

"And I'm glad to be out there again too. Let's go. We're having food catered in for after the concert for all the people who were invited, but I also asked that there be something for us earlier, and for security, the rest of the band and the techies."

James opened the door and Thomas followed him out into the hall and closed the door behind him. They began walking down the hall to the elevator.

"Vegetarian, right?"

"Of course. It's a rule for anyone who works for me. You know that."

"I thought it was more of Mum's rules than yours."

Thomas pushed the elevator button and the doors opened.

"Well, I supported her in it, so I'm carrying it on for her as much as for myself. I don't know why you quit being vegetarian. You were raised as one."

James pressed the panel to the lobby floor.

"I know, but that violinist I dated for almost a year when I was studying in music school wasn't vegetarian, and I spent a lot of time with her family and got used to eating meats. I find I quite like them and having more variety."

"Your mum would have been disappointed if she'd found out, you know."

"I know, but she didn't find out."

The elevator doors opened onto the lobby and the two men stepped out. Thomas froze and grabbed his dad's arm as he saw the blonde girl and her mother enter the hotel restaurant on the other side of the lobby.

"Dad! There's the women I told you about…the Americans I saw check in."

James looked across the lobby, but the women had already vanished through the restaurant door. Thomas wanted to follow them, but James said if they were staying in the hotel, there would probably be a chance to see them later. His mind was focused on the concert and he was anxious to get to the Dusky Club. Being the perfectionist he was, everything had to be just right, especially for his first appearance in over two years.

The two men walked out the lobby doors onto the street then down to the Dusky Club where they could see crowds of people standing out in front. They ducked into the alley that had security people lined up across the front, James limping along with his cane and Thomas with his head looking down in case anyone might recognize the son of one of the most famous musicians on earth. A short time later, they entered the door to the practice room above the stage area.

⌒♡

"I think I'll run up to our room to use the bathroom and check my make-up," Susan said, sipping the last of her wine. "I'll be back in a few minutes."

She stood up and picked up her purse.

"Your make-up looks fine, Mom. You hardly have any on. Quit fussing over yourself," scolded Michelle.

"I can fuss if I want to fuss. Plus, I want to change my shoes. I'm just not a high heels person anymore. All those years of dancing wrecked my toes, and these shoes you talked me into buying this morning are too tight."

"Okay, fine…just don't take too long. The concert is supposed to start in a half hour. I know it only takes ten minutes to walk there, but we should get there a little early."

"I won't be more than ten minutes…"

Susan kicked off the heels as soon as she got in the hotel room door and headed to the bathroom. When she was done, she studied herself in the mirror above the sink. While it was true she'd aged quite a bit since James had last seen her in her 22-year-old body, at age 54, she was still a looker. Her golden blonde hair hadn't faded and she didn't have one gray hair on her head. Her waist was still trim and her breasts, even though they weren't as perky, were still ample and nicely rounded. A generous amount of cleavage peeked out the neckline of her emerald green dress.

She almost laughed. The dress looked identical to the infamous green one she'd worn back in November, 1962, when James had thrown such a snit at her spending her own money. She recalled the consequences she'd had to endure that day and rolled her eyes. Oh my God! He'd been so damn bossy and controlling in those days. And, he hadn't changed one bit when she'd gone back to July, 1967 to be with him again. She wondered if he was still that way and then laughed again. Probably so…did a leopard change its spots?

Looking at her watch, she knew she had to hustle and that Michelle would be getting impatient down in the hotel bar. She slipped on a pair of ballerina flats that had been on her feet when she arrived the day before, locked the hotel door behind her and headed to the elevator.

Michelle was in the hotel lobby waiting for her, both of their coats over her arm. They slipped on the coats and walked out into the cold December air and down to the Dusky. There was a large crowd out front, and the two women had to work their way through to the entrance where Michelle presented their tickets. They were shortly inside, down the steps and passed by the small bar that was still at the back of the club. The room was packed to the gills, standing room only. Susan glanced to the front at the stage area and a chill went down her spine as memories of the past invaded her brain.

She was speechless as she and Michelle handed their coats to the cloakroom girl and were given paper tokens to get them back after the concert.

"Mom! Take my hand…I'm moving us to the front," said Michelle as she started expertly maneuvering through the crowd. Having been to many similar concerts, she was adept at getting to the front, and before Susan knew what was happening, she was right in front of the stage area, but off to the side against the wall, the same place where the small bar table had been when she first came into the past all those years ago.

As was her habit, she began playing with the silver chain of her necklace, twisting it nervously between her fingers. Her hands were shaking. Michelle noticed immediately.

"Where's the ring? What did you do with James's engagement ring?"

Susan blanched. She'd taken the ring off her necklace the previous night. She'd slipped it back on her finger and cried into her

51

pillow for most of the night after Michelle went back to her room. But, she knew she had to get it back to him somehow…it's what needed to be done. She just wasn't sure how.

"It's in my purse. I'll…I'll see if maybe I can get close enough to him after the concert like you suggested. I'll ask for his autograph, and while he's signing, I'll bend down then back up and say I found it on the floor."

Michelle nodded her approval and was just about to say something else when James's band walked out onto the small stage. The audience began to clap. A moment later, James himself walked out, slipped the strap of one of the guitars that was sitting on the stage up over his head and walked up to the microphone. The small crowd roared. Susan felt faint.

⌒♾

Thomas ate dinner with his dad, his bandmates and the support crew up in the old practice room, then left to go down into the club five minutes before the concert was due to start. He leaned up against the stone and brick wall on one side of the club and looked out on the audience, waiting for James to come onstage.

Then he froze. Directly across from him, against the opposite wall were the two American women he'd seen at the Claridon. Both had their long blonde hair tied back in ponytails. Both looked ravishing, the youngest most of all.

She was talking animatedly to who he knew was her mother, and who was clutching what appeared to be a chain or necklace of some kind on her chest. The mother's eyes were riveted on James as he walked onto the stage area, almost as if she were cast under a spell and Thomas chuckled.

She must be one of his dad's long-time fans. They all had that faraway and dreamy look on their faces…the look of yearning that he'd come to recognize over the years. His mum had done her best to ignore those looks when she and James had performed in concerts together, but he knew that she found it annoying…all those girls and women wishing they were in her place. In one way, it made her feel smug, knowing he belonged to her and only her. In another, she recalled hearing about his womanizing days and was always on the lookout to see if his eyes wandered. They did, of course...after all, he was a man...but she had always believed he was faithful to her and his family, and that's what really mattered.

The daughter glanced around the club as James burst into his first song, and for a brief moment she made eye contact with him. He sucked in his breath, but then she looked away again and he saw her elbow her mum. He wondered how he might be able to slip through the crowd to the other side of the room. He was now determined to find out her name.

Then he saw both women glance over in his direction before turning their attention back to the stage.

⌒⌒○

"Mom...look over there...on the other side of the room. It's the guy I told you about that I met at the hotel...the one who gave me the newspaper."

Susan glanced at the audience briefly before looking back at James as the first song ended. "I don't see anybody."

"You didn't even look! Mom! I think he's staring at us..."

"Shhhh...I want to hear James!"

Michelle turned her attention back to the stage as James spoke to the audience, thanking everyone for coming and saying how nostalgic it was to be back in the Dusky Club. He then nodded to the band and the notes of *"Hug Me Too"* began to fill the room.

Susan's knees felt weak. She closed her eyes and listened to James as he sang...

> *"Hug, hug me too...*
> *You know I want you...*
> *Please don't make me blue...*
> *So pleeeeez...Hug me too...*
> *Whoa, oh...Hug me too..."*

It was as if she were once again in the year 1962, listening to the most famous band of all time before they became world famous. She remembered their scruffy look the first time she'd been at the club, and how James had insisted they clean themselves up to look more professional. By the time she'd come back again later that year, they were all cleaned up, wearing white shirts and ties instead of the leather they'd worn in the earlier days.

James voice had changed since then, sounding deeper and more mature, but it didn't matter to Susan. To her, just hearing his voice made her heart beat faster in her chest. It made her feel all tingly inside…in fact, as she looked at him, she began to tingle all over, other memories of him washing into her brain.

His face was still the handsomest she'd ever seen, and she was close enough to see that he still had his captivating hazel eyes with the perfectly arched eyebrows above them. His hair was longer and swept down over his collar in back and she could even see some silver in it, giving him more of a distinguished look. His stature hadn't changed at all. He wasn't quite as slender, but near enough. To her, he was breathtakingly gorgeous.

James was wearing dark blue trousers, a long-sleeved white shirt open at the collar, a blue jacket and had loafers on his feet. His foot was tapping to the music. The audience was clapping along. Susan and Michelle began to clap too.

They were both so involved in the music, that Michelle didn't notice Thomas start to worm his way through the crowd as James finished his tenth song and took a moment to drink some water. When Michelle turned her attention away from the stage to look across the room to see if the newspaper guy was still there, she was startled to see him standing right in front of her.

Thomas smiled at her broadly before extending his hand. She looked even more beautiful today than she had the day before in the hotel lobby. Her sea green eyes almost made him stutter.

"I'm Thomas," he said politely. "I'm afraid I didn't catch your name yesterday…"

Michelle raised her eyebrows. "Thomas? Your name is Thomas?!" She sounded shocked for some reason.

"Yes...yes, it is...that's all right, isn't it? I mean, I've never considered it a bad name..." His voice trailed off.

"Oh no! I'm sorry...I didn't mean it that way...It's just that I know someone else named Thomas...and...um, well never mind...Sorry, my name is Michelle." She took his hand and shook it.

She felt like an idiot all of a sudden. His hand was warm and he had a firm, manly grip. For some reason she found it disconcerting. Her fiancé, Thomas, suddenly didn't seem so manly. And, oh my God! As she looked at him again, he looked so much like James that she had to blink a couple of times. And, those eyes of his...

As if he sensed he was making her nervous, he released her hand.

James started into another song. Susan didn't take her eyes off the stage.

"Are you enjoying the concert?" Thomas asked over the loud guitars.

Michelle leaned in closer to him. "Yes...very much! I actually know most of these songs anyway...My mom...I'll introduce her when I can get her to take her eyes off James for a couple of seconds...played his music all the time when I was growing up."

"Ah, so you know my dad's music then..."

If she'd been drinking something, she'd be choking on it. Her eyes opened wide and she gave a small gasp. Of course, he was James's son! The resemblance was obvious!

"You're...you're...ah...James's son?! As in the guy up on the stage?!"

He smiled. "Is that okay?"

"Uh...well...holy shit! I mean...excuse me...I'm just in a little bit of a shock here..."

"That's not normally the reaction I get."

"I apologize...I'm really sorry..."

"No need to be, Michelle...by the way, that's a beautiful name. My dad even wrote a song by that name a long time ago."

"Yeah...I know...Mom named me after that song."

"So, your mum was a fan of the band then?

"Uh…you could say that…" She thought to herself, "*That* would be an understatement!"

Thomas and Michelle were inches apart now, needing to be close to hear each other over the music.

"I'll be happy to introduce your mum to Dad after the concert. I imagine people will be swarming about him, but I can get her up close and personal to maybe even say a few words…"

Michelle almost choked again. "I…ah, think my mom would like that very much. In fact, I think she'd really love to get his autograph."

"Oh, no problem at all! Dad's really good giving autographs. He rather enjoys making his fans happy."

"Why that's very nice of him. Especially considering how famous he is. So, why did he decide to give this concert? And why did he pick here? There can't be more than a hundred people in this place."

"Oh, you wouldn't know, I suppose, but this is where he started. I mean, he and his bandmates played other places before this, including clubs in Germany, but this is where they got their foot in the door, so to speak. Where they were discovered."

"Back in 1962, right?"

"Oh! You *do* know then! Your mum likely told you."

"Oh yes…she told me all about it actually…"

"So, anyway, he decided this would be a good place to give his first concert since my mum died. It's been over two years now since we lost her…Dad finally agreed it was time to get back to music. It's what Mum would have wanted him to do…so this is like a new beginning for him."

"And this place likely holds good memories…"

"As a matter of fact, I quite think it does. Dad got here a few days ago to poke around and visit places he hasn't seen in years, including the house where he grew up. He even drove out to the countryside to check on his auntie's cottage. I think he spent time there when he was younger."

Michelle turned her head to glance at Susan to see if she might be listening in on her conversation with Thomas, but her attention was rapt on James, plus the music was too loud. Michelle turned her head back to Thomas, remembering Susan's story of Auntie Annabelle's cottage, figuring it must be the same one James had gone to visit. She couldn't say anything to Thomas, however.

"Well, it's healthy to reacquaint yourself with your past sometimes...remember good things..."

"It is, isn't it?"

By this time, Thomas realized James was well more than halfway through the concert. He pulled a copy of the set list out of his pocket and glanced at it, then handed it to Michelle.

"I don't know why he decided to sing so many songs, but once he gets started, well, there's no stopping him. Looks like the next song is, *'Your Love Amazes Me.'* I hope he can get through it. He used to sing it to Mum on stage when they performed together. I don't think he's sang it since they last were on stage together, probably over three years now."

Both Michelle and Thomas turned their attention to the stage as James sat down at the piano that had been rolled from the side over to the center, and started to sing.

"Your love is so deep and strong...
Without you, I could not go on...
Your smile reaches into my heart...
Knowing we never will part...
You are the light of my life...erasing all strife...
Your love dazes me...
Your love amazes me..."

Michelle looked over at Susan again, who had a sad smile on her face, her focus never leaving James. It was obvious Susan knew James had written the song for his wife, and she knew that her mom felt melancholy at his loss despite her feelings for him. Looking at her mom's face, she suddenly realized how much Susan loved him...had always loved him.

Thomas followed Michelle's gaze as Susan reached both hands up to her chest to clutch the ballerina shoes hanging on the end of her necklace. The intensity of her feelings was written all over her face, her lips slightly parted and the sparkle of tears brimming on her eyelashes. He looked back at Michelle but said nothing. They both returned their eyes to the stage.

"I know I haven't been perfect for you...
But my heart and my soul have always been true...
You've stood by me when I wasn't fair...
And you promised me you'd always be there...
Your love crazes me...
Your love amazes me..."

Thomas could hear the quivering in his dad's voice and knew he was having a difficult time singing. There were tears brimming in his eyes as he continued to play and sing.

"You are the reason I get up each day...
The reason I laugh and I cry and I stay...
For without you I wouldn't be much of a man...
It's you who makes me all that I am...
Your love blazes me...
Your love amazes me...
Your love covers me with wonder...
It simply amazes me...amazes me...
And it always will..."

As the final piano notes drifted away, James tilted his head back and closed his eyes. The audience was overwhelmed at the emotional rendition of the song everyone knew he'd written for his Susan, and the clapping and shouting became louder and louder. James stood up, dabbed at his eyes, then turned to get more water and collect himself while the piano was being rolled away. As he came back to the microphone, he shrugged off his jacket, tossed it to the side then unbuttoned the cuffs of his shirt and rolled up the sleeves. He gave a small nod of his head before taking another guitar from one of his bandmates and slipping the strap over his shoulder.

"All right then! Are you ready to rock?!"

The audience enthusiastically responded with a raucous, "*YES!*" and James burst into an old Elvis tune, followed by a few more rock 'n roll numbers that had the audience swaying, clapping and singing along.

Michelle was impressed. She hadn't realized James's musical abilities had such a wide range. Her mom was right that he had talent that went above and beyond the best of the best. He truly was a phenomenon.

Sweat was pouring down James's face as he finished the last number and moved into a slower tune. Thomas knew it was one of his dad's best-known songs and realized he really was trying to do a compilation of his greatest hits, not just for the crowd in attendance but for the video that was being recorded.

Halfway through the song, James looked out at the audience searching for Thomas. When he located him, he did something he'd never done before in a performance. He stopped. It was only for a few seconds, but it was an obvious halt in the singing, so much so that the crowd noticed and started to follow his gaze.

The band behind him picked up again on the notes he'd missed, and James continued to sing, but he was clearly shaken. The crowd turned their attention back to him, not understanding what had happened.

When he'd spotted Thomas, he also spotted the two blonde women standing next to him. In fact, they were only about fifteen feet away. The one standing closest to the wall was staring at him so intently, it was as if an electrical current was emanating from her towards him, and when her green eyes locked with his for just the briefest moment, he felt the electric charge hit him full force, leaving him momentarily stunned.

He used all the will he had to turn his mind in another direction and concentrate on the song. He was somewhat successful, but his voice was unsteady through to the last notes, and when he was done, he excused himself, saying he had a bit of a frog in his throat, joking it must be his advancing age. He walked to the back of the stage, where he drank more water, his hands shaking slightly and took a full two minutes to compose himself.

Susan.

He knew that's who the woman standing against the wall was. He felt it so intensely that it almost made him feel weak in the knees. Why it was affecting him so strongly was a mystery. She was so far in his past that she meant nothing…nothing…

At least that's what he kept repeating to himself as he sipped at the bottle of water. Finally, he felt calm enough to return to the microphone. He signaled the band to start in on the next song on the set list. He only had five more to go, and for some reason felt relieved. He'd only been on stage for a little over an hour and a half, and normally, he was just starting to get warmed up by this time; the more he played and sang, the more pumped up he felt, especially if the audience was in sync with him.

But Susan had ruined all that. Where had she come from? Why was she here? When he glanced in her direction again, he saw her reach up to grasp a silver chain around her neck and almost startled again, knowing it was her damn necklace, confirming that the woman was indeed the Susan from his past, the one who had nearly destroyed him with her lies and duplicity, not just once, but multiple times.

Even though he'd been thinking of her for the past several days, he felt angry and resentful that she would dare show up in his life again, and he was equally upset that she'd caused him to falter in one of his best songs. Damn her! Now, he'd have to figure a way to re-do the song for the video or take it out altogether. The more he thought about her, the angrier he got, wondering how she dared to show her face to him again.

Susan knew the minute James's eyes met hers that he recognized her and she was taken aback by it. He hadn't laid eyes on her in thirty-two years. He'd married and had a family, become tremendously successful and wealthy. He'd even been knighted and was now officially "Sir James." Why and how would he have remembered her? What had made him recognize her?

Then she sucked in her breath as she realized she'd been toying with her necklace when James eyes locked with hers and she knew it had probably given her away. Damn!

Thomas was puzzled as to what had overcome his dad and made him come to a dead stop in the middle of one of his best songs. It wasn't something that he'd ever witnessed before in all the years he'd been at his dad's performances, including the ones he'd attended as a child when his mum and dad toured together. The family always came along on tour.

"Well, that's a first!" he remarked to Michelle as James finished the song and went to the back of the stage and picked up the bottle of water again. "Something seems to have upset Dad for him to stop in the middle of a song like that!"

Michelle glanced over at Susan, whose face was pasty white then looked up at the stage where she could see James drinking water and looking in Susan's direction. Her lawyer's brain, which was quite adept at reading facial expressions, immediately surmised that James had somehow recognized her mom and had been unnerved by it.

"Maybe he saw a ghost," she responded jokingly. "It's been over thirty-six years since he's been here, right? Maybe it's one of his old bandmates who showed up for the concert in spirit."

"Ah...could be! Dad's always saying he feels Derek around him from time to time."

Thomas glanced over at Susan as James started into the next song.

"Your mum looks pretty pale all of a sudden. Do you think maybe the heat in here is getting to her? She doesn't look well."

Michelle moved away from Thomas and nudged Susan in the side. Susan startled.

"Wha...wha...! What are you doing? Why did you poke me like that?!"

"Cool it, Mom. I think James recognized you and I don't want to have to explain why to Thomas."

"Thomas?! Thomas is here??!! How did he get here? I thought he was back in San Diego, and...Oh my God!"

Susan looked past Michelle's shoulder and saw a younger version of James standing directly behind her. She was speechless.

Michelle decided to make introductions.

"Mom, this is James's son, Thomas. He's the one who was nice enough to give me his newspaper at the hotel yesterday. He's actually been standing here for close to a half hour now, while you were...I mean, while your attention was riveted...rather, you were paying attention to..."

"Pleased to meet you," interrupted Thomas, extending his hand. "It's not often that I get to meet two such beautiful women at one time."

Michelle never blushed, but she could suddenly feel the heat in her face.

"Ah...well, thank you..."

Just then, James finished the song and began thanking the audience for attending, adding that he had one more special song to sing. Thomas pulled out the set list again and looked at it.

"He's skipping the last four songs on his list?!"

He looked at his dad with his eyebrows raised. James looked back at him briefly before looking back out at the audience.

"It's been thirty seven years since I first played here," said James into the microphone. "And it's great to be back. There are so many memories here, I can almost feel them seeping out of the walls. I remember the nights we played here and the doubts we had about our future. I remember the small group of fans we had back then and how kind and supportive they were. I recall standing on this very stage all those years ago and looking out into the crowd through a haze of smoke, seeing familiar faces and then new faces as more and more people came to hear us play...But most of all, I remember the music and the tunes Derek and I wrote together as well as the ones we wrote separately but later collaborated on. And, I'd like to close tonight with a tune that I wrote in the summer of 1962, one that was first performed here...on a night I remember so well...one that seemed to be filled with sparks...a night I'll never forget..."

Both Michelle and Thomas looked amused as James spoke to the band for a minute then came back to the microphone, slipping the strap of his bass guitar over his head.

Susan's face drained of all color and she had to lean full back into the wall to keep her knees from buckling out from under her.

"He wouldn't dare...!" she whispered to herself.

But he did...staring directly at her as he sang.

"Close your eyes while I touch you...
You know how I love you...
Remember me while you're away...
And then while you are gone...
I will try to go on...
And send all my kisses your way..."

Michelle instantly recognized the song. Her mother must have played it a thousand times while she was growing up. And she'd also told her about how James had written it for her on her first journey into the past.

"I'll remember your sweetness...
Our moments of sheer bliss...
And know that you'll come back to me...
And I'll also remember your tender surrender...
So sure that we always will be...
All my kisses I will send to you...
All my kisses...
Only meant for you..."

She turned and looked at Susan then at James. He was singing the song directly to her mom. When she looked back at her, she saw her face start to crumple along with her body that began to slide slowly down the wall.

"Close your eyes while I touch you...
You know how I love you...
Remember me while you're away...
And then while you are gone...

I will try to go on…
And send all my kisses your way…"

Susan put both hands over her face as she sank onto the floor. Michelle and Thomas rushed over to her, both going down on their knees, one on each side.

"All my kisses…
All my kisses…
All my kisses…
Only meant for you…"
Susan had fainted.

Chapter 7

James Gets His Revenge

James saw Susan go down and almost stopped playing again, thinking to rush off the stage to her, but knew it would create a backlash of speculation and questions. He used all his self-control to finish the song before saying into the microphone, "Thank you all again for coming! Stick around for some drink and refreshments. I'll be back in just a bit for the promised interview and to answer questions about my up and coming album."

Before the crowd could converge on him, he escaped into the stairwell that led up to the practice room above. Thomas was right ahead of him, climbing the stairs with Susan in his arms and Michelle beside him. When Thomas got to the top, he laid Susan on the cot at the back of the room. James pushed him aside and went down on his knees next to the cot, taking Susan's cold hand in his and looking down into her face.

"Get some water!" he yelled over his shoulder to Thomas.

Michelle went down on her knees next to James. "How could you??!!" she ranted at him. "How could you sing that song, knowing what it meant to her?!"

Thomas came back to the cot with a bottle of water in his hand and unscrewed the cap. He handed it to James with his eyebrows raised and looked at Michelle.

"What about the song?"

"It's the song he wrote for her...all those years ago when they first met here...before the band became famous."

Thomas looked stunned. "You know Michelle's mother??" he said, looking down at his dad.

James turned his head and looked up at him as he took the water bottle from his hand.

"Yes," was all he said before pouring a small amount of water into his palm then sprinkling it on Susan's forehead. He laid his hand on her brow and smoothed it back over her hair. Her eyes fluttered open and she looked up at him.

Michelle looked over at James, and what she saw in his eyes made her speechless. It was a look so tender and full of love that she was taken aback by it. Looking at her mother's face, she saw the look returned.

Was it true then? Did you always remember your first true love? Despite the number of years that had passed? Despite what had happened since the last time you were together? Was it something you could never let go of?

Michelle stood up and looked at Thomas. "I don't know what to say about all this..."

"Please leave us..." James whispered, not taking his eyes from Susan's.

"But all those people down in the Club...they're waiting for you, and..."

James turned his head and looked up at Thomas. "Make my excuses...Say I've come down with a putrid throat...whatever you need to say..."

"But, Dad..."

"Do it, please...and have a car called around into the alley. I'm taking Susan back to the hotel..."

"I'm going with you," interrupted Michelle.

"No...please," begged James. ""Stay here with Thomas, please... I'll make sure she's okay...It was my fault she fainted after all..."

Michelle bit her lip. "I don't know...I think I should stay with my mom..."

"It's okay," whispered Susan, looking away from James. "I'll be all right."

"Are you sure, Mom?"

Susan nodded. "I'm sure…" She looked back at James and squeezed his hand. He squeezed back.

Michelle set Susan's purse on the bottom of the cot. She'd rescued it from the floor where it had fallen when Susan fainted.

"Okay then…I'll see you back at the hotel…"

Thomas grasped her hand and they both left the practice room and headed down the stairs, closing the door behind them.

Michelle didn't really notice that Thomas was holding her hand until they got to the bottom of the stairs and walked out onto the stage area. When she did, she tugged it away and felt heat come into her face again.

Thomas looked over at her and grinned a choirboy grin reminiscent of the photos she'd seen of a younger James. She smiled back. Oh my! He was so charming, and so incredibly good looking. She suddenly realized why her mother had been so obsessed with James when she was young. These men were certainly something to behold!

As Thomas stepped off the stage area, helping Michelle down, the crowd surged around him asking when James would be back. Thomas expertly fielded their questions, explaining that the concert had somewhat strained his dad's voice after being away from performing for so long and that he needed to give it a rest. He further explained that James was getting ready to record a new album, which sent a wave of enthusiasm across the room and resulted in more questions. Thomas handled them all efficiently, and after a half hour, as the audience indulged in more of the free drinks and refreshments that were provided, he and Michelle were able to slip away and walk back to the hotel unnoticed.

When they got to the hotel lobby, Michelle wanted to go up to Susan's room to check on her, but Thomas suggested they go into the hotel dining room instead, adding that Susan was most likely up in the penthouse suite with his dad rather than in her room.

Michelle stared at him. "I'm not sure if that's a good thing or a bad thing."

"Well, as far as I'm concerned, it's a *very* good thing. Dad's been in the doldrums ever since Mum passed. Carrie, Robert and I were wondering if he'd ever come out of it. This might turn out to be the best thing that's happened to him since we lost Mum."

"Carrie and Robert?"

"Oh, sorry...my sister and brother. Carrie stayed with Dad at the family retreat in Colorado for a few months after Mum died. Then, Dad came back to his house outside of London, but always wanted to be alone. We've all been worried about him; his grief all but consumed him. Carrie's always been closest to him. She's what pulled him back to life and coaxed him to start thinking about music again. Then he did a huge favor for me by writing a piano concerto. It's certainly bolstered my career..."

"You're a concert pianist?!"

"Yeah...must be music in my blood, you know...I just ended up loving classical rather than pop or rock 'n roll."

A waiter noticed them standing at the entrance to the dining room and directed them to a table for two set back in the corner of the dining room. Thomas held out a chair for Michelle and she sat down, placing her purse on the floor. Two menus were placed in front of them. Thomas ordered a bottle of wine and continued.

"My brother, Robert, just graduated from chef school in September. He's head chef at a posh vegetarian restaurant in London now called Le Fonda. He wanted to be here tonight for Dad's concert, but wasn't able to get away because there's so much of a demand for catering this time of year and this is his first Christmas season as head chef."

"What about your sister, Carrie?"

"She's an inveterate traveler, almost like a vagabond. Has a hard time sitting still. I don't know how she was able to spend so much time with Dad for the past two years without going stir crazy, but she's always adored him, so..."

"Does she travel just for the sake of traveling and seeing new places?"

"Oh no! She's into ancient artifacts and antiquities as well as being an artist. She likes to explore old castles and villas, that sort of thing. Her boyfriend, David, goes with her on her 'hunting trips,' as she calls them. We all keep wondering when they'll get married, but Dad said she told him they're too good of friends to ever get married."

"She sounds interesting."

"Well, I hope you get to meet her someday."

Michelle raised her eyebrows. "Well, that's unlikely. I don't really know how much longer we're going to be here, and now that the concert's over..."

Thomas looked thoughtful. "So, what is it that brought you to Brighton? Did you come just for the concert then?"

Shit! How am I going to explain it? Michelle muttered silently. *No way I can tell the truth...*

"Yes, actually, we did come for the concert. We...ah...won tickets, and Mom wanted to come just for old times' sake. You know...just for the memories...She didn't think your dad would recognize her or remember her after all the years since she last saw him..."

"I see..." He looked at her questioningly, sensing there was more, but just then the waiter returned with the wine and presented the bottle to Thomas. He nodded and the waiter uncorked the bottle, setting the cork on the table and pouring a small amount of wine into a glass for Thomas to taste. Thomas swirled the wine around in the glass, sniffed it then took a sip. He nodded and the waiter poured two glasses.

"Would you like to order yet?" he asked looking first to Thomas then to Michelle.

"Oh no!" responded Michelle, opening the menu. "I haven't even looked yet."

Thomas opened his menu as the waiter described the specialties of the day, then bowed and left, saying he'd return in a bit.

Thomas looked back at Michelle. "So...it was obvious to me that Dad not only recognized your mum, but he was rather dazed by it. And then, for him to alter the set list and play that *'All My Kisses'* song to end the concert...well, it was most unusual!"

"Yes, well…"

"You said back at the club that he wrote the song for your mum. Is that true?"

"It is…"

Michelle took a sip of her wine, wondering just how much she should tell Thomas about her mom…about how she'd been an American history student who came to Brighton all those years ago… about how his dad had fallen in love with her…

⌒◯

After Thomas and Michelle left the practice room, there was dead silence for a full minute as James and Susan gazed at each other. Then, wordlessly, James sat down on the edge of the cot and pulled Susan up into his arms, where she wrapped hers around his waist and buried her face into his shoulder.

He stroked her back and rocked back and forth, pulling her in tighter to him, but it was as if neither of them had anything to say to each other or simply didn't know *what* to say to each other.

When there was a knock at the door leading to the alley, James knew it must be the car that had been sent for to take them back to the hotel. He stood up, still holding Susan, then released her to take her hand. She picked up her purse and they headed to the door. They were soon on their way back to the Claridon.

James didn't bother putting on his disguise as he hurriedly pulled Susan through the lobby and into an elevator. He hoped he hadn't been recognized, but there wasn't anyone in the lobby other than the desk clerk. When they arrived at the penthouse floor, James led Susan down to his suite and inserted the door key into the lock. They still had said nothing to each other, both of their minds swirling with random thoughts and memories.

When James kicked his shoes off, Susan followed suit, and as he led her across the main room into the bedroom, her heart felt as if it would pound out of her chest. What did he think he was doing? He hadn't said a word to her! Did she really think she was going to let him make love to her? With no conversation? With no words of endearment or consideration as to how she might feel? Without even kissing her first?!

Evidently, that's exactly what he thought as he released her hand and reached up to unbutton his shirt, his eyes never leaving her face. She sucked in her breath as she saw the amber highlights sparking in his eyes, and her knees felt weak with the memory of what that meant. She was frozen to the spot.

He shrugged off the shirt and it fell to the floor at his feet. Before she knew what was happening, he advanced towards her, putting his hands on her shoulders then spun her around and quickly unzipped her dress and pushed the sleeves off her shoulders. The dress puddled on the floor around her feet. He unhooked her bra and it soon joined the dress on the floor along with her panties that he pushed down and over her hips. She gasped as he reached around her and pinched her nipples, pushing himself up against her. She could feel the hardness of his erection against her bottom.

James buried his face in her hair, inhaling the scent of it, remembering how much he loved the smell and taste of her. While she was still slender, her older body was fuller in both the hips and breasts, giving her more of a voluptuous feel rather than the hard, muscled body of her dancing days, but to him it seemed perfection…her skin, silky to the touch, her whole body from head to toe, warm and desirable. He was out of control with lust and overcome with want and need.

"James…please, no…" she muttered as he began to trail kisses down the side of her neck to her bare shoulder, where he bit her a little too roughly. She gave a small cry.

"Shut up!" he panted into her ear as he began rubbing his stiffness between the cheeks of her bare bottom. He still had his trousers on and she could feel the zipper scratching her. She wiggled to get away, but it was futile as he encircled her waist with one arm while moving the hand of his other arm around her front and down between her legs. His fingers probed and rubbed the most sensitive and intimate part of her body and she heard his breath catch as he inserted a finger into her and felt how wet she was.

She felt as if her body were betraying her. It wasn't supposed to happen this way...she wasn't ready for this. There was no point in denying that she wanted him...but not like this! *Shut up?!! He'd told her to shut up?!!* Why weren't they exchanging words of love, talking softly to each other, getting to know each other again? Why was he doing this to her?!

James really didn't know why he was reacting this way. After years of abstinence...well not quite...he'd taken care of his needs himself over the past couple of years...he suddenly felt he had no control over his lust. And seeing Susan again had flamed it into a fire that needed to be quenched. Memories of their intimate encounters flooded his brain like a tidal wave and he almost thought he'd come right in his trousers rubbing against her bottom.

Before she had a chance to protest, he pulled her over to the bed and pushed her down onto her back, spreading her legs open with his knees. He opened his trousers and shorts then thrust forward into her warmth, stopping for just a moment to savor the feel of her around his shaft. He was breathing heavily as he began the rhythmic pumping in and out of her, not noticing the tears on her face, her near choking sobs or pleas to stop.

His thrusts increased in intensity, becoming faster and faster. She writhed beneath him, beginning to feel the pleasure she'd always felt with him. Her breaths became shorter and shorter, but just as she felt her own release approaching, he tilted his head back and moaned loudly, spilling himself into her. He fell forward over her, panting heavily, his palms on the bed and his arms straight, holding himself above her. With a grunt, he stood back up, pulling out of her and turned his back, running a hand through his hair and shaking his head.

He said nothing as he pushed his softening member back into his shorts and trousers and zipped up. He picked up his shirt off the floor and slipped an arm in one sleeve then the other. Walking towards the door, he picked up Susan's green dress, bra and panties and tossed them at her as she sat up.

He turned to look at her, his eyes piercing hers. "Get dressed and get out," he said in a cold voice that chilled her to the bone. When the door closed softly behind him, Susan sat in stunned disbelief on the edge of the bed before hugging herself tightly then rocking back and forth trying to hold back more tears that she knew were about to pour out like a broken dam.

Finally, she was able to collect herself and stood up to get dressed. She could feel James's ejaculation running down her inner thigh and looked around for a tissue to wipe herself, but saw nothing. She slipped on her panties anyway, the leg band wiping most of him off as she pulled them up. She put on her bra then her dress, struggling to get the zipper up, but finally managed it. Picking up her purse that had fallen off her shoulder by the bedroom door when James had dragged her in, she opened the door and went out into the main room of the suite.

James was in front of the window, looking out at the night sky, his back turned towards her, a wine glass in hand. Slowly she walked towards him, slipping her feet into her shoes on the way.

"James…" she whispered in an agonized voice.

"I told you to get out," he said without turning around. "You just got what you wanted, didn't you? You wanted fucked and I fucked you…"

She inhaled sharply, shaking her head as his crude words sent a jolt through her. "No…James, please…that's not why I came here… it's not!"

It was impossible to hold back the tears any longer. Her face crumpled and they poured down her face.

"Get out!" James screamed, turning to look at her, his face mottled in anger. "Get out of my sight…now!!!"

Susan swallowed and started to back away from him, a pain so sharp and deep inside her, that she felt as if she'd been stabbed with a knife. Without saying another word, she turned and ran to the hotel room door, wrenched it open and ran at full speed to the elevator where she punched frantically at the buttons.

Chapter 8

Michelle Explains

"You know, I'm really not very hungry," Michelle said as the waiter stopped by for the third time to see what she and Thomas might want to order.

"Me either," said Thomas, closing his menu. "I ate with Dad right before the concert, so I really don't need anything else."

He excused the waiter, who picked up the menus after re-filling both of their glasses with the rest of the bottle of wine.

"So, I guess maybe it's fate or something that brought your mum here to meet up with my dad again. I saw the way they were looking at each other. It kind of made me feel good inside to think that maybe Dad could find love again."

"I…ah…kind of felt the same way. But, I'm not so sure it would work out between them…"

"Why not? Is your mum still married to your dad or something?"

Michelle bit her lip. She hated lying, but she didn't want to ruin things for her mom. She might lose the opportunity to give the ring back to James.

"No…no, she's not married," she lied. "It's just that something horrible happened the last time she was with your dad…"

"The last time? How many times was she with him then?"

"Um…actually, it was before I was born, so I don't know all the details…but I think she was with him three, maybe four times…"

Thomas leaned back in his chair, swirling the rest of the wine in his glass. "So what horrible thing happened? Do you know?"

"Yeah, she told me about it…and…well, I think she hurt him badly, the last time more than the others…"

"She's hurt him more than once?!"

"Maybe I shouldn't tell you…you'll probably change your mind about feeling good that they might be back together again."

"No, no…don't worry…it was long ago, right? And, I'm sure maybe there were extenuating circumstances or…"

Michelle interrupted him. "Actually, there were reasons…"

Thomas finished his wine and leaned forward again, waiting for Michelle to continue.

"So," she went on. "The first time my mom met your dad was in June, 1962 in the Dusky Club. She was a student here on a history tour. She got into Brighton before the rest of the students and ended up going to the club, where your dad saw her. They ended up having an affair…"

She paused to take a sip of her wine. "But then she had to leave for the tour, and your dad didn't want her to, but she went anyway and it really upset him. That's when he wrote the '*All My Kisses*' song for her…Anyway, she came back again in November of the same year and brought her brother…uh…my Uncle John, with her. Your dad and my mom resumed their love affair…and your dad asked Mom to marry him…"

Thomas's eyes opened wide in surprise. "He did?! Wow! Dad's never spoken of it! Didn't she want to marry him?"

"I think she was shocked when he asked her. She knew that the band was on the brink of being famous. A lot of girls fawned over him all the time and, well…she told me he had a wandering eye and had slept with a bunch of other girls during the time she was gone…"

Michelle was doing her best to have the story make sense. There was no way she could tell Thomas the truth about time-traveling or the explosion in the hotel room when James had proposed to her mom and discovered her deceit. And, she didn't want to bring the necklace into the story. *That* would be even harder to explain.

"Anyway, she refused him and then she and Uncle John came back to America. Your dad was even more upset. She said she knew she broke his heart…but that it couldn't be helped…that he would have married her, the band would have become famous and he would have been on tour, cheated on her…well, she didn't think she could handle it…"

Thomas nodded understandingly. "Yes, I know Dad was quite the lady's man in those days…I suppose she had to make the decision that was right for her…I don't find what she did so horrible…"

"Well, it was actually the last time she was with him that was the worst…"

Thomas sat back in his chair again. "And?"

"So…she came back to England in July, 1967 to do an internship with the Royal Dance Company of England…she used to be a ballerina…Two of her girlfriends came with her. One of them was also an intern with the RDC, the other an intern actress with the theatre company. Their dorm room and classes were in the same building where your dad's band recorded. My mom got a part-time job with Cherry Studios and hooked up with your dad again. She ended up moving in with him…and, well…from what Mom said, they were madly in love with each other. He asked her to marry him again…and she accepted…"

"Dad was married before he met my mum??!!"

"No, no…something happened…"

Michelle paused for a few seconds, finishing off her wine and taking a deep breath. "Her friends betrayed her on their wedding day. They…ah…kidnapped her…drugged her, I think…and your dad and the rest of the family were in the church and everything…and she never showed up. Her friends brought her back to America…"

"How is that possible?! Why would they do such a thing?!"

"I don't know…Mom won't talk about it," she continued the lie. "I guess it really tore her up…"

"Why didn't she get a hold of my dad when she got back? He probably would have come to get her! If they were both so much in love, they would have found a way, wouldn't they? It doesn't make sense."

"I know, I know…but she won't talk about it, and your dad obviously never said anything about it to anyone…Maybe when he was left standing in the church he figured she'd changed her mind and didn't love him after all…Maybe he was angry because she'd left him before when he asked her to marry him…"

Thomas gave a heavy sigh. "What a horrible and sad story. No wonder Dad faltered in his song when he recognized her tonight. But I'm curious as to how he would have recognized her after all these years. That doesn't make sense either…"

"Well, maybe it does…I look almost exactly like my mom did when your dad last saw her, and I was standing next to you, remember? Plus, she has green eyes…not a lot of people have eyes like hers…But, not only that…"

She thought now would be the time to casually bring the necklace into the conversation.

"Mom was wearing her necklace tonight…in fact, she never takes it off. She was wearing it all those times she was with your dad. It's a silver ballerina necklace that my great-grandfather gave her on her twelfth birthday. She told me she'd given it to your dad when they were first together…in fact, she left it with him, but he gave it back to her the second time she was back…"

"She gave him her necklace?

"Yeah…he had it for the months she was gone in 1962 and she said he wore it the whole time she was gone. I think he must have recognized it tonight. She always plays with it when she's nervous. He must have noticed. He would have known for certain then that she was the girl he met all those years ago. I just didn't think it would matter to him."

"I'm stunned, Michelle, really stunned. Dad's never spoken of your mum…and to think she has the same name as my own mum… why that's pretty incredible!"

"It is, isn't it? …Well, I think I should go up to my room now…I'm right next door to Mom…I wonder how she is or if she's back yet…"

Her face began to flush, thinking she might still be with James up in his penthouse suite.

Thomas's face turned a light shade of pink along with Michelle's. "Uh, well...I suppose she might still be with my dad...the way they were looking at each other back in the practice room..."

"You're probably right...but, ah...I still think I should go up to my room. It's been a long day and I'm still on a different clock than you are. There's an eight-hour difference, you know."

"Oh, right! Sorry, I wasn't thinking."

He signaled the waiter and gave him his room number for the wine bill then stood up. Michelle reached down to the floor, picked up her purse and stood up. They left the dining room and crossed the lobby where Thomas pushed the elevator button. When they were inside he asked Michelle what floor she was on.

"Four," she replied.

"Oh, me too!" he said, pushing the panel inside the elevator.

When they got to the fourth floor, Thomas stepped out with her. "What room number"

"Oh! I think it's 4128. Mom's in 4130. It's down that way." She pointed down the hall to the left.

"I'm in 4029...it's down the other way. I'll just walk you to your door...make sure you get in all right and all..."

Michelle blushed again. "Okay..."

When they got to her door, she fished in her purse for her room key and inserted it into the lock. She turned back to face Thomas. "Well, I've got to say we've sure had an interesting night..."

"I can't argue with that...the only thing is that we've done nothing but talk about your mum and my dad. I don't know anything at all about you!"

"That's true, isn't it? And I don't know much about you either, other than you're a famous concert pianist."

"I'm not quite as famous as you think. I'm a newbie, actually, but I love what I do. I'll have to play for you sometime..."

She smiled as she looked up into his eyes. "That would be very nice."

"And," she thought to herself, "it would be very nice indeed!" His eyes were locked onto hers, sending shivers down her spine, and she wondered if her mom had experienced the same unnerving feelings for James when he first looked into her eyes with such intensity. The golden embers mixed in with the sapphire blue was simply hypnotic. She felt as if she could stare into them forever. As she continued to gaze, she almost thought that the gold in his eyes intensified into tiny flames and she felt chill bumps on her arms.

Thomas couldn't tear his gaze away from hers. He'd discovered that she wasn't only the most beautiful girl he'd ever met, but intelligent as well. And, her voice was like sweet music to his ears; he could listen to it forever. There was no denying his attraction to her.

"So," he said. "Might I see you again tomorrow? Maybe even meet you in the dining room for breakfast?"

Her smile turned brilliant, lighting up her whole face. "Yes, I think I'd like that very much…"

"Is 8:00 too early? I'm an early riser."

"That's fine."

"Well…I'll see you then…I'm looking forward to it."

"Me too…"

She turned and unlocked her hotel room door then walked inside. She looked back at him for a brief moment. "Good night, Thomas."

"Good night, Michelle…"

As the door closed, Thomas wanted to kick himself. He was so close to asking her if he could kiss her goodnight. But then he thought she might find him too forward and was glad he didn't. There would be opportunity for kisses later, he thought as he walked down the hallway.

When he got to the elevator, he suddenly remembered that he'd left notes on a new piano composition up in his dad's suite on the coffee table. He debated for a moment as to whether he should go up, not wanting to interrupt any romantic interlude his dad might be having with Michelle's mum. But, then he thought they'd probably be in the bedroom and it would only take a few seconds to grab the notes and leave. He pushed the "up" button on the elevator.

When the elevator doors opened, Susan was shocked to see Thomas standing inside. He saw that her face was ghostly white and had tears running down from her eyes, the mascara staining her cheeks. She pushed past him and hit the panel for the fourth floor.

"What's wrong? Are you okay?" he asked, concern on his face and in his voice.

"Just please…leave me alone…" she begged, pushing him out into the hallway. "Please…"

Thomas didn't know what to think or do as the elevator doors closed in his face. He turned and walked down the hallway to his dad's suite. The door was open. When he walked in, he saw James staring at the open doorway, an unreadable expression on his face. He couldn't tell if it was anger or pain or a combination of both.

He flinched as James flung his wine glass, some wine still in it, against the wall, where it shattered into pieces, then his shoulders drooped and he covered his face with both hands and began to sob.

"What's happened, Dad?!" Thomas blurted out as he watched James's shoulders move up and down. "Are you okay? I just saw Michelle's mum in the elevator, and…"

James stumbled over to the sofa and sat down, pulling his hands down his face. He tilted his head back for a moment, giving a loud groan then looked at Thomas.

"I just did something terrible," he choked out. "I don't know why, but…" His voice hitched and he closed his eyes, putting his hands on his face again and shaking his head back and forth.

"I don't know what came over me when we got back here from the Club. I thought we'd talk and…maybe get to know each other again… that maybe she'd explain why she left me all those years ago…broke my heart in a million pieces…"

Thomas said nothing, sitting down on the sofa next to his dad.

"But holding her in my arms at the Club after she woke up from her faint, and then in the car on the way back here…so many memories came back…and I kept looking at that damn necklace she's still wearing…and remembering what she did to me…" James sucked in a deep breath. "I wanted to hurt her! I wanted to make her pay for what she did to me all those years ago…I wanted her to feel the same pain I felt when she abandoned me at the altar of the church…"

So, thought Thomas. *Everything Michelle told me about Dad and her mum was true then…*

"When I found you in the audience at the Club and saw the girl standing next to you, she looked so much like Susan from all those years ago. I thought I was imagining it…that she was a ghost from the past. Then, when I saw the woman standing next to her against the wall…and she was twisting a silver chain in her hand…it all came back to me…I knew it was really Susan, the American history student that I fell in love with…who I thought loved me just as much…"

Thomas just nodded, continuing to listen.

"I was so angry…Seeing her made me stop in the middle of one of my best songs…I felt that she'd ruined the filming of the concert… And, I wanted her to know that I'd recognized her…"

"Is that why you sang *'All My Kisses'* to end the show…why you didn't do the last four songs on your set list?'

"Yes…Even though I knew it was really her, I wanted to make certain. As I sang and looked into her face, I knew for sure…but I didn't think she'd faint like that…I felt rather bad about it…"

"Until you got back here, that is…"

"Yes."

"What did you do to her, Dad? I don't think I've ever seen anyone with a look so full of anguish before."

James covered his face with his hands again. He stood up, dropping them to his sides and walked towards the window where he stood with his back to Thomas.

"When we got upstairs and she started toying with that necklace again, I decided to skip any talking…I just dragged her into the bedroom…and, and…I had my way with her…"

He turned around to face Thomas. "She didn't protest…at least not very much…just a little…I didn't *quite* force myself on her…"

Thomas stood up, staring at his dad in disbelief. "What do you mean she didn't protest *very much?!!* Did she tell you 'no?' Did you force her anyway?!!"

James turned back towards the window and looked out into the darkness.

"Yes," he whispered. "She was crying and begged me to stop, but...I did it anyway...it was over quickly...Then I told her to get out... to get out of my sight..." His shoulders slumped again.

"How could you, Dad?!" Thomas yelled, his voice getting louder. "How *could* you?!!"

With that, he snatched the notes he came for off the coffee table and stormed out of the suite, slamming the door behind him.

James went back to the sofa, where he sat down, leaned over and put his head in his hands. The image of Susan as she looked at him when he'd told her to get out, burned in his brain. It wouldn't go away...

⌒◌

Michelle tossed her purse onto the dresser in her hotel room then went and sat on the bottom of her bed.

What in holy hell was she doing?! What had she been thinking when she agreed to meet Thomas for breakfast?! She was engaged! She had no business going out to breakfast with another man! In fact, she had no business drinking wine with him like she'd done.

She was an intelligent woman. She was an attorney, schooled to control her emotions at all times. To be aloof, non-emotional, focused on facts and not on fantasy like her crazy mother. She'd come here to help her mother get rid of a ring and nothing more. It was a job she had to do, just like taking on a case for a client. You did your job, the judge or jury decided in favor of your client and that was the end of it. Hopefully, her mom was giving the ring back to James right now.

She screwed up her face in disgust as she thought about what else her mom and James might be doing. Yech...old people having sex... it didn't bear thinking about.

Then she thought about James's son, Thomas, again. She knew she shouldn't be thinking about him, that she should put him out of her mind, forget he existed...

83

But, she couldn't. His handsome face, tempting lips...Oh my God! Did she just think about his lips??! His warm hand and engaging smile...but most of all...yes, most of all...those captivating eyes...eyes you could swim in until you sank into the depths...drown in them...

Ugh! She stood up and started pacing the room, hands clasped behind her, just as she did in the courtroom. But, it didn't work to put Thomas out of her mind. Not one bit. She sighed as she went into the bathroom to wash her face, brush her teeth and change into her nightgown. She thought she might watch a little t.v. before trying to fall asleep.

Then she heard the door to her mom's room open and wondered what she was doing back so soon. Maybe she was able to give the ring back to James right away, and then they could get the hell out of here. She was relieved to know Susan wasn't spending the night with him and...well, she didn't want to think about two old people rolling around in bed together.

When she opened the connecting door to her mom's room, she saw Susan stretched out on the bed on her stomach. She had her head under a pillow and knew it was to stifle the sound of her crying. Her shoulders were heaving up and down.

"Mom!" she yelled, coming over to the bed and pulling the pillow off Susan's head. "What happened?! Why are you crying?! The way you and James were looking at each other back at the club...I thought you'd be...well, I thought you'd be getting reacquainted, whispering words of love to each other..."

Susan just moved her head from side to side to indicate "no" before sitting up and turning her tear-stained face towards Michelle, but she couldn't speak.

"Oh Mom! Maybe you were right and we shouldn't have come here! Maybe I made a mistake!"

"No, Michelle...no...It's okay..." Susan sniffed before reaching for the box of tissues at the side of the bed.

"But it's *not* okay! First he sings that song to you in the club that makes you pass out on the floor...then he does...whatever else he did just now upstairs...to make you so upset that you're crying your eyes out! Did you ever think that maybe you're some kind of poison to each other? I mean...your damn necklace goes back and forth between you...you break his heart...he breaks yours..."

Susan wiped her eyes and blew her nose.

Michelle continued. "I was just in the dining room with Thomas, James's son. We were going to have dinner, but neither of us was hungry. He kept wanting to know about you and his dad. I had to make things up..."

Susan sniffed again. "Like what?"

"Well, I told him about you being a student and all that, and how you and his dad fell in love and that he asked you to marry him, and..."

"You told him all that??!"

"Well, I hedged as much as I could, but then I mentioned that you'd done something horrible, which was why his dad sang that song to you that made you faint...and I ended up telling him that your two girlfriends kind of kidnapped you on what was supposed to be your wedding day...and that you woke up on a plane, and..."

Just then, Michelle heard pounding on her hotel room door.

"What the hell?!" she exclaimed, standing up. She walked through the connecting door, looking back over her shoulder at Susan. "Stay right there, Mom..."

"Where in the hell else would I go?" Susan said, mostly to herself, trying to absorb what Michelle had said to Thomas.

When Michelle opened the door, she was surprised to see Thomas standing there. He came in the room, closing the door behind him. "I need to talk to you about your mum..."

Then he noticed the connecting door to the room next door was open. "Is your mum okay?"

His face was flushed and he seemed out of breath.

"Well, actually..." Michelle began, but Thomas was already through the connecting door. Susan was sitting on the edge of the bed, tissues clutched in her hands. She looked up at him questioningly. Michelle was behind him and grabbed his arm.

"What's this all about, Thomas?"

"Dad told me what he did to you," Thomas said, ignoring Michelle and looking straight at Susan. "I wanted to make sure you were okay... I don't know what to say other than I'm very sorry...He hasn't been himself since Mum died...I know that's no excuse, but..."

"Did what?!" Michelle interrupted.

Susan held up her hand. "It's okay, Thomas...really...I'll be okay..."

"But he *forced* himself on you!! He told me you said, 'no' but he did it anyway..."

"He did *what?*!!" Michelle screeched.

"Your dad's done things like this to me before...it was a long time ago...he really hasn't changed all that much..."

Thomas inhaled sharply. "He's forced himself on you before?!"

Michelle gasped, covering her mouth with her hand. "Oh my God, Mom! He *raped* you?!!!"

Thomas turned towards her. "I don't know what to say, Michelle. There's no excuse for what he did...I'm ashamed."

"There's no reason to be ashamed," said Susan quietly, dabbing at her eyes. "And...and, he didn't force me...I gave in...I always give in to him..."

Michelle and Thomas looked at each other, neither of them knowing what to say.

At that moment, the phone rang. Everyone turned to the nightstand next to the bed where it was sitting. Susan sucked in her breath, staring at it and licked her lips. There was only one person who would be calling her.

She looked at Michelle and Thomas and waved her hand at them, indicating she wanted them to leave. Michelle started to protest and headed towards the phone, thinking to pick it up.

"If that's your dad," she said scathingly, glaring at Thomas, "I have a few choice words to say to him!"

But Thomas grabbed her arm and pulled her back into her room through the connecting door and closed it behind them.

By the time Susan gathered up the courage to answer the phone, it stopped ringing. But then it started again. She picked it up, slowly putting the receiver to her ear.

"Hello," she said in a quavering voice. It was almost a whisper.

"Come back upstairs, Susan," said James on the other end of the phone. "Please come back upstairs…I'm begging you…please…" His voice was just as unsteady as hers.

She sighed heavily, and James could hear her breathing as she thought. He held his breath, his hand shaking, waiting for her response. Never in his life had he wanted anything more than for her to say, "Yes."

"Okay," she whispered before slowly returning the receiver to its cradle.

Slowly she got up from the bed and went into the bathroom where she splashed cold water on her face, wiped off the mascara on her cheeks, released her hair from the messy ponytail it was tied up in and brushed it out. She walked over to the connecting door and opened it. Thomas and Michelle, who'd been talking heatedly, both turned to look at her.

"I'm going back upstairs," she said softly. Before either of them could utter a word, she closed the door again, picked up her purse that was laying on the floor by the bed, and left the room.

Moments later she was standing in front of the door to James's suite. When she raised her hand to knock, the door opened as if he knew she was already there.

She fell into his arms.

Chapter 9

James and Susan Together Again

"What the shit do you think you're doing?!" Michelle ranted at Thomas as he released her arm after closing the connecting door between her and her mom's hotel room.

"I'm letting your mum make her own decisions, that's what I'm doing," responded Thomas, crossing his arms over his chest.

"Well, I don't think she's rational enough to make her own decisions...especially in regard to your high and mighty, arrogant, egotistical and abusive dad!!"

Thomas uncrossed his arms. "Damn it all! He's not any of those things!"

"Well, he is if he thinks he can just drag any woman he fancies off into the bedroom any time he wants a quick fuck!"

"That's not what he did!"

"*You're* the one who said he forced himself on her!"

"And she denied it!!"

"So then, what was she doing bawling her eyes out when she came back downstairs? He obviously did *something* horrible to her!"

"He told her to get out...he said he never wanted to see her again..."

"Yeah, after getting a quick fuck..."

"Your language is disgusting..."

"Your father is disgusting!"

"I suppose you find me disgusting as well?"

"Maybe I do…like father, like son…isn't that the expression?!"

"You think I'm like my father?! You know nothing about me!"

"You look just like him!"

"And what does that have to do with anything?! That's just simple family resemblance! You look quite a bit like your mother…does that make you just like her?!"

"We're not talking about my mother!"

"Well, that's how this whole fiasco started, isn't it? Your mother decided to just pop back into Dad's life out of nowhere! She ruined his concert, you know…"

"What?! How can you say such a thing?! She was just standing there in the audience along with everyone else!"

"But she's *not* just like everyone else! He was going to marry her, remember?!"

Michelle folded her arms across her chest and turned her back on him.

"Of course I remember…"

Thomas's shoulders slumped. "I don't want to fight with you, you know."

"I don't want to fight with you either."

He walked up behind her, put his hands on her shoulders and turned her around.

"I'm sorry," he said, gazing into her eyes.

She bit her lower lip, looking away from him for a second before turning back towards him. "I'm sorry too…it's just that my mom is stupid crazy over your dad. She's never been able to forget him after all those years…I'm thinking now we never should have come here…"

"*I'm* glad you came here," he said softly.

She looked away again, stepping back from him. "I don't know what to say to that…You don't even know me…We know virtually nothing about each other…"

"Well then, why don't you say something like, 'I'm glad to be here too because now that I've met you, I'd like to get to know you better' or, 'Why. Thomas, I'm so very glad to have met you, and I'd love to spend more time with you,' or…"

Michelle looked back at him and smiled. It lit up her whole face and her eyes sparkled with amusement. Thomas was captivated once again.

"All right then, Thomas...how's this...I'm delighted to have met such a charming Englishman, who may just sweep me off my feet if he's not careful..."

Thomas tilted his head back and laughed before looking into her sea green eyes again and becoming serious.

"I think I'd very much like to sweep you off your feet," he said, locking his eyes onto hers.

When she thought he might have the idea to kiss her, she moved away again. What in hell was she thinking, leading him on like this?! She must be crazy! So what if he was devastatingly attractive, much more attractive, in fact, than her fiancé, Thomas....

"I...ah...I'll have to think on that..."

"Are we still on for breakfast tomorrow?"

She looked at her watch. "You mean today...it's half past midnight already."

"Okay, today then?"

"Sure...I guess so..."

"8:00 still okay, or is that too early?"

"Maybe a little too early...how about 10:00?"

"All right...10:00 in the hotel dining room."

He walked towards her door and put his hand on the knob before turning back to look at her. He let go of the door knob and came back to stand in front of her.

"I don't suppose you'd let me kiss you goodnight, would you?"

She looked into his eyes, wanting so say "Yes," but knowing she needed to say, "No." Impulsively, just as her mom had done all those years ago in the lobby of this same hotel, she extended her hand for him to kiss.

He reached forward and took her proffered hand in both of his, bringing it up to his lips and brushing them across the top of her hand before turning it and pressing a kiss on her palm. Shivers traced themselves down her spine, her mouth opening in a small "oh!"

He stepped back and gave her a bow, just like he did when in concert before taking the piano bench or afterward as he stood to the applause of the audience. Then without uttering another word, he went out the door, closing it softly behind him.

Michelle went over to her bed and sat down on its edge, placing the hand Thomas had kissed onto her lap and looking down on it. A slow smile spread across her face.

When James opened the door, Susan's tear-stained face punctured his heart and he wanted to kick himself for his cruel words as well as what he'd done to her earlier. Self-loathing washed over him in waves.

He kicked the door closed with his foot as he continued to hold her tightly in his arms, running his hands soothingly up and down her back. She wrapped her arms around him just as tightly and buried her face into the front of his shirt, breathing him in.

Slowly, they both released their grip on each other. Susan looked up into James's face, her eyes piercing his, but she couldn't find any words to say to him. He was equally speechless as he brought his lips down on hers in a soft and gentle kiss, brushing them back and forth across hers before claiming all of her mouth in a scorching kiss. His tongue invaded her mouth and she could taste the wine on it. Both of their tongues commenced an erotic dance evoking memories of long-ago kisses, and they became breathless.

James was dazed at Susan's melting and compliant response to him after what had just recently happened, and he could feel an erection growing in his trousers. Before she aroused him any further, he ended the kiss, released her from his arms and led her over to the sofa.

"Sit," he said to her. "I'm getting us some wine."

She gave a weak smile, doing as he instructed, shaking her head, amused at his command of "sit." She felt like an obedient dog, but realized that not only was it unlikely he'd changed his controlling ways over the years, but that fame and fortune had probably even worsened them. He was obviously accustomed to getting his way in anything and everything…waited on hand and foot. She wondered if his wife, Susan, had been the submissive female he always seemed to want. She probably had.

James came back to the sofa carrying two glasses of white wine and handed her one before sitting down next to her.

"Chardonnay," he said, smiling. "I've never forgotten."

She smiled back at him, suddenly feeling shy. "Neither have I…"

He looked down for a moment before looking back up into her eyes. "I'm sorry, Susan…I'm so very sorry…for…for earlier…"

"It's okay…I understand…"

"It was unforgivable…"

"No, James…don't you remember me telling you once…all that time ago…that everything is forgivable…" Her voice trailed off to a whisper.

"You did, didn't you? I did some terrible things to you."

"Not as terrible as what I did to you."

"I think I'm going to agree with you on that."

"Will you forgive me?"

"Here," he said holding up his glass. "Let's make a toast to forgiveness!"

She bumped her glass up against his. "To forgiveness."

They each took a sip of wine before setting the glasses on the coffee table.

"Why, Susan?" James asked quietly. "Why did you leave me waiting in the church like you did? I've asked myself that question a thousand times…I thought you loved me…I thought you wanted to spend the rest of your life with me…"

Susan hung her head and bit her lip before gazing back up at him, trying to think of how she could truthfully answer the question. There was no way she could tell him the real truth, about time travel. Then she remembered the lie Michelle had made up for Thomas and figured it would have to do, especially if their stories were to be in sync.

"Joy and Alice, my friends who were with me…they betrayed me… Alice gave me something to drink when we were in the bedroom at the

Vicar's house getting dressed…and…and that's all I remember until I woke up on a plane…"

"They kidnapped you??!! How?! Why???!"

"I don't really know how…they must have hired a car or something to take us away…and Alice told me that she'd lied to me about why you gave me the necklace back. At first, she told me that you gave it back to me so I could wear it in the wedding…to make me feel like my grandpa was there, since he's the one who gave it to me on my twelfth birthday…But, later on the plane, she said it was because you'd changed your mind about getting married…that you realized we wouldn't suit…"

Tears brimmed at the back of her eyes. "I…I believed her…"

"What about our child?"

"I lost the baby within a week of getting home…I wanted to call you, but Alice said you made it clear that you never wanted to see me again…I went into a…a decline, I guess you'd call it…I couldn't eat…I couldn't sleep…"

"And you believed her??!! After all that we meant to each other?? You really believed her?!"

"I didn't want to…"

James ran his hands through his hair, a pained expression on his face. "I don't know how you could have, Susan…I'll *never* understand…" He shook his head.

"Looking back, I don't know how I could have believed her either… But, that's not all…"

James focused on her face again.

"Joy told me that Ryan had talked to you and said marriage would be too distracting for you…that the band would break up…that your career would be ruined…She said Derek and Ian and Blue agreed, that Ian even confessed to you that he slept with me one afternoon when I skipped class… She said they'd all been talking to you…and, and…that's why none of them came to the wedding…they knew you weren't going to go through with it anyway…"

All James could do was shake his head in disbelief.

"And then...Alice sent me a tabloid a couple of months later that showed you with a bunch of women at a party at your house, a bachelor having the time of his life. It said you had a houseful of women and girls and fancied yourself a real ladies man. Joy said you'd also got back together with Tracie, the airline stewardess...I didn't want to believe any of it, but there were pictures, and..."

"Oh, Susan!" he exclaimed, taking both of her hands in his. "I don't know what to say...none of that was true...I mean, about Ryan talking to me or Derek or Ian or Blue, especially Ian being with you...I would have throttled him..."

"But it doesn't really matter now, does it? You married someone else and she made you happy. You made music together. You have wonderful children and a charmed life...Even if it wasn't true and my friends betrayed me, it's all in the past now and we can't go back and change anything."

James nodded his head. "You're right...I know you're right, but now I can't help but wonder how our lives would have changed if you'd married me. So," he said as he looked at her left hand. He noticed earlier when she was in the practice room after fainting, that she wasn't wearing a wedding band. "I know you have a daughter. Do you have any other children?

"Yes, I have a son named Steven. He's a writer."

"And your husband? Are you married now?"

Oh no! The question she was dreading! What to say? What might Michelle have told Thomas? She felt like she needed to confirm that before she answered.

"He's...he's not with me now..." she hedged.

"So you're divorced then?"

She nodded, hating that she had to lie. But it was true that she wasn't with him, wasn't it? When she left, Donald had been staying downtown in the condo near his office and she'd been staying in their mountain house alone. She wondered what Michelle might have told Thomas...or if the question had come up...

James seemed relieved.

"I'd rather not talk about it..." she said with a pleading look on her face.

He started to say something, but then changed his mind, picking up his wine glass again and taking another sip. She did the same.

"Another toast?" he proposed.

"Okay."

"To getting reacquainted..." He tapped his glass against hers.

"And to leaving the past behind?"

They bumped glasses again. "Yes...to leaving the past behind..."

After taking a few more sips, they both set their glasses down again. They were silent for a minute, both not knowing what to say next. The chemistry between them, however, began to warm.

"Did I tell you how beautiful you are? Still are?" James asked, piercing Susan with his eyes.

She blushed. "And did I tell you how devastatingly handsome you still are?"

He smiled before leaning in to kiss her softly. She moved closer until their thighs were touching and put her hands on his chest. He wrapped his arms around her as his kiss deepened and their tongues invaded each other's mouths. When their faces drew apart, Susan could see the familiar sparks flaming in James's eyes and felt a sudden clenching between her legs. A soft gasp escaped her and James smiled wickedly as if he knew what she was thinking and feeling.

"I promise I'll make it good for you this time," he whispered in her ear as he moved in close again to plant kisses on the side of her neck. Then, he took her hand and placed it on his crotch, where she could feel an impressive erection growing in his trousers. She squeezed the bulge gently then moved her hands up to begin unbuttoning his shirt.

He chuckled. "You're always so anxious, aren't you, Susan?"

"I can't help it...when it comes to you, I've always been anxious... you know that..."

"I seem to recall that, yes..."

He nipped at her earlobe and she gasped again. Pulling away from her, he stood up, took her hand and pulled her up into his arms. They kissed deeply and hungrily. James slipped his hands up under her dress and squeezed the cheeks of her bottom as he pulled her tightly into him. The feel of his throbbing shaft poking into her belly was intoxicating as she thought of how it felt inside her. There was a throbbing need between her thighs, and when the kiss ended and they looked into each other's eyes, she knew he felt the same.

Wordlessly, they walked into the bedroom and James closed the door behind them. The two small night lamps on each side of the bed were turned on, and James used the sliding switch on the wall to lower the lights to a soft glow. Susan finished unbuttoning James's shirt and ran her hands up and down his chest, pausing at his nipples to pinch them with her thumb and forefinger. He gasped before shrugging out of the sleeves. The shirt fell to the floor.

He kissed Susan again as he reached behind her and unzipped her dress, pushing it off her shoulders and down her arms where it dropped onto the floor around her feet. She kicked it away then slipped out of her shoes. James was already barefoot.

For a moment, James froze, his gaze focused on the necklace then he reached forward and lifted the silver ballerina slippers hanging on the end into the palm of his hand. He stared at it for a few seconds before looking down into Susan's eyes.

"Do you think this holds some kind of spell?" he whispered. "Is it magic? Is this what keeps bringing us together and breaking us apart?"

Her eyes never left his. "I don't know James...maybe it does... other than me, you're the only one who's ever worn it..."

"Would you let me wear it again?"

She sucked in her breath. "Would you want to wear it again?"

"I'm not sure...let me think about it...I have something else in mind right now..."

She gave a sigh of relief as he dropped the ballerina shoes back onto her chest and pushed down the straps of her bra. She slid her arms out of them and lowered the bra down to her waist and over her hips taking her panties along with them. She kicked them out of the way before reaching forward and squeezing the bulge in James's trousers again. Then, before he could respond, she went down on her knees in front of him and unbuttoned and unzipped his pants, pulling them down over his hips and onto the floor. She reached both hands up to his crotch, one fondling his balls and the other his stiffened member through the fabric of his shorts. He gave a loud moan, placing his hands on her shoulders and tilting his head back.

She looked up into his face as he gazed back down on her and he could see the lust in her eyes and in her flushed face. She reached up to the waistband of his shorts, and pulled them slowly down over his hips, her eyes never leaving his, her lips parted. His hands tightened on her shoulders and he moved them up into her hair. They gripped the sides of her head as she brought her mouth down on his swollen shaft, taking every inch of it deeply into her throat.

"Oh, my God!" he panted, beginning to rock his hips as she moved her mouth on him.

She knew she didn't want him to come in her mouth, at least not now. The throbbing need between her legs was hard to bear. As he pumped into her throat, the muscles of her sex squeezed and unsqueezed, making her feel as if she would climax right then and there. She pulled away from him, panting and breathless.

James pulled her up into his arms and they kissed feverishly, rubbing their bodies against each other, Susan's breasts full and warm against his chest, her nipples hard. He reached behind her and squeezed and fondled her bottom, pulling her into him and smearing his slippery wetness into her bare belly.

He pushed her backwards towards the bed, and when the backs of her thighs hit it, he thrust her onto her back, her legs still hanging over the edge. And this time, he went down on his knees in front of her, spread her thighs apart with his hands and gazed at the flowering petals of her most intimate part.

"No! James…please!" she begged, trying to sit up. "I'm ready to explode! I want you inside me…please…"

But, her feeble protests were for naught as he bought his mouth down on her, his tongue darting out with teasing little licks on the nub of her desire.

She screamed and tried to buck up off the bed, but he held her thighs firm in his grip and continued the sweet assault. Her hands clenched and unclenched the bed covers while her head rolled from side to side and she moaned her gratification. As his mouth and tongue quickened on her, she felt waves of pleasure wash over her in in jolt after jolt. She dug her fingers into his hair, tugging and pulling his face into her then screamed her release as he sucked mercilessly on her. Her whole body quivered and shook...

And then he was inside her all the way up to her very core. Her sex was still in the throes of spasms and he thought, as he held still inside her for a moment, that it would throw him over the edge. He brought his mouth down on hers to silence her screams, moving his hands to her breasts and massaging them.

Finally feeling he'd regained control, he began to move slowly inside her, pulling nearly all the way out of her hot, wet sheath, then pushing slowly back in until his balls pressed against her bottom. Her breath hitched as his shaft pushed deeply in and she wrapped her legs around his waist to bring him in even deeper. She could feel the throbbing beginning anew and knew that he was holding back in order to bring her to her peak again.

And he was...he was determined to make it good for her...

When he felt her tightening around him once again, he increased the speed of his thrusts, making them smooth and rhythmic, almost as if he were singing to her, but he didn't know how much longer he could hold on before exploding. Reaching one hand down between them, he began to finger her, knowing it would bring her release sooner and slowed his thrusts down once more. She moved her hips in small circles beneath him intensifying the pleasure for both of them.

When she screamed his name again, reaching up to wrap her arms around his neck, pulling his face down to hers and lifting her bottom up off the bed, he spilled himself inside her, moaning his own release. Her tongue thrust deeply into his mouth and he sucked on it while pumping the last drops of himself into her. Their chests were both heaving and their bodies molded together as closely as they could, merging themselves into one.

As the beating of their hearts slowed, James put his hands on each side of Susan's face and planted soft, feathery kisses across her cheeks, nose and eyelids. Her eyes fluttered open and she looked into his, her desire for him clearly reflected there. He returned her gaze with equal desire before rolling them both on their sides and pulling her into him again. He stroked her back and smoothed her hair. He could feel her soft, full breasts pressing into his chest.

She felt him soften inside her and moved her hands to his shoulders, gently squeezing them.

"Wow..." she said, smiling. "I think that was *more* than good..."

"Was it?" he smiled back at her, giving her a quick kiss. "Maybe we could try it again sometime..." He raised his eyebrows.

"Any time you like, James...any time you like..."

Chapter 10

Back to Auntie Annabelle's Cottage

Thomas paced back and forth in his hotel room, pausing by the phone on the bedside table now and then and debating whether he should call his dad and see if things were okay between him and Michelle's mum.

He decided it wasn't any of his business, hoping they had reconciled. It was time his dad left his grief behind and found some happiness again. While he knew there would never be anyone he would love as much as his mum, maybe this woman from his past, who had most likely been his first love, could bring him joy once more. It was time.

Then he thought about Michelle, the lovely and feisty American girl he'd so recently met and was, incredible as it seemed, beginning to fall in love with.

But, how could such a thing be possible?! There was no such thing as love at first sight, was there? No! Of course not! He was a sensible young man and, like his father before him, quite used to pretty girls casting their eyes at him. Unlike his father, however, he didn't bed them all, and had, in fact, only one steady girlfriend for a period of time when he was in the music academy.

But, the opportunity for a relationship was always there, and he knew it. It was just that his music was more important to him than women, and the dedication it took to be a successful concert pianist left little, if any, room for an affair of the heart.

So, why couldn't he get Michelle out of his mind then? Her face, with the enchanting sea green eyes, just wouldn't go away.

He kicked off his shoes then sat on the edge of his bed to take off his socks before padding into the bathroom to brush his teeth and change into the pajamas he'd unpacked earlier and placed on the sink counter. He looked at himself critically in the mirror. Yes, the resemblance to his father was quite remarkable. He had the same dark hair, mouth and nose along with the distinctive arched eyebrows. His eyes, however, were a unique combination of both his mother and father, the blue in them from her and the golden glints from him. He wondered for a moment if Michelle found his eyes as interesting and different as he found hers.

He poured himself a glass of water, turned off the bathroom light and went back into the hotel room, setting the glass on the nightstand. He pulled back the covers of the bed, flicked off the bedside lamp and laid back on the pillow, staring into the darkness.

Tomorrow he would find out everything he could about Michelle. He decided he would even ask her out to a movie or maybe even the theatre if something was playing in town. A nice dinner with some wine before, then maybe stop by a club on the way back to the hotel for some music.

Would he be able to kiss her on those tempting lips of hers? He thought she just might let him. At least he hoped so as he drifted off to sleep.

He didn't give his dad and Michelle's mum another thought.

Michelle tossed and turned, unable to get comfortable or fall asleep. She kept waiting for the sound of her mother coming back to her room, but when she looked at the bedside clock and saw it was almost 4:00 in the morning, she figured her mom wouldn't be coming back, at least not until much later. She scrunched up her face and turned her thoughts in another direction.

But, the direction they turned in, wasn't one where she wanted them to go.

Thomas.

Not her fiancé, Thomas…but, Thomas, son of James, the pop icon, rock star…no rock God, a former member of the most famous band of all time…

Shit! Why was she thinking of him? She *shouldn't* be thinking of him. She didn't even *want* to think about him! He looked too damn much like his father, well known for being one of the biggest womanizers of all time. And she knew that her own mother had fallen prey to that devastatingly pretty and handsome face…

Was Thomas a womanizer too? If so, staying away from him until her mom gave the ring back to James, needed to be her first priority. No way would she want to get involved with a man who wanted to screw every pretty face he came across.

But, was she being fair? Maybe it wasn't "like father, like son." Maybe Thomas was different.

His eyes were certainly different, and she realized with a start that she'd been sucked into their vortex just as her mom had been with James's mesmerizing eyes.

Then she thought again of her fiancé. Compared to *this* Thomas… well, there *was* no comparing him to this Thomas. Her Thomas had blonde hair that had first reminded her of gold, but which was in fact rather drab under the lights of the courtroom and beginning to gray at the temples. Plus, he was already balding a bit. At first she thought it gave him a more mature air, but now it seemed in her mind, to give him an "old" air. This Thomas had a full head of dark, silky hair, just like his dad when he was younger. Her Thomas's eyes were a pale blue and couldn't even be compared to this Thomas. In fact, she began to picture them in her mind as being rather fishy looking…

"Stop!" she screamed at herself, sitting up and turning on the bedside lamp. She got up and began pacing, her hands clasped behind her back and her face focused on the carpet. Her dad called it her "courtroom stride," and swore he was the one who taught it to her, but she'd perfected it and made it her own. Her mom found it annoying because she always knew Michelle was going to scold her about something when she started to do it when she visited.

After ten minutes of pacing, Michelle didn't feel any more resolved in her conflicting emotions. She sat back down on the bed, propped up the pillows and turned on the t.v.

"Might as well watch an old movie or something," she muttered to herself. Maybe it would take her mind off the two Thomas's…

⌒◯

"Susan, wake up," prodded James, nudging her in her side under the covers.

"Hmmmmm…" she moaned sleepily, having fallen asleep a couple hours earlier after another bout of lovemaking.

"I have an idea." He sat up and turned on the lamp next to the bed.

Susan rolled over and blinked her eyes up at him. She glanced at the bedside clock. It was just a little after 4:00 in the morning.

"Let's get up and get dressed then drive out to my Auntie Annabelle's cottage…you remember the cottage, don't you?"

Susan sat up, clutching the bed covers up over her bare breasts. "The cottage? Of course I remember…how could I *not* remember!"

She felt heat coming into her face with the memories. And, crazy as it was, it had only been a year and a half in the past for her, while it was 37 years in the past for James.

"She's still alive? She still lives there?"

"Yes, she's still alive, but no, she doesn't live there anymore. She moved in with Auntie Ginny over in King's Head last June. The stairs were getting to be too much for her, and most of her friends in Little Dippington have passed on. Both she and Auntie Gin are up in their eighties now. Uncle Albert also passed a couple of years ago."

"So, no one's living in the cottage now? She hasn't sold it?"

"No. When I found out she was moving, I told her not to sell it and I bought it from her. It was always a bit of a sentimental place for me. We all used to go there when I was a lad, and I have a lot of good memories of the place…"

She looked at him, feeling suddenly shy. "I don't suppose they would include memories of me?"

James smiled wickedly, yanking the covers out of her hands to expose her breasts. "As a matter of fact, they do…"

"Stop that!" she yelled indignantly, snatching them back.

"Why?" He pushed her down on her back and rolled on top of her then lowered himself for a kiss.

"Stop it, James…I mean it!" She said, pushing up on his chest then wriggling under him trying to get away. When she realized the effect her wriggling was having on him, however, she stopped.

"I have to go pee…let me go…"

He didn't move off her.

She tried her best to push him away again. "I mean it…I really need to go…badly…"

He rolled to the side and she immediately raised up, moving her feet over the edge of the bed. He reached out and grabbed her hand. "I'm only letting you go if you promise to come right back…"

"Okay, okay…I promise…"

She looked back over her shoulder at him as she went into the bathroom. He'd pulled the covers off and was wagging his stiffened erection at her teasingly.

"James! What in the hell do you think you're doing?!"

"Just giving you a visual…so you'll hurry back…"

She couldn't help but laugh, closing the door then quickly using the loo. She was back in bed within two minutes…

A half hour later, James leaped out of bed, picked up the telephone and dialed room service, ordering a carafe of coffee and a couple of to-go cups.

"Come on, Susan. Time to get up and get dressed. We can stop in Little Dippington for some breakfast on our way to the cottage."

Susan, who was just about to doze off again, rolled over and looked at him bleary-eyed.

"But what if I don't *want* to go to the cottage right now? Besides, I need to talk to Michelle and tell her, and…"

"You can leave a note. I'm going to write one to Thomas right now and slip it under his door on our way out. You can do the same for Michelle."

"But what if I don't *want* to write her a note? What if I want to talk to her in person and...?"

"She'll be fine with a note. You can copy mine when I'm done. Now, come on and get up."

He reached to the floor, tossing her the green dress she'd been wearing the night before, along with her bra and panties, before opening the bedroom door and going out into the main room of the suite.

"But..." she protested, frowning as she climbed out of the bed. She snatched the underwear and bra off the side of the bed where they'd landed and went into the bathroom to use the loo again and wash her face. When she came out and was slipping on the dress, James came back into the bedroom, an impatient look on his face.

"The coffee got here five minutes ago. What's taking you so long?"

When he saw her struggle to zip up the back of her dress, he came over to help. "Why do women always have to take so long..." he muttered under his breath.

"I do *not* take too long!" she protested as he briskly walked out into the other room with Susan trailing behind.

James ignored her remark, going over to a desk at the side of the room, picking up a tablet and pen and handing it to her.

"Here...write a note to Michelle." He also handed her another piece of paper, which was the note he had written to Thomas. "Just copy what I wrote."

"But James, I told you I want to talk to Michelle, not just leave her a note..."

"It's not even 5:00 in the morning. She'll still be asleep. Do you want to wake her up then? Of course not! Just write the note."

She looked back at him defiantly, tablet and pen in one hand, his note in the other. They had so obviously slipped back into their familiar roles of Mr. Bossy and Miss Rebellious, that it was almost uncanny.

"Your bossiness never ceases to amaze me!" she spit out.

"And your being disagreeable hasn't changed much either over all these years…!"

They glared at each other for a moment, before Susan angrily pulled out the chair in front of the desk, sat down and copied James's note. As she finished, James came up behind her, brushed her pony-tail to the side and began to plant soft kisses down the side of her neck.

"I just want to be alone with you again, Susan…totally and completely alone…I want us to get to know each other again…" His voice was dark and seductive.

Shivers raced up and down her spine as his arms wrapped around her and he tweaked her nipples through the fabric of her dress. She squirmed in the chair and gave a sigh. When she turned her head to look at him, he pulled her up out of the chair into his arms and sealed his mouth with hers in a hungry kiss that left her breathless. The tablet and pen fell to the floor. The note he'd written to Thomas fluttered after them.

"Tell me you want to be with me again…" he whispered into her ear before blowing in it gently and tugging her earlobe between his teeth.

"Of course I want to be with you," she whispered back, her knees feeling weak.

He smiled his devastatingly handsome smile at her before picking up the tablet, pen and note, and tearing her note off the tablet. "Let's go then…"

"But what about my clothes and make-up and toothbrush and all my other stuff?" she asked as he picked up his own small suitcase and handed her the bag containing the coffee carafe and cups.

"You can pack a small bag when we stop by your room and buy anything else you need in Little Dippington when we stop for breakfast. Besides, you don't need many clothes…maybe I'll just keep you naked…"

She poked him in the side as he opened the door. "No way! Not at my age!"

"I think you look quite fine for your age…"

"I don't care what you think…I'm *not* running around naked!"

107

"We'll see about that…" He smirked at her, the amber in his eyes sparking.

A few minutes later, Susan was inserting the key into her hotel room door. She heard the noise of the t.v. from the adjoining room and wondered if Michelle was awake or had fallen asleep with it on as she'd often done when she was younger and living at home. When she went to knock on the connecting door, however, James stopped her.

"Just slip the note under the door, Susan."

"But she might be awake and then I can tell her and…"

"Just put the note under the door. You can call her from the cottage later."

He grabbed the note from her hand as she took it out of her purse, bent down and pushed it under the door.

Susan scowled at him but said nothing, quickly packing one of her suitcases with some underwear, a few items of clothing and her toiletries from the bathroom.

They were soon back out the door and headed down the hall to Thomas's room, where James slipped his note under the door. Once in the lobby, James asked that his rental car be brought around, and they were soon on the road to Little Dippington.

Susan felt in a daze.

Oh my God! Auntie Annabelle's cottage…her heart gave a lurch.

Chapter 11

Thomas and Michelle

"So what did *your* note say?" Michelle asked as Thomas held out a chair for her in the hotel dining room.

It was a few minutes after 10:00 in the morning, and Thomas had been prompt to knock on her door for their breakfast date right at ten.

He sat down in a chair across from her, reached in his shirt pocket and took out a folded piece of paper.

"It says," he began to read after unfolding it. *"We're going to Auntie Annabelle's cottage. Will be gone a few days, possibly longer. Don't worry. All is fine. Love, Dad. P.S. Don't call us. We'll check in with you. Show Michelle around Brighton and have fun."*

Thomas looked across the table at her, nodding to the waiter to pour them both coffee. "What does yours say?"

"Exactly the same thing, except that you'll be showing me around Brighton and to have fun. Rather presumptuous, don't you think?"

Thomas chuckled. "Well, that's just like my dad. He's quite used to getting his way and ordering other people about…"

Michelle lifted her coffee cup and blew across the top to cool it down. "Uh…well, my mom is used to getting *her* own way and ordering people about as well. Not so sure that bodes well for their little trip to the cottage."

Thomas grinned at her. "Dad loves a challenge…and, it appears he got his way in regard to going to Little Dippington. Appears as if you mum copied his note word for word, doesn't it?"

Michelle smiled back. "Yes, it does…and I can just picture my mom fuming about it under her breath. He'll pay the price later you know…"

"Sounds like they're well suited then…"

"Maybe so…" She set down her coffee cup as a waiter came over to see what they might want to order.

"Just some toast for me…and maybe a bowl of fruit?"

The waiter nodded at her, turning towards Thomas.

"Eggs, scrambled, bacon, some potatoes and toast with jam, please." He handed the menus back to the waiter.

"Aren't you very hungry?" he asked Michelle.

"No, not really…I'm still a bit worried about my mom."

"Dad won't hurt her or anything, you know…"

"Well…he did last night…"

"I think he still has feelings for her."

"I *know* she still has feelings for him. She, uh…never really got over what happened all those years ago. She's kind of clung to the memory…but, hey! Can we quit talking about your dad and my mom for a while? Tell me about you. How is it that you came to be a concert pianist?"

Thomas seemed relieved at the change of subject.

"Well, I was brought up in a house full of music and musical instruments. My dad had me up on his knee at the piano from when I was toddling around. He said his dad did the same to him when he was a wee lad. I took to it right away. I was fascinated at the different sounds each key made."

Michelle sipped on her coffee, listening intently.

"My mum gave me a couple of lessons, but then took me to a piano teacher. He was a concert pianist who'd played all around the world. He told me stories of his travels as well as taught me the piano. He's the one who fostered love of classical music in me. Mum and Dad weren't into it that much at the time. Plus, they were busy with their own band. We traveled a lot, so I missed a lot of lessons, but Mum always made sure there was a piano wherever we went so I could practice. When I turned sixteen, I applied to the Music Academy of London and was accepted. I quit traveling with the family except I did join them for a few vacations. The one I remember most was going to Disneyland in California where you're from. We all loved Disneyland. We stayed there for a few days…It was my parent's anniversary too as I recall…"

"Disneyland? I love Disneyland too! I've been there a lot since we live so close. It's only a couple of hours away. We even lived up near there for a couple of months when I was a teenager. Dad was on one of his first big cases and we rented a condo in Costa Mesa. My brother, Steven, and I used to hang out at a big shopping mall they had there called the Gallery or something like that, plus we went to Disneyland a few times."

"Oh really? I wonder if we could have been there at the same time…Wouldn't that be funny?"

"Do you remember when you were there? I think we were there in February or March, sometime during the beginning of the year. I was twelve, so that would have made it…let me see…1987…"

"1987? Hmmm…If I remember correctly, I was fourteen when we went to Disneyland…yes, I think that's right, because I started at the music academy two years later in January, 1989…We probably *were* there at the same time…interesting…"

"So that would make you 26 now…"

"It would…and that would make you 24…"

Michelle laughed. "Yes, I turned 24 two months ago…So we really could have been at Disneyland at the same time!"

"Or at the big shopping mall you just mentioned. I remember a lot of big shopping malls we visited when we were in America traveling. Nothing like them in the UK…So your dad's a solicitor then?

"Yes, if that's what you call an attorney or lawyer…and, as a matter of fact, that's what *I* am too. My dad and I share an office suite on one of the top floors of the courthouse building."

"I take it that your mum and dad still see each other then?"

"Not so much recently…"

To herself, she thought that really was the truth with her dad at the downtown condo and her mom up at the mountain house.

"So, was their divorce a friendly one?"

Michelle was stumped for words, wondering how much she should say, especially since she didn't know what her mom might have told James.

She hedged again. "They're still on somewhat friendly terms..."

Thomas sensed her reluctance to talk about the subject. "I've heard that a divorce can be harder on the children than it is on the two getting divorced."

"Yes, it can be..."

"So, do you like being a solicitor...I mean a lawyer?"

"Oh yes! I work on discrimination cases, mostly employment-related cases concerning women who've been treated unfairly and also cases of sexual harassment as well as domestic abuse. *That* actually makes my blood boil. It's quite rewarding when I can nail somebody to the wall in a clear cut case of discrimination or sexual harassment, or send a guy to jail for giving his partner a black eye."

Thomas sat back in his chair as their breakfasts were placed in front of them and observed her. Michelle was obviously very proud of what she did, as well as enthusiastic about her work. He unfolded his napkin and placed it on his lap.

"I'll bet it is..."

She scooted her chair closer to the table before unfolding and dropping her own napkin on her lap. "I especially enjoy making arrogant men, who feel they're somehow entitled to sexual favors from a female employee, look about an inch tall and see them squirm on the witness stand...I'm pretty good at bringing them down a peg or two..."

She picked up a piece of toast from her plate then proceeded to spread it with a miniscule layer of jam.

Thomas squirmed a little in his seat. No wonder she was about to pounce on his dad over the phone last night after he said his dad had forced himself on her mum!

She looked over at him and smiled her brilliant smile.

"Am I scaring you off?"

He smiled back. "Are you *trying* to scare me off?"

She bit into her toast, not taking her eyes off him. When she finished chewing and swallowed, she picked up her napkin and patted her lips.

"No...not at all, Thomas...not at all..."

⌒♥

James and Susan drove into Little Dippington just as the sun was coming up over the horizon. James pulled up in front of one of only two of the village's restaurants called *The Brass Penny*. When Susan went to reach for the door handle to let herself out, James reached over and grabbed her arm.

"Now, Susan, is your memory so bad that you don't recall you're supposed to wait for me to come round and open your door?"

"Oh, come on, James...it's stupid! You don't need to play the gentleman thing with me...and besides, it's almost the year 2000! Men don't open doors for women anymore..."

She reached for the door handle again, but James wouldn't let go of her arm.

"Well, *I* do! I always have, and I always will! And, just in case you haven't heard, I have the real title of 'Sir' now...I'm official! You need to show respect for a 'Sir,' you know..."

"Yes, I've heard you're 'Sir James' now...woop-dee-doo! Ask me if I care, because I don't! And, let go of my arm so I can open my own damn door...I'm a liberated woman I'll have you know..."

"Liberated or not, you're going to sit there like a lady and let me come round to open your door!"

"You're being stupid!"

"You're being stubborn!"

They stared each other down, saying nothing for a full minute, each one of them waiting for the other to give in.

"Fine, fine, fine!" Susan muttered, shaking her arm free from James's grasp and glaring out the front window. "Go round and let me out, *Sir* Bossy..."

James tried to hold back the smirk on his face, but couldn't quite do it. When she turned to look at him again, he immediately wiped it off, got out of the car then went around to open her door. She declined his proffered hand, got out on her own and brushed her way past him, heading towards the door to *The Brass Penny*. He smirked again, but she didn't see him.

She waited for him at the entrance, knowing he expected to open that door for her too, even though she was severely tempted to open it herself and breeze into the restaurant in front of him. When he gave a little bow as he pulled open the door, she couldn't help but laugh.

"Okay...so you win again, but don't expect to get your way *all* the time!"

"Oh, but I do, you know..."

She rolled her eyes at him.

They were the first customers of the morning, were quickly seated and handed menus. They both declined coffee, having drank the entire contents of the carafe from the hotel on the drive.

Susan ordered a blackberry scone and a glass of orange juice. James ordered a cheese omelet, toast and a pot of tea.

"I know how to make these..." Susan commented as a plate with the scone on it was set in front of her.'

James lifted the lid on the small teapot that was placed in front of him, dunking the tea bag in and out of the steaming water. "Do you? Might you make them for me then?"

"If you'd like...How well provisioned is your auntie's cottage now that she's moved? Are there any staples, like flour and sugar, still there?"

"Actually, she left everything except her personal things, clothes and the like. She was planning on boxing the rest of the stuff up and donating it, including the furniture, to a charity shop. I'm not so sure about food stuffs, however, but I did notice when I was there a few days ago that the fridge was still plugged in and running. Nothing inside it, though."

"Well, if you want me to be cooking you anything, we'll need to go to a grocery store. Do they have one here? The village doesn't look all that much bigger or different than it did over thirty years ago."

"Villages like this don't change much, but there is a food shop here now that carries most of the same stuff you can get in a bigger town. There are several large estates in the area now that expect more choices. The shop even has fresh fruit and vegetables. I stopped there to get a bag of crisps and a bottle of juice when I was here two days before the concert and was quite impressed with the selection."

"Well then, I guess we'll need to stop there and pick a few things up."

"We can do that after we're done eating, then when we get to the cottage, you can look through the kitchen cabinets and decide what else you might want or need. We can call it into the shop and have it delivered."

"Grocery stores make home deliveries?"

"They will if I tell them to."

She rolled her eyes again. "Of course they will...if *you* tell them to..."

"But, I might have something else in mind first when we get to the cottage, you know..."

His eyes locked on hers as he leaned back in his chair and gave her a wicked grin.

She took the last bite of her scone then tipped her glass to drink the last of the juice. "Don't count on it...the cottage is probably freezing cold...just look outside...it' starting to snow! I'm not taking off any clothes if it's freezing inside the cottage!"

"Who said you had to take off any clothes...?"

"James! We're not teenagers anymore! You think you can just flip my skirt up, pull down my panties, unzip yourself and..."

"Why not? It'll keep you from feeling all cold..."

"Shhh...drop this subject right now! The waitress is right over there. She can hear what we're saying. You're embarrassing me!"

James snickered before turning to look out the glass front door that Susan was facing.

"So it's snowing. I guess we'd better get going then. We might even be lucky and get snowed in...I think I might even recall being snowed in with you there once before..."

Susan felt the heat come into her face again, the memory as fresh in her mind as if it was only yesterday. "You have an awfully good memory..."

"Being back in Brighton brought back a lot of memories for me…and then when I drove out here…well, even more came into my head…I was actually feeling a little guilty about it, remembering my wife, Susan, and all…then thinking about you…"

"I can understand that…"

She looked down at her hands in her lap for a moment. "But…she told you to go on, didn't she? That after she was gone, you needed to go on with your life…to maybe even find someone else with who you could be happy again…"

He nodded. "How did you know?" he asked quietly, his eyes intent on her face.

"It's what I would have said to you…If you love someone deeply, that's what you'd want for that person…"

James was quiet for a moment as if he were contemplating her words. "Are you trying to tell me that you still love me?"

"I…I don't know…yes…maybe…I don't think I ever really stopped loving you…"

"Then how could you have left me like you did? I still don't understand it…"

"I told you…my friends…they…"

"It doesn't make sense to me, Susan…kidnapped by your best friends?! It's too far-fetched…I don't know if I'll ever be able to trust you again…"

You think that's too far-fetched, she thought. *If I told you the truth…*

Instead, she said, "I know how it sounds…and…I'm sorry…I understand why you wouldn't trust me…"

James suddenly reached across the table. "Give me your hands, Susan…"

She looked at him questioningly before bringing both hands up to the tabletop and extending them towards his. He grasped them and gently squeezed.

"Swear to me that you're telling me the truth…you've lied to me before…swear to me that you'll never lie to me again…"

His eyes bored into hers.

She bit her lower lip. "I swear to you that I'll never lie to you again, James..."

He stood then, not letting go of her hands, and she stood too. He brought her hands to his lips and slowly brushed them across her knuckles.

"I don't think I ever stopped loving you either..."

He released her hands, she picked up her purse and slipped on her coat. He put on his own then paid the bill before he opened the door for her to go out to the car.

Chapter 12

Hilary

The polish-remover, soaked cotton ball splatted against the television screen with a vengeance.

"Fuck!" screeched Hilary, reaching for the remote control to turn up the volume.

The late evening news was on showing a reporter standing outside the Dusky Club in Brighton, England. Hilary watched from her most recent client's penthouse near Piccadilly in London as the reporter talked about how James, a former member of the most famous band of all time, was doing his first concert there since the death of his wife, Susan.

"I missed the bloody thing!"

The crowd outside the Club was yelling and singing songs the band had made famous as well as those James had recorded either solo or with his new band.

She turned off the t.v. then angrily tossed the remote onto the coffee table where it slid off onto the floor. Reaching for her pack of cigarettes and a lighter on the end table, she cursed again.

"Shithead, Marcus! He was supposed to get me a pass!!"

She shook a cigarette out of the pack and lit it, inhaling deeply, then blew the smoke out both her nose and mouth.

Her life as a high-priced "courtesan" was becoming boring. The money was good, and the benefits of expensive clothes, jewelry and a nice place to live were definitely perks to the lifestyle, but servicing old, disgusting men with her body was distasteful. Sure, it was a step up from being "Honey Pot" in porn movies, but she'd begun to set her sights higher in the past few months. In fact, she'd deliberately started to search for something more lucrative, something to set her fortunes for life instead of just a few months at a time.

And that's when she'd struck upon James. Not only was he filthy rich and famous, he'd recently lost his wife, which made him available and on the rebound. To top it off, he was quite good looking, in fact more than that. He was hot! Rumors from his younger days indicated that he had a love for women with great bodies, and she had to admit, even if it was a little vain, that at age 36, she had one fantastic body. Not that her face was all that pretty. In fact, it had kind of a "sneering" look to it, but men were prone to overlook a face if the body screamed "sex!" And, hers did. She'd proven it over and over, captivating one man after another both in film and in person...until she'd tired of sucking cocks in front of a camera or working her hand on an old guy's limp rod for hours on end to get him stiff enough to fuck.

She'd done her research on James and knew quite a bit about him. For example, she knew that he'd been happily married to a mousy-looking woman named Susan who'd born him three children and that they'd spent a lot of their married life either living on a farm...how dull...or touring with James's new band. She also knew he was a vegetarian and that he supported a lot of "causes" like protecting wildlife and promoting the arts.

She figured it wouldn't take too much effort to find some kind of cause to support or that she could, at least temporarily, pretend to give up steak and burgers, two of her favorite foods.

"Yes," she thought, stubbing out her cigarette and picking up the phone to call her former pimp and on-and-off boyfriend, Marcus, "I'm sure it won't be a problem to snag James...I just have to figure out how to put my tits in front of him..."

⁓

The "food shop," as James referred to it, was bigger than Susan expected it to be. Not only did it have a butcher counter, which was a moot point due to James being a staunch vegetarian, but it had a rather impressive produce section with a wide variety of fresh fruits and vegetables. It was especially impressive for December, when fresh fruit and veggies were scarce. Her eyes alighted on the strawberries immediately.

James smiled, "Ahhh...I seem to recollect that you love strawberries...I'm quite fond of them myself...especially on top of French toast..."

"You're teasing me with all your memories...I don't know how you can remember so much."

"I'm not sure myself...maybe just being with you again..."

She leaned up and pressed a kiss on his cheek. "I'm remembering too, you know...So, maybe I can make you zucchini pancakes for dinner...that is, if they have any zucchini here..."

"We call them courgettes."

"Well, that's an odd thing to call them! Oh! And look! They have eggplant! Do you like eggplant? I make a really good Eggplant Parmesan..."

"We call them auberrgines."

"Why?"

"Because we do...because that's what they're supposed to be called."

"Well, I disagree...I think they should be called zucchini and eggplant."

"You always disagree..."

"I do not! Not *always*...only sometimes."

She rolled the shopping cart over to the zucchini and eggplant and picked up several of each, placing them in plastic bags that she pulled off rollers next to the vegetable display.

She looked at him. "Potatoes? Yams? Green beans? Cabbage for cole slaw?"

He nodded, grabbing some apples, bananas and pears and putting them in bags. Spying some blackberries, he put a carton of them in the cart along with the other items. Before long, their cart was nearly full of fruit and vegetables.

She rolled the cart out of the produce section and down an aisle. "So, what about rice and beans, pasta, flour, cornmeal, sugar, that kind of stuff? And then, we should get milk and butter and eggs…"

"I imagine there might be things like flour and sugar there, but I didn't really look. Go ahead and load up the trolley with whatever you want, then when we get to the cottage, you can check to see if there's anything else you'll be wanting."

She smiled at him. "This is fun! Spending your money…especially now that you have tons and tons of it."

He smiled back at her and playfully swatted her on the bottom. "I suppose you'll be wanting more green dresses and jewelry next?"

"No! Food is different since I'll be cooking it and you'll be eating it. If I want anything personal for myself, then *I'll* be buying it…not you! Besides, I *hate* jewelry."

"We'll see about that…"

By this time, the cart was near overflowing. Susan maneuvered it towards the check-out counter with James right behind her. As the store clerk rang up the groceries, she bagged them and James paid. They were soon on their way to the cottage with the snow falling thicker by the minute.

When they got there, it was a near white-out. As Susan went to reach for the car door handle, she heard James clear his throat and looked over at him. His eyebrows were raised.

"Fine." Was all she said, crossing her arms over her chest and looking out the front car window.

"Good girl," he said, getting out his side of the car, going around, opening her door and holding out his hand to help her out.

She frowned up at him, extending her hand. "I'm not a girl anymore…"

"You are to me." He tugged her out of the car, smiling at her.

She couldn't help but smile back, suddenly feeling a little nervous and shy about being back at Auntie Annabelle's cottage again. She didn't really know why.

They were soon in the cottage, stamping the snow off their feet. James closed the door and immediately went to the fireplace, where he put wood on the grate from a box sitting next to it, crumpled some paper to put under the wood then lit the fire. Flames licked up into the wood.

Susan walked over to an end table by the couch and set her purse down before glancing around the room. It was the same, yet different. The piano was still in the same place as was the rest of the furniture in the main room. Glancing across into the kitchen, it looked the same also except for a new refrigerator and kitchen table.

James went to the wall by the back door, and she saw him push buttons on a small panel. A few seconds later, she heard a rumble.

"I got Auntie a new furnace a few years ago," he said. "She'd been using an old radiator system that she told me wasn't working very well. She was also having some plumbing problems, so I told her to get in a new kitchen sink and update the bathroom. She didn't want to take my money, but I talked to Uncle Albert and he arranged for it all."

"That was awfully nice of you."

"She's always been my favorite auntie. I spent a lot of time here when I was a lad. Mum and Dad came to visit a lot too."

"I remember you telling me that. It was still nice of you…Should we bring in the groceries while the cottage is warming up?" She started moving towards the front door,

He stepped in front of her. "The groceries can wait…"

She looked at his face and saw a slow, seductive grin spread across it.

"Now, James, you can't be serious about…"

But before she could say anything else, he was pulling her into his arms. He brought his mouth down on hers in short, soft kisses, stealing any more words from her lips, before moving his hands around to the front of her and starting to unbutton her jacket.

She pushed at his chest. "Stop it! It's freezing cold in here."

"It won't feel that way in a minute…" He finished unbuttoning her jacket, spreading it open and placing his hands on her breasts, gently squeezing.

She sucked in her breath as he tilted his head, moved in closer and began kissing her neck. Shivers ran down her spine…and they weren't due to the cold. His lips moved up the side of her neck to her ear, where he nibbled and tugged on her earlobe before swirling his tongue inside. When his hands moved from her breasts to her bottom, she felt a tightening sensation between her thighs and could almost feel herself getting wet.

James moved his lips back to her neck then drew away a moment before pulling her in tighter to him and taking her mouth in a deep kiss. Her arms wrapped around his neck and she reached up to scrape her fingernails through his hair.

He moaned, feeling the bulge in his trousers become stiff and hard. He was surprising himself. He'd made love to Susan four times already in less than twelve hours, and here he was stiff and ready for her again. It almost felt as if he were twenty years old once more and she were seventeen, just like they were the first time they came to the cottage.

Susan was breathing heavily as she broke from James's embrace, took hold of his hand and pulled him towards the back of the couch. When they got there, she turned, reached under her dress and pulled down her panties to her knees. She flipped up the back of her dress, exposing her bare bottom and leaned over the couch.

"Ahhh...I *knew* it, Susan...I knew I could put you in the mood..."

She smiled as she heard him unzip his trousers, and moaned in pleasure as he pushed himself into her from behind.

Firmly grasping her hips, he began slow, deep thrusts, pausing inside her now and then to savor the feeling of being buried in her warmth. But then the slow strokes became faster and more intense. When he reached around to the front of her and circled his finger around her love button, she screamed his name and he felt her passage tighten and pulse around him. He immediately followed her into a shattering climax, groaning heavily as his seed pumped into her. Both of them were panting and their breath made puffs of smoke in the freezing room.

When James pulled out of her, she straightened and turned around, reaching down to pull up her panties. He tucked himself back into his shorts and trousers and quickly zipped up before pulling her into his arms for another kiss.

"All warmed up now?" he teased.

"Yes...quite...You always *do* get your way, don't you?"

"Yes, Susan...I always do...it would be best for you to keep that in mind..."

⌒◯

Hilary was pacing back and forth in her hotel room in the Claridon hotel in Brighton. She'd arrived early that morning, hoping to catch James before he checked out and returned to his house outside of London.

It was the day after the concert at the Dusky. Marcus had assured her that James was registered at this hotel and that he hadn't checked out yet. He had ways of finding things out that she never questioned, but thought it might have something to do with favors owed him, bribes or even blackmail. She shrugged her shoulders. It didn't matter. Here she was in James's hotel.

But James wasn't here.

She'd gone up to his penthouse suite, pretending to be someone new from his London team, using her courtesan charm and body to worm her way past two of James's security people that monitored the penthouse floor. Neither of them knew where James had gone, only that he left word with the front desk to keep the floor reserved for him.

Damn! She'd had her plan all worked out. Knowing James was a staunch vegetarian and animal lover, she decided to take up an animal-related cause. It had taken some thought, since she really didn't give a shit about animal welfare, but she finally hit upon the idea of "People for Pigs – Ban Bacon in Britain." It sounded cute and catchy, and she figured James would find it clever...not that she was actually all that clever, but she was damn good at manipulating men even if there was a bit of deceit involved. Deceit was one of her specialties.

And even though bacon was something she loved, especially on her burgers, she figured she could do without it for the time it took her to lure James into her bed and into her clutches.

When the phone rang, she picked it up on the first ring. It was Marcus.

"He's not here, damn it all!" she screeched into the phone. "And it's not like I want to spend the rest of my life in this musty old hotel!"

"I know he's not there. Calm your tits…I'm working on tracking him down now. But, I did find out something that might interest you…"

"What?"

"One of his sons is also staying there. Name of Thomas. He's a concert pianist with the London Philharmonic. He's in room 4029. You should pay him a visit. He probably knows where his dad is or when he's coming back."

"A piano player for the Phil har mon what? Oh! You mean the orchestra thing that plays all that dull classical shit!"

"He's one of their up and coming talents. James even wrote some concerto for him a few months back. It really made a name for him."

"What else do you know about him?"

"Only that he's 26 years old and is supposed to be the spitting image of his dad."

"That sounds rather nice…Maybe I could snag both of them…"

"Forget it, Hilary. Just use him to find out where James is and work our plan. James is the one with the millions, not Thomas. And don't forget our agreement…"

"Yeah, yeah…you get a smooth million pounds once the wedding ring is on my finger."

"It's a pittance to him. He won't miss it."

"Whatever. Okay, I'll go find this Thomas and make him tell me where James is or at least find out how long I have to wait before he comes back here."

"Stay in touch and let me know what you find out. If I come across more information, I'll let you know too."

"Fine…Bye then."

"Wait! Hil…I've been thinking about you for the past few weeks. We haven't been together much since you've been with that old gent in Piccadilly. How about a little phone sex? Mmmm? Tell me what you're wearing, luv…I've got a hard one in my trousers right now… How about it?"

"Shit, Marcus…You're one horny bastard…Okay, I guess we can do it. Hold on a minute while I get out of these tight jeans…"

Chapter 13

Michelle Suspects

James and Susan soon had all the groceries and their suitcases out of the car and into the cottage, which was warming up nicely due to the new heating system and the burning logs in the fireplace.

After a half hour, they were able to remove their coats. Susan put away the groceries and began to inventory the kitchen. James went to the piano. Looking over at him, her eyes began to mist and she had to pinch herself to believe she was here with him in the same place where their torrid love affair had begun in June, 1962 when she'd come back into the past in her 17-year-old body and he was 20.

She was both touched and amazed at how much he remembered about her and the times they'd spent together after so many years had passed. For her, however, it was all so recent that she recalled every moment, every disagreement, every touch... every kiss...

It was also hard to believe that the mere sight of him, now at age 57, could still make her weak in the knees, and that when he looked at her with those eyes of his, it just about knocked the feet out from under her.

He sensed her staring at him and turned to look at her. Her love for him was clearly written across her face and it tugged at his heart. Could he really love her again? Was it true that he'd never stopped loving her as he told her before they left the restaurant?

More memories flooded his brain as they continued to look at each other, but not just memories of the good times they'd spent together, but also the bad ones.

Could he trust her again? That was the big question. He just wasn't sure.

⌒〇

As Thomas and Michelle were coming out of the hotel dining room after breakfast, Hilary was stepping out of the elevator into the hotel lobby. Her predatory eyes spotted Thomas immediately and she gave a small gasp.

Shit! Marcus hadn't been exaggerating. He looked *exactly* like his dad, but younger and a lot hotter. She moved nonchalantly towards him and the blonde who was walking next to him.

His girlfriend maybe?

She assessed Michelle critically. Not bad looking…in fact she had to admit that she was quite pretty. It was annoying. She hated to see women prettier than her.

But what did it matter? She reminded herself that she wasn't here to snag James's son. Her purpose was to snag James himself.

As Thomas and Michelle came closer, she pretended to stumble and would have fallen into one of the lobby's arm chairs if Thomas hadn't seen her and reached out to grab her arm.

"Oh! How clumsy of me!" she exclaimed breathlessly.

"Are you okay?" Thomas asked, helping her to sit in the chair.

"Yes, yes…I believe so…I must have caught my heel in the carpeting."

Michelle glanced down at the woman's spike heeled shoes before glancing at the woman herself. For some reason, it seemed to her as if the stumble had been contrived. She shook her head. What a silly notion. This wasn't a courtroom and the woman wasn't a witness for the defense. She needed to stop her lawyer's brain from invading her thoughts so much.

"Did you sprain or hurt anything?" Thomas asked solicitously.

"Oh no…but thank you for asking…so very kind of you…"

"Well, if you're sure you're okay…"

"I am...thank you...Um...excuse me for asking, but you remind me of someone."

Thomas smiled but said nothing. Hilary looked up at him, fluttering her eye lashes. Michelle's eyes became shuttered, but she suddenly became very alert. Something was up with this trampy looking woman...

Oh my God! Did she just think "trampy?!" She looked at her again. Yes, that would definitely be the correct word to describe this woman in skin tight jeans, spiked heels and a blouse unbuttoned halfway down to her waist.

Hilary continued, "I mean, you remind me of James...you know, the singer and song writer who was once a member of the most famous band of all time? He was here in Brighton just last night at the Dusky Club..."

"Were you at the concert?"

"Oh no! Unfortunately, I missed it. I had a transportation problem. I just got here this morning. I was so upset having missed it...I'm a huge fan of his..."

"Are you?"

"Yes! Very much so!"

"Well, it's unfortunate you missed the concert."

"Yes," chirped in Michelle. "It was quite fabulous."

"Oh! Were both of you there then?"

"We were," responded Michelle as she looped her arm into Thomas's. For some reason, this woman was making her suspicious.

"I was so hoping to meet him, you know," said Hilary. "I've founded a new vegetarian cause to save animals and I wanted to tell him about it."

"So, she has an ulterior motive," thought Michelle. "I knew there was something..."

Thomas seemed oblivious. Michelle was tempted to elbow him in the ribs.

"My dad is always interested in causes that benefit animals," he said.

"Oh my goodness!" exclaimed Hilary. "You're James's son?!!!" She covered her mouth with her hand, opening her eyes wide.

"Yes, I am."

"Oh!!...Is there any possible way you could introduce him to me?" Michelle rolled her eyes.

"Actually," replied Thomas. "Dad's gone off with a...an...old friend of his for a few days...Just to catch up on old times and memories from when the band first started here."

Hilary's face fell. "Oh dear...I don't know how much longer I'll be staying here...I don't suppose you could tell me where I might run into him? I'd so very much like to share my cause with him..."

This time, Michelle did elbow him in the ribs.

She looked at Hilary. "So. What's the name of your cause?"

Hilary beamed. "It's called 'People for Pigs – Ban Bacon in Britain.' Isn't that a clever name for a cause?"

Both Tomas and Michelle choked back a laugh. Michelle had to turn her head away to stop herself from bursting out in laughter.

Thomas cleared his throat a few times to collect himself. "Umm... Quite clever, yes."

"So might you tell me where your father is?" Hilary persisted.

Michelle turned back around. "Oh, but we don't know, do we Thomas? Mom didn't say in her note where she and your dad were going...Did he say anything in his note to you?"

Hilary stiffened and an annoyed look passed over her face. It was instantly replaced with a disappointed smile. But not soon enough for Michelle not to notice.

Her lawyer's brain kicked into full gear. She ran through her head every move and word Hilary had uttered from the minute she and Thomas encountered her. It was one of Michelle's gifts that had served her well in her budding career. It was almost as if her mind took a film of everyone around her...every nuance of what they did or said, but especially their facial expressions and eyes, which told volumes about them.

The woman was a fake and had something up her sleeve concerning James. She just knew it.

Thomas picked up on Michelle's vibrations and responded to Hilary. "No, he didn't say...No idea where they might be off to... might not even be in Brighton anymore...Sorry I can't be of help."

Hilary looked back at him with tears brimming in her eyes. "Oh dear, I guess my cause will have to wait then…But, seeing as he's still checked into the hotel, did your dad's note say when he might be back"

"Exactly how did you know he hadn't checked out yet?" Michelle questioned, eyes hard and locked with Hilary's.

Hilary's face flushed as she quickly thought up a lie. "Why I over-heard a couple of men who must be James's security guards. They were in the elevator. They were talking about James and wondering when he'd be back to check out."

Michelle noted that Hilary was blinking more than a normal, relaxed person would do, indicative of a person who was lying.

"No, sorry…He didn't say," responded Thomas sounding as apolo-getic as possible. "Umm…If you're all right then, we'll be off…"

He started to walk towards the elevators. Michelle grabbed his arm to stop him and looked into Hilary's face again.

"What's your name? …You know, in case James and my mom come back…We can talk to them and let James know about your cause…"

Hilary began to feel nervous for some reason and abruptly stood up. She needed to get away from this blonde American girl. She quickly gave her first name, adding that she could be contacted through the front desk, then walked briskly towards the hotel dining room.

Thomas and Michelle looked at each other before heading to the elevator and up to the fourth floor where their rooms were. This encounter warranted some discussion.

Chapter 14

Love at the Cottage

James stood up from the piano bench and wordlessly went to Susan and gathered her in his arms, pressing her softness into him and burying his face in her hair. While the question of love was easy to answer, the question of trust was a hard one.

He remembered late in the year 1962, when he'd been so in love with her, had bought a little sparkling engagement ring and started to propose. The truth that there was another man in her life and that she never told him, had deceived him...left him wounded beyond pain. Not only was she his first true love but she was also the cause of his first broken heart.

Then he recalled five years later in 1967, when she'd come back into his life again. He forgave her the past and they fell in love anew, this time even creating a child together. And then she'd vanished on him again...leaving him totally shattered. Other than a different kind of broken heart, the one that he felt when his wife, Susan, passed, this had been the second and last time he ever suffered a crushed heart. Susan had been his first and last broken heart, a heart broken by her deceit and lies.

His mind refocused on the present and he began to run his hands soothingly up and down Susan's back as she melted into him. Here she was back in his life again. His stubborn, feisty and passionate Susan.

Could he...should he...trust her again...? Yes, he decided...at least he would try.

He pushed back from her and she smiled up at him, a stray tear rolling down one cheek.

"Oh, James…I love you so very much…"

He rubbed a finger across her cheek, wiping away the tear then leaned in to kiss her softly on her lips.

"I love you too Susan…I really do…" He released her from his arms. "So, will you be needing anything else in the way of supplies for the kitchen? We can call the food shop if you do."

She looked over to the kitchen table where she had a small notepad with a list of additional items needed, but there was nothing really important.

"I only noticed a few things missing, but I could do without for now."

"But I don't want you to do without…"

"James, it's just things like cinnamon and nutmeg that I like to use in baking and also some canned goods, like tomato sauce and paste, nothing urgent considering everything that was already here as well as what we bought."

"But if you want what's on your list, we can call…"

"No. Look outside! It's snowing like crazy. We'll be snowed in before long if it keeps up like this. The poor shop people could never get through."

"I'm going to like being snowed in with you…" He looked at her with a sparkle in his eye.

"I think I'll rather like it myself…But, for now, let me finish up in the kitchen and then I think I want to take a nice hot bath to get the rest of the chill off me."

"I didn't warm you up enough?"

"Well, yes, you did in one way, but I'd still like to take a hot bath."

"I'll go turn on the tap for you then."

"Why, thank you, James! I see that you *can* be thoughtful now and then…" She tried to hide a smirk.

"Are you implying that I'm not very thoughtful?"

"No…well, actually, you're very thoughtful when it comes to yourself…"

"Now you're insulting me?"

"No, of course not! I would *never* want to insult or even *imply* you were anything less than perfect!"

He crossed his arms across his chest. "I think you're being facetious…"

She looked over her shoulder at him as she opened a kitchen cabinet to finish putting the last of the grocery staples away. "I'm surprised you even know what that word means."

"Of course I know what it means! Now you're implying I'm ignorant!!"

She laughed. "Don't you know when I'm teasing you, James?"

"Well, I don't find it amusing. I'm thinking perhaps I should turn you over my knee for your insults…and your implications…"

He began to advance towards her, but she scooted out of the way, giggling and ran towards the bathroom. He was quicker than her, however, and caught her.

"You wouldn't want spanked now, would you?" he teased.

"Hmmm…Let me think about it…are you trying to get a little kinky with me?"

"Maybe…I might like to see that nice round bottom of yours turning pinkish…"

"I'll let you know later then…"

Before he could respond again, she broke free, ran into the bathroom and closed the door. "I'm taking a hot bath!" she yelled through the door, then went to the tub and turned on the tap herself.

Looking around the bathroom, she saw that it had been remodeled. The claw foot tub was gone and replaced by a new, deep tub with a shower and clear glass shower doors.

Maybe I'll take a shower instead of a bath, she thought as she saw the steam rising from the water pouring into the tub. She quickly stripped off her dress, bra and panties then turned the knob in the tub to make the water jet out of the shower head. She stepped in and closed the door, letting the hot water pour over her head and body. It felt marvelous.

There were bottles of shampoo, conditioner and body wash on a small built-in shelf in the shower, things that had been lacking when she was last at the cottage. She squirted shampoo into her hand, then proceeded to suds up her hair. She rinsed out the shampoo then put some of the conditioner on, rubbing it into the ends of her long hair, which still reached past her waist. Just as she was getting ready to rinse it out and wash the rest of herself, she heard the bathroom door open, and when she turned, she saw James come in and close it behind him. Within a minute, he'd stripped off his own clothes, grabbed a shaving razor out of the bathroom cabinet and was in the shower with her.

"And just what do you think you're doing?" she asked. "I didn't invite you in here!'

"I'm joining you...and it doesn't matter if you didn't invite me."

He reached for the body wash and lathered up his face then began shaving. She watched him as he expertly stroked the razor along his face. The water cascaded down her back, rinsing out the conditioner.

When he was done, he picked up the body wash again, squirted some into his hand then looked at her wickedly.

"Want washed?" he asked, quirking his eyebrows at her.

"Do I have a choice?

"No."

He rubbed his palms together then reached forward and took her breasts into his hands, gently squeezing and rubbing them with the soap before pinching and rubbing his thumbs across her nipples.

She sucked in her breath. "That's not exactly washing, James..."

"Don't you like it?"

"I didn't say that," she sighed as he continued to fondle and caress her breasts with the slinky and slippery soap.

She reached to the shelf in the tub and put some body wash on her own hands and began to rub the soap into his chest, also giving his nipples a little pinch now and then.

He sucked in his breath and when she looked into his eyes, she saw the amber highlights in them sparking as they always did when he became aroused.

His arms reached around her and he pulled her in for a kiss, turning her so the water ran down over both of them. She pressed her breasts into his chest and began to seductively rub them against him, while at the same time bumping her hips into his thighs. She felt his erection grow against her belly as her own body responded with a tightness and throbbing sensation between her legs.

Their kiss deepened and their tongues danced the erotic dance they both knew so well. Before long, their hands were roaming all over each other, from arms, to back, to buttocks then back up again and they both began to pant heavily

"I want you, James," Susan murmured into his ear, reaching down to enclose his stiffness with one hand. She squeezed gently and began moving her hand up and down, making him groan.

Without another word, he reached behind her and turned off the shower then opened the shower door and pulled her out. Opening the bathroom door, he tugged her, both of them still dripping wet, into the main room and over to the fireplace. She saw that he'd brought the bedding, comforter and pillows out from the bedroom and laid them on the floor in front of the blazing fire before coming into the bathroom.

She needed no urging to lay down amongst the pillows where he quickly joined her, covering her dripping body with his. They moved rhythmically together, savoring the feel of their skin against each other from shoulder to toe. Susan wrapped her arms around James's neck and pulled his mouth down to hers, kissing him deeply and hungrily.

When he pulled away, her chest was rising and falling and the need to have him fill her was almost unbearable. But he wasn't about to let her have him just yet.

He trailed soft kisses down one side of her neck, then the other, stopping to nibble on her earlobe and blow little puffs of air into her ear. The sensation sent shivers down into her nether region, causing her to squeeze her thighs together and writhe beneath him.

"Stay still, dammit!" he whispered hoarsely. "Or you'll make me spill myself on your belly."

"Then let me have you *now!*" she implored, her breath coming in soft gasps as he moved his tongue down to her collar bone then down to her breasts where he took turns taking each nipple into his mouth, suckling her. Her nipples were already taught, but now they hardened into tight buds.

His mouth continued to move on her, going lower to her belly, planting small kisses from side to side then swirling his tongue in her belly button, making her near swoon with pleasure.

"James, *please...*" she begged.

But he was deaf to her words, continuing his erotic assault on her body. When he spread her thighs and moved his head lower, she instinctively raised her hips upwards, exposing her most intimate part to his eyes. Reaching between her legs, he spread the lips of her womanhood wide, exposing her throbbing nub before softly flicking his tongue at it. She grabbed his hair and screamed.

She closed her eyes as he continued the gentle torture, but when he began to swirl his tongue around her bud, increasing the pressure and the speed, she couldn't contain herself any longer and went over the top into a climax that made her entire body shudder and convulse. Her hips pumped up into his face and her hands pulled on his hair while she screamed his name over and over.

Before the throes of her orgasm were over, he was up on his knees and drove his now throbbing member deeply into her to the very core, where he stilled for a moment then began urgently stroking in and out. She felt as if she might faint, but wrapped her legs around him and met each thrust hard and fast until she felt another climax building within her.

He grunted out his pleasure with each stroke and she knew he was doing his best to hold back for her to experience a second pleasure. When she saw him squeeze his eyes shut and try to slow down the thrusts, she reached behind him and dug her fingernails into his buttocks. It threw them both over the top with James pounding several more times into her then spilling his hot liquid deep into her warmth.

He collapsed onto her then rolled them both to their sides, where their chests heaved against each other.

James grabbed her chin in his hand and brought his mouth to hers, passionately at first, but then he slowed to soft, feathery kisses, moving from her lips to her cheeks, her nose and her brow. Their breathing began to slow.

"That was quite fabulous, James" she whispered breathlessly, gently running her fingernails across his chest then down his arms. "In fact... that was the best ever..."

He hugged her to him for another quick kiss before reaching for the comforter to cover both of them.

"I can do even better, you know..."

"I don't think so..."

"Are you trying to argue with me...?"

"No, James...I know that it's quite useless to argue with you..."

"As you should, Susan...as you should..."

They both closed their eyes and drifted into a contented sleep, bodies entwined, as the fire crackled next to them.

Chapter 15

Michelle Falls for Thomas

When the elevator doors opened at the fourth floor, Michelle stepped out before Thomas and motioned him down the hallway to her room. Her steps were quick and determined as her brain analyzed what had just happened in the hotel lobby. She was soon inserting the key into her hotel room door. Thomas followed her in.

Michelle flung her purse onto the bottom of her bed. "Something is up with that woman, Thomas, and it's not something good."

"What are you talking about? She's just another fan of my dad's that thinks she has an animal rights related cause that he might be interested in."

"With the ridiculous name of 'People for Pigs? Ban Bacon in Britain?' You've got to be kidding me! Even you had a hard time holding back a laugh."

"Well, it did sound rather clever..."

She shot him a look. "Clever or not, that woman has intentions towards your dad that have nothing to do with animals or any rights."

"I still don't know what you're talking about..."

"Well, no, you wouldn't. I saw your eyes glued to her chest the entire time we were with her and..."

"I did *not* have my eyes glued to her chest!"

"You did, you know...Remember, Thomas, I'm a *very* observant person...It's my job. If I were less observant of people and didn't attend to every detail and nuance, I wouldn't win cases."

"And you like to win and nail the guilty to the wall in your cases, right?"

"It can bring a sense of satisfaction, yes…But that's not what we're here to talk about. That woman has something else in mind regarding your dad other than her so-called 'cause.' And, I was making her extremely nervous."

"How can you know? We just spent five minutes with her!"

"Because I *observed*! Think! First off, I saw her focus on you as we came out of the restaurant and she came out of the elevator, then I saw her eyes and face light up, as if she recognized you. It was obvious that she deliberately maneuvered herself towards you before she pretended to snag her heel on the carpet"

"You think she only pretended to catch her heel?!!"

"It was as clear as night and day, Thomas! The carpet is flat and solid. You *can't* catch your heel in it! The hotel could be in for a zillion lawsuits if it was the kind you could trip on or catch your heel in. All she did was stumble right when she knew you'd reach out to catch her."

"You mean she recognized me and figured it would be an easy way to talk to me and see about presenting her cause to my dad?"

"You still don't get it, do you? She has no cause! She just wants to *get* to your dad…the thing is, I don't know exactly why, but I have a suspicion."

"Which is?"

"She has designs on him."

"Which means?"

Michelle gave an exasperated sigh. "For heaven's sake, can't you even figure that out?!"

Thomas bristled. "I'm not stupid, Michelle!! But, I have no reason whatsoever to believe that someone would deliberately trip herself just so she could get to my dad to seduce him somehow. Is that what you're implying?!"

"It's *exactly* what I'm implying. Consider this: Your dad is back performing again. He's still attractive. He's filthy rich. And, he's on the rebound from having lost your mom. He's what you'd call 'ripe for the plucking' for any gold-digging woman."

"You think she's after Dad's money?"

"I can't be certain, of course, but it's my first thought. Did you notice her face when I said my mom was off with your dad? It was plain as day that it pissed her off. A hard look came into her eyes and her mouth formed into a straight line. If all she cared about was her 'cause,' why would she react that way when I mentioned Mom was with your dad?"

"And then she knew he was checked into this hotel and hadn't checked out yet...Yes, I do recall her saying that...But she said she overheard Dad's security people in the elevator."

"Bullshit is what that is! Her eyes were blinking so fast that I thought they were hummingbirds."

When Thomas looked confused, she added, "When people are lying their eyes tend to blink a lot."

"You scare me, Michelle."

"Why?"

"You observe too much about people! Not saying you're wrong about that Hilary woman, but it makes me rather disconcerted to think you're looking at me like some kind of...some kind of specimen in a jar!"

"I haven't been observing you...all that much, that is. But I was sure observing Hilary! I'm sure she'll be asking you about your dad again, and I don't like it. My mom would have conniption fits if she started making moves on your dad. She has a horrible jealous streak in her."

"I wouldn't worry about it. I think Dad's fallen in love with your mum all over again. I don't think that woman could pry him away from her." He thought for a moment then gave a quirky little grin. "Even with those impressive breasts of hers..."

Michelle, who was reaching for the water glass on her nightstand, picked up one of her bed pillows and tossed it at him. It caught him unaware as it hit him full in the face. She laughed at his startled expression.

"Watch it, Thomas...I just might have a jealous streak in me as well!"

"Ah...does that mean you care a bit for me then?"

Her face tinged pink. She had no idea why those words had come out of her mouth. She was left speechless for a moment, something that was foreign to her.

"Cat got your tongue?" he smirked at her.

"No…I…I just don't know why I said what I did…I mean, about having a jealous streak…"

"Do you have one?"

"I don't really know…that is…I never thought about it…"

"So, back to my other question…Do you care a bit for me? I know we haven't known each other long, but from my side, I think you've rather captivated me…"

Her eyes flew to his. "I have?"

Her heart began to beat fast in her chest even though she told it to stop.

"Well, Miss high and mighty lawyer and observer of people…what do you see when you look at me now?"

Her breath caught in her throat as he pierced her with those incredible eyes of his. He was so damn good looking! And, she hated like hell to admit it. He was the spitting image of his father at the same age…the same dark, silky hair, the same arched eyebrows, perfect nose and sensual lips. He was also, however, a few inches taller and had a more muscular build than his dad. He was quite perfect.

She remembered, when she was growing up, making fun of her mother for her James obsession, even scolding her about it, telling her how ridiculous it was…telling her he really wasn't all that "cute," as her mother referred to him.

She recalled going to see her mother just a few weeks ago and giving her a really hard time about her "James thing," then having to listen to her mother recount her crazy time-travel tale and how it was impossible to resist him…especially those eyes…

But, oh, now…to be confronted by the devastatingly handsome man who stood in front of her, eyebrows raised, eyes piercing hers with the golden glints sparking within… And, she suddenly realized and understood what her mother had felt, and still felt, for James for all those years.

She swallowed before biting her lower lip and moving towards him. Her eyes never left his. "I see you looking at me as if you want to take me in your arms and kiss me..."

His smile made her knees weak as he reached for her and gathered her in his arms. When he brought his lips down on hers, she twined her arms around his neck and pressed herself into him, kissing him back with a fervor she'd never felt before.

And, it wasn't as if she hadn't experienced other men. She had, in fact, experienced many of them. None, however, including her fiancé back in the future, made her feel the way she was feeling now, as if little jolts of electricity were singing in her veins.

When the kiss ended, both looked at each other with wonderment in their eyes. They stared silently at each other for a full minute before Michelle reached forward and began to unbutton Thomas's shirt.

⌒◯

"Shit, shit, shit!" Hilary hissed into her mobile phone, making her voice as low as possible. She was in the hotel dining room after encountering Thomas, James's son in the lobby. "Some bitch has already got her claws in him!!"

"Who?" asked Marcus, picking his teeth with a toothpick on the other side of the call.

"James, you idiot! He's off with some woman somewhere. I don't know who, but she's the mother of an American girl I met out in the lobby. She was with Thomas, James's son."

"Did you find out her name?"

"No, damn it all. She was making me nervous as shit, the way she was staring at me. It's almost like the bitch could read my mind or something."

"What did she look like?"

"Why, Marcus, do you think you might be interested? She was good looking enough...tall, blonde, and her eyes were really a funny color of blue and green combined. I thought they were creepy, like seaweed."

"Is she staying at the hotel? If so, I can find out from my contact at the front desk who she is, and if her mum is staying there, I can find that out too."

"Well, obviously the mum isn't here *now*, she's off somewhere with James. I prodded Thomas to tell me where I could find his dad, but the American bitch put him off me."

"I already told you he's in room 4029. I'll have my contact at the front desk get you a key to his room. Do what you usually do, and wait for him in his bed. I'm sure he'll tell you where his dad is."

"What if he doesn't come back to his room? What if he's staying with that girl he was with?"

"Just let me do more checking and I'll call you right back."

She slammed her phone onto the dining table. A waiter, seeing that she was off her phone, came over and asked if she'd care for anything for breakfast. She'd already ordered and been served a vodka and orange juice, and drank it down in five swallows.

"Just get me another screwdriver…make it a double…and I'll have a hamburger, no chips."

"I'm sorry, ma'm," he responded. "But we're still serving off the breakfast menu. Luncheon won't start until 11:00."

"I don't care when your fucking luncheon starts. Bring me a god-damn burger! I'm sure it's not so hard to make one!"

The waiter gave her a hard look before giving a small nod of his head. "Very well, ma'm, I'll see what I can do."

She waved him away impatiently and looked out the window next to her table.

Her phone rang again five minutes later, just as she was polishing off her second drink.

"So what did you find out?" she barked impatiently.

"Mother and daughter checked in in the afternoon, the day before James's concert. Mother's name is Susan and the daughter is Michelle. Both from California. I couldn't find out anything about the mother, but the daughter put down a number in the states for emergency contact when they checked in. When I called it, the woman who answered said it was a law firm. I thought quick and said I was a solicitor in

England and needed to check on a case the firm was handling for one of my clients. She seemed puzzled but put me through to some chap, name of Donald. He started asking too many questions, so I said I must have the wrong law firm, apologized and hung up."

Hilary was thoughtful, jiggling the ice cubes in her glass. Right then the waiter set a plate with a hamburger on it in front of her and she waved him away.

"A law firm, huh? No wonder the girl seemed so high and mighty. She's probably a solicitor working there. So do you know if they came for the concert or if they're just here on holiday? And, how does Thomas know them?"

"According to the desk clerk, they went to the concert, but he doesn't know how either James or Thomas came to know them. He saw Thomas talking to the daughter out in the lobby right after she and her mum checked in. He thinks maybe they knew each other before. They were in the dining room together after the concert…Thomas and the girl, that is. No one's seen the mum or James and no one saw them leave the hotel, but my contact is only on duty during the day."

"Well, that's fucking great…I guess I'll go pick up that key to Thomas's room and think on how to make him tell me where in the hell they went or at least when they're coming back. Try to find out more about the Susan woman. I need to know what I'm up against."

"No problem, but I need to make a lot of calls, so it might be a day or two. In the meantime, work your charm on Thomas. I'm sure you'll have no problem with him."

"Yeah, well, I'm not so sure, but you know I always try my best. Men are pretty fucking easy to manipulate…including you, Marcus… including you."

She disconnected, picked up her burger and took a giant bite wishing she'd ordered some bacon on it.

Susan woke up as the sun was beginning to set and when she looked out the window, she saw it was still snowing, the snow building up in drifts.

She shivered a little as she pushed the comforter aside and noticed the fire in the fireplace was nearly out. Only glowing embers remained.

Looking over at James, she saw that he was still sound asleep. Her breath caught in her throat as she gazed at him. She couldn't get over how attractive she found him, more so now that when he was younger. How that was even possible, she didn't know and she had to shake her head to clear it before getting up and putting more wood on the fire.

Picking up a pair of bellows, she fanned the embers back into flames and the wood caught. James still hadn't budged, so she went into the bathroom to use the loo, slipped into a pair of jeans and a long-sleeved top she'd packed in her suitcase then went into the kitchen to start something for dinner.

Figuring James would be hungry, since they hadn't eaten anything since breakfast, she decided on zucchini pancakes, steamed maple carrots and a spinach salad. Originally, she thought of making her Eggplant Parmesan, but it took too long and would have to wait until tomorrow.

It seemed surreal being in Auntie Annabelle's kitchen cooking again, but she felt right at home. It was comforting.

As she was shredding the zucchini, James came into the kitchen and wrapped his arms around her. He'd also slipped on a pair of jeans but was bare-chested. He nuzzled the back of her neck.

"Cooking for me, are you?"

"As always."

"And what are you making?"

"Zucchini pancakes. I made them for you once before, but you probably don't remember…"

"But I do! I think they were green and I teased you about it…You said you were making me healthy."

She smiled before turning in his arms and planting a smacking kiss on his lips. "Now I'm going to *keep* you healthy."

"Are you vegetarian then?"

"I guess I am now…"

"But you're not really?"

"Actually, I refer to myself as a 'Pescatarian," which means I don't eat meat, but I do eat fish."

"If you're going to be with me, you need to give up fish too. They suffocate when they're pulled out of the water, you know...Pretty horrible death to suffocate."

"I know that, James. It's not a problem giving up seafood." She paused, turning her head to look out the window for a moment before turning back to him. "I'll be anything you want me to be...anything..."

He hugged her tight into him for a moment before pushing her away. "I'm starving. How fast can you get dinner ready?"

"As fast as you can go over to the piano and sing me a few songs."

He slapped her on the bottom before going into the other room and sitting down on the piano bench.

"As you wish, m'lady..."

It was late afternoon when Hilary decided to knock on Thomas's door and try to talk to him, but when she did, there was no response. Looking over her shoulder and up and down the hall in each direction, she inserted the room key that she'd got from Marcus's contact at the front desk into the lock and let herself in. She closed the door softly behind her and flicked on the light. It was already getting dark outside and the rainy weather wasn't making it any brighter.

Looking around the room, she saw an opened suitcase laying on the bed, and going over to it, she rummaged through. Only clothes. Going into the bathroom, she saw shaving gear and some other toiletries, so assumed Thomas was just out somewhere and planning on coming back. If he was staying with the blonde bitch, Michelle, his stuff probably wouldn't be here.

She contemplated her next move. Slipping naked into his bed and waiting for him was her first thought, but then Michelle might very well be with him when he came back, and that could make things awkward. No, she needed to think of something else, but what it was, she wasn't sure yet.

She slipped back out the door, locking it behind her, and went down to the hotel bar. She figured she could hang out there near the entry to the hotel lobby and watch for Thomas, and if Michelle wasn't with him, she could approach him again. It would also give her a good vantage point if James came back, with or without the Susan woman.

⌒☉

Thomas had never experienced such passion before in his entire life. Gazing over at Michelle after their third bout of lovemaking, left him spent, dazed and amazed.

Her aquamarine eyes were half open as she trailed her fingertips across his bare chest and smiled a Cheshire cat grin at him.

"You're quite remarkable, Thomas," she purred.

And, indeed, she thought he was. Her mind was in a whirl, while her body was still tingling from the most intense orgasms she'd ever experienced. The fact that she'd been the one to initiate their intimate encounter made her blush, but her face was already so flushed from what had just happened over the previous two hours that it wasn't even noticeable.

Thomas was speechless as he gazed into her sultry eyes. He'd experienced several women over the years, a few of them married women in high society who were patrons of the Philharmonic. And, he'd had a steady girlfriend for about a year while he was attending the music academy. But none of them came close to what had just happened between him and this captivating American girl. He felt overwhelmed.

"Maybe we could sleep a little bit?" Michelle asked. "I didn't sleep much last night."

Thomas smiled. "I didn't either…and to be honest, it was because I was thinking about you…"

"I was thinking about you too." She leaned in and gave him a kiss on his nose. "Cuddle with me?"

He pulled her in tighter to him. "Gladly…"

Within a minute, they were asleep entwined in each other's arms, Michelle's golden hair trailing across the pillow next to Thomas's dark, silky locks.

Chapter 16

James Loses Control

Susan was shocked when James offered to help her with the dinner dishes, but she didn't turn him down. She washed while he dried then they both put things away. When James went out to the car, making his way through the deep snow to get his guitar, Susan took the bedding from in front of the fireplace back into the bedroom and made up the bed. Making love and taking a nap on the floor in front of the fire was one thing, but getting a good night's rest, now that she was older, required a real bed. She blushed. Not that she was going to get a good night's rest anyway with James's over-the-top testosterone levels, but she had to admit that she was feeling sleepy, even after their long nap in front of the fire and a nice cozy bed with a soft mattress sounded very nice.

She heard James come back in and stamp his feet inside the front door to get the snow off his shoes. A few minutes later, as she was finishing making the bed, she heard him strum the strings of the guitar. She leaned her head out the bedroom door.

"Are you going to write another song for me?"

He was sitting on the couch and turned around to look at her. "How did you know?"

She smiled at him. "Just because."

"Put a few more logs on the fire and come listen then."

"Okay, but let me get our suitcases unpacked first."

She tossed hers on the bed, opened it and started putting away the few things she'd been able to pack before they left the hotel. When she was done with her suitcase, she did the same to his.

Then she spotted her purse that she'd brought in from the main room and put on the dresser in the bedroom. Even though there was a landline phone at the cottage, she wondered if she could use her iPhone phone to give Michelle a quick call. She knew that Marta had set up their phones to be able to text back to the future or to stay in touch with each other.

But dare she use it? What if James caught her with it? What would she say? What would he think? She knew he had trust issues with her already and that she was on shaky ground with her kidnapping story. She decided it would be best to hide it. But where? She looked around the bedroom, but didn't see any good hiding place. Moving quietly out of the bedroom with the phone behind her back, she slipped into the bathroom and closed the door, telling James she had to use the loo then would be right back out to put the logs on the fire and join him on the couch.

He ignored her as he picked out notes on his guitar and scribbled on a tablet.

Glancing around the bathroom, she opened the cabinet under the sink and saw a pile of towels. Quickly, she pulled out a hand towel and wrapped the phone in the towel. She then shoved it behind the pile of bath towels and hoped James would have no reason to remove all the towels and come across her phone.

Not that there weren't mobile phones in 1999. In fact, James had a new Nokia phone, but she had an iPhone6 and thought it best he didn't see it. Apple iPhones didn't exist in 1999.

When she came out of the bathroom, James was intent on creating the new song. She saw the concentration in his eyes as a tune took shape and he made more notes on the tablet. Moving over to the fire-place, she opened the screen and added more logs to the fire before closing it and going over to the couch. She sat down on the end opposite James, tucked her feet up under her and quietly observed him.

Watching him create and develop a new song was mesmerizing to her. She had to pinch herself to even believe she was here, let alone having become his lover again. Intense feelings washed over her. She loved him so much at that moment that it hurt.

And looking at him make her toes tingle. She couldn't stop herself from thinking again how incredibly handsome he was, with his full head of hair, longer in the back than it had been before, curling down past his collar, with tiny streaks of silver in the dark, almost black hair. He still had the baby face of his youth and the sensual lips, but it was his eyes that still drew her in, made her breathless and set her heart to beating double-time.

Suddenly, he stood up and tossed the tablet he'd been writing on towards her. It landed on the floor by her feet. He threw the guitar down on the floor next to the couch and walked into the kitchen. She immediately sensed his anger and was puzzled by it.

"Read what I wrote," he tossed over his shoulder, shaking his head and running his fingers through his hair. She could see that his hands were trembling.

It was as if the entire mood and atmosphere in the cottage had changed from warm and cozy to cold and uncomfortable. Susan felt it immediately and a freezing chill ran through her. What was it? Why the sudden change?

Slowly she reached down to the floor and picked up the tablet he'd tossed at her and began to read the beginning song lyrics he'd written.

"I loved you like no other...
I knew it from the start...
But you lied and you deceived me...
After capturing my heart...
I wanted to believe you...
And honestly I tried...
But you never could be truthful...
When I found that you had lied..."

She gave a small gasp and swallowed. Those certainly weren't the words of a love song! They were painful and hurtful, and she realized through the mist forming in her eyes that he couldn't let go of the past, of the memories of what she had done to him all those years ago.

What to do…what to do…

She turned to look at him again. His back was still turned towards her and was ramrod straight, fists clenching and unclenching at his sides and she began to feel frightened. It was as if a red rage had suddenly enveloped him and she thought he must be dwelling on the words he'd just written. It was impossible, however, to know his exact thoughts and she didn't know if she should stand up and go wrap her arms around him or if she should wait for his inner storm to pass.

She wondered if maybe she should try to tell him the real truth about her…that she was really 63-years-old, even though she was now in her 54-year-old body, and that this was the fifth time she'd time travelled into the past to be with him…that she'd loved him all her life, and that this time…really and truly…this time, she would stay with him, never leave him, give her heart and soul to him, do anything he asked.

She could plead and beg and explain it all, show him her mobile phone, get Michelle to confirm that what she was saying was true…

But, no…It wouldn't wash. He'd never believe her now or believe something so fantastic and unreal. She was in too deep…so deep that digging out of the morass of past lies would be impossible. If she had any chance of keeping him and staying in the past with him this time, she would have to stick to everything she'd already told him, not faltering in the slightest detail. She'd have to work to earn his trust again, and this time keep it.

When she looked at James again, he hadn't moved a muscle. It was like she was looking at a stone statue. But, she knew she had to do something to diffuse the negative energy emanating from him. Slowly she got up from the couch and approached him.

When she was a foot away, she reached out and tentatively placed a hand on his back.

"James," she whispered.

Without warning, he spun around and backhanded her across the face, knocking her to the ground. She fell onto her side, her cheek slamming into the kitchen floor, dazed and uncomprehending. But then, before she had a chance to even think or recover, he reached down and pulled her up into his arms, gathering her so tightly into him that she could barely breathe.

She was stunned and in shock, and her cheek and eye stung from his blow and from hitting the floor.

"Susan, oh my God, Susan," he wailed, moving his hands up and down her back before taking one hand and pulling the back of her head into his shoulder. "What have I done to you???! What have I done??!!"

She could feel him shaking as his tears fell onto the side of her face. He continued to hold her and she slumped in his arms, feeling as if her knees would give out from under her. Her face crumpled and she too began to cry.

James was thunderstruck and confused at what he'd just done. He had *never* in his entire life struck a woman...*Never!!!* ...except for...except for Susan. In fact, he'd never laid a hand on another woman in anger, including his wife of 28 years. *Never!* ...except for this Susan. He knew he'd always had a short temper and he'd thrown things numerous times and even punched holes in walls, but to strike a woman...Never! He had *always* been able to control himself.

But not with this Susan...

He recalled all those years ago, whacking her on her bottom in outrage over her buying an expensive dress. He remembered grabbing her and even shaking her, even forcing himself on her...things he had never, ever done to another female.

Why? What was wrong with him? What was it about this one girl/woman that made him lose complete control of himself...to lose *all* self-control...to become an...an abusive monster...?

As he continued to hold her, James searched his mind for answers.

Yes, it was true that he still had pain in his heart from losing his wife, Susan, the love of his life, the mother of his children, the most caring, talented and wonderful woman he'd ever met or known. He would always love her. The pain would always be there.

But it was also true that, even though he waxed nostalgic over the good memories of old times in Brighton, he also remembered the hurtful ones…and the hurtful ones *all* had to do with the Susan he was now holding in his arms.

Thoughts of her had been invading his mind since the trip to Paris, even more so since he'd arrived in Brighton, and when he laid eyes on her at his concert at the Dusky, he'd resented her coming back into his life so suddenly and unexpectedly. She had no right to invade his life as she did, to catch him unaware, to re-awaken all he'd felt for her all those years ago…a love so intense it had almost destroyed him…No! *She* had almost destroyed him! Didn't the song lyrics he just penned say exactly that?!

Then he remembered what he'd just done to her the night before… when he brought her back to the hotel after she'd fainted at his mini concert. He'd been cruel and heartless, wanting to punish her…hurt her. And, he had taken her against her will when she begged him not to. But he hadn't stopped his cruelty there. He'd cursed her and told her to get out of his sight…to hurt her even more…to make her feel the pain he'd once endured because of her.

Intense feelings of shame and self-loathing washed over him in waves, and he felt as if he would drown in both of them. He had to get a grip on himself, rein in his emotions, think coherently. Didn't he just tell himself earlier in the day that he would try to trust her again? Didn't he promise himself a long time ago that he would never be violent with her again? And what had he just done? Would she…could she forgive him? Could he make things right between them again? Or were they meant to ride this roller coaster of emotion forever?

Slowly and gently he released her from his hold and set her away from him, looking deeply into her eyes. What he saw there made him hate himself even more. It was anguish so deep that it made him swallow and hug her to him again.

This time, she pushed him away with tears running down her face.

"You won't ever forgive me for the past, will you James?" The words choked out of her between sobs. "I've loved you my whole life, you know…I've never stopped…not for one moment…No matter what you do to me…I can't imagine life without you…"

He was speechless as he searched her eyes for the truth. And, he knew then that she *was* being truthful with him.

Silently, he took her hand and led her into the bathroom, where he turned the cold water tap on in the sink, took a washcloth off the shelf below the mirror and wet it. Gently, he placed it on her face. Her cheek was beginning to bruise along with her eye. He had to choke back a sob as he realized how hard he'd hit her, but she didn't flinch, just stared into his eyes as if she was trying to reach into his soul and understand him and why he'd reacted the way he did.

Finally, he found his voice.

"I don't know what to say to you, Susan. What I did was..."

But before he could say anything else, she put her finger on his lips and shook her head.

"No...I understand...I do...really...please, can we just try to start over again? Can we put the past behind us? Please..."

He looked away from her penetrating and begging gaze before turning back to her.

"I'll try...I promise you that I'll try..."

He took the cold washcloth off her face and leaned forward to give her a gentle kiss. When she turned around and looked in the mirror, she gasped.

"I'm sorry, Susan...oh my God, I'm so sorry..." he wailed.

"It's okay...really..." She paused.

But was it okay? Her thoughts were in a turmoil. Had what he'd just done to her been her fault somehow? She knew she was always making excuses for him whenever he said or did something bad to her. It was the price she paid for putting him up so high on a pedestal. It was also the bare truth that she would do anything to keep him this time...anything, including allowing him to abuse her. Admitting it made her cringe. She hated herself for being so weak.

That was so, so wrong...and on so many levels. What kind of woman would allow a man to abuse her? It went beyond being weak. It verged on being demented.

But maybe that's what she was. He was her obsession and the thought of losing him again sent her into a panic. Knowing he was single and available again and that hundreds...no more likely *thousands* of women would soon be after him once he was again out in public, was frightening. She was in her 54-year-old body, and although she knew she wasn't bad looking and that James assured her she was still desirable, there were so many more women, a lot of them younger and more beautiful than her that would cast her in the shade. Was that why she was so desperate to please him…to allow him to boss her around…and yes, to even abuse her?

How else would she be able to keep him? His past reputation with women, his penchant for cheating…and, even though it was said he never cheated on his wife, Susan, she didn't believe it for one minute… Would she be able to satisfy a man like him with such an insatiable sex drive? Or, would he tire of her and tryst with other women behind her back? Could she accept that along with everything else?

Sadly and pitifully, she thought that if it really came down to it, she would.

Then she thought of Michelle.

"James…I have to tell you something."

He raised his eyebrows.

"My daughter, Michelle, well…I can't let her see this…She would go crazy. She's an attorney, you know, a solicitor as you call it…She specializes in discrimination against women, and sexual harassment… and ah…domestic abuse…"

James looked shame-faced.

"So…we might need to stay here until…well, until these bruises fade…" She reached up to touch her face and winced. "Or unless I can make up a story about how this happened…"

"I'll stay here with you forever if you want."

"Well, that might be too long, but I think black eyes can last up to two weeks or more. Do you think we can put up with each other, cooped up here, for two weeks?"

She smiled at him, trying to break the gloomy mood.

He thought for a moment, his mood instantly brightening. "I can think of things we can do to occupy two weeks."

A small smile spread across her face as she looked at him from the mirror. "I'll just bet you can…"

Chapter 17

James Regrets

Thomas and Michelle, neither of them getting much sleep the previous night, dozed until mid-afternoon. Michelle was the first one to wake up, feeling something warm and stiff poking her in the hip. A slow, seductive smile spread across her face. She nudged Thomas and reached under the covers.

"Why, what's this...hmmm?"

His eyes fluttered open and he smiled back. "A present for you maybe?"

"I like presents..."

Playfully, he rolled her onto her back and moved on top of her, capturing her lips with his.

A half hour later, Michelle was in the shower and Thomas was back in his room down the other end of the hall to pack his suitcase and move in with Michelle. She'd shyly hinted that it would be quite nice if he decided to stay with her and he immediately agreed.

"What am I doing?! What in the hell am I doing?!!" Michelle asked herself for the dozenth time as water cascaded over her. "I'm engaged for Christ's sake! I shouldn't even be here! I should be back in the future planning my fricking wedding!!"

She poured some shampoo into her hand then rubbed it into her hair. She was truly in a quandary and it was all her mother's fault. Her and her damn James's obsession! If it weren't for that, she wouldn't be here. She'd be where she was supposed to be, back at her job and

159

taking care of the wedding plans. Her well-ordered life would be proceeding on track. She'd soon be a married woman, and even though she'd just turned 39, there was still time to have at least one child. Her life would be complete, a nice package tied up in a bow.

…With boring, fishy-eyed, balding Thomas, the attorney for drunk drivers…

But damn, damn, damn! Here she was back in her 24-year-old body and falling in love…with all people! James's damn son!

Yes, she had to admit that it was true. She *was* falling in love with this Thomas and there was no denying it. She wasn't even sure how it happened. Maybe it started when he gave her his newspaper and she first looked into his eyes. Maybe it was during the mini concert at the club when he came over and formally introduced himself. Or, maybe it was when he came to check on her mom to make sure she was all right after his dad had done whatever horrible thing he'd done to her. She didn't really know. It crept up on her and took her unawares. And that was something that literally *never* happened to her.

"So now what?" she questioned herself. Her mom was off at a cottage somewhere with James and she had no idea when they'd be coming back. Knowing how desperately in love her mom was, she might never come back! And then what?

She chastised herself. She should have taken the ring from her mom and just given it to James instead of leaving it for her mom to do. Then they could have skipped out of here. Oh, but no, that wouldn't have worked! Marta said that Susan had to be the one to give it to him. But would she ever do it? That was the million dollar question. For all she knew, it was likely James would be wearing her mom's ballerina necklace again and her mom would have the engagement ring back on her finger. Talk about complicating matters!

Then her mind floated off into the future. She should text her dad and tell him that she and Mom were having a great time on their trip and ask if he was handling her clients okay. Then she should text her fiancé, Thomas, and tell him how much she missed him.

Ugh! The truth was that she *didn't* miss him. In fact, after being with James's son, she couldn't even stomach the thought of marrying the Thomas back in the future! Crap! Had she really just thought that? She leaned her head back under the shower spray and rinsed the shampoo out of it then put on some conditioner and proceeded to wash her body before also rinsing that out and turning off the tap.

As she stepped out of the tub and wrapped a towel around her, she heard Thomas come back. She hadn't closed the bathroom door and he peeked his head in.

"Too late to join you, I see."

"And what makes you think I would have let you join me?"

"Maybe I wouldn't have given you a choice..."

"Is that so? Does that mean you *are* like your dad then? My mom says he's bossy and always has to have his way."

He smirked at her as he unbuttoned his shirt and tossed it on the floor. "I'm not very bossy, but I do tend to get my way...at least most of the time..."

She could see a bulge growing in the front of his trousers.

"You've got to be kidding me, Thomas! Again already?!"

He just smirked once more as he advanced towards her and ripped the towel away.

"I can't help it, Michelle...you just have this crazy effect on me..."

Hilary stayed in the hotel bar for a couple of hours, smoking her way through half a pack of cigarettes and drinking a half dozen cocktails. By the time she got up to leave, she was half drunk and stumbled rather than walked to the elevator. When she got to her room, she passed out on the bed.

Her mobile phone ringing woke her up three hours later. It was Marcus.

"I found out more about James and the Susan woman from the desk clerk."

"What?"

"He wasn't on shift at the time, but the other clerk who was on night shift, said James came in not long after his concert ended with a blonde woman in tow. Said she looked unsteady on her feet and was very pale."

"Was she drunk or something?"

"How would he know that?! My contact just pried the information out of the other clerk!"

"Go on then."

"Well, he also found out that James called for his rental car to be brought round at 5:00 in the morning. James left with the Susan woman a short time later."

"Did he know where they were going?"

"No. Nothing was said. They just left."

"Well, that's fucking crazy! Where would anybody be going at that ungodly hour?!"

"Who knows? I assume it might be somewhere a distance away and they needed to leave early."

"Shit! That's kind of what Thomas, his son, hinted at. He mentioned they might not be in Brighton anymore. Maybe they went to his house outside of London. Think I should go back to London?"

"But he's not checked out of the hotel. We can only assume he'll be coming back."

"Well, I can't spend my whole fucking life waiting here!"

"What about the son? Did you lay in wait for him in his room?"

"No. He wasn't there. I used the room key I got from your contact to get in the room then I checked through is suitcase that was on the bed. His razor and stuff was still in the bathroom, so I assume he's coming back. I think he must be with the daughter, Michelle. She scares me for some reason."

"Someone scares *you*?! You're funning me!"

"No…it's like she can read my brain or something. She makes me nervous."

"Well, stay away from her then."

"Did you find out anything else? Anything about who this Susan is or Michelle?"

"Not yet, but I should have something by tomorrow. They live in California and there's an eight hour time difference. Don't worry, you know you can rely on me."

"Yeah, especially if a million pounds is on the line, right Marcus?"

"Yes luv…I won't deny it."

"I think I'll wander up to Thomas's room again and see if he's back. I just hope that bitch isn't with him."

"You do that, and I'll talk to you tomorrow."

Within minutes of disconnecting with Marcus, Hilary was back at Thomas's hotel room door. She knocked and waited then knocked again before using the key to let herself in. She cursed loudly when she saw that his suitcase and items from the bathroom were gone. Shit! He must have either checked out or moved in with the blonde bitch.

Then she spotted a piece of paper on the bed next to where the suitcase had been. She picked it up and began to read. It was the note that James had written to Thomas and slipped under his door that morning. Hilary smiled wickedly. Sooooo…James and the Susan woman were at Auntie Annabelle's cottage, wherever in the hell that was.

But it was a start. She figured Marcus could track them down with this bit of information. And now, she wouldn't need Thomas for anything, which also meant she wouldn't have to see that creepy Michelle again.

Yes, this would all work out…and once she was able to get rid of Susan, James would be all hers…along with his millions of pounds…

James led Susan out of the bathroom and told her to sit on the couch while he went to get some ice out of the freezer for her eye. Instead of ice wrapped in a wash cloth, however, he brought back a bag of frozen peas.

"I didn't see you put these in the trolley this morning when we were at the food shop. You didn't remember that I don't care for peas?"

"I remembered."

"Then why did we buy them?"

"Because I thought you might have changed your mind since you've become vegetarian." Then to lighten the mood between them, she added. "Or, maybe because I wanted to annoy you."

He handed her the bag of peas and she put them on her face and eye.

He played along with her comment, wanting more than anything for things to return to normal between them...if there were such a thing as "normal" for them...

"I think you rather enjoy annoying me..."

"I do when you do stupid things like make me wait in the car for you to come round and open the door for me."

"It's not stupid. It's gentlemanly."

"I'm capable of opening the door for myself."

"I didn't say you weren't capable. But I will say that you're stubborn."

"Am not."

"Yes, you are. And you're too damn independent. Don't you know that women are supposed to be taken care of by men? Guided as well?"

"I can guide my own damn self. You're a chauvinist..."

"My wife, Susan, let me guide her."

"I'm sure she did, but I'm not your wife, Susan."

"You could have been..."

The words were out of his mouth before he could stop them. She froze at the comment, almost feeling as if she'd been slapped again. The silence in the room could be measured by the beats of their hearts.

She looked at him and suddenly the teasing attitude in the room changed.

He sat down next to her and took her hand in his. "We need to talk, you know...I want so much to trust you again...I really do..."

She swallowed. "I want you to trust me again. I want that more than anything in the world...But, James...?"

He looked into her eyes. "Yes?"

"I...I need to trust you too...You get so out of control angry, that you scare me...I thought that when you got angry with me all those years ago that it was just because you were young and hot-headed…and, I know I did things to upset you…but now, you're a grown man, and…"

He let go of her hand and abruptly stood up. "You don't need to remind me, Susan…you don't need to throw what I just did to you in my face!"

And she knew that she'd upset him again. She stood up and put her hand on his arm, "Oh please…I'm sorry for mentioning it… please…I wasn't trying to throw anything in your face…"

He shook her hand off before taking a deep breath and tilting his head back with closed eyes.

"Then why did you feel you had to bring it up?"

She stared at his back for a moment and suddenly began to feel her own anger bubble up from inside herself. His mercurial moods were so hard to deal with.

"Because you said we needed to talk, damn it all! ..And I'm just being honest! Don't you care how I feel? Is this just all about you and no one else?!!!"

He paused before turning around, gathering her in his arms and burying his face in her hair.

"I'm sorry, Susan…I don't know what comes over me sometimes. There's never been another woman in my whole life who affects me like you do. It frightens me sometimes. It's like there's something crazy between us that makes me lose control…"

He drew back and his eyes focused on her necklace. He reached forward and lifted the silver ballerina shoes in his hand. "Are you sure this necklace of yours doesn't have some kind of power over us?"

"I…I don't know…sometimes I think it might…but I don't know…"

"Give it back to me then. Maybe I feel the way I do because you're wearing it and not me."

She broke away from him and turned her back, twisting the chain in her fingers. "No…no…I can't…"

"But you can, you know. You say you love me. If you really do love me, you'll give it back to me…"

And before she could utter a word, he'd pinned her hands behind her and ripped the necklace up and over her head.

165

She gasped and spun around, reaching out to him, but he stepped back and slipped the necklace up and over his head. She could see the ballerina slippers hanging on his chest.

"Give it back to me, James," she sobbed, reaching out to him. "You're not meant to have my necklace!! Don't you know??? When you wear it, it keeps me tied to you, and I don't want to be tied to you other than..."

"Other than when you decide you *want* to be tied to me, isn't that right? You want to pick and choose when you want to be with me and when you want to vanish, isn't that right, Susan?"

She shook her head at him, knowing he was right, but not wanting to admit it.

He continued. "It's why you came back to see me all those years ago at the Ted Flannagan Show, isn't it? And, it's why your friend, Alice, begged me to give it to her so you could wear it in our wedding...You know it binds us together somehow, but you won't tell me the reason..."

"I don't know the reason! I swear to you, I don't know!!"

He grabbed her by the shoulders, bringing his face just inches from hers. She could read the pain in his eyes.

"Why should I believe you, Susan?! Tell me why I should believe you? Convince me, please...I want to believe you and trust you again, but there's something about you that just doesn't seem right...You're in my life then you disappear without a trace...then you're there again, almost as if you conjured yourself up somehow, then you vanish again...and every time you disappear, it's like my head's in a fog, I can't think straight for days or even weeks on end and the pain in my heart is unbearable!"

She swallowed. The thought of coming clean and telling him about time travel flew into her head again, but just as quickly flew back out. Telling him the truth would only emphasize the fact that everything else she'd ever told him about herself was a lie. She couldn't do it. She'd have to tough it out, make him ask her questions, then answer them until he had no more.

"Let's sit back down, James." She tried to forget the panic that was building up inside her by not having the necklace around her neck. She took his hand and led him back to the couch, but before he sat down, he spotted the tablet with the song lyrics he'd just written. He ripped the sheet off the tablet, balled it up, went to the fireplace and tossed it into the flames. A moment later, he sat down beside her.

This time, she took his hands in hers. "Ask me anything...I promise I'll be truthful with you. I want the past to be cleared up between us...I love you so much..."

It was over an hour later, after James peppered her with questions, most of them related to the day she'd vanished moments before their wedding, when he finally seemed satisfied that she was telling him the truth. The kidnapping story still seemed fantastical to him, but she was able to repeat verbatim what she'd told him before, and it was so far in the past, that his own memory of that day was a bit vague. He remembered the anguish and the pain more than what had actually happened.

He pulled her into his arms and rocked her back and forth. "Please, Susan, don't ever vanish on me again...I couldn't bear it..."

"I won't ever leave you again, James...I'm yours forever..."

And this time, she meant it.

Chapter 18

Carrie Wants to Know

"**D**amn you, Thomas! Now I feel like I need another shower again!" Michelle rolled off the bed and reached down to the floor for the towel he'd ripped off her before once again taking her to heights of passion she'd never experienced before. Much more of him, she thought, would make him an addiction, just like her mom was addicted to his dad. Damn!

He sat up and leaned back against the pillows, grinning a choirboy grin. "Want me to join you?"

"No!"

The bathroom door slammed. He heard the lock turn and laughed. Then he got up and took his mobile phone off the dresser. He thought about calling his dad, but James had made it clear that he didn't want disturbed, and he knew his dad would call him when he was ready. He figured Michelle's mom was getting a bit of the same he was giving Michelle and smiled again. It would be so great if his dad could find love again, and it would be especially wonderful if it was with Susan, which would ensure that Michelle would be close at hand.

He had to admit that he was more than captivated with her. He was entranced. She was beautiful, brilliant, feisty and an incredible lover, all wrapped up in one lovely package. He thought he might like to keep her.

Then he thought of his brother, Robert, and his sister, Carrie. He'd love for them to meet Michelle. He punched Robert's number into his mobile phone.

Robert answered on the first ring. Thomas could hear pots and pans banging around in the background.

"Hello, Thomas! I've been waiting to hear from you or Dad to find out how the concert went."

"It went great! Are you at the restaurant doing your chef thing?"

"How could you tell? Noisy rather, isn't it? So, how did Dad do? Was he nervous? I was expecting a call from him this morning, but so far nothing. Carrie called me a bit ago and wanted to know how the concert went and if I'd heard from Dad."

"Like I said, the concert went great. And, no, Dad wasn't nervous. He carried it off as he always did, and the people who were there couldn't get enough of him. He even made it through the song he used to sing to Mum all the time. Got a little teary-eyed, but the people at the concert went crazy over it."

"You mean he actually sang *'Your Love Amazes Me'* and made it through the whole thing without breaking down?"

"Yeah, Mum would have been proud of him…But, he did falter once during the concert. It was during one of his other most well-known songs."

"He did? Why? What happened?"

"Well, you're not going to believe this, and actually it's a long story, but a woman from his past was there at the concert, someone he'd met when he and the band first started at the Dusky thirty-seven years ago."

"And?"

"Well, when he saw her in the audience and recognized her, he faltered in the song, actually quit singing for a few seconds. It was obvious he was shocked to see her."

"How could he have recognized someone he knew 37 years ago? That sounds crazy."

"Well, like I said, it's a long story, but the bottom line is that they were in love all that time ago, so much so, that he even asked her to marry him. She refused, however. It was way before he met Mum."

"But how or why did he recognize her? She'd be a lot older and wouldn't look the same."

"That's where things get complicated. She was at the concert with her daughter. Her name is Michelle and the mum's name is Susan. They're from America. Her daughter, evidently, is the spitting image of what she looked like when she was young, and Dad saw them both together. But not only that... The mum, Susan, has this silver necklace that she once gave to Dad, but he ended up giving it back to her, and he recognized the necklace. He even changed his set list at the end of the concert and played a song he'd written for her back in the day. It upset her so much that she fainted dead away."

"That's all amazing, Thomas. I wish I could have been there. So, what happened after the mum fainted, and how did you get to know the names of these women?"

"I met the daughter, Michelle, in the hotel lobby. She and her mum are staying in the same hotel as Dad and me. I gave her my newspaper right after she checked in."

"You gave her what?"

"My newspaper. She was coming into the hotel gift shop for a paper as I was going out and I took the last newspaper. So I gave her mine. And then I saw her again at the concert and decided to go over and introduce myself."

"I can hear from your voice, that you're not telling me everything."

"I think I've fallen in love..."

Robert began to laugh on the other end of the call. "You've actually fallen in love with a girl you just met?! And what about Dad? What happened after the mum fainted?"

"I carried her up to a room above the stage area at the club and Dad was there seconds later pulling her into his arms. They were like two lost souls that had just found each other again. Dad took her back to the hotel and didn't even go back down to the club to talk about his new album. I had to go cover for him."

"I'm shocked. I don't know what to say! So, where is Dad now?"

"Out at Auntie Annabelle's cottage with Susan, the mum. They left early this morning and left notes for Michelle and me."

The mum's name is Susan?!"

"Yes…same as our mum…interesting, isn't it?"

"I'll say! So you're with the daughter, Michelle, now?"

"She's in taking a shower."

Robert whistled. "Well, I have to say I'm truly shocked at all this news. Have you told Carrie what happened?"

"No, I called you first. I'm planning on calling her next. Then I'm thinking I might ask Michelle to come back to London with me. I'd like you to meet her. If Carrie's around, I'd like her to meet Michelle too."

"What about Dad?"

"He's still checked into the hotel, but who knows if or when he and Susan will be back. I've never seen Dad so love struck before…other than with our mum, of course."

"Do you think he can be happy again with this Susan then?"

"I have no idea, but the way they were looking at each other has given me hope. I'd like to see Dad happy again."

"So would I…Well, Thomas, I need to get back at it. Bring your Michelle by the restaurant when you get back in London and I'll cook you up something special. If you talk to Carrie, tell her to come too."

"I will, Robert."

They disconnected as Michelle was coming out of the bathroom. She had on her bra and a pair of thong panties. Quickly, she ran to her suitcase, pulled out a pair of jeans and a pullover sweater and slipped them on.

Thomas smiled at her. "Worried I might try to ravish you again."

"As a matter of fact…"

"I just talked to my brother, Robert. I told you he's a chef at Le Fonda in London? He invited us to stop by and said he'd cook up a specialty for us. I was thinking we might leave here and go to London. I have a rather nice flat there."

"You mean check out? What about my mom and your dad?"

"I think they're old enough to take care of themselves."

"You don't know my mom…"

"Well, if she can't take care of herself, I'm certain Dad will do it for her."

"Yeah, and that's what I'm afraid of…"

Just then, Thomas's mobile phone rang. It was James.

"Hey Dad, I guess you made it out to the cottage okay then. I heard that it was snowing up there. Is all right and tight with you and Michelle's mum?"

"As right and tight as it can be. I just wanted to tell you we might decide to stay here for a couple of weeks…"

"A couple of weeks!! What about the new album you wanted to start on? I thought you were going right back to London after the concert!"

"Well, I changed my mind. Susan and I are working through some…ah…issues from our past. We're taking time to get to know each other again. The recording will wait. It's all set to go, the songs all written. I'll need to do a few things before I call in the others anyway."

"I'm still surprised you'd want to stay at the cottage that long. Not much to do there, is there?"

James cleared his throat, but said nothing else.

Thomas blushed and Michelle, who was only hearing one side of the conversation, looked at him quizzically.

"Ah…so then…will you be coming back to the hotel? I think Michelle's mum still has some things in her room. And, just so you know, I was planning on checking out myself along with Michelle and taking her to my flat in London."

James wanted to laugh but held his tongue as Susan stared at him, also only hearing one side of the conversation. "So, you've been captured by an American girl too, have you?"

"Yes, I believe I have, and I'm hoping the feeling is mutual."

"Well, if she's anything like her mum, I have to warn you that you're in for quite a ride. Feisty and stubborn and argumentative is what her mum is…"

Susan kicked her bare foot at him, frowning. "Let me talk to my daughter."

James grinned at her. "Speaking of Susan, she'd like to talk to Michelle. Have a good time in London and tell Michelle to pack up her mum's stuff and take it. I've already called my team and told them to check me out and take my stuff that I left at the hotel to my house outside of London. Maybe we can meet you there in a couple of weeks."

"Sounds like a plan, Dad. I think Carrie will be coming back around about that time. She was making plans for Christmas if you recall."

"I recall. Okay, here's Susan for Michelle." He handed the phone to her.

She went into the kitchen and sat down at the table. When James started to follow her, she waved her hand at him, indicating she wanted some privacy. He frowned but went and sat on the piano bench, pretending to look through some music that was sitting on top of the piano. Susan knew he was listening in.

Michelle took the phone from Thomas and went into the bathroom, closing the door behind her and telling him she wanted some privacy for "girl talk." Thomas opened the adjoining door to Susan's room and threw over his shoulder that he was going to pack up the rest of her mum's stuff to take to London with them.

"What's this about a couple of weeks, Mom?! Are you planning on staying at Auntie What's-her-name's cottage for two whole weeks?!"

"Yes, like James told Thomas, we're working on some issues from the past. And, did I hear correctly that you've captured Thomas's heart?"

"Maybe..."

"And has he captured yours?"

"Maybe..."

Susan laughed. "And here's my high-and-mighty, attorney daughter, who thinks she knows everything, making fun of *me* all this time!! Ha! So, you're not immune either, are you?!"

"You don't need to rub it in, Mom!"

"Okay, I won't...but it's not saying that I don't want to..."

"So, Mom..." Michelle's voice turned to a whisper. "I have a question for you."

"What?"

"Um…when you were with James when he was young…you know, when he was Thomas's age…um…did he, ah…have a rather strong libido?"

"What are you asking?"

"Did he have an over-the-top, out-of-control sex drive?!"

Susan burst out laughing. "He still does, Michelle! He still does!!"

"Mom!!! I asked you a yes or no question!!! You didn't need to tell me that! I don't want to know that!!"

"I'm not on the damn witness stand, Michelle! I'm your mother! I can say whatever I want to! So, are you telling me that you and Thomas have been having non-stop sex?"

"Maybe…"

"Ha! Well, if he's anything like his dad, then I'll bet he's damn good and has you dropping your drawers just with one look of those gorgeous eyes of his. Am I right?"

"I'm not saying…"

"That means I'm right."

"Oh, Mom…he's just so wonderful…But…what about Thomas… you know, my fiancé back in the future? What am I going to do? What's going to happen when I have to go back?"

"Then don't go back…you don't have to go back, you know…"

"Of course I have to go back!!! How could I *not* go back??!!" What would Dad think? What would my fiancé, Thomas think?!!"

"Maybe you should follow your heart, Michelle, instead of your head. I plan on following mine…"

"What do you mean?"

"I'm not going back this time. I'm staying with James…" She looked over at him and knew he was listening. "I can't bear to leave him again. I love him with my whole heart…"

"Oh, Mom! You can't do that!!! What about Dad?"

'Hush."

"Oh, is James listening?"

"Yes."

"Well, maybe we can talk about it later, like when James is asleep or something."

"There's nothing else to talk about. I'm staying and that's the end of it."

"So, why are you staying out at that cottage for so long? Why can't you come to London with us? Thomas says his dad has a house outside of London."

"I told you...because we're working out trust issues we have from the past...besides, we're having some fantastic sex."

"Gaw!! Mom! I don't want to hear about old people having sex... it's...it's disgusting!"

"So, you think you're supposed to get to a certain age and just give it up or something?"

"I didn't say that!"

"Well, fine...I won't talk about it anymore then, but to answer your original question...yes, he had a very over-the-top libido. I rather enjoyed it..."

"Okay, Mom end of subject."

"Fine with me...end of subject."

"So, is it okay if I call you when we get to London?"

When Susan didn't answer, she added, "From Thomas's mobile phone to James's, that is."

"Sure, I'd like to know that you got there okay."

"I'll ring you when we get to London then, but if it's the middle of the night, I'll call first thing in the morning. It sounds like Thomas wants to leave now."

"Okay, Michelle; I'll be here. Love you..."

"Love you too, Mom!"

They both disconnected. Susan set James's mobile phone on the kitchen table and got up to go to the bathroom.

"My cheek and eye are starting to throb a little. I want to splash some cold water on my face. I put the bag of peas back in the freezer. Can you get them out again for me, please?"

James began to feel bad again about her face. "Yes, of course. Then come back out and I'll rub your shoulders for you, okay?"

"That would be nice...I'll be back in a few minutes. I need to use the loo too."

She closed the bathroom door behind her, sat on the closed toilet seat lid and thought about her conversation with Michelle. So, her daughter was falling in love with James's son, was she? She was somewhat amused but at the same time concerned. How could that possibly work out? Or would Michelle be doomed, just like she had been, to love someone she might never get to have, someone she'd be forced to leave and then pine after for the rest of her life? The last thing she wanted for her beautiful and caring daughter was to have her heart broken.

Susan quickly used the loo, washed her face with cool water, pinned up her hair with a clip and came back to the couch where James was waiting for her with the bag of peas. He looked forlorn, staring at the bag sitting on his lap. He met her eyes as she sat down next to him. He picked up the bag and gently laid it on her face and eye.

"Susan, I'm so sorry for what I did to you. I didn't mean to...it was just a jerk reaction...and I was thinking about the lyrics I wrote...and when you touched my back..."

"It's okay, James...really...let's just forget it, okay?"

"But every time I look at you..."

"Well, tomorrow I'll try to put some makeup on it or something. Does it make me look too terribly ugly?"

"You'll never be ugly to me...never! Here...turn around and let me rub your shoulders."

Obediently, she swiveled around and he placed his hands on her shoulders, gently squeezing at first, then rubbing his thumbs into her shoulder blades in small circles. She closed her eyes and sighed. He could certainly be nice to her when he wanted to.

After a couple of minutes, she removed the bag of peas from her face and set it on the coffee table then dropped her hands into her lap as James continued to rub. When she felt his lips graze the back of her neck, shivers traced down her spine, and when he started to plant small kisses from one side of her neck to the other, chill bumps popped up on her arms and she gave a small sigh.

"And just what do you think you're doing now?" she purred as he removed his hands from her shoulders and slipped them up under the long-sleeved top she was wearing.

"I want to feel your soft skin," he murmured in her ear before tugging on her earlobe with his teeth and swirling his tongue inside. She gasped, suddenly feeling a familiar tightening sensation between her thighs and sucked in her breath as his hand moved around to the front of her and cupped her breasts, squeezing gently. She squirmed and heard him chuckle.

"And I think I might know what you want as well..." he whispered, moving to her other ear and repeating the tug and tongue swirl. She arched up and leaned back into him as he began to pinch her nipples through the fabric of her bra with his thumbs and forefingers.

She wiggled to get away, but he pulled her back tight into him where she could feel his erection growing against her bottom.

"Might you want to retire to the bedroom and our nice cozy bed?" he suggested now blowing little puffs of air into her ear.

"I might..." she said breathlessly as his hands traced patterns on the bare skin below her breasts.

When he reached down the front of her panties, moving his hand lower and seeking her most sensitive spot, she renewed her efforts to break away from him, but it was futile. He had one hand securely around her waist, his lips and tongue moving erotically on one side of her neck as he continued to kiss and taste her.

Dipping his finger in and out of her now wet passage, he could feel her tighten with every finger thrust. She arched her hips upward to give him better access. Her head tilted back onto his shoulder, her eyes closed and mouth open as he rubbed her nub in small, light circles, increasing the pressure until he thought she might climax, then moved back to finger thrusts. When he returned to the rubbing movement, he slowed down the circling for a full minute as she thrashed on the couch. He could hear her panting. Increasing the pressure once more and the speed of the circling, it wasn't long before she screamed his name out loud and he felt her whole body shudder. When he plunged three of his fingers inside her, he could feel her convulsing around them and his erection began to throb against her bottom.

As the final throes of her climax washed over her, he spun her around and pulled her face to his, bringing his mouth down on her opened one, where he stroked in and out with his tongue as deep as it would reach. She began sucking back on his tongue in a parody of lovemaking, nearly causing him to explode in his trousers.

"Enough!" he moaned, grabbing her hand and pulling her into the bedroom, where he quickly unzipped and removed both his trousers and shorts before pulling her top up over her head and pushing her bra and panties down over her hips.

She wasted no time in laying down on the bed on her back, but when he went to knee open her legs to enter her, she shook her head and told him to move his now pulsating member up to her bosom. She reached her hands up, squeezing him between her ample breasts, and he began to slowly rock his body back and forth, bringing the tip of his erection up to her chin then sliding it back down again between the soft warmth of her globes.

Susan tilted her head downward and as he moved up towards her face, she flicked out her tongue to lick the tip of him. The space between her breasts became slick with his own wetness as his movements increased. When he paused on an upward stroke, she took the tip of him into her mouth, swirling her tongue around him. He groaned in pleasure, his head tilted back in ecstasy.

She knew he was on the brink of exploding as she saw sweat on his face and chest. His mouth was open but his eyes were half-closed in concentration while his breathing became louder and louder. When she knew he was going to come, she let go of her breasts and grabbed his bottom, pulling him forward into her mouth all the way up to his balls. He convulsed and she could feel and taste his hot, salty liquid as it shot down her throat.

She sucked him dry as she continued to grasp his bottom and dig her fingernails into the soft flesh. When he lowered his arms and placed his hands on the bed above her head, she released him from her mouth and tilted her head up to look at him. He smiled down at her.

"You little vixen! I wanted to save a little for your love tunnel and pleasure you again. You drained me of every drop…"

"I wanted to drain you of every drop. I'm tired and want to go to sleep."

He moved off her and laid alongside, turning and pulling her into his arms. "I'd almost forgotten what a wanton you are."

"But I know you don't mind…"

"I don't mind one bit, Susan…" He kissed the top of her head and released the clip from her hair that was all askew. Her still golden locks cascaded onto the pillow and he ran his fingers through them before giving a satisfied sigh and closing his eyes. Susan was already asleep, a sweet smile on her face.

Chapter 19

A Love Song for Susan

It was three days after James's mini concert, and Hilary was checking out of the Claridon hotel. Marcus had informed her that James's had been checked out by his "team" and also that Thomas and Michelle had left. He could only assume that James, and probably the Susan woman, had gone back to his house outside of London. He had no idea where Thomas had gone and didn't know where he lived as he hadn't provided that information when he checked in.

Hilary was fit to be tied. She was running low on funds and now would need to have Marcus find her another rich old gent to shack up with for a bit while she figured out where James was. But, she also knew she could go back to the old pervert near Piccadilly, who had begged her not to leave and promised her a very lovely diamond ring and bracelet if she would come back. She didn't have to think too hard that the best choice was the diamond ring and bracelet, which she could turn into cash if she had to, even if it meant sleeping with the old turd.

She smiled at the desk clerk as she handed in her room key. Damn! He was pretty hot looking! If she'd noticed him before, she could have enjoyed a few hours with him up in her room, which certainly would have alleviated the boredom of this trip.

After ordering up a cab to take her to the train station for the trip back to London, she wandered into the hotel gift shop and browsed around for a magazine to pass the time on the train. She ended up with a couple of fashion magazines, not that she was all that fashionable even though she tried to be, and smiled when she spotted an entertainment magazine with a picture of James plastered on the front cover. Flipping it open, she saw there was an article on him and his dead wife, his family and something about his getting back out in public and performing again. There was a picture of him performing at the Dusky Club along with photos of the audience, which included his son, Thomas, and few other celebrities. She sucked in her breath when she saw Thomas in one of the audience photos. He was standing next to the blonde bitch, Michelle, and on the other side of Michelle was an older woman who was her spitting image, blonde hair and all.

Well, well…must be the mum, Susan. She looked more closely at the picture and didn't like what she saw. The woman was, damn it all, beautiful! And, she hated beautiful women, especially if she was in competition with them. But then she remembered that Marcus had told her that Susan was 54-years old, and here she was only 36-years old. Pictures could be deceiving. Her face might be pretty for an old broad, but her body was likely saggy and getting wrinkly, while she knew her own was firm and toned, even if some of it was due to a few little cosmetic procedures. Stand her and Susan naked, side-by-side, and she knew James would choose her any day. She'd just have to figure out how to get her naked body in front of James's eyes.

She bought the entertainment magazine along with the others and went out to catch the cab. She was soon on her way to the train station, her mind working feverishly with plans in regard to her "cause" along with convincing James to dump the American slut in place of her. She just needed to find out more about Susan and Michelle, knowing her success would rely on finding out what secrets they might have. Everyone, after all, had a few dirty secrets, and once she found out theirs, it wouldn't be too hard to discredit them. Susan, most of all…She thought that she'd rather enjoy it…

∽੭

Thomas and Michelle arrived at Thomas's London flat shortly after 1:00 in the morning. Michelle decided to wait and call her mom and James later. They'd driven straight through from Brighton in Thomas's Audi, only stopping once for petrol and a couple cups of coffee. When they got to his flat, both were hungry, having skipped dinner the previous evening.

"So, do you have a well-stocked kitchen?" asked Michelle as Thomas showed her around.

He flicked on the kitchen lights, revealing state-of-the-art appliances, stark white cabinetry and a bar-type island with four stools along one side.

"I actually have someone come in to do the cooking for me three times a week, and I'm sure she keeps it well-provisioned. Her name's Meredith. I'll introduce you to her tomorrow. My brother, Robert, recommended her to me. She works at the restaurant with him."

"Well, in the meantime, let's see what I can scrounge up for us. Maybe an omelet?"

"You enjoy cooking then?"

"Well, that *is* one thing where I can certainly say, 'like mother, like daughter.' I was in the kitchen making bread from scratch with my mom when I was five years old. I remember I used to make fresh yeast rolls for Thanksgiving and Christmas and I got mad if she tried to help me. Then I used to make butter in the food processor from whipping cream and turn it different colors with food coloring."

"I guess you can manage an omelet then. I can barely boil water for a cup of tea. Go ahead and make yourself at home....but no purple butter in the omelet, okay?" He grinned at her. "I'm going to take a shower if that's okay."

She laughed. "Sure. It'll take me time to figure out where things are anyway...and maybe I'll make the omelet with blue butter..."

She started opening and closing cabinets, making a mental note of where things were. Before she opened the refrigerator, however, Thomas came over and grabbed her from behind, cupping her breasts and planting little kisses on the side of her neck.

"I'm glad you agreed to come to London with me. I don't know what I would have done if you'd told me no," he whispered in her ear.

183

She turned in his arms and looked into his eyes. "Are you kidding me? After being with you and getting to know you, there was no way I would have said no."

She put both of her palms flat on his chest and pushed him away. "You better go take your shower before we start to think of something other than food…"

He laughed, gave her quick swat on her bottom and left the kitchen. She smiled as he walked away. She was most definitely falling in love. Damn it all!

⟳

James dozed with Susan entwined in his arms for only about an hour before he opened his eyes and disentangled himself from her embrace. He didn't know why, but he felt wide awake. When he looked down at Susan's face, he cringed and had to look away. The lamp next to the bed was still on and it appeared that the bruise on her cheek and eye had turned darker in color. It didn't matter what she said or felt, what he'd done to her was unforgivable and he hated himself for it.

Quietly, he slipped out from under the covers and shivered. Even though he'd turned on the heating system in the cottage, there was still a chill about the place. He pulled on his boxer shorts and jeans then slipped into a long sleeved shirt and pullover sweater that Susan had taken out of his suitcase and hung in the closet.

Closing the bedroom door softly behind him, he went into the main room where he re-kindled the fire in the fireplace and added a few new logs. The wood in the baskets next to the fireplace was almost all gone. He'd have to go out to the woodshed when it got light and get some more.

He sat down on the couch and reached for the blank tablet on the coffee table, the one he'd written the lyrics and notes to the new song on right before he'd struck Susan. He would make it up to her. He'd write her a true love song, one that he'd put on his new album as a tribute to her and to their newfound love.

His mobile phone that was still on the kitchen table began to vibrate, and when he answered it, Carrie's voice was on the other end.

"There you are, Dad! I thought you were going to call me right after your concert was over! I've been dying to know how it went!"

"Hi, sweetheart. How are you? Are you still in Italy?"

"No, David and I are in Bangkok now. There were some jade figurines we heard about that I wanted to check out. You know that painting I started working on? Well, I want it to have an Asian influence, and these figurines are supposed to be not only spectacular but available for sale. I'm hoping to be able to buy them."

"Do you need more funds then? Just transfer what you need from the main family funds."

"No, no...I'm okay. You know I don't squander money. I'm hoping to get a deal on just a pair of the figurines. We're going to see them tomorrow, and then we're going back to Italy for a week before I head to London to your house. I told you I was going to arrange a Christmas celebration this year, remember?"

"I remember...So, isn't David coming back with you?"

"No, he promised his sister he'd spend the holidays with them in Scotland."

"So, I guess no wedding plans for the two of you then?"

"No, I told you, Dad, we're just friends and that's all. Neither of us are interested in anything else, so quit asking. I'm quite happy being free and single. You'll have to rely on Robert or Thomas for grandchildren for the time being. So, tell me, how was the concert? Did everything go well?"

"Quite well, actually. Thomas was there, but Robert was too busy at the restaurant in London. You haven't spoken with Thomas then?"

"No, he was next on my list to call. I actually forgot what time it is where you are, and when your phone started to ring, I figured I'd just be leaving you a message. Isn't it the middle of the night there?"

"A little after 3:00 in the morning as a matter of fact...but I was a bit restless...couldn't sleep..."

"Well, I know you stay up late, but 3:00 is even a bit late for you. Is there something wrong? Are you feeling well?"

"I'm feeling quite well...it's just that...something unusual happened at the concert..."

"Unusual? Okay, Dad, don't get all mysterious on me and make me pry the information out of you. What happened that was unusual?"

"I met someone...someone from my past, from when me and the band first started playing at the Dusky...I was so shocked to see her in the audience that I choked up right in the middle of a song."

"*You* choked up??! Really?! You're the most focused person I know when you're performing. I can't imagine anything could shake you. So, you said, 'her...' I assume this person from your past was a woman then?"

"Yeah...She was a wee bit of a girl when we first met...an American history student in Brighton for a history tour. She was only seventeen. I was twenty at the time."

"You're sounding rather nostalgic, Dad."

"How can you tell?"

"I know every nuance about you and you know it, even how your voice sounds when you're feeling different things."

"Yeah, I guess you do know me quite well."

"So, don't keep me in suspense...go on. What about the girl you met way back when?"

"Well, I never told you...I never told anyone actually, even though Derek, Ian and Blue were all there at the time...but this girl and me... we fell in love..."

"I heard you fell in love a lot, like almost daily..."

"No, this was different...this girl wasn't like the others...but anyway, I was with her twice in 1962, the first time in June and the second time around the end of the year...November, I think. Then I was with her again just briefly when the band and me went on our first American tour. The last time I was with her was in 1967 in London..."

"Sounds like she popped in and out of your life then?"

"You could say that...the first time she left, I never thought to see her again, but then she suddenly showed up with her brother...the last time she stayed longer..."

"Okay, so? Now you're sounding melancholy. What does this have to do with your concert? Are you saying that this girl, who would obviously not be a girl anymore, showed up at your concert?"

"Yes...along with her daughter...her daughter looks exactly like she did when she was young. I thought I was seeing a ghost...then I looked at the woman standing next to her and realized it was her...the girl from my past..."

"And her name would be?"

"Her name is...Susan...the same as your mum."

There was silence on the other end of the phone while Carrie tried to absorb and make sense of the information her dad was telling her.

"And, her daughter's name is Michelle...Thomas is rather taken with her..."

"Thomas??! Thomas is interested in a girl?!! I'm rather shocked! It's always seemed his piano was the most important thing to him and that he has no time for women!"

"He did have that girl from the music academy that he was with for almost a year, and I know he has quite a few women chasing him. I noticed when we were working on the piano concerto I wrote for him. I think he went out with a few of them."

"But he's ignored girls for the most part! What's so special about this American? Is she pretty? Have you met her? And what about her mum?"

"Michelle's very pretty, stunning in fact...an image of her mum when she was younger and we were together."

"And what about the mum, Susan? Why, she must be in her fifties like you by now! Is she still pretty?"

James sighed and Carrie heard the wistfulness in his voice. "She's still beautiful...quite beautiful in fact..."

Carrie was thoughtful for a moment then she smiled. "I'm hearing something else in your voice now dad. Could it be that you and Susan have, how should I put it...re-connected? For some crazy reason, I'm suspecting it's why you didn't call me after your concert? Might she even be with you now, Dad?"

James smiled into the phone and Carrie could almost hear the smile in his voice. "Yes...but she's asleep now. We're at Auntie Annabelle's cottage near Little Dippington..."

"Ah...I recall you telling me about the cottage. Isn't that where you used to go with grand-da and grandma when you were young? Didn't you say that Auntie Annabelle moved over to Kings Head with Auntie Ginny? Speaking of which, I haven't seen either aunties in over a year when they both came to London to visit some friends. I should invite them to our Christmas celebration this year."

"I'm sure they'd love that."

"Okay, so I'm not letting you off the hook here. Tell me more about this Susan and her daughter, Michelle. And, when can I meet them?"

"There's too much to tell you over the phone in the middle of the night. I'll be bringing her back to London in a couple of weeks and you can meet her then. But I can also tell you that the daughter, Michelle, is at Thomas's flat in London right now. I talked to him earlier."

"You're kidding me, Dad!! Didn't he just meet her at your concert last night...or was it the night before...the time difference has me confused?!"

"Well, yes...but they obviously hit it right off...that can happen you know..."

"And there you are with the girl from your past out at Auntie Annabelle's!! I think I might skip going to back to Italy and head home straightaway. This is *much* too interesting. I'm thinking maybe these American women must have cast spells on both you *and* Thomas!"

"It's possible...I know Susan cast her spell on me all those years ago when I first saw her at the Dusky..."

"Well, I won't pepper you with any more questions then, but I'm seriously considering skipping Italy. I'll let you know when I decide. Maybe I could even drive out to Little Dippington and meet Susan..."

"No! ...we're...we're getting re-acquainted...and we need time to sort through some issues from the past..."

"Now you have me *really* curious! Okay, I'll wait until you bring her to London then, but I'm definitely paying a visit to Thomas to meet her daughter!"

"You'll like her, I'm sure. I didn't have much of a chance to talk to her…"

James recalled the brief moments he'd been with Michelle up in the practice room at the Dusky and where she appeared to be quite unhappy with him over the *'All My Kisses'* song and her mum fainting. But, if Thomas was besotted with her, she was most likely very much like Susan, and he *knew* how easy it had been for him to fall in love with her all those years ago.

"If Thomas likes her so much to take her back to London with him, she must be special."

"Hell yeah, she must be! Okay, Dad, I'll catch you later. Behave yourself out there at the cottage okay?"

He could hear the wink in her voice and chuckled. "I sure will, Carrie…Love you, sweetheart."

"Love you too, Dad…Oh, and…" She paused. "I'm happy for you, you know. I want you to be happy again…Bye."

The call disconnected before he could respond.

He went back to the couch and sat down, picking up the tablet again and tapping his chin with a pen.

He needed to write a love song, one that would erase all the bad memories from the past, one that would reflect the renewed love he felt for Susan and one that would bring tears of happiness, not pain, to her eyes when she heard it.

Could he do it? Could he write a love song for a woman other than his wife, Susan? From the moment they had come together, all of his songs had been written for her and only her. Would he be tarnishing her memory by writing a love song for another Susan, the girl who had captured his heart years before he'd met and married the love of his life?

"Well," he thought to himself. "I *did* write *'All My Kisses'* for this Susan, didn't I?"

He pulled his guitar up off the floor where he'd tossed it earlier, checked to make sure nothing had been broken and began to pick out a tune.

An hour later he was done.

Susan had woken up when she heard James talking to someone on his mobile phone. She couldn't hear what he was saying because he was in the kitchen, and she didn't feel right opening the bedroom door and trying to eavesdrop, so she put a pillow over her head and tried to go back to sleep.

When she heard him start picking out notes on his guitar, however, her curiosity got the better of her. She climbed out from under the warm covers, slipped on a pair of panties and a pullover sweater then cracked open the door. All she could see was the back of his head as he sat on the couch. His concentration was intense, and she thought she'd just stay peeking through the door watching and listening, until she saw him put a tablet and pen down on the coffee table.

"Come on out, Susan," he said without even looking over his shoulder.

He didn't know why he suddenly sensed her behind him, but he did. It was almost like they had an unspoken language between them.

She opened the door the rest of the way and came to sit beside him, leaning over and kissing him on the cheek, but she didn't say anything, feeling a little anxious about what he might have written this time.

He could see the worry in her eyes and leaned towards her and kissed her full on the mouth.

"Don't worry; this time I *did* write a love song. Do you want to hear it? Still needs some polishing, but I think it's rather nice."

She nodded at him and he picked up the tablet and set it next to him. Settling his guitar on his lap, he strummed a few notes then began to sing.

"I just wish you knew...
How much you mean to me...
I need you to understand now...
My love is true...

You are all I want...
You are all I need...
You are all I long for...
Just you... 'Her eyes started to mist.
"Please remember this...
Love is so real, it's true...
And from now on there will be time...
For me and you...
I just need to ask...
Ask one thing of you...
That you'll never leave me...
Our love, like new..."

When he looked over at her for a moment, she could see his eyes were also moist.

"And time goes by so quickly...
When I'm in your arms...
I want to stay forever...
To enjoy your charms... 'She smiled and he smiled back at her.
"Love, you must know this...
As we work things through...
Our hearts will beat together...
Time for just us two...
You are all I want...
You are all I need...
Susan, please remember...
I'll be true to you...
Because I love you...
Just you..."

As the final notes of the song faded away, Susan reached up and wiped a tear off her cheek. James set down the guitar and pulled her into his arms. Neither of them said anything for a full minute, just holding each other and feeling their hearts beat against each other.

It's where they wanted to stay...forever...

Chapter 20

Hilary Continues the Hunt

"**I**'ve got quite a bit of information for you, luv," purred Marcus into his mobile phone.

Hilary, who was now back with her old gent outside of Piccadilly, lit a cigarette and leaned back against the couch cushions.

"I'm waiting. It's been a whole damn week. I don't know what took you so long."

"Just cool your tits, Hil. First off, I found out about James's Auntie Annabelle. She lives over in King's Head north of Brighton with her sister, Ginny. So, I think that's likely where James and the Susan woman are. Seems James is rather fond of his aunties."

"Well, isn't that so sweet," she remarked sarcastically. "But, damn it all, that means he's nowhere near London, and I can't go dashing off to Brighton or this Kings Head place at the moment."

"It also appears that James left word at the studio where he records… Cherry Studios, it's called…that he might be back to start work on his new album the week before Christmas, which is only a couple of weeks away."

"Hmmmm…that should give me time to get a few diamonds out of the old gent. He's being very generous since I've come back."

"Well, get what you can because you don't want to come across to James like you're after his money when you meet up with him."

"I know. I need to pitch my pig cause at him."

"Along with your body. Rumors say he loves a woman with nice breasts, and I have to say Hil, yours are quite…"

"Yeah, whatever," she interrupted him. "So what did you find out about Susan and her daughter? I need some good dirt to discredit them."

"I couldn't find out much about Susan, but, the daughter, Michelle, just passed the exams two years ago to become a solicitor. She was the youngest in the state of California to ever have passed. She's with some women's law firm. They specialize in discrimination cases, women's rights and all that. I'm trying to figure out what connection there is between Michelle and Donald, the solicitor chap I spoke with. The phone number of his law firm is what she put down on the hotel registration. He's possibly a relative, maybe even her dad. Susan also has a son, Steven, who's a writer. He has three published books, even though he's only two years older than Michelle. The books are related to environmental issues. Steven is 26 and Michelle is 24."

"Well, that's all pretty boring. I need to know more about Susan. Did you find out anything about how she and James know each other?"

"Actually, yes. I tracked down a chap from another band called the Stingers that played at the Dusky at the same time James and his band were there back in 1962 before they became famous. He remembered Susan when I described her. Said she was the prettiest thing he'd ever seen and all sweet and innocent looking. James grabbed her up straightaway and was besotted with her."

"He knew her that long ago??!"

"Seems so, but what that has to do with now, I'm not sure. I'm suspecting she found out he was going to have a concert at the Dusky and decided to come see him again, and knowing his wife died, maybe she has her own designs on him."

"Shit!"

"And I also found out something that happened at his concert last week in regard to Susan. She fainted dead away at the end of the concert and Thomas, James's son, carried her off somewhere with the daughter following. James was supposed to stay and talk to the audience about his new album, but he vanished right after Susan fainted and never came back. Thomas talked to the audience instead. I suspect that James took Susan back to the hotel, which is what I told you.

Remember the night clerk telling my source that James came in shortly after the concert with a blonde woman who looked ill."

"Yeah, I remember. Must have been Susan then. Well, shit! Now what should I do? And I need some dirt on Susan. Can't you dig anything up on her?"

"I've been trying, luv..."

"Well, I guess I'll have to make something up then...set her up somehow...I'll start thinking on it now. So, you think I should wait to approach James with my 'cause' when he goes to Cherry Studios? Or, do you think I should try to slip away for a couple of days and hunt him down in wherever it is you said he is now?"

"You mean Kings Head with the aunties? Well, that actually might be an easier place to approach him. There's likely to be a crowd of fans at Cherry Studios when word gets out he's there recording again, plus security."

Hilary stubbed out her cigarette. "Okay, I might as well try that first then. Get me the address for the aunties and I'll figure a way to go there. I might even see if the old gent would take me to Brighton on a short holiday. I know he has an old war buddy of his who lives there. While he's with his friend, I could slip up to Kings Head."

"What about Susan?"

"What about her? I'm just going to try to pitch my cause to James and check her out. You know, see what my competition is...get her measure."

"Clever girl."

"Yes, I am, aren't I? Okay. I'll check in with you in a few days and let you know how things went at Kings Head. In the meantime, keep looking for some trash on Susan, or even her daughter. I'd like to send both of them packing back to America with their tails between their legs, if you get what I mean."

"I get it, Hil. Fine then. Bye."

Hilary disconnected and lit another cigarette. What could she do to discredit Susan? She'd have to meet her first. Pry out a weakness and then put her head to work. It shouldn't be too hard.

⌒◯

Thomas and Michelle were both amazed, not only at their "love at first sight" reaction to each other, but also at how comfortably they had settled into a romantic and domestic relationship that could almost be described as pure bliss.

Unlike James and Susan, they had no issues from the past to overcome, so spent most of their time getting to know each other and finding out that they were quite well-suited on many levels. Both were intelligent and could discuss just about any topic whether it be current events or something related to history. Both loved music, and Michelle surprised Thomas when she sat down at his piano one evening after dinner and began to play *"Fur Elise,"* which she'd memorized since she was a child when Susan forced her to take piano lessons.

He applauded when she was done. "Is there anything you can't do? Every day, you do something else to surprise me!"

"Well, I have to tell you a funny story about what I just played."

"Yes?" He swirled the wine in the glass he was holding.

She picked up her glass that she'd set down on the top of the baby grand piano in Thomas's living room, took a sip and turned towards him.

"I just *hated* my piano teacher. I remember she was so fat that I thought she might break the piano bench. After a month of lessons with Mrs. Butz, I decided I didn't want to learn how to play the piano after all. But, my mom wouldn't let me quit. She reminded me that I'd begged her to buy the piano and now that we had one, I was going to learn to play it whether I liked it or not. I got really mad, and the next time Mrs. Butz showed up, I refused to come out of my bedroom."

"What a stubborn little girl you were! How old were you?"

"I think I was 10. Anyway, when mom realized I was going to hide in my room every time Mrs. Butz showed up, she relented and told me that if I learned how to play *'Fur Elise'* perfectly, straight through before Mrs. Butz was due to come again, then she'd cancel the lessons. I think I drove my mom, dad and brother crazy playing *'Fur Elise'* over and over again, morning, noon, day and night for the next week, and the day before Mrs. Butz was due to come for my lesson, I played it straight through without missing a note."

"Like I said, it sounds like you were a stubborn little girl..."

"Okay, I admit that I can be stubborn sometimes... But, oh my God, if you want to talk about stubborn, my mom should have the word tattooed on her forehead! I've never known anyone as pig-headed as her!"

"I know somebody like that...my dad..."

Michelle laughed. "Well, it might be fun to be a fly on the wall at the cottage then. My mom is also impulsive, doesn't listen real well and jumps to conclusions. But most of all, she just *hates* being bossed around. That's where her stubborn streak kicks in."

"And my dad is used to bossing people around..."

"Might be a little stormy inside the cottage then."

"I was thinking 'steamy' would better describe it..."

Michelle blushed. "Yeah, well, let's not get onto *that* topic! I don't need to know about it."

She took her last sip of wine and stood up. "I have Beef Bourguignon on the stove for dinner. I best check on it."

"I knew something was smelling delicious in here. I'll come in the kitchen with you and get us more wine. Maybe you could make more of those yeast rolls that are your specialty? I don't even think Robert can make rolls as good as yours."

"I made a dozen two days ago. Don't tell me you ate them all!!"

Thomas grinned a sheepish grin. "Well, they're so good...I've been having them with your green butter and jam. I had the last one this morning."

"Then you should have told me this morning! It's too late to make them for dinner now."

"I did mention something to you this morning."

"You didn't ask me to make more rolls."

"But I said it would be *nice* if you made more."

"That's not the same as *asking* me to make more! And you didn't say you'd eaten them all!"

"Well, it's the same thing to me!"

"No Thomas, if you want something, you don't hint about it, you just out and out ask."

"I think you should have gotten the hint."

"Well, I didn't, and I don't respond to hints. Hinting about something that you want is just plain stupid."

"Are you calling me stupid?"

"I'm not calling you anything. Quit being so overly sensitive."

"I'm *not* being overly sensitive, but I think you're being rude."

"I'm never rude. I think now that *you're* being rude and trying to start an argument."

"Why would I want to start an argument?"

"Because you're overly sensitive…"

"I'm not…never mind…it's pointless talking to you when you're being stubborn…"

"I'm not being stubborn."

"You told me about your piano lessons and what you did. I'd call that stubborn!"

"I was 10-years old, Thomas!"

"You said your mom is stubborn, and she's 54-years old…"

"I'm not like my mother!"

"Could have fooled me!"

She slammed the lid down on the pot of Beef Bourguignon and tossed the spoon she'd been stirring it with into the sink then trounced out of the kitchen, across the living room and into the bedroom, slamming the door behind her.

Uh oh…their first argument…and it was stupid. Was she like her mother? Oh God, *please*, no! Was Thomas like his father? Well, how would she know? All she knew about James was what her mom had told her. And he sounded like a bossy, control freak unable to manage his temper or emotions. At least Thomas didn't appear to be a control freak. But then again, she wasn't a pushover like her mom, and she wasn't about to take crap from any man. Even if he was so devastatingly handsome that it made her knees weak. Even if he seemed sweet and kind and was over-the-top awesome in bed. Even if…

Just then, there was a soft knock on the door. She gave a heavy sigh before saying, "Come in."

The door opened slowly and Thomas stood in the doorway.

"I'm sorry, Michelle. I don't want to argue with you...not about anything...You've come to mean a lot to me over this past week...I don't want to ruin things between us you know..."

She moved forward and fell into his open arms. "I don't want to argue with you either, Thomas...and I'm sorry too. I guess I think too much like a lawyer and need to think more about being just a girl who's...who's falling in love..."

She felt Thomas stiffen at her words and thought she shouldn't have said them, that now he'd be scared away. But, he put her away from him, holding onto her shoulders and looked deeply into her eyes.

"I think I'm falling in love with you too, Michelle...I truly do..."

Chapter 21

A New Dress for Susan

J ames took Susan back to bed after singing his new song to her, but he didn't make love to her. They were both tired and simply cuddled up under the warm covers and fell asleep in each other's arms.

The days passed quickly at the cottage. It snowed straight for three days after they arrived, then the sun came out to glisten on the fresh fallen snow. James and Susan ventured out, trudging up the hill to the tree where they'd first had their picnic all those years ago, then down to the pond, that was sealed over in ice.

They spent hours sitting on opposite ends of the couch, a blanket over their legs and feet, reading books and talking in front of a cozy fire. Every now and then, one of them would start a game of "footsie," which often led to a bout of lovemaking.

Susan made Eggplant Parmesan, cheese souffles, a polenta casserole, Spinach Lasagna, and baked fresh bread and yeast rolls along with blackberry scones and chocolate chip cookies. The cottage was constantly filled with delicious smells and James complained that Susan was going to make him fat. She just told him to shush and enjoy it.

They'd been at the cottage for a week when James suggested they brave a walk into Little Dippington to browse the shops. He was itching to buy Susan something other than groceries, but she knew it and was equally determined that he buy her nothing. He finally coaxed her into going, hedging around her insistence that if she saw something she liked that *she'd* be the one buying it.

She did her best to cover the bruises on her face and eye, which were starting to fade somewhat, covering them with make-up. It did a good job of hiding them, and she didn't think anyone would notice.

The weather was fine when they left the cottage late morning, and most of the snow had melted off the road. The first shop they came to when they entered the village was Emily's old shop that sold teacups and the like. Emily, Auntie Annabelle's friend, had passed away some years before and James told her that her granddaughter, Angie, had moved back from America and taken over the shop.

The bell tinkled over the door as they entered and they could see a middle-aged blonde woman near the back, unpacking items from a box that was sitting on the floor. Hearing the bell, she straightened up to see who her customers might be then immediately froze, bringing her hand up to her mouth, her eyes as big as saucers. James seemed amused; Susan seemed puzzled.

"Oh, oh, oh...!" exclaimed the woman, who Susan assumed must be Angie. "Is it really you...or am I dreamin'?!" Her voice, with a very obvious Southern drawl, was breathless.

It was instantly apparent that Angie was a fan of James's and was somewhat overwhelmed to see him in her shop.

This was the first time Susan had been with James on this trip to witness fan adoration first hand, and she was a bit put off by it. She looked Angie up and down, trying to determine if she might be a threat, but then told herself she was being ridiculous. She slapped jealous thoughts out of her head and composed herself. Angie was certainly an attractive woman, with blonde hair and bright blue eyes, and she couldn't help but think that James, as fond as he'd always been of women, was checking her out. She bristled slightly, reaching over to tuck her arm under James's.

"Are you...are you really...really *James?!*" Angie gushed. "Live and in person?! Oh, oh, oh! I swear I can't believe it!!" She moved towards James and Susan, her eyes focused on James, as if in a trance.

"Can I...can I touch you?" she pleaded, her voice in a whisper, her face flushed.

James just smiled at her as she continued to advance on him.

When she reached out her hand to put it on his chest, Susan wanted to slap it away, but James squeezed her arm in his, giving her the signal to behave herself. She smiled at Angie sweetly.

Angie touched her palm to James's chest then pulled it away as if she'd touched a hot stove burner.

"Oh...thank you!" she said excitedly. "I can't believe I really touched you! I can't believe you're in my shop! What can I do for you? What can I get for you?" Her mouth was running a mile a minute, she was so excited. "Can I get you to sign something for me? Would you like a cup of tea?"

"No, no thank you...no tea," replied James. "And yes, I'd be happy to sign something for you."

"Oh, oh, oh...thank you!" she murmured, running to the back of the shop and returning a moment later with a pad and pen.

"What would you like me to write, Angie? That's your name, right? You're Emily's granddaughter. Emily was my Auntie Annabelle's best friend."

Angie was shaking as she handed James the pad and pen. "Yes! Yes, I'm Emily's granddaughter. I've been runnin' the shop for almost five years now since she passed. I divorced my good for nothin' husband back in North Carolina and moved here lock, stock and barrel. Would you...would you write 'To Angie' on the top of the pad?"

James grinned at her, took the pad and pen and proceeded to write what she asked. He looked back at her and lifted his eyebrows, waiting to hear what else she wanted him to write.

But Angie was speechless. She just stared at him, mouth half open. Susan thought she might start to drool and suddenly felt sorry for her.

"Write something sweet for her, James," she suggested.

Angie looked over at Susan as if she just noticed her for the first time, but then she focused back on James.

"Write me a little sugar...sure would be nice..." Angie said, batting her eyes. Susan rolled hers.

James began writing on the pad again, nearly filling up the whole page while Angie waited breathlessly. He then signed his name with a flourish and handed the pad and pen back to her.

Angie's eyes scanned the page and her face flushed. Oh my, darlin', thank you so much! I'll cherish this forever…I surely will!"

"Nice to meet you, Angie," nodded James.

"Same here," added Susan.

They turned and left the shop before Angie had a chance to say anything else, the bell tinkling again over the door as they left.

When they were outside, Susan looked over at James. "So what did you write to her?"

"You want to know?"

"I wouldn't have asked if I didn't want to know."

"I wrote, 'To a charming and lovely Southern belle with the prettiest blue eyes I've ever seen. Maybe I'll write a song for you someday. Stay sweet and pretty. Always, James.' You told me to write something nice…"

"The prettiest blue eyes you've ever seen?!!!"

"Yours are green, Susan…"

"I know that, but…"

"Don't go getting all jealous now…"

"Hmphhh!"

James chuckled, grabbing Susan's hand and they continued to walk down the cobblestone street into the village proper.

There were new shops, but then Susan spotted the clothing shop where she'd bought the two infamous green dresses. James noticed her looking at the shop window.

"Might you need another green dress?" he asked teasingly.

"No!" she snapped back at him. "I have enough green dresses."

"I like you in green dresses. They match your eyes."

"Well, I don't need any more of them."

James moved to the entrance of the shop, tugging Susan after him and opened the door. "Maybe you'd like a pink or blue one then…"

"If I do, you're not paying for it."

"We'll see about that."

"Then I won't look at anything." She shook her hand free from his and turned to go back out the door. He grabbed her elbow and pulled her back just as an elderly woman approached them from the back of the shop.

Even though she was thirty-seven years older, Susan instantly recognized her. It was Thisbe, the woman who had sold her a slinky green dress in November, 1962. She'd helped her hide it in the bottom of her purse so she could sneak it into the closet before James found out. Susan didn't want to mention that she'd recognized her, however. She didn't want to dredge up the green dress fiasco where James once again threw a snit fit over her buying it with her own money.

"Hello, luvs," said Thisbe with a wide smile on her face. "Might you be looking for something special?"

Susan sighed in relief when she realized the woman didn't recognize her. Well, holy crap! Why would she remember her anyway? She'd been a 17-year-old girl when she last saw her!

Thisbe also didn't seem to recognize James, which was a relief as neither of them wanted a repeat of an over-zealous and love struck fan.

"A pink or blue dress would be nice," James responded.

Susan elbowed him. He looked over at her. "What's it to be, Susan? Pink or blue?"

"I don't need a new dress, thank you, James."

"But I told you I'd buy you a new dress. Would you prefer pink or blue?"

"I said I don't want a new dress!"

"Pink or blue?"

Susan gritted her teeth. "What!...Are we in the Sleeping Beauty Castle at Disneyland or something? Pink. Blue. Pink. Blue. And besides, after I sang to you and you asked me what color Sleeping Beauty's dress was at the end of the movie, I told you it was pink..."

Her face paled as she felt the words spew out of her mouth. Oh my God! That day she'd met him at Disneyland in the Sleeping Beauty Castle when she was 16-years-old!! It was something she'd never mentioned to him, and not something she wanted mentioned. Her age at that time wouldn't make sense if it was compared to her time travel ages.

She looked over at James and saw the puzzled expression on his face and could tell he was searching his memory in regard to Sleeping Beauty's dress color.

Quickly, before he had a chance to think real hard, she said, "I much prefer pink over blue."

She looked at Thisbe. "Might you have any pink dresses?"

Thisbe smiled. "Of course, Luv. I have quite a few of them, nice ones too. Come this way."

This time, Susan tugged on James's arm and pulled him towards the back of the shop where Thisbe pointed to two round clothes racks packed with dresses. She sorted through them, pausing to look at the pink ones, before pulling out a pale pink one with false buttons down the front. It was long-sleeved and made from stretchy material, something Susan always liked because it clung to her curves.

"I'll try this one," she said, handing it to Thisbe who led her to the very back of the shop to a small curtained-off area. Thisbe slipped it off the hanger and pulled the curtain aside for Susan to enter the fitting area. She hung her purse on a hook on the wall, then took off her jeans and sweater and slipped the dress over her head, wiggling into it. When she looked in the mirror, she was happy with what she saw. The dress fit perfectly. It had a scoop neck, which revealed just a bit of cleavage, long sleeves, and the hem came down to mid-calf. The material was thick enough to provide some warmth; it was a perfect winter dress.

She trounced out of the fitting area and twirled in front of James. He looked her up and down twice before shrugging his shoulders.

"A bit long, isn't it?"

"Well, I'm not a teenager anymore, you know! Plus, it's winter and this covers more of my legs."

"But I like to look at your legs…"

Susan blushed as she saw Thisbe smile. "You see enough of my legs. And besides, this is nice and warm. I think I'll take it. I can wear it when we go to London."

She motioned for Thisbe to follow her back into the fitting area, telling James she'd be back out in a minute.

Thisbe helped her pull the pink dress up over her head, telling her how lovely she looked in it, but before she went to open the curtain to leave, Susan put her hand on her arm and whispered to her.

"I want to pay for this myself. My uh…man friend keeps wanting to buy stuff for me, but I…ah…don't want to feel *obligated*, if you know what I mean…"

Thisbe winked at her. "Och! Of course I understand, Luv! Men rather enjoy making women feel they owe them something, don't they? One reason I never married."

Susan reached for her purse hanging on the hook and took out enough money to cover the price of the dress and handed it to Thisbe. "Keep the change, okay?"

Thisbe accepted the money, laid the dress over her arm and left the fitting room. Susan heard James ask her the price of the dress, but then he and Thisbe moved out of ear shot. Susan quickly slipped her jeans and sweater back on, hooked her purse strap over her shoulder and exited the fitting room.

James was standing at the counter at the back of the shop where Thisbe was folding and laying the dress in a box with tissue paper. When he turned and she saw the expression on his face, she almost ran back behind the curtain of the fitting room.

But then she thought to herself, "This is bullshit!" Instead of cringing at his angry stare, she lifted her chin, squared her shoulders and strode up to the counter just as Thisbe was placing the lid on the box.

"Is there a problem?" she asked innocently, looking James straight in the face.

His eyes locked on hers, his mouth set in a straight line. "Yes, Susan, there is."

"And what would that be, James?"

"I was just told you paid for the dress instead of letting me pay for it. I thought I made it clear that I would buy you a new dress if you wanted one."

Susan picked up the box off the counter. "And I made it perfectly clear that if I decided on a dress, that *I* would be buying it and not you."

She headed towards the door, then turned. "Thank you for your help," she said pleasantly to Thisbe. "I just love the dress!"

James went to grab her arm, but then thought better of it, briskly walking in front of Susan and opening the door for her.

"Ta!" Thisbe yelled after them.

When they got outside, James started to grab her arm again, but Susan saw the move coming and stepped back.

"Don't you dare, James! I mean it! You better get it through that thick head of yours that I'm *not* going to be controlled by you. Or told what I can or can't do! We've spent the past week talking about issues from the past. Maybe we need to spend the next one discussing the present and the future."

She tucked the box up under her arm, turned on her heel and began walking back down the street with the intention of going back to the cottage alone if he was going to act all pissy at her. James soon caught up with her, hands shoved deep down into the pockets of his coat.

"Why do you have to be so damn obstinate?! I just wanted to do something nice for you and instead you have to be all disagreeable..."

They continued walking.

"I'm *not* being disagreeable! I'm simply telling you that I'm an independent woman. I think you're living in the dark ages. Did you miss the women's liberation movement entirely?"

"I thought it was a bunch of balderdash...burning bras and all that stuff...rubbish!"

"It wasn't just about burning bras. It was a statement to let men and the whole world know that girls and women aren't 'objects.' We're real people with brains and the ability to make decisions ourselves. We don't need a *man* making decisions for us!"

"Is that what you want? To make all your own decisions? Don't you think that if you love someone that the other person should have a say in the decisions?"

"Of course the other person should have a say, but that's not what this dress argument is all about and you know it!"

208

"Exactly what is it about then, Miz Independent Woman who doesn't think she needs a man for anything?!"

"Quit putting words in my mouth! I didn't say women don't need men for anything! I simply was trying to say that I can make my own decisions...especially when it comes to buying a dress for myself!"

"But I have money to buy you a hundred dresses!"

"I don't *want* a hundred dresses! I don't *want* you buying me things!!"

"Why not?"

"Because...because I don't want to feel *beholden* to you, that's why! I'd like to feel that I have control over one small thing here and there. You want to control *everything!*"

She could feel tears brimming at the back of her eyes. "Can't I just have a little bit of independence, James? I'm not asking for much... just a little..."

They were passing Emily's shop and Susan saw Angie peering out the window in the door. Suddenly it all seemed too much.

"If you want someone to fawn all over you and kiss the ground you walk on...and to boss around and buy a hundred dresses for, why don't you just go be with Angie then?! Look, she's oogling you from her shop window. Why don't you go take up with her, and I can leave and go back to America and..."

She started to run down the road to get away from him. Damn it all! Why did she and James always seem to get in arguments over the dumbest things? Was it possible they would or *could* ever get along? If she stayed in the past with him this time, were they destined to constantly be at each other's throats about something? It didn't bear thinking about.

James caught up with her within seconds and they walked side-by-side back to the cottage in silence.

When they got there, James unlocked the door and Susan went in before him, tossing the box with the dress angrily on the floor then walked past it into the kitchen. She grabbed the tea kettle off the stove, filled it with fresh water, slammed it on the stove and turned on the burner before taking two mugs out of a cabinet and placing them noisily on the counter.

James observed her, still saying nothing. But his anger with her had vanished. She was just being her Susan-ish self and he knew she'd end up calming down as she always did after thinking things through. And, he knew she'd be contrite, want to pretend nothing untoward had happened then make up with him.

He had to admit that he rather enjoyed the making up part.

Chapter 22

More Love at the Cottage

Thomas and Michelle enjoyed the Beef Bourguignon along with another bottle of wine for a late dinner after being delayed in the bedroom for an hour, for a little 'make-up sex,' after their argument. Thomas surprised her by bringing candles into the kitchen, lighting them and turning off the kitchen lights. They ate and talked in the candlelight, savoring not only the food but the conversation as well.

It was after 9:00 when Thomas suggested they watch a movie before bed, but then his mobile phone rang. It was his sister, Carrie.

"I just tried to reach Dad, but he didn't answer his phone," she said. "I wanted to let him know that I'm on my way back from Italy. I was going to stay longer, but my curiosity about Dad and the Susan woman got the better of me. Are they still out at Auntie Annabelle's cottage? I'm also dying to know about you and the daughter, Michelle. What's she like? Is it true she's staying with you?"

"Slow down, Carrie! I can only answer one question at a time! When are you going to be back? Can you save your questions until then? Michelle and I were just about to watch a movie."

"Oh! So she *is* staying with you then! Well, sorry for disturbing you, but after talking to Dad last week, I've been dying to know what's going on with both him and you and the American women who went to his concert."

"You can meet Michelle when you get here. So, when *are* you going to be here? Are you going to stay out at Dad's house?"

211

"I'm flying in from Rome tomorrow morning. And, no, I won't be staying at Dad's house. I rented a flat in London a few months ago. I've only stayed there once, but I plan on going there. Well, especially if Dad has a girlfriend he'll be bringing to his house. Three's a crowd, you know..."

"Do you need picked up at the airport? Is David going to be with you?"

"No, he's going from Rome to Edinburgh to be with his family for the holiday. I can catch a cab when I get in, don't worry about me. I'll call you when I get to my flat. So, I was thinking about something... When I get there, why don't we drive up to Brighton and then over to Little Dippington and surprise Dad and Susan? I don't want to wait another week to meet her, plus I can get to know Michelle on the drive."

Thomas raised his eyebrows. "Well, Dad seemed pretty specific saying he wanted to be alone with Susan so they could work out some issues from the past..."

"What kind of issues?"

"Carrie, Michelle knows more about them than I do. Why don't you ask her when you get here?"

"I still think we should go to Brighton and then out to the cottage. We can stay in either Brighton, or maybe they have a small B&B in Little Dippington."

"I don't know...I don't want to upset Dad..."

"He won't be upset. Hell, they've had a whole week alone together! I'd think that would be long enough to resolve whatever issues they had."

"Let me think about it then, and we can decide when you get here tomorrow. It's a three hour drive to Brighton from here, you know."

"Yeah, I know, but like I said, I could get to know Michelle on the drive. I'm quite shocked that you have a woman in your life. After that girl you were with while you were at the music academy, I never thought you'd find another one you liked so well."

"I'm rather shocked at myself as well, but when cupid strikes, you know..."

Carrie laughed. "Okay, Thomas, I'll let you get back to your movie. Talk to you tomorrow, okay?"

"Okay, Carrie. See you tomorrow. Bye."

Thomas disconnected.

"Your sister?" Michelle asked, sorting through the pile of DVD's she found in the cabinet below Thomas's t.v.

"Yeah. She's flying in from Italy tomorrow morning and is dying to meet you. You'll really like her. I think both of you will hit it off right away."

"Well, I have to admit to being a little nervous about meeting the rest of your family. We were supposed to meet Robert on three different occasions this past week, but he keeps cancelling."

"It's just because the restaurant is so busy and he keeps getting special requests from high profile people and food critics that want to check out the restaurant. Plus, it's close to the holidays. He said their catering orders are overwhelming him. It's why Meredith hasn't been able to come cook for me."

"Well, with me here, there's no need for her to come cook anyway."

"I know that. So, Carrie has an idea in her head that she wants the three of us to drive to Brighton then out to Little Dippington to surprise Dad and your mum. What do you think?"

"Really? Wow! I'm not so sure that would be a good idea...but then again, they *have* been there for a week already. And, I wouldn't mind seeing the cottage. Mom told me that's where your dad took her right after they met the first time."

"Really?"

"Yeah, I thought I'd told you. I...ah...think he popped her cherry there..." Her face tinged pink.

"Popped her?? Oh!! You mean he breached her maidenhead!"

Michelle turned a deeper shade of crimson. "Well, those are terms you don't hear too often these days..."

Thomas laughed. "I suppose not. I told Carrie we'd let her know tomorrow about going to Brighton. I'm up for going if you are."

"Do you think we should call your dad and my mom and let them know we're coming?"

"No, let's make it a surprise."

"What if they're...ah...you know..."

"We'll knock real loud and give them plenty of time to answer the door."

"Well, okay...I guess it'll be all right then. And, I am rather looking forward to meeting your sister. So then, what movie do you want to watch? I'm up for something funny. How about you?"

"I'm good with funny. You pick one out and I'll go make some microwave popcorn."

He got up and went into the kitchen. Michelle laughed when she saw Thomas had a copy of one of her brother's favorite movies, *"Blazing Saddles."* It was an oldie, made in 1974 and terribly politically incorrect. She slipped it into the DVD player then hit pause while she waited for Thomas to come back with the popcorn.

She was a little worried about showing up at Auntie Annabelle's cottage unannounced, but then figured what the heck. She was anxious to know how her mom and James were getting along. She also wanted to get her mom aside to find out if Susan had given the ring to James and what the both of them were going to do about the future. It was daunting to think about. She felt like she was trapped in a spider's web of gargantuan proportions and there was no way out.

Hilary and her old gent checked into the Sheraton hotel in Brighton a couple days after she spoke to Marcus. He hired a limo to drive them there in style and gave her a diamond studded watch on the drive. Part of the payment, however, was that she give him a blow job in the back seat of the limo. She obliged, feeling disgusted as she always did, but then thought she'd soon be doing the same thing to James in the back seat of his limo, assuming he had one. If not, she'd talk him into getting one. It cheered her up considerably.

Upon arriving, the old gent contacted his old war friend immediately and arranged to spend the afternoon and evening with him. He told Hilary she could rent a car if she wanted to and do whatever she pleased as long as she was back at the hotel by midnight when he planned on being back himself.

She was soon motoring her way to King's Head, hoping James and Susan were still staying with his aunties. When she got there, however, it took her almost an hour to find their house which was located down a maze of country roads that all seemed to dead end. She was irritated and pissed by the time she finally arrived at the address Marcus had given her.

But there was no one home. She banged on the door for a full five minutes before giving up and going back to sit in her rental car. She pounded on the steering wheel furiously. Should she stick around to see if someone would come home or should she just go back to Brighton and try again tomorrow?

In frustration, she punched in Marcus's number, but all she got was his voice mail. She left a scathing message for him and told him to call her back as soon as possible. After waiting another ten minutes, she started the car back up and drove into the town of Kings Head where she located a bar and decided to go have a drink. Shit! She had the whole evening ahead of her and nothing to do.

The bartender was chatty, but when she asked if he knew anyone named Auntie Annabelle or Auntie Ginny, he just shrugged his shoulders and said he'd never heard of them. He asked if she knew their last names, but she didn't. Frustration began to set in, but her mood was quickly improving with each cocktail she drank.

After she finished her fifth, the bartender, who was just getting off his shift, asked if she'd be interested in going to his flat which was above the bar. She shrugged her shoulders. Why the hell not...

He helped her off the barstool and they went up some narrow stairs behind the bar. Within five minutes, they were rolling around naked on his single cot, and a couple of hours later, feeling sexually satisfied and sobered up, Hilary drove back to Brighton and the Sheraton. James and Susan and the aunties would have to wait until tomorrow.

❧

When Susan set the cup of tea down on the coffee table in front of him, James tried to keep a straight face. He could see she was feeling a little remorseful for blowing up at him about the dress, but he was determined to keep a cool silence to see what she would do.

"I made your tea just the way you like it...two sugars and just a spot of milk," she murmured, sitting down next to him then lowering her eyes. She'd set her own cup of tea on the table next to his then put her hands in her lap where she was wringing them back and forth.

His silence was unnerving. Had she gone too far exploding at him like she did and insisting she was an independent woman and wanted to make her own decisions? She didn't think she had. She was just trying to be honest after all. Isn't that what he wanted from her? Honesty? That's what he'd told her anyway.

When he reached over and laid his hand on hers, her eyes flew up to meet his and she sucked in her breath. It was obvious he was no longer mad or upset with her, and the way he was looking at her sent chill bumps up and down her whole body. Oh my! It was *that* look, with the amber highlights in his eyes sparking out at her, his pupils beginning to dilate. She squirmed on the couch. Damn it all! Why did he have this effect on her?! It just wasn't fair!

And he knew the effect he had on her. She was so easy to read. He wasn't even surprised she'd slipped behind his back to pay for her dress. He almost knew it before she did it. It was like her to thwart him at every turn, but it kept him on his toes as well as made life interesting. He knew very well that if he insisted on having his way or if it was something really important, he could get her to back down. As long as he could keep his own temper in check, that is. And, he was finding, since he'd unintentionally struck her a few days ago, that it wasn't as hard as he thought it would be. Maybe he had matured over the years after all. Or, maybe what he did to her, and having to look at her bruised face every day for the past week had sent a message to his brain that it was time he started trying a little harder to rein in his temper. Whatever it was, he felt that it boded well for their future.

When he moved in to brush his lips against hers, she closed her eyes and leaned in towards him. He moved his soft and tantalizing lips

216

back and forth across hers a few times before moving them from her
mouth to her cheek then down the side of her neck to her collarbone
where he licked his tongue back up her neck and up to the front of
her ear.

Her fingers fluttered in her lap and he grasped them tightly,
scraping his fingernails against the palm of one of her hands. It sent
more chill bumps down her arms causing her breath to hitch in her
throat.

When he released her hands and pulled her into his arms for a
deep and hungry kiss, she melted against him like a ragdoll, tilting
her head back and then moaning as his mouth left hers and he licked
his tongue down her neck to where her breasts peeked out of the top
of her sweater. He loved the taste of her skin and could feel a bulge
growing in his trousers.

Moving his hands around to the front of her, he slipped them up
under her sweater and squeezed her breasts gently, teasing her nipples
with his thumbs through the fabric of her bra.

In return, she reached towards his chest and began to open the
buttons of his shirt before pulling the shirt tails out of his trousers.
Placing her hands on his bare chest, she rubbed her palms in circles
on his breasts, pausing now and then to pinch his hardening nipples
between her fingers.

He moaned his pleasure into her ear before reaching up to the
back of her head, where he pulled the clip and hair tie from her hair,
causing it to spill down her back and across her shoulders. He ran his
fingers through it, savoring the feel of its silkiness.

"Should we go into the bedroom or would you prefer me right
here on the couch? You have me burning for you, Susan…"

She pulled out of his embrace, stood up and held out her hand. "I
prefer the bedroom," she said coyly, kicking off her shoes.

Before standing up and taking her hand, he leaned over and took
off his own shoes and socks. She pulled him around the couch and
towards the bedroom. His eyes focused on her tantalizing bottom out-
lined by her tight jeans and an idea suddenly popped into his head.
He smiled to himself wickedly. While he wanted to take her quickly

and passionately as was their wont, he pushed back his ardor, released his hand from hers and swatted her on her bottom.

Her head spun around to look at him as they passed through the bedroom door, a surprised look on her face.

"Oww! What was that for?!"

"The sight of your bum in those tight jeans has me thinking..."

Anxious as always to have him inside her, she quickly striped off both her jeans and panties. When he swatted her bottom again, she squealed.

"Just what do you think you're doing?!!"

He just grinned at her mischievously before pushing her down onto the foot of the bed face down. Before she had a chance to respond, he brought his hand down on her bottom again then again, and when she protested and tried to get up, he put one knee up on the bed next to her and held her down with one hand on her back.

"Stop it, James!!" she screamed.

"You don't like being spanked? You don't recall me telling you that if you crossed me again that I just might turn you over my knee...?"

He swatted her several more times. The sight of her nicely rounded bottom turning pink set him on fire and he could feel his erection straining against the front of his trousers.

"Oww! You've got to be kidding me!! Oww!"

He ignored her protests, continuing to swat her before slipping his hand between her legs and seeking her entrance. Inserting a finger into her, he could feel her dripping wetness and gave a low chuckle.

"Why Susan, it appears you might enjoy being spanked..."

"I do not!! Oww! Stop it right now!! Oww!!"

Staring at her bottom, which was now a brighter shade of pink, almost sent him over the edge. He removed his hand from her back, and went down on his knees behind her then began planting small kisses on her now red globes. They were stinging from his blows, but his kisses not only soothed the sting, but began sending waves of desire through her entire body.

She squirmed as his tongue licked its way down the cleft between the cheeks of her bottom, lifting up off the bed to give him better access to her most intimate part. He teased her love bud with his tongue before moving back up to kiss her bum again.

Both of them were breathing heavily now, and James didn't know if he could hold out much longer before he exploded into his trousers. Standing up, he unbuttoned then unzipped and his stiff shaft sprung out at the ready. A second later, he entered her from behind, grasping her hips with both hands and moaning as he felt her tight sheath envelope him.

She screamed as she felt him push deep inside her to her very core, where he stilled for a moment, savoring the feel of her. He then began slowly withdrawing before pushing back in again, then again and again.

When he swatted her bottom a few more times, the stinging sensation brought her a pleasure so unexpected and intense that she could feel herself throbbing around his member, screaming again as he continued to spank her. She felt wave after wave of rapture wash over her bringing her into a shattering climax. James, feeling her tighten around him, soon followed, spilling himself into her before collapsing over her back.

Parting her hair as his breathing slowed, he began to kiss her neck with soft, downy kisses. She closed her eyes and sighed contentedly as her heartbeats slowed.

"So, Susan…did you learn your lesson not to cross me then?" he murmured into her ear.

"Absolutely not, James!" she responded. "If those are the consequences for crossing you, I might just be doing it again…"

He chuckled above her and she smiled.

Chapter 23

Hilary Harasses the Aunties

Carrie called Thomas shortly after arriving back at her London flat. It was 10:00 in the morning and she was anxious to meet Michelle and find out more about Susan and how she came to be with her dad out at Auntie Annabelle's cottage. She was also anxious to drive out to Little Dippington and meet Susan in person as well as see her dad. She was sorry to have missed his first concert since her mum had passed and was just about dying of curiosity as to how he so quickly fell into a love affair.

"You really want to drive to Brighton today?" asked Thomas, answering his phone and hearing Carrie's voice.

"Yes, Thomas. I told you that yesterday. Let's just do it. We can stop for a bit of luncheon on the way. I checked maps and we could actually drive straight to Little Dippington. I also found out there's a bed and breakfast there, so we could skip Brighton all together. Or, maybe we could even stay at the cottage with Dad."

"I wouldn't count on that, you know…"

"Okay, well, maybe not…especially if we're surprising him…"

"I'm still not so sure this surprise is such a good idea. Dad made it very clear he wanted to be left alone with Susan."

"That just seems so weird that she has the same name as Mum's, don't you think?"

"Yeah, a coincidence for sure."

"Well, I'm anxious to meet her as well as your Michelle."

"Then head on over when you're ready and we can take my Audi. We're packed and ready to go whenever you are."

"Sounds good, Tom-tom...See you in a bit...'"

"Don't call me that, Carrie! It's embarrassing!"

But, Carrie had already hung up.

Susan was up early the next morning making more of the blackberry scones she'd promised James when they were at breakfast in Little Dippington the week before. The coffee was done and she was on her second cup when James came in wearing only his boxer shorts, wrapped his arms around her and kissed her on the back of her neck. She turned in his arms and kissed him back.

"Something smells good," he remarked.

"I'm making you blackberry scones."

"Again? Will these be as good as the last ones you made?"

She pushed at his chest. "Of course they will! You haven't complained about my cooking since we've been here..."

"I'm just teasing you. I told you that you're going to make me fat. I don't need all the food you cook up for me. Neither do you..."

"Are you implying that *I'm* getting fat?!"

"No, not at all, but we'll both be fat if you keep up the three meals a day along with baking."

"But you *love* chocolate chip cookies..."

"I can do without them. We aren't getting any exercise with the weather being so bad."

She smiled up at him. "We're getting *some* exercise..."

"Well, yes...I know what you're referring to now, don't I...but we're not burning enough calories."

Susan harrumphed.

He turned the tea kettle on the stove before going over to the piano and sitting down.

"Any special requests?"

"How about something classical, like maybe the piano concerto you wrote for Thomas?"

"Well, that's rather complicated and long. Why don't you come over and play something while your scones are baking?"

"Me?"

"Yes. As I recall you know how to play the piano."

"It's been a long time...:

Susan thought to herself, "I wonder if I can still do this...but I did ask Marta for the same talents I've had all the other times..." She picked up her cup of coffee, went over to the piano and opened the bench as James got up. Flipping through the music, she saw Tchaikovsky's *'Piano Concerto'* and put it up on the piano before sitting down and handing her cup to James. He leaned his hip against the side of the piano and watched her as she laid her hands on the keys.

She played expertly and beautifully. As she watched her hands move on the keys, she felt as if she were in a trance watching someone else's hands. The piece of music was long, and James turned the pages for her until the timer for the scones went off. She stopped playing, but James motioned for her to continue. He went into the kitchen, got the oven mitts Susan had left next to the stove and took the scones out of the oven. The tea kettle started to whistle at the same time. He turned it off and made himself a cup of tea before coming back into the other room and sitting on the couch.

As the final notes faded away and she turned on the piano bench, he clapped.

"Very nice. You could give Thomas a run for his money with your playing, you know."

"I seriously doubt that, but thank you anyway."

"So what do you want to do today, besides spend more time in bed with me?"

"I *don't* want to spend more time in bed with you. I feel like I'm getting honeymoon cystitis."

"Making excuses already, are you?"

"No, but you do have a rather over-the-top sex drive, you know. I thought maybe you would have slowed down being older."

"*You* don't seem to have slowed down..."

"Well, you just have that effect on me...I can't help it..."

"I know..."

Before she could say another word, he was in front of her, pulling her up into his arms for a kiss. She could feel the bulge in his boxer shorts growing against her belly.

He released her and started tugging her towards the bedroom. "And you seem to have the same effect on me."

⟶

Hilary drove back out to Auntie Gin's house late the next morning, after servicing her old gent and fortifying herself with a couple of drinks in the hotel bar. This time, the aunties were home.

When Auntie Gin opened the door and saw the platinum blonde standing there, she blinked her eyes. Hilary was decked out in a pair of green skin tight jeans, high heels and a clingy red sweater studded with rhinestones. She looked like a Christmas ornament.

"May I help you?" she asked politely.

Hilary tossed her head. "Oh, I hope so! I was told that James's aunties lived here and that he might be visiting you. I talked to his son, Thomas, and he told me I might find James here..."

Auntie Gin just looked at her but said nothing. She'd become accustomed over the past several years to having fans or favor seekers try to pry information out of her as to James's whereabouts or how to reach him. And, as she looked this woman up and down, she didn't care for what she saw.

Hilary continued her lie. "Thomas said James would be interested in my cause related to animal welfare. I so want to help innocent animals and just hate seeing them slaughtered unnecessarily and in such an inhumane way, solely for the purpose of being food. It's been my lifetime quest to change this, and..."

Auntie Gin interrupted her. "You need to contact James's organization in London, dear. You can reach them through his office at Cherry Studios. I'm afraid I can't put you in contact with James myself."

"Oh, but Thomas assured me you could! He was very excited about my cause…it's to save pigs, those lovely and friendly creatures that end up as bacon…just horrible, you know. He even told me James was here visiting you and that I should come straight away!"

Auntie Gin squinted her eyes at Hilary. She was very adept at smelling out lies, and it was obvious to her that this painted up woman was lying.

"If he were here, I wouldn't be able to tell you, dear. You really do need to go through his organization. If your cause is something James would be interested in, they will certainly put you in touch with him."

"But Thomas said…"

"And just how did you come to know Thomas?"

"I…I met him at James's concert in Brighton a little over a week ago, and we struck up a conversation. He was extremely excited to hear about my cause. It's called 'People for Pigs – Ban Bacon in Britain' – isn't that clever?!"

Auntie Gin tried not to roll her eyes or laugh out loud.

"Ah, yes…quite clever."

"So is James here or not?"

"I told you, dear, that I can't give you that information. James would be upset with me if I did. I'm sorry, but I think you need to go now."

Hilary stared at her, her polite mask dropping from her face for the briefest of moments, but Auntie Gin didn't miss it.

"Oh, please…maybe you could just go ask him? I'll only take a few moments of his time…"

"I'm sorry, but I really can't."

She started to close the door, but Hilary still wasn't about to give up.

"Are you sure? I know how important animal welfare is to James… and also his dearly departed wife, Susan. I just *know* he would want to support my cause…"

The door closed in Hilary's face.

"Fucking bitch!" she muttered under her breath as she turned away from the door, but it was still loud enough for Auntie Gin to hear. She shook her head. She hoped this horrible woman would never track James down.

◦⌒◦

Carrie and Michelle hit it off right away when Carrie pulled her into a warm hug the minute she spotted her. James's family had always been affectionate, freely giving hugs and kisses, even if they were a little annoyed with each other. It was something their mother had taught them from a young age, admonishing them with the phrase, "Love, love, love, always love. We are family and the most important thing we have is each other. Never forget it."

Carrie took it to heart more than her brothers, and sometimes made people feel a little uncomfortable at first with her overwhelming affection. Michelle was a little nonplussed by the sudden embrace, but Carrie's smile was so warm and welcoming, she couldn't help but be pulled in by it.

Carrie held Michelle out by her arms and looked at her before turning her head to face Thomas.

"Why, Thomas! You have a regular beauty queen here!"

Michelle blushed.

He smiled lovingly at Michelle and his sister. "I rather do, don't I?"

"Are you all packed and ready to go then?" asked Carrie.

Both Michelle and Thomas nodded as he picked up their suitcases, one in each hand, and Carrie opened the door. Michelle picked up her purse and slung the strap up over her shoulder.

"I told the concierge to bring your car up from the parking garage and put my case in the boot," said Carrie heading out the door in front of Thomas and Michelle.

When they got to the elevator, Carrie smiled at Michelle once again. "I can't tell you how happy I am to meet you! I'm just thrilled that Thomas has a girlfriend. He's been too wrapped up in his music and I keep telling him he needs balance in his life. I hope you can be that balance."

Michelle blushed again, feeling a bit awkward. She didn't think she'd ever blushed so much in her entire life as she had since coming back into the past with her mom.

"Well, I have to admit, Carrie, that your brother has quite swept me off my feet, not that I want to admit it, but..."

"And apparently you've done the same to him! I look forward to talking to you on the way to Little Dippington, and I also have to admit that I have a burning curiosity to hear about your mum. Sorry, but I'm quite thrilled that Dad might have found love again. We've all been quite worried about him."

"I'll be happy to tell you anything you want to know," responded Michelle, hoping Carrie wouldn't ask too many probing questions.

Just then, the elevator doors opened and all three went inside; Thomas pushed the button to the lobby and they were soon on their way to Little Dippington.

Susan left James dozing in bed after yet another episode of lovemaking. It amazed her that they couldn't keep their hands off each other. It was almost like they were teenagers again. She wondered if Auntie Annabelle's cottage held some hormonal magic of its own. After gazing lovingly at James again, she decided now would be a good time to take a warm bath. Quietly, she closed the bedroom door and went into the bathroom where she turned on the tap before looking at herself in the mirror above the sink.

The bruise on her cheek, along with the black eye, was starting to fade. It was no longer black and purple but was still very noticeable, now being more of a rainbow of the colors, blue, red and yellow.

She'd been covering it up with makeup when they went out for walks, but when they stayed in the cottage, she didn't bother. A wicked little part of her wanted James to be reminded of his lack of self-control and to think real hard on it. She saw him wince now and then when he looked at the bruise and thought it served him right.

Plus, it seemed to make him somewhat contrite. Not completely of course. James would always be bossy and controlling James, but she could tell he was trying hard to not jump at her when she said or did something he found "annoying," which could be the tiniest little thing. She didn't think she'd ever known someone so moody or unpredictable and was starting to get a good idea how his wife, Susan, must have acted with him, kowtowing to his every whim. She suspected that he was trying to make her into his other Susan.

And, she didn't like it one bit.

That just wasn't her…it would never be her. Despite her fears of losing him and despite her believing that she *could* be like his wife, Susan, if she put her mind to it. She was her own person and always had been. Donald had accepted it all the years they'd been together, and he even encouraged her in it. To think on her own. To have her own opinions. To be independent, self-reliant and to make her own decisions. They shared the same values and the same moral and political views, exchanging their thoughts and often having long conversations on a variety of topics, including the books they read.

Well…at least they *used* to, that is until Donald's case loads increased to the point where he had no time for her and she rarely saw him. His high profile clients had become the most important thing to him and she felt as if she'd been cast aside. In a lot of ways, he'd become like James over the past few years, puffed up with his importance and success. If Susan was anything to him, she was an afterthought.

Could she ever reach a level of understanding with James? Or would he always expect her to live in his shadow and ask "how high?" when he said "jump!"

Loving him as much as she thought she did, could she ever accept the role his other Susan had? Could she submit to his will in anything and everything as he seemed to expect? Would she be able to accept his moodiness and volatile temper?

Sometimes she thought she could, but she really didn't know.

Chapter 24

The Surprise Visit

M ichelle, Thomas and Carrie arrived in Little Dippington shortly after 3:30 in the afternoon, after stopping for lunch on the way. They located the B&B that Carrie had found in a phone directory, checked in, unloaded their suitcases and were soon on their way to Auntie Annabelle's cottage.

The weather had turned bleak, with dark storm clouds moving in, and there was the smell of snow in the air. By the time they arrived at the cottage, fat flakes were beginning to fall.

Susan was in the kitchen starting dinner and James was dabbling at the piano when there was a knock on the door.

"Who could that be?" asked Susan as she diced potatoes into a pan with some onions and peppers. She was planning on making a vegetable frittata for dinner. She'd made fresh yeast rolls that morning, one of James's favorites. In fact, she had to scold him for sneaking three of them right after they came out of the oven.

James got up from the piano bench. "Not sure. I know I told the food shop yesterday we needed a few more things, but said we'd pick them up and not to bother delivering them."

He looked out the window. "Looks like it's starting to snow... maybe someone is lost or had a car breakdown..."

"Surprise!" three voices chorused as James opened the door.

Susan spun around, a potato and the paring knife still in her hand. Carrie rushed to her dad, wrapping her arms around him, a giant smile on her face.

Thomas looked on, taking off his coat, also smiling at his dad as Carrie planted a smacking kiss on James's cheek then Thomas moved in to hug his dad as well. They began chatting.

Michelle, after shrugging off her jacket, immediately spotted her mother in the kitchen and started to walk towards her, grinning, but then she froze and their eyes locked. Susan quickly turned away, laying the potato and knife on the kitchen counter, knowing Michelle had seen the bruises on her face.

"Mom!!!" Michelle screeched, running the rest of the way into the kitchen and grasping Susan by the shoulders. She spun her around, her eyes wide and questioning.

Susan's face drained of all color as she put a hand up to her cheek and eye to try and hide the colored hue. Michelle reached up and pulled the hand away.

Thomas and Carrie turned at Michelle's scream and stared at the two women in the kitchen. James face also paled, realizing everyone was now staring at Susan's bruised face. His gaze slowly followed that of the others.

Michelle was not only shocked but livid. She couldn't believe what she was seeing and had to blink her eyes a few times. She squeezed Susan's shoulders. "What did he do to you, Mom!!? What the fuck did that bastard…"

But before she could finish, Susan broke away from her grasp and interrupted her. "It was an accident, Michelle! An accident!!"

She brushed past her daughter and ran to James, wrapping her arms around his waist and burying her face into the pullover sweater he was wearing. He pulled her in tight.

"Hold me, James…hold me…" she begged. "Tell them…tell them it was an accident…"

Carrie and Thomas were speechless, glued to the spot. But Michelle was boiling like a kettle ready to whistle and blow steam.

"An accident?! An accident!!?"

She advanced towards James and her mom. "Don't you think I've seen enough broken faces from all the abuse cases I've handled over the years!? Don't you think I can recognize an *accident* from bruises from a back-handed slap!!?"

Susan moved her head from side to side, feeling sick, but still kept her face pressed into James's chest. "Say something James..." she murmured. "Tell them it was an accident...or that it was...it was my fault..."

Michelle heard her mother's last words and any self-control that still remained inside her vanished. If her mother hadn't been in James's arms, she be launching herself at him. Thomas sensed her anger was about to escalate out of control and pulled her away back into the kitchen.

"Calm down, Michelle...I'm sure there's an explanation...your mum even said..."

But Michelle wasn't about to listen. "*Your fault!!!*" she exclaimed incredulously. "You're fucking insane, Mom!!! First he sings a song that makes you faint and almost crack your head open on the floor of that club, then he rapes you in the hotel...and...and now you have a black eye from being smacked...and don't you *dare* deny that he struck you! How many other bruises do you have? How many more times has that... that...*monster* raped you!!? Is that why he brought you here...to..."

Carrie's eyes grew as big as saucers.

"Stop it, Michelle!" Thomas yelled over her ranting. "Stop it right now!!" He pulled her back into his arms so quickly that the breath was knocked out of her.

And suddenly she began to cry, something she didn't recall doing since she was a small child. Thomas turned her in his arms and gathered her in close.

"Oh god, Mom...we never should have come here..." she muttered into the front of Thomas's shirt. "You were right...It was a mistake to have brought you here..."

After watching the scene unfold before her in stunned silence, Carrie finally gathered herself together and went to stand next to her dad and Susan, a confused look on her face.

"What's going on, Dad?" she asked softly, laying a hand on his shoulder. "What's Michelle talking about?"

"It was an accident that I struck her…" James responded just as softly. "I didn't mean for it to happen…and Susan wasn't to blame. It's me who holds the blame."

Thomas overheard. "Is this why you wanted to stay here so long?" he asked, still holding tightly onto Michelle, who was now openly sobbing.

Susan lifted her head up from James's chest and turned to face Thomas and Michelle. She nodded at the same time James said, "Yes."

"We thought the bruise would be gone by the end of two weeks…" Susan muttered. "No one would have known but us…"

Other than the sound of Michelle's crying, the silence in the room was palpable. It was as if all the characters in a play had suddenly forgotten all their lines.

They all stared at each other. Michelle's sobs turned to sniffles. She pushed out of Thomas's arms and turned to look at her mother. What she saw there made her wince. Susan and James were wrapped so tightly together, it was as if they were one body instead of two. She saw anguish in both of their eyes and realized it was because they wanted to keep the "accident" a secret between themselves. That they were both embarrassed at being discovered like this.

Carrie sensed the same thing. "I'm so sorry, Dad…We shouldn't have just popped in on you like this…we should have at least called first…"

Thomas looked down at the floor, silently agreeing with his sister. Michelle walked over to her mother and James. She sniffed a few more times and wiped her eyes with the back of her hand.

"I'm sorry if I jumped to conclusions, Mom…James…it's just that…"

"It's okay," said Susan, sighing with relief when she realized Michelle wasn't about to launch into another verbal attack on James.

Then Michelle froze again, looking at Susan's neck and seeing that she wasn't wearing her necklace. Susan had on a sweater with a scooped neck, and if she'd been wearing the ballerina necklace, it would be hanging on her chest. Her eyes met her mom's.

"Where's your necklace?"

Susan instinctively placed her hand on James's chest where she could feel the necklace beneath his sweater. Michelle saw the movement and sucked in her breath.

"You gave it back to him?! Oh, Mom, no! Please don't tell me you gave it back to him!"

Susan nodded.

Michelle groaned. "Did you at least give him back the ring?"

Susan's face turned even paler. James felt her stiffen at Michelle's words and looked down at her. She swiveled her head back from Michelle to look up into his eyes. Her lips parted, but before she could speak, James released her, dropping his arms to his side.

"What ring?"

Susan turned to Michelle and shook her head, indicating she wasn't to say anything else. She walked past James into the bedroom, all eyes following her, where she went over to the dresser and fished in the bottom of her purse that was sitting there. A few moments later, she located what she wanted and took it out, holding it between her fingers. Closing her fist around it, she walked back out into the main room. Everyone was staring at her, but no one said anything.

Susan walked up to James, stopping in front of him. She opened her hand, extending it towards him and he gasped as he saw what she held in her palm. He recognized it immediately, even after all this time. He knew it was the engagement ring he'd tried to give to her once back in a hotel room in November, 1962 and again placed on her finger in anticipation of marrying her in August, 1967. The one he'd called the *little sparkler*.

His eyes blurred with tears as his focus moved from the ring to Susan's face.

Before he or anyone else could comment, she pulled her hand in toward herself and looked down at the ring.

"I've never been able to forget you, James…in all of the years we've been apart…I've never been able to forget you. I've worn this on my necklace every day since the day…the day we were to be married…Just like you, I've been tormented about that day ever since…"

She paused and swallowed. "Michelle wanted to help me…a few months ago, I became very depressed…I told her about us and what happened in the past…she thought that if I went to your concert, you wouldn't recognize me after all this time, and if I could somehow get this ring back to you…it would break the hold you have on me…You asked me if my necklace has some kind of magic or spell attached to it, remember? Well, I think this ring does as well…"

"Do you want me to take it back?" he asked softly. She could hear the pain in his voice.

She looked up at him. "Only if you want to…" she whispered.

"Well…I don't want to…"

He took the ring from her palm then looked into her eyes. "I want you to wear it again…"

And before Susan could respond, he lifted up her left hand and slipped it onto her ring finger.

She gasped, looking down at her hand in disbelief, then looked back up into his eyes questioningly, right before he pulled her into his arms and brought his mouth down on hers.

Thomas and Carrie looked on with bemused expressions on their faces, but Michelle tilted her head back and moaned before she did something else she never recalled doing before. She fainted.

Chapter 25

Susan and James Engaged...Again

Hilary stifled a bored yawn as her old gent droned on about the meeting with his elderly army buddy. They were on their way back to London from Brighton, and she wished he'd just shut the fuck up and go to sleep or something.

She needed to think. Going out to James's aunties had been a waste of time. The old bat hadn't been willing to share one small morsel of information on James's whereabouts.

And, as of yesterday, Marcus still hadn't been able to dig up any dirt on the Susan woman, or her daughter, Michelle either, so she was doing her best to come up with something creative to discredit them in James's and Thomas's eyes. She'd done a lot of discrediting in her life, so she figured it wouldn't be too hard. The only difference in this case was that her victims were too damn "good." It was frustrating. Her typical targets were people who generally had a dirty secret or something to hide.

Finally the old guy dozed off. She knew he slept like a rock, so she took her mobile phone out of her purse and punched in Marcus's number, hoping maybe he'd learned something on either James's whereabouts or some dirt on Susan and her creepy daughter.

But, the only other information Marcus had was that James's other son, Robert, was head chef at an exclusive restaurant in London called Le Fonda. He suggested she go there and see if she could worm some information out of him.

"Oh, I suppose…" she said unenthusiastically. "This hunting James down is wearing me out. I guess I can have the old gent take me there. We go out most of the time anyway since I hate to cook…"

"Well, Hil, you hate it because you don't know *how* to do it. Doesn't your old guy have a personal chef also?"

"Yeah, but she only cooks up healthy, tasteless crap. Even the old gent hates it, but his doctor dictates the menu, so it's no problem talking him into going out. And quit insulting me about my cooking talents. I can boil water for tea just fine…I'll suggest Le Fonda as soon as we get back to London. If we don't go tonight, I'll make sure we go tomorrow. Keep trying to find out what you can about that Susan woman. Once I find James, I want to move in quick and strike before she knows what hit her."

"Fine. I'll keep you posted. I'm quite looking forward to my own reward once you've snagged James, you know…"

"Oh yeah, Marcus, I know, I know…"

Carrie went to get a washcloth with cold water as Thomas carried an unconscious Michelle over to the couch and laid her down. Susan rushed over to her, went down on her knees and took her hand. A few seconds later, Michelle's eyes fluttered open.

"Wha…what happened?" she mumbled.

Carrie handed Susan the wet washcloth and she laid it on Michelle's forehead.

"You fainted," responded Susan.

"I never faint! I've never fainted in my entire life!"

"Well, you just did. It's why you're laying here on the couch."

Michelle looked away from Susan and saw Thomas, James and Carrie all looking at her with concern on their faces.

"Well, shit…I guess there's a first time for everything…" Her head started to clear and she looked back at her mother. "Did I imagine it, or is it true that James is wearing your necklace again and that you've got the engagement ring back on your finger?"

Susan held up her left hand.

Michelle rolled her eyes. "Oh God, Mom! What are you getting yourself into!? What happens when we have to go home?"

"I told you, I'm not going home. I'm not leaving James again...I can't...I won't..."

Michelle removed the washcloth from her forehead and slowly pushed herself up into a sitting position. Thomas came over to sit beside her and took her hand in his.

"I don't want you to leave either, Michelle..."

Michelle looked at him and sighed. Truth be told, she'd been thinking of staying in the past with this Thomas as well...at least for a bit longer. But what about her dad? What about her fiancé, Thomas? What about her career, her brother, all her friends back in the future?

Could it somehow be arranged that both she and her mom could stay in the past and that maybe news could be sent back to the future saying they'd been killed in an accident while on vacation?

It made her head spin to think of all the complications if they were to stay in the past. She blinked her eyes a few times before responding to Thomas, but instead of saying anything, she simply wrapped her arms around his neck and kissed him softly. When she drew back, they smiled at each other.

"I'd love to stay longer and talk some more, and I'd especially like to get to know you, Susan," said Carrie turning from the window and looking at her. But it's snowing like crazy now, and if we don't leave, we'll be snowed in here with you and Dad."

"Well, that would be okay," said Susan. "Wouldn't it James?"

He didn't seem enthusiastic. "Of course, of course they can stay if they want to..."

Thomas stood up, taking Michelle's hand and pulling her up with him. "No, I think it best that we return to the B&B in Little Dippington. Enough has happened here today that I think you two need to be alone. Besides, all our stuff is at the B&B."

"Maybe if the weather clears tomorrow, you could come into the village and we could all go out to dinner?" Carrie offered.

"Or, you could come back here and Susan could make dinner for us," responded James.

Susan shot him a look that said, "You could have asked me first, you know…" but he ignored her.

Michelle shook her head, seeing her mother's frown. How in holy hell could her mom stand that bossy man? It was sickening to watch. She'd never put up with that from her dad!

Thomas went over to the coat rack by the door and retrieved his coat and Michelle's jacket. "Well, just call me on my mobile tomorrow then, Dad."

Carrie picked up her coat from the reclining chair where she'd tossed it when they first came in.

After hugs and hurried goodbyes as the snow began to fall faster and faster, James and Susan were once again left alone in the cottage.

"Well, I sure wasn't expecting all of *that*!" said Carrie as their car inched the way down the road to Little Dippington.

"Neither was I!" exclaimed Thomas.

"Sorry," said Michelle, "but I thought I was going to kill your dad. When I saw my mom's face, I lost it…"

Thomas took his eyes off the road for a second and looked over at Michelle. "We understand, don't we, Carrie?"

"Of course." She leaned forward from the backseat. "It's just that Dad has never, *ever* done anything to physically hurt someone before. He never laid a hand on our mum. Sometimes he yelled at her, and I recall him punching a hole in the wall once, but he never struck her that I know of."

"Well, she was probably more accepting of his bossiness," remarked Michelle. "My mom has a tendency to buck up against anyone who tries to boss her around or tell her what to do. She considers herself an independent woman."

"Our mum wasn't interested in being an independent woman. She was just a gentle person who went along with dad on everything," said

238

Carrie. "She was what I would call nurturing, almost like a mother to him. She understood his moods and knew when to keep her thoughts to herself."

"When they first met," continued Thomas. "He was killing himself on drink and drugs. He was depressed over the pending breakup of the band and living like a bum, going on terrible binges."

"She saved him," added Carrie. "Pulled him out of his depression...then he got her pregnant with me and they got married."

"She sounds like a paragon of a woman," remarked Michelle. "I'm not sure my mom could ever measure up to her."

"Well," said Thomas. "Dad needs love in his life again..."

Carrie continued. "And I think he's found it with your mum."

"She was, after all," said Thomas, "his first true love from all those years ago. I think they'll end up doing fine together. Maybe some fireworks along the way..."

"And maybe Dad needs to be challenged," added Carrie. "He's used to being famous now and it's gone to his head a bit. Your mum could bring him down a peg or two..."

As if that would ever happen... Michelle thought.

"Well, I know for a fact that my mom has never forgotten him," said Michelle. "As I told you, the reason we came here was because she'd become despondent thinking about him again. And, when she told me that the ring she'd been wearing on her necklace for all those years, was the engagement ring he'd given to her, well, that's when I thought maybe if she got rid of it, it would break her tie with him."

"It just all seems so odd and everything," interjected Carrie. "Her wearing that ring on her necklace all that time and not telling anyone about it."

"She didn't really tell me about it," said Michelle. "I found out from her friends. When my dad and her...uh...when they separated, that's when she started thinking of your dad again...and...uh, once the divorce was final..." Michelle cringed at the lie, but couldn't turn back now. "She started to play with the necklace and the ring and got all depressed with memories of your dad..."

239

"How fortunate then, that you came to the concert!" said Thomas. "And even more fortunate for me that I got to meet you!"

Carrie smiled. "Oh yes, Thomas…I think I'm as happy for you as I am for Dad!"

Michelle blushed before reaching over and squeezing Thomas's hand. Other than James, who she wasn't quite sure if she liked or not, Carrie and Thomas were delightful people…especially Thomas…

～◌

James followed Susan into the kitchen. Her mind was in a whirl and the kitchen always seemed to be her safe haven. She looked down at her left hand at the ring that was back on her finger and her heart wrenched. She started to pick up the potato and paring knife again to turn her thoughts, but James stopped her, taking both from her hands and putting them back on the kitchen counter.

"Dinner can wait, Susan. I need to talk to you."

She turned and he led her into the main room where they sat on the couch. He pulled her into his arms and began stroking her back.

"I'm not angry or upset with you, but why didn't you tell me you had the ring? Why did it take Michelle mentioning it? If she hadn't said something, would you ever have told me?"

Susan took a deep breath, pushing out of his embrace. "I…I was worried it would upset you…especially after…after…"

"You mean after I struck you?"

"Oh, James! Can we please forget that!? It was an accident! You didn't mean to do it…you even said so!"

She twisted her hands in her lap again, focusing on the ring that was back on her finger. "I wasn't sure if I should show it to you or not…I just didn't know how you'd react…or…or if you'd be angry remembering what happened at the church…"

He sighed heavily. "Do I really frighten you that much that you're afraid to talk to me…tell me things?"

She looked up at him. "No…yes…sometimes…"

240

"I don't want you to be frightened of me…I want you to be able to tell me anything, not hide things from me. You promised to be honest, remember?"

"Of course I remember, but I find you unpredictable now…your moods change for reasons I don't understand…"

"I have a lot on my mind. Until I decided to perform again, I'd been at odds and ends with my life…like a boat lost at sea…then you suddenly popped back into my life… it threw me."

"I understand that. It threw me too when I realized you recognized me."

"I'm glad I recognized you…but I'm also sorry for what I did to you when I took you back to the hotel."

She looked at him searchingly for a moment before giving a shy smile. It wasn't something she wanted to remember or talk about. "Oh, but you made up for it later…"

"You think so?" He smiled back.

"We've both changed, James, and yet we're still a lot like we were all those years ago. You're still bossy…"

"And you're still contrary…"

"I am *not* contrary!"

"You are, my sweet little independent woman! Don't deny it! And I love every stubborn little bone in your body…" Leaning in, he gave her a quick kiss on her nose before taking her left hand in his and lifting it up. "You know what this means, don't you?"

Her eyes opened wide.

He smiled. "It means you're going to marry me."

Her face paled slightly at his words, but he didn't seem to notice.

How could she marry him!? She was already married! And, she'd also been a married woman in the year 1999, where they were right now. It would be bigamy if she were to marry him! Even if she figured a way to make a quick trip back to the future to file for divorce, it would take months, plus she knew that Donald would never agree to it. And there was no way she could backdate a divorce 16 years from 2015 to 1999.

Oh, what a conundrum!

But then she pondered some more, her thoughts following those of Michelle's, even though Michelle and her hadn't spoken about it. A message could be sent into the future saying she'd been in a boat accident, drowned and her body lost at sea while on vacation. James would never know. No one in the current time period would know.

But...Wouldn't Donald and Steven demand proof to know the story was true? Wouldn't Donald question the matter, file an insurance claim, want to sue the owners of the boat? And what would happen when the year 2015 rolled around?

Her head started to hurt. When James spoke again, it jolted her out of her confused thoughts.

"You do want to marry me, don't you?" His eyes looked pleading.

She wrapped her arms around him, burying her face in his shoulder and inhaling his familiar scent. "I do, James...I do..."

He squeezed her. "Well, what do you say to a Christmas wedding then? Just us, Thomas, Carrie, my other son, Robert, and Michelle? We can get married at my house outside of London and..."

"So soon?" she interrupted. "That's less than two weeks away!"

"So? Carrie was planning to have us all celebrate Christmas together this year." A pained look came over his face for just a moment then was gone. "I haven't been much into Christmas for the past two years...ever since..."

"I understand...ever since you lost your Susan...Are you sure you want to marry me, James? Is it too soon for you?"

"No...no, it's time...she would want me to be happy again, to find love again..."

"But will I be able to make you happy? I'm not like your other Susan. You even said I was contrary, and you know I'm going to argue with you if you try to boss me around...and..."

"I love you, Susan. You've been deep down in my heart since the day I first saw you at the Dusky all those years ago..."

And with that, he captured her mouth with his, invading it with his tongue in a passionate kiss.

"Let's forget about dinner for now," he whispered, laying her back on the couch and planting kisses down the side of her neck. When he slipped his hand up under her sweater and squeezed a breast, she sighed beneath him then reached her hand down between them and grasped the front of his trousers where she could feel something stiff growing.

She smiled up into his face and nodded.

Chapter 26

Hilary Confronts Robert

Robert was extremely busy in the kitchen at Le Fonda. The catering orders before Christmas were almost too much to handle, and he'd had to turn a few requests down. The restaurant itself was booming with customers and reservations had to be made days in advance to get in. Having a strictly vegetarian restaurant had been a risk for the owners, but their bet had paid off with Robert; his imagination and culinary skills were quickly becoming a legend.

He felt somewhat annoyed at the special request from one of the prominent London millionaires to come to the restaurant without a reservation and to personally meet with him to order dinner. But, he also knew that if Le Fonda was to continue to be successful, he needed to cater to the wealthy who made up a large majority of patrons. Whether they came to try a gourmet vegetarian meal or out of curiosity, he didn't know, but he basked in his success and was dying for his dad to come sample a meal.

When the maître de came into the kitchen to inform him that the rich, elderly gentleman had arrived and been seated along with a young woman, he sighed, took off his chef's hat and went out into the dining room, where the maître de led him to their table. He still had on his apron.

He saw that they'd been served wine already, so that at least relieved him from the task of discussing wines and recommending one based on what they might decide to order.

The young woman immediately brightened when she saw him approaching the table. He was a bit taken aback by her being with the old gentleman, immediately surmising him to be what Americans would refer to as her "sugar daddy," or that she was his "trophy girlfriend."

Whatever the case, he just wanted to get this over with as quickly as possible and get back to the kitchen where there were several soufflés in the process of being made for other patrons.

"Why, here's the chef, darling!" the woman purred at the old man. "Isn't he so...so 'chef-like,' don't you think?"

"Eh...eh?" remarked the old guy. "Yes, yes...quite looks like the chef and all."

"So what wonderful delicacies might you prepare for us special like?" she asked, looking Robert up and down from head to toe then back up again.

Robert felt like he was being inspected and began to feel uncomfortable. Looking more closely at the woman, he felt a sense of disgust. Women like her preyed on wealthy old men for only one reason...to grab their money. He rather felt sorry for the old guy. Despite her obvious physical charms, this woman had a hard look about her, as if she'd been around the block a few times.

Oh well, it wasn't any of his business.

"A nice red, juicy steak would suit me fine!" said the elderly man. "Haven't had a good one in a while now. Damn doctors telling me what I can and can't have..."

The woman reached over and touched his hand. "Now, now, darling, you know we all just want to keep you healthy. But..." she giggled. "I guess you can splurge tonight and have whatever you desire..."

The old guy's eyes lit up and Robert knew he wasn't thinking of the steak or food. Yech...disgusting...

"I'm not sure if you're aware or not," he interrupted, "but this is a vegetarian restaurant. We don't serve meat here, or seafood either for that matter."

Both the old man and the woman stared at him.

"No meat!?' the old guy exclaimed.

"Well, surely you can make an exception for us," the woman remarked as if it would be no big inconvenience. "My name is Hilary, by the way. I was referred to your restaurant by your brother, Thomas, who I met in Brighton the week before last. It was at your dad's concert…"

Robert raised his eyebrows. This floozy knew Thomas!?

"Then he most certainly told you Le Fonda is a vegetarian restaurant."

"Oh, well no he didn't…or it must have slipped his mind."

"No meat?" the old man said again.

"No," responded Robert. "But I'm quite certain we can prepare something to your liking. We offer quite a few egg dishes, some wonderful pasta dishes…the pasta is made fresh daily and we use only the finest ingredients along with newly picked greens and vegetables. Might I suggest a winter greens salad with radicchio, pine nuts, shaved Parmesan with an apricot balsamic vinaigrette for starters? For your main course, I can offer a mushroom risotto, which is one of our most popular dishes, with grilled lemon asparagus or one of the pasta dishes…"

"I want a steak!" interrupted the old man, banging his fist on the table.

"I'm sorry, sir, but we have no meat of any kind on the premises. We don't serve meat here at all."

The old man looked accusingly at Hilary. "You didn't tell me all they served here was a bunch of vegetables…"

"I wasn't aware, darling," she cooed at him. "Why don't we just enjoy our wine, have a taste of the salad that Robert is suggesting, then we can go get you a steak somewhere else?"

He harrumphed, but immediately cheered up when Hilary reached under the table and squeezed his knee.

She looked up at Robert. "The salad sounds wonderful! We'll both have it, I think. And, oh, by the way, I heard your dad is going to be recording a new album soon. I'm so excited about it! I'm a huge fan of his…"

Robert shifted from foot to foot uncomfortably. Now that he had their salad order, he was anxious to get away.

But Hilary continued. "I was also talking to Thomas about a cause of mine that I'd like to present to your dad. He said he was certain your dad would want to hear about it. I don't suppose you could tell me if he's back in London yet?"

She batted her eyes at him. Robert wasn't impressed.

"What is your cause?" Robert asked politely.

Hilary hedged, not wanting to get into a long conversation about something she didn't know much about, and for some reason she didn't think Robert would be as impressed about her "Save the Pigs" motto.

"Oh, it's related to animal welfare, something I'm very passionate about. I just thought if your dad was in town, I could meet with him and explain my cause..."

"Well, he's not back in town that I know of."

"And even if he was," Robert thought to himself, "you're the last person I'd let know." There was definitely something about this Hilary woman that he didn't like, but he wasn't sure what it was.

A black look came over her face for the briefest of moments before it cleared. "Well then, maybe you can just provide me with his phone number?"

"I would never give his phone number out," Robert said in an annoyed tone of voice. "If you'll excuse me now, I'll get your salads..."

"Oh, come now, Robert...you know how concerned your dad is about animal welfare. I won't give his number to anyone else."

"I'm sorry, but I can't give it out."

"Quit badgering the man, Hilary!" interrupted the old man again. "Let's just eat the damn salad and get out of here. I can almost feel an attack of the gout coming on..."

Hilary frowned before pasting another smile on her face.

"Whatever you say, darling..."

She turned back to Robert and he could see she was angry that he wouldn't divulge his dad's phone number to her. Although she was obviously a beautiful woman with a very shapely body, her angry stare made her face seem ugly. Robert shivered before bowing and beating a hasty retreat to the kitchen.

⁓◯

Thomas, Michelle and Carrie were relieved when they finally arrived back in Little Dippington and found their way to the B&B. It was past dark by the time they got there, the falling snow impeding their drive.

"I think I could use a hot toddy," remarked Thomas, stamping his feet just inside the door of the B&B. "That was a rather harrowing drive…"

"Me too!" chorused Michelle and Carrie together. All three shrugged off their coats and hung them on a coat stand next to the fireplace where a burning blaze lit the room. A beautifully decorated Christmas tree with blinking lights was next to it in the corner. The fireplace mantle was also decked out with a festive garland.

Thomas held his hands to the fire. "Rather stupid of me to forget my gloves in weather like this. My hands are frozen."

"Well, I forgot mine too," added Carrie, also moving closer to the heat.

"I was just lucky that mine were in the pocket of my jacket," said Michelle.

"Good place to keep them…very sensible…" remarked Thomas.

"Well, I'm just a sensible type of girl, you know," she teased back.

"You might just be *too* sensible for me…"

"I doubt that!"

"Thomas needs a sensible woman," interjected Carrie, leading the way to the dining room. She looked at Michelle. "Tom-tom can be a bit of a bumblehead…"

"I'm not a bumblehead! And quit calling me that!"

Michelle nudged Thomas in his side. He winked at her.

There were eight tables arranged around the room. Only one was occupied by a young couple who appeared to be finishing their meal. Carrie led Thomas and Michelle to a table near another fireplace that had a cozy fire burning on the grate.

As soon as they were seated, a plump, rosy-cheeked woman in a Christmas sweater entered the room and asked what she might get for them.

"Hot apple cider with some rum for me," said Carrie.

"Sounds good. Same for me," said Michelle.

"Coffee with a bit of whiskey for me please," responded Thomas.

"Be right back then, luvs," said the woman. "My name's Hilde by the way. I'll tell you what's for dinner tonight when I bring your drinks."

She bustled off and was soon back with three steaming mugs.

"We've got a nice brisket this evening with roasted potatoes and carrots. Cabbage salad, and for dessert, sour cherry tart." She beamed at them.

Carrie shrugged her shoulders. "I guess it's just cabbage salad and some cherry tart for me. I'm vegetarian; don't eat meat."

"Och!" Hilde exclaimed. "I have some boiled potatoes and turnips leftover from last night. I'd be happy to make you a nice mash with some butter and cream."

"Mmmm...that sounds fabulous!" chimed Michelle. "I'm also vegetarian...at least most of the time. Sometimes I eat fish." She turned to Thomas. "Are you vegetarian too?"

"No. I used to be, but ah...gave it up a couple of years back..."

"Because he had a meat-eating girlfriend," interrupted Carrie. "Our mum would have been disappointed."

"Well, she never found out. Dad was giving me a hard time about it when we were in Brighton too."

"You could always switch back, you know."

"Maybe I will...but not tonight." He turned to Hilde. "I'll have the brisket, please."

Hilde looked at the two women. "Potato and turnip mash for the both of you?"

Carrie and Michelle nodded and Hilde bustled off again.

Michelle took a sip of her drink. It felt great going down and warmed her whole body. She turned towards Carrie.

"I want to apologize again for going all crazy when I saw my mom, and I'm sorry you didn't get to really meet her or talk to her. She means a lot to me. She has her faults, but my brother and I had a good childhood. I have no complaints."

"What about your dad?" asked Carrie. "You don't have to talk about it if you don't want to, though."

Michelle sighed, not wanting to say much but feeling she had to answer the question.

"He's an attorney like I am, except he's well-known and in high demand, especially by important politicians. In the past few years, he's taken on a lot of high profile cases and has to travel a lot. He pretty much is all wrapped up in it and didn't have time for Mom anymore. He even bought a condo...I think you call them flats here... downtown near his office and started staying there instead of coming home. Then...uh, there was an affair he had with one of his paralegals named Melanie...."

Carrie nodded her head in understanding. "Ah, so sad for your mum. I'm sorry for you and your brother, Steven, who you told me about on the drive. Our mum was always worried about Dad straying on her, but to my knowledge he never did, isn't that right, Thomas?"

Thomas nodded and Carrie continued. "Whenever we went places as a family, there were always women throwing themselves at him. I don't know how Mum put up with it, but they loved each other deeply up until the day she passed..."

"And it drove the tabloid people crazy," interjected Thomas. "They were always trying to dig up dirt on Dad. He had a pretty bad reputation regarding women in his younger days, and I guess they figured he'd likely be cheating on Mum, but he never did...at least not that we know of..."

"We were all worried about him," added Carrie, "after Mum died. He went into a severe depression. I stayed with him in our Colorado retreat where she passed, and I was finally able to convince him to close up the house there and come back to England. The house he has outside of London is one he bought when Mum was sick. He thought he'd be bringing her back to it to recover…but she never got to see it."

Michelle could see tears in Carrie's eyes and reached out her hand to touch Carrie's. "I'm sorry for you and your family too then. It must have been very hard for all of you."

Just then, Hilde arrived carrying a tray with platters of food on it and set everything on the table. "There you go, luvs. I hope you enjoy it. I'll bring out some glasses of water. Let me know if you need or want anything else."

They all thanked her and Thomas wasted no time digging into his meal. All three of them were hungry as they'd only grabbed a quick luncheon of sandwiches and crisps on the way from London.

"Delicious!" exclaimed Michelle, taking a bite of the potato turnip mash. "I don't think I've ever had this before."

"We make a lot of mashes here in the UK," responded Carrie. "You can do it with just about any vegetable and potatoes. Mum used to make them from time to time, but Dad never cared for them. He would tease her about her mushy mash."

Thomas laughed. "He did, didn't he?"

Carrie took a bite of the cabbage salad, declaring it to be quite good. "I remember she wanted to put a mash recipe in her cookbook, but Dad said 'No.' She was disappointed."

"Your mom wrote a cookbook?" inquired Michelle.

"Oh yes!" exclaimed Carrie. "It was one of the things Mum did put her foot down and argue with him about. He thought he should be able to approve all the recipes she put in it, and it had to be things only he liked. She ignored him."

"And," interjected Thomas. "He was jealous of the bloke who came to take the food photos. Whenever he came to take pictures, Dad always made sure to be around and to mosey into the kitchen. I thought it was funny."

Michelle smiled, enjoying the family stories. "My mom loves to cook too, and so do I. She was teasing me that we should write a cookbook together someday, but we never made time…"

"Maybe you can make time now!" said Thomas, starting on his salad.

"How? Where?"

"Maybe at Dad's house outside London. We're all going there for Christmas as I told you, and now that your mum has that ring back on her finger, well…"

Carrie took a sip of water. "Or, maybe at Robert's restaurant. He might even help…but the cookbook would have to be vegetarian, of course."

Michelle started to feel uncomfortable, but the hot toddy she'd drank right before the food was served also made her feel mellow. "I'm not sure what to say…I mean, I have a job back in the states…I have clients…Dad is covering for me, but he has his own clients. I can't expect him to do my work for me. We're partners in the firm."

A forlorn look passed across Thomas's face. "But I don't want you to leave, Michelle…you have to at least be here for Christmas with us and your mum…then maybe I can fly back to the states with you and meet your dad and brother. We can have a holiday in California, maybe even go to Disneyland again, and then…well…"

Michelle suddenly started to feel a bit panicky. "I…I guess I can stay for Christmas then, but…after that, well…it would be better if I went back by myself at first…and…uh, you could come a few weeks later. I'd need to work and do some catching up before I could do any vacationing…"

Oh my god! Had she really just said all that!? There was no way she could get on an airplane and fly back to the future any more than there was a way that Thomas could follow her a few weeks later!

Deftly, she changed the subject. "I really like the cookbook idea, and I'm also looking forward to meeting your brother, Robert. I'm sure my mom would like the idea too."

"Maybe you could put in your butter recipe," Thomas teased.

Carrie raised her eyebrows.

"Stop it, Thomas," Michelle said, blushing.

"She makes butter in a rainbow of colors," Thomas continued, ignoring Michelle's pink face. "I think the last time she made it a few days ago, it was blue…"

"No, it was orange," said Michelle, smiling.

Hilde arrived with the cherry tart and removed the empty platters. The three diners immediately took spoons and dug in for a taste.

"Lovely," commented Carrie. "But I'm stuffed to the gills. I think when I'm done with this, I'll go up to my room and leave the two of you alone. It's been a long day for me flying in from Italy this morning and I'm quite knackered."

"I might have another hot toddy and sit in front of the fire in the main room," remarked Thomas, taking another bite of the tart.

"That sounds good to me," said Michelle.

They talked some more until the tarts were consumed. Carrie excused herself for bed, gave both Thomas and Michelle a hug then headed upstairs to her room. Thomas and Michelle ordered their hot toddies and went to sit in front of the fire next to the Christmas tree.

Chapter 27

Thomas Asks Michelle to Marry Him

Susan retrieved her pieces of clothing that were scattered about and around the couch and re-dressed herself after James's most recent sweet assault on her body. He was softly snoring there and she covered him with a blanket before going into the kitchen to resume dinner preparations. It wasn't long before the smell of frying onions, potatoes and peppers filled the cottage and woke James up. He pulled on his jeans and came to stand behind her.

"Mmmm...you were quite delightful, you know..." he murmured in her ear while at the same time planting soft kisses down each side of her neck.

"Thank you...you were quite fine yourself..."

Chill bumps shivered down her body. She elbowed him in the stomach. "Stop that! You're making me feel all tingly again, and I don't want to feel all tingly again..."

"Why not?"

He wrapped his arms around her and began tickling her ear with his tongue.

"Because I'm cooking...and...ahhhh...ohhhh...because..."

She broke free from him and turned around. "And because you're hungry!"

He smiled at her wickedly.

"I'm not all that hungry...for food, that is..."

"I mean it James, let me finish making dinner."

"Are you denying me?"

"Denying you what!? We just did it! How could you want more right now!?"

"Maybe because I'm Mr. Rabbit…do you remember calling me that?"

"I remember very well…"

"Good."

He reached behind her and turned off the stove burner before spinning her around and grabbing her in an embrace then claiming her mouth with his. The spoon she'd been using to stir the potatoes clattered to the floor. She could feel his erection poking into her belly. When she wriggled to try and get away, he just held her tighter with one arm and put his other hand on the back of her head so she couldn't pull away from his kiss. When his tongue invaded her mouth, she slumped and gave in to the passion that was once again building up inside her.

Damn the man for what he did to her!!

Releasing her, he took her hand and pulled her over towards the kitchen table, lifting up the sides of her sweater then pulling it up over her head in one swift movement. A moment later, her bra was unhooked, her jeans and panties pulled down and off and he had her naked on her back on the kitchen table.

Looking up at him, she could see the fire smoldering in his eyes and when her gaze moved down, she saw his stiff member spring out of his jeans as he unbuttoned them.

She was stunned at his over-the-top libido that she thought to be quite unusual for a man nearing sixty years old. But, on the other hand, she knew from being with him for the past week that it took almost nothing, sometimes just a look, to make him want her. It was quite wonderful actually, her own libido being a match to his.

She screamed when he entered her, wrapping her ankles around his neck and scooting her bottom forward to him to take him in deeper. Her chest was heaving at the intense pleasure she was feeling and she could sense herself throbbing around his shaft as he slowly withdrew then plunged back in again inch by slow and tortuous inch.

The slow speed of his thrusts made her anxious and she urged him to speed up, wiggling her hips up against him, but he refused to cooperate, looking into her half-closed eyes then reaching forward to fondle her breasts and tweak her nipples.

Her head thrashed from side to side on the hard wooden table, her hands gripping the edges. She was so close to her release, the angle of his strokes hitting the back side of her pleasure point. A fleeting thought passed through her brain that it must be what was called the "g-spot," and James seemed to know exactly where it was and how to manipulate himself inside her to give her the most pleasure possible.

But, he kept stilling inside her, holding himself back to prolong their love-making. It was driving her near mad and she knew very well that he was aware of what it was doing to her.

She pleaded for him to speed up again, crying out for release and an end to the sweet torture.

"Beg me some more, Susan..." he hissed, stilling inside her again, tilting his head back and closing his eyes.

She could see his nostrils flaring as he sought to stay in control and dominate her.

Susan screamed again as he began to pick up the pace. "Yes! Oh my God, yes!!!"

But then he stilled once more and leaned over her pinning her arms to the table. The angle of his body brought him even deeper inside her and it almost felt as if there was a sliver of pain mixed in with the pleasure.

"Beg me, Susan...tell me what you want..."

She looked up at him in a daze, throbbing for the need of her release.

"Beg me! Say it!!"

Her head tossed from side to side.

"Say it!! You know what I want you to say!"

Any and all self-control she had remaining, left her. "Fuck me, James!!! Pleassseee! Fuck me!!!!!"

Hearing the profane words, words that she told him she would never say, threw him over the top and he began to frantically pump

257

in and out of her. She met each and every thrust, lifting her bottom off the table, and within seconds they were both loudly groaning out their climax as he spilled his hot liquid into her.

Panting heavily, he collapsed on top of her, her ankles slipping off the back of his neck and her legs flopping down around his hips.

Susan's eyes were closed as her whole body continued to convulse and quiver. She had never experienced pleasure, combined with torment, to this level ever before in her entire life and she felt totally spent and undone by it.

A minute passed before James pushed himself up and off her, standing up and pulling her into his arms as he always did after he made love to her.

He rubbed his face with his five o'clock shadow across her cheek before kissing her deeply and passionately. His hands roamed up and down her bare back.

When he gently pushed her away from him, their eyes locked.

"Your enthusiasm never ceases to amaze me, Susan. I could love you over and over and over and never stop..."

"I can't help myself...you do things to me...and I have no control..."

He smirked at her. "I liked hearing you beg...saying those words..."

She blushed, remembering what she'd yelled and feeling embarrassed about it. They'd come unbidden and out of the blue. She'd never used those profane words with him in regard to sex before, just in general cussing. In fact, she'd told him that she didn't like that word used related to intimacy, insisting on the words, "love-making."

"Hearing how much you wanted me sent me over the edge, you know...I just might be having you beg me again sometime..."

She felt the heat in her face and bit her lip, suddenly not knowing what to say. She wasn't so sure she liked being so out of control and at his mercy. And she knew he'd pushed her to say words she didn't want to just to demonstrate the control he had over her.

He pushed his jeans off his hips and down to the floor where he kicked them off, leaving him naked before her.

"Let's just forget about dinner for now and have a bit of a lay down. I just want to hold you and feel you against me."

She yawned. "Okay…but no more sex or begging for now, okay? And please, James, don't make me say those words again…"

He smirked before taking her hand and leading her into the bedroom.

"Of course, Susan…of course…but I'm not promising…"

He winked and squeezed her hand. She wasn't amused.

⤳

Thomas and Michelle talked for two hours in front of the fire, enjoying another hot toddy and the Christmas music that the B&B had playing in the background. Although they were both tired, they felt keyed up after what had occurred at Auntie Annabelle's cottage, especially Michelle.

"I'm still in shock over my mom and your dad. I'm still furious over whatever happened to her face, and then seeing your dad put that ring on her finger…well, I just can't believe it really happened!"

"I was a bit shocked myself. Like I said, I've never known my dad to strike a person, and I'm sorry it upset you. I understand how you would feel, considering your job ad all…But, you know what the ring means, don't you?"

Michelle looked down at her lap, twisting her fingers. "Yes…but… but…"

"But what?'

She took a deep breath before looking up into his face. The few drinks she'd had were loosening her up. Should she tell him the truth about her and her mom…about time travel? That her mom was married? That she herself was engaged? Would he believe her…?

No!

She caught herself just in time. "I…I think he expects her to replace your mom, and…and, that she should be just like her…but she's not and…"

Thomas took her hands in his. "You think too much and you're just complicating things. Shut off that solicitor's brain of yours. Dad knows your mum is different. I think he likes that she's different."

"But what if she pisses him off again and he…"

Thomas put his hand over her mouth before she could say more. "Let's not talk about your mum and my dad anymore, please?" He gave her a pleading look before removing his hand.

"Okay."

"I'd much rather talk about us."

"Okay. What about us?"

"Well, I realize we haven't know each other that long, but…" He squeezed her hand. "What if I were to slip a ring on your finger, Michelle…?"

Her eyes opened wide. "What are you saying!?"

"I think I'm saying…I'm saying that I've fallen head over heels in love with you…and that I want to marry you…"

Michelle just stared at him.

"Not marry right away, of course…I'd want to do the right thing… go see your dad and ask for his blessing and all…"

She was still left speechless, her thoughts whirling in her head like a tornado.

He stood up and looked down at her. "I do recall you telling me you were falling in love with me too?" he asked, a worried expression coming over his face. "Please tell me you meant it…Please tell me that you have…"

"Oh Thomas!" she wailed, leaping out of her chair and throwing herself into his arms.

His mouth came down on hers and they kissed hungrily, their hands roaming over each other, up and down arms and backs.

Michelle was the first to draw away, so caught up in her own emotions that she could barely think at all.

"I do love you, Thomas…I do!"

They kissed again before Thomas put an arm around her waist and led her upstairs to their assigned bedroom.

Chapter 28

Hilary Closes In

Hilary was extremely agitated. She was getting nowhere in her quest to track down James and put herself in front of him. And, she knew that as each day went by and he was with the Susan bitch, the harder it would be to capture him.

She paced the flat of the old gent's impatiently, waiting for Marcus to call her. It was mid-afternoon the day after she'd gone to Le Fonda and tried to worm information out of James's other son, Robert. Marcus had called her that morning to let her know that he might have discovered some information on Susan that she would find most interesting and that would ensure that Hilary could replace her in James's life.

When her phone rang, she answered right away. "Well?" Smoke blew out her nose from the cigarette she was smoking.

"Good news at last, Luv...The Susan woman is married!" He paused waiting for Hilary to absorb his words. "As in...she's not available. She's not even separated. I suspect James doesn't know..."

Hilary stubbed out her cigarette and sat down, a satisfied grin on her face. "Oh really? That *is* most interesting. So, how did you find out? And, what's she doing here then?"

"I called the solicitor's office again and spoke to some receptionist girl. Made up a story about having a jewelry gift ready to deliver for Donald's wife...you remember that was the name of the solicitor bloke I spoke to? It was the phone number that the daughter, Michelle put on the hotel registration at the Claridon in Brighton. I just had a hunch…and it paid off! Susan, the mum, is married to Donald."

"Very clever of you, Marcus. What else were you able to find out?"

"The receptionist was very chatty. Told me she was just filling in for the regular one who was out sick. Anyway, we started talking and I found out that Susan is Donald's wife and that they've been married for 29 years."

"Go on."

"She then told me something that I found quite odd. She said that Susan was expected in the office later and that she and Donald were going out to luncheon together. She suggested I drop by with the jewelry delivery while they were both out and that she'd give the package to Donald later in case it was a surprise for Susan."

"Maybe it's not the same Susan then! She can't be over here in England and in California at the same time!!"

"No, no…it *is* the right Susan. I verified that the daughter is also a solicitor named Michelle and that there is a brother, Steven. Has to be the right one!"

"Well, that does seem terribly strange. Since the girl is just filling in, maybe she has it wrong about Susan coming in. Must be looking at an appointment calendar wrong or something."

"Most likely. She did sound rather young and scatter-brained, and to give all that information to me, a stranger, well…"

"Who cares?! You found out what I needed to know. James is fucking a married woman and she's not available. I imagine she wouldn't like her husband to find out…"

"Most likely not."

"Thanks, Marcus. I think I can take things over from here then. I was able to find out that James is expected back at Cherry Studios the day before Christmas for an interview on his new album. The news is actually in the tabloids. I imagine the paparazzi will all be there hounding him. The Susan woman will most likely be with him…And I will most certainly be there myself!"

After an hour of cuddling and dozing, Susan coaxed James into letting her get up to make dinner. After they ate and Susan cleaned up the dishes and kitchen, she went into the main room and sat next to James on the couch. He had his guitar and was testing out the melodies he'd be recording the week after Christmas and wanted her to listen.

She settled back into the cushions, her bare feet up on the coffee table next to James's while he played and sang, losing herself in every note and in the sound of his voice.

She must be the luckiest woman in the world, being here with him like this, listening to the most talented musician and most handsome man in the world, who had just placed an engagement ring on her finger. As she gazed at him and listened to his voice, she had to pinch herself to believe that this was real. That after all the heartbreak she'd endured because of him...and all the pain he'd endured because of her...that at long last, her dream was coming true.

She'd already made the decision to stay in the past with him this time and nothing or no one was going to stop her. There were complications to figure out as far as her life in the future was concerned, but she was sure that if she and Michelle put their heads together, they'd be able to figure it out. She knew that Michelle now understood her obsession with James and wanted her mom to be happy.

She looked down at the *little sparkler* on her left hand and her heart gave a lurch as her newfound happiness and love for James washed over her. Being back at the cottage with him had rekindled so many memories for her, and even though not all of them were good, the good ones were the only ones she thought about.

She remembered James playing ballet barre music for her as he watched her do plies right before she put the *Sleeping Beauty* record on and danced around the room to her favorite '*Once Upon a Dream*' song. She remembered cooking for him, walking down the lane to Little Dippington holding hands, sketching pictures up on the hill above the cottage and their picnic under the tree.

But most of all, she remembered the time they spent in each other's arms, holding and loving each other.

He truly was her obsession.

James finished playing his last song for the new album and was staring at Susan, who appeared to have her head in the clouds.

"A penny for your thoughts..." he said, startling her.

She blinked then smiled at him. "I was just remembering back to all those years ago when you brought me here...our picnic up on the hill and how I almost fell in the pond..."

"But I rescued you...and we came back to the cottage where you let me make love to you for the first time..."

"*You* remember too? I didn't think you would...I mean, men don't remember back that far, do they? And besides, with all the other women you..."

"You were my first and only virgin, Susan. You gave a precious gift to me...how could I have forgotten? How could I ever forget? And... men *do* remember things you know...especially their first true love."

"Was I your first true love?"

"Yes. I believe I told you so before."

They gazed into each other's eyes for a moment, their love for each other written clearly on their faces. It was as if they were frozen in time and wanted to keep it that way.

James broke the silence. "So, what would you have me play for you now?"

She thought for a few seconds then smiled. "How about '*Not Before You?*' It's always been one of my favorites."

He strummed the strings of the guitar before starting in.

"I saw stars in the sky but I never saw them shining...

No, I didn't see them before...not before you..."

Tears welled in her eyes, but she didn't break hers away from his as she joined in.

"And there was sunshine...

And beautiful sweet peas...

That sent out fragrance reminding of you...

There were birds all around...

264

But I never heard their chirping…
No, I didn't hear them before…
Not before you…
Not before you…"

James was overcome with emotion as he gazed into Susan's emerald green eyes that hadn't changed one bit in the years they'd been apart. It had been one of the first things to mesmerize him when they'd first met and he still found them captivating.

In fact, from a physical sense, he still found her quite captivating and excessively desirable. Yes, the word would be "excessively." He seemed to be in constant need of her, wanting to touch her, feel her, taste her…be one with her. The way she molded herself against him when they slept brought him comfort. The way she writhed and wriggled beneath him as he thrust himself inside her drove him near insane with desire. The way she screamed her release and quivered beneath him in throes of passion made him lose his senses. And he wondered if she knew to what extent it was *she* who controlled him in their physical relationship and not the other way around.

He smiled. Well, he didn't think that was something he really wanted her to know…that she had something over him…

Once they were married, he'd make it clear to her that *he* would be the one in charge, and there would be no argument on it. Her opinions would always be welcomed and considered, but all final decisions would be his. That's the way it had always been with his other Susan and that's the way it would be with this one too. It's what he was accustomed to.

And he was quite certain she would come to accept it without too much of a fuss. He knew that, just like she had a hold on him, he had one on her as well. He reached up and touched his chest, feeling the necklace beneath his shirt and wondered if he should give it back to her.

Could the necklace cause him to have some kind of hold on her? And did the ring tie them together in some way as well? He didn't really believe in magic or the supernatural, but it was certainly something to think about. If the necklace did bind her to him in some way, he wasn't sure if he wanted to give it back to her.

She noticed the gesture to his chest and looked into his eyes. It was almost as if they could read each other's thoughts.

"You'd like me to give your necklace back to you, wouldn't you?"

She nodded. "I've told you before that my grandfather gave it to me when I was twelve years old...it's sentimental to me..."

"It is to me as well... Do you really think it holds some kind of magic that ties us together somehow?"

"I told you I don't know...but if it does, then so does the ring..." She looked down at her left hand. "Until the night of your concert at the Dusky, I'd worn it on the necklace...I'd worn it there for..." She counted the years back in her mind. "For 32 years...so, I think it must hold the same magic...if there is such a thing..."

He thought for a moment then slowly reached up around his neck and lifted the chain of the necklace up and over his head. "Then you can have this back, Susan. I shouldn't have ripped it away from you like I did, but I thought it would make sure that you'd never leave me again."

She gave a sigh of relief as she bowed her head for him to slip the chain over her head. The necklace slid down onto her neck, the silver ballerina shoes once again resting on her chest.

"You don't have to worry about me ever leaving you again. Magic or no magic, James...I'm yours forever this time..."

Thomas loved Michelle over and over again throughout the night before they both fell into an exhausted and satisfied sleep entwined in each other's arms.

The sun was just coming up when Michelle untangled herself from Thomas's embrace and got out of bed to use the loo. Coming back into the room, she saw that the sun was shining and went to sit on the window seat, a hair brush in one hand. She looked out the mullioned windows onto the glistening snow as she slowly pulled the brush through her hair.

Glancing at the bed, her breath caught in her throat at the sight of Thomas who had his face turned towards her on the pillow, his sensuous lips slightly parted, his long eyelashes sweeping down onto his cheeks, his dark silky hair spread out around his head. He was the most gorgeous and desirable man she'd ever seen.

The resemblance to his dad was remarkable. It was as if he was a younger version of the man her mother had fallen so deeply in love with all those years ago.

Unlike his dad, however, he was accepting and understanding of her independent nature, admiring her accomplishments and interested in her ideas and thoughts. He was a good listener, had a quiet yet sunny disposition without an ounce of arrogance. And, as an added bonus, he was a fantastic lover, bringing her to heights of passion that she didn't even know were possible.

How could so many wonderful things be wrapped up in one man?

And, how could she ever bear to leave him? How could she accept going back to the future, knowing what awaited her there, while she had the opportunity to experience immeasurable joy, passion and happiness here in the past?

Sensing her presence and that she was staring at him, Thomas blinked his eyes open. A slow, seductive smile spread across his face as his eyes met hers.

Taking his hand out from under the pillow, he crooked his finger at her. The hair brush fell from her hand to the floor as she stood up and smiled back at him. A moment later, she was back under the covers with him.

Susan also got up as the sun was rising, padding into the kitchen on bare feet to put on a pot of coffee. There was a chill in the cottage, so she checked the thermostat for the heating system and turned the heat up a few degrees. She thought of going back to bed to keep warm until the coffee was done, but knew she'd likely wake James up and he'd then keep her there.

They'd stayed up the previous night until the wee hours, something James was accustomed to doing. He was definitely a night owl and told her that the early morning hours were his most creative and productive time when it came to his music.

And, she was an early bird, loving to watch the sun rise over the horizon with a hot, steaming cup of coffee in one hand, hearing the birds chirp and seeing morning dew on the plants and flowers.

She sighed as she stretched her arms up over her head. Was she going to have to change her sleeping habits to conform to James's? Or, would he be willing to compromise?

She didn't think the word "compromise" was in his vocabulary. She would likely have to get used to being a night owl along with him. A frown found its way onto her face as she sat down at the kitchen table, coffee mug in front of her, and looked out at the sparkling snow. She would miss the early mornings and watching the sun rise.

Just how much would her life have to change once she was married to James? Could she accept his dictates? Would she fit into his style of life?

While it was true he seemed content and happy to be with her at the cottage, she could tell that he sometimes seemed restless, and knew he was used to living in a much larger space. She also knew that he was accustomed to having hired help jump at his every request and provide him with all the household services that she was now doing for him. He'd remarked a few times that she shouldn't be scrubbing floors or cleaning the bathroom, that he could get someone to come in from the village to do it.

But she didn't want someone to come in from the village to do things she was used to doing her whole life and that she didn't mind doing. Back in the future, Donald had told her on several occasions to hire a housekeeper to come in once a week, and for a while, she had one. But, truth be told, she didn't mind doing the cleaning herself and, besides keeping her busy, she got a certain sense of satisfaction from it.

Was James's house outside of London a monstrosity of a mansion, bigger than the one he had back in 1967 when she was last with him? Would it be filled with servants and butlers and grounds keepers? She hoped not, but thought it likely was. He probably even had a personal chef who would ban her from the kitchen.

Susan loved their cozy little love nest at Auntie Annabelle's cottage, and when James got up a couple of hours later and told her he wanted to go back to London the next morning, she was severely disappointed.

"We'll need to make wedding plans, you know," he said, sitting down at the kitchen table as she placed a cup of tea in front of him. "It's only 11 days until Christmas, plus I need to go into Cherry Studios on the 24th to check on the setup and to give an interview to the press about the new album."

"But, I like it here! I thought we were going to stay until my bruise went away."

She spread butter and jam on his toast before setting the plate on the table in front of him along with a cheese omelet she'd prepared.

He took a bite of toast, chewed and swallowed. "You can put some makeup on to cover it up. You'll be needing to settle into the house and meet the staff, plus we'll need to go to the Registry Office for a marriage license. There's a requirement for blood tests now too, so we'll have to get that done as well."

She sat down across from him as he dug into the omelet. "Please, James, can we just stay here a few more days, like maybe until the weekend? I like being alone with you and talking to you and having you sing to me like you did last night, and…"

"I can still spend alone time with you, talk to you and sing to you at my house. No, Susan, we'll leave tomorrow morning. I'll call to have the rental car picked up and hire another one to drive us back. It's a good 3 hours from here to London, or if Thomas, Carrie and Michelle are going back tomorrow, maybe we can ride with them."

"But I have a lot of cleaning to do and we have stuff in the fridge and…"

"I'll have someone from the village come in to take care of it all, maybe even that Angie woman that took over Emily's shop. All you need to do is pack our clothes and personal things."

Susan's face scrunched up at the mention of Angie. She was quite certain Angie would just *love* to do anything for James as besotted with him as she was.

Just then, the phone rang. It was Thomas.

"So, Dad...Michelle, Carrie and I just had breakfast. Michelle and I are going to do the tourist thing around Little Dippington today, look in the shops and stuff, and then we thought you and her mum might want to come into the village for dinner at the B&B. I can request a special vegetarian meal for the five of us."

James took his last bite of toast. "Oh no. I think I mentioned last night that Susan would be cooking dinner for us." He winked at Susan. She scowled back, but he didn't notice.

"I hate to put her to all that trouble."

"It's no trouble. She loves to cook, and..." he winked at her again. "She's a very good cook to boot."

Susan scowled again, grabbed his empty plates off the table and marched over to the sink where she noisily deposited them before turning on the water.

So! Was this the way it was going to be then? Being bossed around and told what to do or not do every minute of every day? As she finished washing and rinsing each dish, she clattered them loudly into the dish drainer on the kitchen counter and noisily tossed the silverware in the drawer tray after drying them.

James ended his call with Thomas and leaned back in the chair observing Susan's stiffened back, knowing she was angry or upset about something, but not knowing what it was.

"Are you angry about something?"

No response.

"Don't you want to make dinner tonight? You love to cook so much, I thought you'd like to, especially with Michelle. Remember, you told me how you taught her to cook and that you always had so much fun cooking together when she was growing up?"

"I remember."

"So, what's the problem then?"

"There's no problem."

James put his tongue in his cheek, knowing she was lying and was upset about something, but before he could say anything else, she trounced out of the kitchen and went into the bathroom, slamming the door behind her. He immediately got up from the kitchen chair and went over to knock on the bathroom door. He was starting to feel irritated.

"Susan, what's wrong?"

When he received no response, he knocked again before opening the door. Susan had a spray bottle of cleaning fluid in one hand and a cleaning rag in the other. She was furiously polishing the mirror above the bathroom sink. She glanced over to look at him when the door opened, but then turned and resumed cleaning the mirror. When she was done, she sprayed fluid in the sink and continued cleaning, ignoring him completely.

James pursed his lips. "I told you I'd have someone come in from the village to do the cleaning."

"And I told you I wanted to do it myself."

"I don't want you cleaning and scrubbing floors like some kind of washer woman."

"Well, I don't care what you want. I'm doing the cleaning myself!"

James pursed his lips again before grabbing the spray bottle and rag out of her hands, tossing them into the bathroom sink and dragging her out into the main room where he pushed her down onto the couch. When she started to jump up, he pushed her back down, putting his hands on each side of her head on the back of the couch.

"Quit being so obstinate, Susan! I mean it!! I don't know what it is about you sometimes. It's almost like you deliberately want to thwart me!"

Susan crossed her arms over her chest and turned her head away from him.

He signed in exasperation. "Do you think you're going to be scrubbing floors at our London house after we're married? Do you

271

know how inappropriate it would be? I have an army of people to take care of those things!"

He began to lose patience with her when she refused to respond again. "Susan! Look at me, damn you! Your life is about to change! Drastically! I've been living a different lifestyle than you since we were last together. I have staff to take care of my every need. I have security around me constantly. You're going to be part of my life and are going to have to accustom yourself to the way I live. Don't you understand that?!"

She turned to look at him. "I understand." Then she turned her face away again.

It was the last straw for James. He pushed back from the couch and looked down at her. "Do you really want to marry me or not? My concert at the Dusky was just the beginning for me getting back out there. To involve myself in my music again. It's a new beginning for me artistically as well as for you and me together. I want you to be a part of my life, but if you don't want to, then tell me now, dammit! … you can give me the ring back and go…"

She gasped and turned to look into his face. What she saw there frightened her. His eyes were blazing. He meant what he said.

And, she realized he was right. His life had changed a thousand fold compared to hers, which actually hadn't changed at all. He was rich and famous, pampered and sought after. Guarded and protected. And, now that he'd come out of seclusion, he was also back in the public spotlight and in all the newspapers and tabloids. After they were married, she would be in the public eye as well. It suddenly seemed very daunting to her.

She stood up and moved forward to place her hands on his chest.

"I *do* want to marry you! I *do* want to be a part of your life! There's nothing I want more!!" Tears welled in the back of her eyes. "I'm sorry, James…I'm so sorry…You mean the world to me…you…you can call someone in from the village to clean the cottage then…I'm sorry…I just feel…so…so *inadequate!*"

He enfolded her in his arms, rubbing his hands up and down her back, as she softly cried into his shoulder. A moment later, he gently pushed her away and they both sat down on the couch. He took both of her hands in his.

"I know it's not going to be easy for you to adapt to my way of life, and sometimes I wish I didn't have to live the way I do, but there's nothing I can do about it. I need you to understand that. There are things you need to learn and do, not just to conform to my lifestyle, but to keep yourself safe as well."

She nodded at him and he continued.

"Another reason I want to get to London sooner is because you'll be needing to get new clothes as well as get to know the staff and my security people."

"New clothes?! What's wrong with my clothes?!"

"There's nothing wrong with your clothes, but once you're out in public with me, everyone will be looking at you as well as the staff who do our laundry and who will know the quality of what you wear. Word will get out that you get your clothes from a charity shop. It will embarrass us both."

Susan's mouth dropped open as she looked down at the Sears jeans and Mervyn's sweater she was wearing.

James lifted her left hand up.

"And this ring...when people see this ring, especially the paparazzi, you'll be laughed at. You can wear it when we're alone together, but when we're out, I'll need to get you something bigger and nicer to wear along with some necklaces and other jewelry." He looked at her ears. "And we'll need to get your ears pierced so you can wear earrings."

She began to shake her head. This all seemed to suddenly be too much. She snatched her hand away from him. "No! I'm *not* taking off this ring!! It means too much to me! To *us*! Please, James...please don't make me take off the ring!" She looked at him imploringly.

He sighed. "Well...okay. You can keep that ring on, but you can wear another, bigger one along with it in addition to a wedding band. I'll need a wedding band as well."

He looked her up and down again, but before he could say anything else, she spoke up. "Please don't make me change my hair or cut it off...please..."

He smiled at her before pulling her into his arms. "No, no...you don't need to change a thing about your hair. I love your long hair... especially when you're naked and it falls down around you like Lady Godiva..."

He planted several kisses on the side of her neck before reaching up to the back of her head where there was a clip holding her hair up in a knot. He removed the clip and it fell down around her shoulders and arms. He loved taking the clip out of her hair. He loved it even more when she stood in front of him after stripping her clothes off, and did it herself with a seductive and knowing smile on her face.

Susan pressed herself into him, wrapping her arms around his waist as he continued to press small kisses on her neck, then her cheek, before capturing her mouth with his. His hands roamed up and down her back tantalizingly, and they both began to feel a familiar stirring in their nether parts.

"I think I want to ravish you..." he panted into her ear, nipping on her earlobe.

"I think I'd like to be ravished," she responded, reaching down to the front of his trousers and giving his crotch a squeeze.

Chapter 29

Plans for a Double Wedding

Thomas, Michelle and Carrie arrived at the cottage for dinner shortly after 4:00 in the afternoon. They brought a half dozen bottles of wine with them. One was a bottle of champagne that Carrie insisted on bringing to celebrate her dad's engagement to Susan. All three assumed that when James slipped the ring back on her finger the afternoon before, it meant they were engaged. The fact that James hadn't actually *asked* Susan to marry him didn't seem the least bit odd to Thomas or Carrie, but Michelle had been a bit annoyed about it.

Susan, as usual, was in the kitchen when the knock came on the door. She was chopping lettuce for a salad. James was putting more wood in the fireplace. The day had turned gloomy again and it looked like more snow was on the way. He went to answer the door.

"You sure have lousy weather here," commented Michelle, taking off her gloves and shoving them into her jacket pocket before taking it off and hanging it on the coat rack next to the front door.

"You don't need to rub in that you're from the land of sunshine, you know," responded Thomas, shrugging his coat off. After hanging it up, he went over to the fireplace and gave James a hug.

"Hey, Dad, need any help with the wood?"

"No thanks. I brought more in this morning."

After hanging her coat up, Carrie gave her dad a one-armed hug and a kiss on the cheek, holding up the champagne bottle in one hand.

"Look what I brought! It's to celebrate your engagement!"

Michelle joined Susan in the kitchen then also gave her a hug after setting two sacks on the kitchen counter next to the fridge. Susan raised her eyebrows.

"What did you bring? We really don't need anything at this point. James informed me we're leaving here and going to London tomorrow."

Michelle sensed she wasn't very happy about it. "You are? What about your eye?" She looked critically at her mom, who had obviously gone to great lengths to cover her bruises with makeup and had to admit that it was barely noticeable. She opened the door to the fridge.

Susan saw her take bottles of wine out of the sacks and start to put them in the fridge.

"Remember only white gets chilled, not the red…"

"I know, Mom. Do you think I forgot or that I'm just stupid?"

"Neither! I was just reminding you is all. And my eye is looking a lot better. I don't think anyone will notice. But…" Her voice turned to a whisper. "I still don't want to go to London tomorrow. I was really wanting to stay here longer."

"But, you have no choice, do you?" Michelle whispered back. "I'm assuming James told you that you're going to London, so you're going to London."

"How did you know?"

"Well, maybe you can't, but I can read him like a book. I can spot a control freak a mile away…Are you sure you know what you're getting into, Mom? You would never in a million years let Dad treat you the way you do James."

But, Susan couldn't respond as James, Thomas and Carrie came into the kitchen, Carrie in search of wine glasses to pour up the champagne.

Michelle located the cabinet with glasses. There were at least a dozen wine glasses on the top shelf too high up for her to reach. She looked at Thomas, pointing to them, and he reached up and took down five.

"Ugh…dusty…looks like they need washed."

He carried them over to the sink and turned on the water. Michelle took over and washed them. Thomas dried. Carrie popped the cork on the champagne and, as Thomas handed the glasses around, she carefully filled each one.

"So, Dad, how about if you propose the toast?"

James went to stand next to Susan, a tender smile on his face. He held his glass up and everyone followed suit.

"To a Christmas wedding!" he said, bumping his glass first against Susan's then against the other three, who all suddenly raised their eyebrows in surprise. James and Susan took a sip, the others following.

"Christmas!!?" exclaimed Michelle. "That's only...only 10 days from now!"

James looked at her. "Which is why I decided we need to get to London sooner than we originally planned. I had my rental car picked up this afternoon and hired a car to drive us there tomorrow morning."

"You're going back tomorrow?" Carrie looked at Susan's face to check for signs of the bruise and saw that it was no longer noticeable but she didn't comment on it, not wanting to bring up the subject.

Thomas took another sip of champagne. "We were thinking of staying another day and driving out to King's Head to visit the aunties tomorrow. I'd like to introduce Michelle to them."

"I'd like to see them again," interjected Susan. "I haven't seen them in forever, and..." She looked at James. "Please, James...can we stay one more day and go with them to see your aunties?"

"We're going to London tomorrow morning, Susan. It's all arranged."

"But, it would only be for one day more...Please?" She looked at him pleadingly and Michelle felt disgusted hearing her mother beg. She schooled her face into a blank stare.

"No, Susan. Don't ask again."

Thomas and Carrie, hearing their dad's tone of voice, knew that was the end of the conversation but felt uncomfortable when they saw Susan's disappointed face. It was very similar to what they'd sometimes seen on their mum's face when James put his foot down about something.

Michelle's hand tightened on her wine glass, but she said nothing averting her eyes from her mom's face.

"I invited them to come to your London house for Christmas, like I said I would," said Carrie, trying to change the atmosphere in the room. "They said they'd be delighted. So, that means they can come to the wedding!"

Thomas, also sensing Susan's disappointment as well as Michelle's simmering anger over watching her mom being dictated to, emptied the remaining contents of the champagne bottle into each glass and proposed another toast to a happy future.

"So, what are we making for dinner, Mom," asked Michelle, setting her empty glass on the kitchen counter and changing the subject entirely away from the engagement, the wedding or the aunties.

Susan brightened. "Scalloped potatoes, curried cauliflower, a salad, and I thought we could bake homemade yeast rolls like we used to do together. I also made a peach and blackberry cobbler for dessert."

"I've come to be quite fond of Michelle's yeast rolls," commented Thomas.

"And I like her mum's as well," chimed in James. He'd seen the disappointment on Susan's face when he refused to change their plans for tomorrow and knew it cheered her up when he complimented her on her cooking.

"I made the dough earlier," said Susan to Michelle. "It's on its first rise. We can make it into rolls any time then they can rise the second time before we bake them."

"Okay if we make knots, Mom?"

"I've been making clover leaf for James."

"I've been making knots for Thomas."

"Half knots and half clover leaf then," suggested Carrie.

Michelle and Susan went to the sink to wash their hands and make the rolls while Thomas went to the fridge where he took out a bottle of white wine and opened it. James opened a bottle of red and glasses were re-filled. James, Thomas and Carrie went into the main room to discuss the details of the Christmas celebration along with wedding plans.

Susan and Michelle made the rolls, covered them with a dish towel and set them to raise. They then sat at the kitchen table together and peeled and sliced potatoes for the scallop then made the curried cauliflower ready to pop into the oven.

As they pared and sliced, Michelle looked at her mom, who seemed to be just a bit melancholy. She almost wished she couldn't read people so easily, especially her mother. It made her more sensitive to her feelings and then she felt she had to do or say something if Susan was feeling down. In fact, truth be told, it's why they were here back in the past. Discovering how depressed her mom had been in the future, and then finding out why, was what prompted this trip. She sighed.

"Mom," she said in a lowered voice, looking over her shoulder into the main room where James was talking animatedly. "I'm worried about you. Are you *sure* this is what you want? Do you really, really think you can...can *tolerate* that man!? Once you're married to him, you'll be at his mercy. He'll jerk you around like a puppet on a string...that's not *you*, Mom! You're a free thinking and independent woman and...and, I'm sorry, but I think he's an...an abuser!"

Susan held up her hand. "He's not, Michelle! He's just...just moody sometimes...and...and he has a lot on his mind after losing his wife and...he's an *artist*...you know how temperamental an artist can be...and he made clear to me, my life is about to change... drastically..."

"Really! And you're just going to accept that!!? Are you constantly going to make excuses for the way he treats you!!?'

"You don't understand, Michelle...his life is different than ours. He's rich and famous and in the limelight constantly. He has a team of people who manage his finances, his homes, his security. It's a life foreign to me. He understands it and I don't. If I want to be with him, I have to understand...and to...to change my way of thinking... to accept things..."

She folded her hands in her lap and looked down at them.

"I love him...I truly love him...despite the way he is. I know deep down inside of me that he loves me too. We've loved each other for a long time, even though we've been apart and lived different lives.

I trust him to know what's best for us...what's best for...for...me..."
Her voice faded to a whisper.

Michelle reached out a hand and touched her mom's.

"I want you to be happy...I really do...and...and, if you think James will make you happy, then I'm okay with it...but, oh Mom! I just don't know about him..."

Susan abruptly changed the subject. "What about you and Thomas, Michelle? It looks like you've fallen in love with him, just like I did with his dad all those years ago..."

Now it was Michelle's turn to look down at her hands in her lap before she lifted her eyes back to her mom's. "Yes...I believe I have... and, I don't know what to do about it."

"Stay in the past here with me and follow your heart just like I'm following mine. I never thought you'd be happy with your Thomas in the future. He just didn't seem...dynamic enough for you..."

"But I thought he'd 'do,' you know what I mean? My biological clock was ticking and he seemed nice enough."

"But there was no passion, am I right? When I spoke to you last week, you seemed rather overwhelmed with this Thomas's over-the-top libido. Assuming he's like his dad, I'd venture to say you've found passion. Do you really want to give that up?"

"No, I don't. It's just that I keep thinking of Dad and my career, aside from the fact that I don't know *how* I could stay back here in the past. The same goes for you. If we're to stay here, just *how* do we do it?"

"I've been thinking on it. I think we do or say nothing. It will be like we just vanished into nowhere."

"But Dad and Steven will try to track us down. I told dad I was taking you on a vacation to try and find out what was wrong with you and help you out of your depression."

"Did you tell him where we were going?"

"Actually, no. I told him I'd check in, but then so much has happened here, that I feel like I've been swept out to sea on a tidal wave. I keep thinking about sending him a text, but just haven't done it."

"Well then, don't send one. It can be like we just disappeared. It happens sometimes, you know. Two women alone, maybe in some foreign country..."

"Oh, Mom! How cruel is that!? To have Dad and Steven, and even Thomas, my fiancé, have to worry and wonder what happened to us!"

Susan sighed and hung her head. "I know it is. It's mean and horrible and selfish. I admit it...and I feel ashamed...but I wasn't making your dad happy anymore and his work became more important and interesting than me a long time ago. As much as it hurts to say it, I'm sure he could find someone else to replace me if he wanted to."

"I find that hard to believe, but maybe you're right, and other than my career and my feelings for Dad, I really don't have anything to go back to that I find very exciting. And, at this point, you're correct, I don't think I want to give up the passion and happiness I've found with this Thomas."

Susan and Michelle hadn't noticed Thomas come back into the kitchen.

"What's this about giving up passion and happiness?" he asked, directing the question at Michelle.

"She looked up at him. "My mom and I were talking about my having to go home, and I was telling her how hard it will be to leave you."

"But what about what we talked about last night? I was just telling Dad and Carrie about it. About you and me..."

"And that he was going to marry you," interrupted Carrie, coming into the kitchen with James close behind.

"A double wedding is what we can have," prompted James as he went to stand behind Susan, resting his hands on her shoulders and squeezing gently.

She looked first up over her shoulder at him then at Michelle.

"You didn't tell me Thomas asked you to marry him!"

Michelle blushed. "Well, he didn't actually *ask* me..."

"Oh, like Dad then," said Carrie. "He just told you he was going to marry you."

Michelle smiled, looking at Thomas. "Not quite like that...he just said something about putting a ring on my finger, and..."

"And," continued Thomas, "I told her I wanted to marry her."

"Did she agree?" asked James.

Thomas blushed. "Well, not in so many words...we became a bit distracted...but I believe she did..." He went over to where Michelle was sitting and pulled her up into his arms. "You will marry me, won't you, Michelle, ma belle?"

She laughed before leaning in to kiss him. "Yes, Thomas...I believe I will."

Chapter 30

Off to London

Dinner was a happy occasion, with more wine being consumed along with the dinner Susan and Michelle prepared, followed by dessert and coffee. There was much discussion related to wedding plans, and it was past 9:00 before Thomas, Michelle and Carrie left the cottage to go back to the B&B.

Susan took a long, hot bath before going to bed, while James stayed up, reviewing the notes he'd made on new songs as well as looking over the schedule for the new album. The official announcement would be made on Christmas Eve day with a press conference in front of Cherry Studios where the recording would take place beginning the first of the New Year. The media had all been invited to the press conference, and news of the event had already hit the newspapers and tabloids.

Before joining Susan in bed, James made several phone calls to his team, discussing what he wanted done in the next few days. He made his most trusted members aware of his and Thomas's upcoming nuptials, swearing them to secrecy and giving them specific instructions. It was past 2:00 in the morning when he climbed under the covers with Susan and settled against her warmth. She was breathing softly, her golden hair spread across the pillow. The sight of her took his breath away.

"Yes," he thought to himself. "I truly have found happiness again." Thoughts of his departed wife, Susan, passed through his mind, and he felt as if she were looking down at him from "the other side" and giving her blessing for his future with another Susan. He smiled contentedly and fell into a deep and satisfying sleep.

Susan was up early, as usual, to watch the sun rise through the kitchen window as she sat at the table with a cup of coffee.

Nine days from now, the dream of her lifetime would come true. James would belong to her and she would belong to him. They would work together to make their marriage a success, even if it meant that she would have to buckle under and accept the fact that James would be the one calling the shots. She could adapt. She could accept her new role in life. She loved him more than life itself. She would do her utmost to make him happy, and they would grow old together.

And, then she thought of Michelle, who had agreed to marry Thomas and stay in the past with her. Michelle was only 24 in this time period. She didn't have to worry about any biological clock ticking. She and Thomas could give her and James grandchildren, something she had always wanted, but never thought to have from her daughter. She knew that Michelle would make a wonderful mother and Thomas a great father. And, she also knew that James would be a loving and fantastic grandpa. She smiled contentedly.

James came into the kitchen about an hour later and tried to coax Susan back to bed. He teasingly pointed to his erection poking into the front of the boxer shorts he was wearing, but she shooed him away, saying she needed to make breakfast and had other things to do before they had to leave. He smirked at her, saying jokingly that she'd pay the price later for her refusal to take care of his "needs," then got dressed and came back into the kitchen for Belgian waffles with blueberries.

At precisely 9:00, a limo pulled up to the cottage and the driver knocked at the door along with one of James's security team. A second car pulled up behind the limo.

"A limousine, James!? Isn't that rather extravagant!? And what's with the other car?" Susan asked as their suitcases were carried out of the cottage and put in the boot.

James helped her into the back of the limo. "I always travel in a limo or SUV, at least most of the time unless I feel like driving myself.

And the other car is for the security team who've been staying down the lane from us in another cottage as well as two of them that were staying in Little Dippington."

"We've had security people spying on us!!!"

"Not spying, Susan...protecting us. Yes, that's the way it is. It's something you'll need to get used to."

She leaned back into the soft faux leather seat, real leather not allowed due to James's stand on animal welfare, and looked out the window as the limo driver closed the door.

"This just all seems so unreal to me. Everything seemed so 'normal' at the cottage, and...and now I feel like I'm some kind of princess or something...like Sleeping Beauty when she found out she was really a princess and not a peasant girl and was taken to the castle..."

He smiled at her. "You *are* my princess, Susan, and I *am* taking you to my castle."

She looked back at the cottage as they pulled away. "I'm going to miss being with you at Auntie Annabelle's cottage..."

"I'll miss it too, but we can come back whenever we like...when the crazy world I live in becomes too much for us and we want to truly be alone. I promise you, we'll come back..."

Susan wrapped her arms around him and put her mouth to his. "Thank you, James...that means a lot to me..."

She kissed him again, this time deeply and hungrily, and it wasn't long before their bodies began to move against each other sensually, Susan rubbing her breasts into the front of James's shirt.

"You recall that you refused me this morning, don't you, Susan?"

"Mmmm...maybe..." She gently bit his lip before kissing him again as her hands moved to his shirt buttons and she began to undo them one by one. "I can make it up to you now if you want...I've never made love in the back of a limo...in fact, I've only been in one once in my life when a bunch of girlfriends and me went to the horse races."

Undoing the last button on his shirt, she pulled the shirt tails out of his trousers and scraped her fingernails up and down his bare chest. He moaned, deepening their kiss, their tongues now swirling together in the familiar dance they both knew so well.

James moved his hands under the sweater she was wearing, reaching around the back to unhook her bra then moved them around to the front, palming her full breasts in his hands. He loved her generous breasts, wanting to suckle them while squeezing them and pinching her nipples.

Before things went further, however, he reached forward and latched the window between the driver and the back of the limo then pulled a curtain across the window. Before laying her down on the seat, he pulled the sweater up over her head and pulled off her bra, tossing both onto the seat opposite.

The soft seat was cool against her back even though it was obvious the back of the car had been heated for their comfort. Susan reached up and wrapped her arms around James's neck and tried to pull him down on top of her, but he grabbed her wrists and pinned them above her head.

He brought his mouth down on hers, kissing her once again then moved his tongue down the side of her face to her neck, tasting her skin and sending waves of pleasure through her, chill bumps raising on her arms. She squirmed deliciously beneath him as he continued to lick and nip at her neck and ears, moving his mouth like a hungry animal enjoying a feast.

Her eyes were closed and her lips, swollen from his kisses, were slightly parted as she moaned softly and repeatedly. The sensation of her hands being pinned up above her head and feeling helpless against his erotic onslaught sent a throbbing need down low in her belly, and she knew she was becoming dripping wet in anticipation of having him inside her.

When he released her hands and moved them down to cup her breasts, she lifted her hips up towards him, moving them in slow circles. She spread her legs and could feel his rock hard erection even though both of them still had their jeans on. Inhaling sharply at her movements, he took one nipple into his mouth and sucked it into a stiff peak, while he pinched the other between a thumb and forefinger. She let out a breathless cry, arching her back and neck and pushing her hips harder up into him as she wrapped her legs around his upper thighs.

In response, he moved his mouth to her other breast, nipping her already hardened nipple with his teeth before taking it into his mouth and sucking. Now that her hands were free, she reached down and ran her fingers through his hair, tugging and pulling on it, her head tossing from side to side. When she unwrapped her legs from around him and tried to reach down between them to feel his crotch, he pulled his mouth off her breast and lifted himself off of her.

"I need you now, Susan…right now!" he panted looking down at her flushed face.

Without hesitation, they both kicked off their shoes, pulled off socks, jeans and underwear. James shrugged off his shirt, pushed Susan back onto the seat and entered her in one swift stroke. When she screamed and lifted up her hips to take him in deeper, he felt as if he would explode inside her with just the one thrust. He stilled for a moment, but when he felt her passage throb around his shaft, he began the rhythmic slide in and out of her, pausing now and then to keep from coming too soon. But, when she wrapped her legs around him again and began moving beneath him, rubbing against his pelvis in a circular motion to bring her own release, he had to grit his teeth to hold on and wait for her. It wasn't long, however, and a moment later, he could feel her entire body quiver as her sheath contracted tightly around him, her orgasm sweeping him into his own. Pumping the last of his seed into her, he collapsed on top of her. Both of them were breathing heavily from the exertion, eyes closed, savoring the last of their release.

James rolled them onto their sides where they smothered each other with feathery kisses, murmuring words of love, until their heartbeats slowed.

"I can't wait to marry you, Susan," he whispered in her ear. "To know you'll be mine forever…to have you share my life and my bed until the end of time…"

"Oh, James," she sighed back, wrapping her arms around his neck and pulling herself more tightly into him. "I *want* to be yours forever and ever. I promise I'll be a good wife to you…to support you and love you with my whole heart and body and soul…"

They laid together in silence for the next ten minutes, holding tightly to each other and thinking their own private thoughts of their future life together. Not one stray thought of the past wandered into their heads.

⌒♾

Auntie Annabelle and Auntie Gin fell in love with Michelle within minutes of meeting her, and in a short time the aunties and their three guests were sitting on the couch, each with a cup of tea in hand.

The aunties were thrilled to hear the news about James and Susan and said they'd be pleased as punch to attend the wedding and join the family for Christmas. When Carrie told them that Thomas and Michelle would also be tying the knot along with her dad and Susan, they were doubly pleased.

"You're quite the spitting image of your mum, you know," remarked Auntie Annabelle. "Lovely little thing she was."

"Yes, I recall James and her coming for dinner all those years ago. She was quite helpful as well, right there in the kitchen with us as if she was accustomed to it, added Auntie Gin.

"Both Susan and Michelle love to cook…and are quite good at it," added Thomas, casting an adoring look at Michelle.

The aunties smiled, thinking to themselves how wonderful young love was…and old love as well, when they thought of James finding happiness again. They'd both been quite worried about him since he lost his wife and were thrilled to find out that his first true love had come back into his life.

Thomas, Michelle and Carrie stayed with the aunties for well over two hours, chatting amicably, Michelle sharing amusing stories about being a solicitor and Carrie telling everyone about her recent travel adventures. Right as they were getting ready to leave, Auntie Annabelle remembered the platinum blonde in the tight pants and sweater that had stopped by the previous week trying to worm information from her as to James's whereabouts. When she described the woman and related their conversation, Michelle instantly perked up.

"Did her name happen to be Hilary?"

Auntie Annabelle thought for a moment. "I don't recall that she mentioned her name, but I thought her to be a quite horrible person. Pushy she was, and decked out like a harlot, if you ask me. She said she had some cause related to saving pigs that she wanted to talk to James about. I referred her to his organization, but she wasn't happy about it."

"Must be the same woman we met at the hotel in Brighton!" said Thomas. "The one who tripped on the carpeting."

Michelle looked at Thomas. "She *didn't* trip on the carpeting, and you know it! She just pretended to on purpose so you'd catch her. Then she tried to pry information about your dad from you. It must have been the same sleazy woman."

Thomas was puzzled. "But why would she think to find Dad here in King's Head? And how would she have known that the aunties are related to him?"

Michelle was thinking. "I don't know, but I find it very suspicious. I told you what I suspected about that woman…that she was out to track down your dad for purposes other than her 'pig cause.' It was obvious."

"Well, I certainly found her awful," chimed in Auntie Annabelle. "And, I hope she never tracks him down. She looked like the type that would be after a man for his money…"

"Which Dad has plenty of," added Carrie. "And now that he's available again, I imagine every gold-digging woman in the world will be after him in short order."

"Looks like Hilary has beat everyone to the punch then." Michelle shivered.

"She hit a dead end here, that's for sure," said Auntie Annabelle. I shut the door in her face when she kept pressuring me for information."

"Good for you," said Thomas. "Hopefully, that will be the end of her."

Michelle looked serious. "Don't count on it. Women like that don't give up very easily. I hope you're right, though…"

The three made their goodbyes to the aunties and were soon on their way back to the B&B for one more night before heading to London the next morning. Michelle had agreed to the double wedding with her mom and James for Christmas day, telling Thomas that she'd spoken to her dad and brother, and they were happy for her. When Thomas asked if he could speak to her dad or if he and Steven would be flying over for the wedding and to spend Christmas, she told him that Steven had a family he needed to spend Christmas with. She said her dad was travelling to Washington, DC and unavailable at the moment, and that he certainly wouldn't want to come to England to see his ex-wife getting married again, even if his daughter was getting married at the same time. Thomas was disappointed but figured he'd get to meet the rest of Michelle's family when they traveled to California later.

Chapter 31

Susan is Overwhelmed

James and Susan arrived at James's home outside London early in the afternoon. The first thing he did when they arrived was to introduce Susan to his staff, which included a head housekeeper by the name of Mrs. Bodkins, which she found funny, remembering the lady from the dorm back in 1967, who had the same name. She wondered if they could be related and thought she might ask later. She was also introduced to the housemaids, the kitchen staff, including James's personal chef, the grounds keepers and James's personal secretary. Everyone had been lined up and waiting in the entry hall when they arrived, like a scene from one of Susan's Regency era novels.

As if sensing her awkwardness, Mrs. Bodkins stepped forward and grasped her hand warmly. "While your things are being brought in, why don't I show you about the place, Luv? Then I'll set a nice luncheon up for you and James in the yellow parlor that looks over the gardens in the back."

James was engrossed talking to his secretary and just nodded at Susan and Mrs. Bodkins. Then, on second thought, he went to Susan and gave her a quick kiss. "I'll see you in about an hour then, okay?"

She nodded at him dumbly as he turned back to the secretary and they went down a hallway together. Knowing that all eyes were on her, she smiled broadly at Mrs. Bodkins. "Thank you; I'd love for you to show me around." She turned to the rest of the staff, who were still lined up and standing at attention. "It's lovely to meet you all…

um…thank you for being here to greet me…I appreciate the warm welcome…"

When they all smiled back in a friendly manner, she sighed a relief, but they remained standing in the line. Recalling what she'd read in the Regency books, she added, feeling a bit ridiculous, "Don't let me keep you standing…please, um…feel free to go about your…your jobs…"

A few of the staff smirked at her, sensing not only her discomfort but her naiveté as well when it came to upper class behavior, but the rest smiled and nodded before they all moved off. Susan could feel the heat flood her face. Mrs. Bodkins noticed and led her towards a large curving staircase. "Don't worry, Luv. You'll soon get the hang of things. Sir James actually keeps a quite informal house, but some of the staff are used to working for the titled and wealthy and have airs about them.

When they got to the top of the staircase, Mrs. Bodkins turned left and Susan followed her down a long hallway to a pair of double doors at the end. Opening them with a flourish, Susan entered what appeared to be a large living room with a sofa and two reclining chairs, a small dining table, a baby grand piano, a large fireplace and French doors leading out onto a balcony. Her eyes became as big as saucers, despite trying to school her face into an impassive stare.

"Yes, it is rather large if you're not used to such a house, but you'll soon adapt, I'm sure. This way to the bedroom." Mrs. Bodkins trotted across the room to another set of double doors.

When Susan entered, there was a young woman with dark hair unpacking her suitcase and laying the items out on the large four poster bed which dominated the room. Susan got chill bumps on her arms, knowing this was the bed where she and James would be sleeping together…and, of course, making love.

"Lucy," said Mrs. Bodkins. "Meet your new mistress, Susan, soon to be Lady Susan."

Lucy bobbed a curtsy.

"Oh my god!" thought Susan. "That's right! James is a 'Sir' now. In nine days' time, I'll be a Lady!"

"Good to meet you, Miss," responded Lucy. "I've just been unpacking your things. Will your trunks or other cases be arriving soon?"

Susan felt the heat flood her face again and recalled what James had said to her back at the cottage about the hired help talking amongst themselves about what kind of clothes she had. She thought they'd have a lot to laugh about later when Lucy related what she unpacked for the new mistress.

But, Susan had never been one to be intimidated for long. She lifted her chin. "Actually, the rest of my wardrobe is back in America. I only came here a couple of weeks ago on a holiday, then when James and I met up again, well... Anyway, that's all I brought with me. I'll be doing some shopping for new things in the next few days..."

Mrs. Bodkins smiled approvingly, leading Susan back out of the bedroom. "Handled very nicely," she commented. "But Lucy is a quiet one, doesn't gossip like the others."

An hour later, after Susan had been shown most of the house, including the kitchen that she looked at wistfully, she was led to the yellow parlor and told to make herself at home while tea was being prepared. A moment later, James entered the room. Susan immediately ran to him and wrapped her arms around his waist.

"Oh James! This is so overwhelming! This giant house and all these servants or whatever you call them! It seems too much! I wish we were back in Auntie Annabelle's cottage!"

He patted her on the back. "You'll get used to it, Susan. This is the way I live now, the way I've lived for quite some time. My other Susan didn't care for it much either. We had a farm that we lived on most of the time when the children were growing up, but when we came to London, we had a house, not this one, but another. It was smaller but I sold it after she passed."

He looked sad for a moment. "Like I promised you, we can go back to Little Dippington and the cottage from time to time. Even though this is what I'm used to now, I know how much you like being at the cottage and...waiting on me hand and foot..."

She pushed at his chest. "Who said I like to wait on you hand and foot!? I do not!"

"Yes, you do...and you like baking clover leaf rolls for me and scrubbing floors on your hands and knees and..."

She gave him a small punch in his belly and he pretended it hurt. "Ooof! Watch it or I might just have to take you over my knee for that..."

"I dare you..."

A wicked look came over his face and she could see the amber highlights in his eyes sparking.

Uh oh...

Just then, the door opened and Mrs. Bodkins came in followed by two girls in white aprons. One carried a tea service and the other a tray laden with small sandwiches and other delicacies. They were set on a table by a pair of French doors that looked out on the garden. It was too cold to have the doors open this time of year, but it was still a pleasant view looking out onto the garden, especially since the sun was shining today.

James winked at Susan before he leaned over and whispered. "I'll save the spanking for later then..."

She blushed.

"Would you like me to pour?" asked Mrs. Bodkins after dismissing the two girls in aprons.

"Oh, no thank you," responded Susan. "I think I can handle it... but thank you anyway..."

Mrs. Bodkins smiled and left the room, closing the door behind her.

Susan poured James a cup of tea. "There you go, sweetheart...just the way you like it...two sugars and a spot of milk."

"Why do you and Carrie have to say that every time you make me tea?"

"Oh! Carrie says it too!? I guess because we want to make sure we got it right!"

He smiled and shook his head at her. "Susan, Susan, Susan...do you know how much I love you?"

She smiled back at him, pouring herself a cup of tea and sitting down across from him.

"No...I don't...tell me..."

Thomas and Michelle arrived back at Thomas's flat late the next afternoon with Carrie going straight to her flat, which wasn't far from Thomas's. Carrie called Robert at Le Fonda and made arrangements to go there for dinner that night. James and Susan were also invited but not sure if they'd be able to make it as they were busy working with the household staff to prepare the house for Christmas and the wedding.

They had decided to hold the ceremony in the entry hall in front of the massive fireplace that dominated the space, with the brides walking down the curving staircase to meet their grooms.

James and Susan had also gone to the Registry Office to get their marriage license, and remarkably Susan discovered that Marta had provided her with a passport containing the correct dates and information to match the current time period she was in. Blood tests followed. James told Susan to go shopping the next day with Michelle and Carrie for a wedding dress and a new wardrobe. She wasn't really feeling enthusiastic about the new wardrobe, not really knowing what kind of stuff she was supposed to buy, but James told her that he'd have one of his female team members go with her to help. She still didn't look excited.

"Most women would *love* the opportunity to buy a new wardrobe!" complained James, seeing what he considered a stubborn look come over Susan's face.

"Well, I'm not other women. I don't want an expensive wardrobe or to spend your money on over-priced clothes that are over-priced just because of the tag they have on them or because the store is some snooty place where rich people go…"

"We discussed this before, Susan. I have an image to maintain."

"Maintain for whom? Who's going to see the tags inside the clothes I wear?"

"No one will see the tags, but everyone will *know*. I can't have my wife dressing in rags."

"I don't want to dress in rags either! It just seems stupid to pay ridiculous prices for clothes!"

"Be a good girl and don't argue with me. You're going shopping for a new wardrobe tomorrow and that's the end of it. The day after, we'll go pick out some jewelry for you."

Susan pouted, but when she looked at James and saw the stern expression on his face, she quickly removed the pout. Hadn't she told him that she'd be a good wife to him…that she'd support him? Yes, she had!

"Okay…fine…I'll buy a new wardrobe and bankrupt you doing it…but I don't want a lot of jewelry…I hate jewelry! And I'm *not* taking off the engagement ring no matter what! And not only that, I don't like having a personal maid hovering about all the time and…"

James jerked her into his arms and brought his lips down on hers, silencing her. When he pulled away, he looked down at her, a wicked gleam in his eyes.

"I don't believe I turned you over my knee yesterday like I said I would…but I believe I'll do just that now… It excited me to see your bottom turn all pink and then I can kiss it all better…"

With those words, and before Susan could respond, he took her hand and pulled her up the staircase to their room.

Robert had a dining table set up in the kitchen at Le Fonda for Thomas, Michelle and Carrie, and was actually able to join them off and on during the course of their meal to chat. The restaurant was becoming more and more popular as the days went by and Robert was exhausted.

"I'll be glad when Christmas and New Year's has come and gone," he lamented. "I've been putting in 20-hour days and sleeping on a cot in the pantry behind the kitchen. "Not sure how much longer I can keep it up."

"Well, you don't *have* to come cook for the wedding if you don't feel up to it and need a day of rest, you know," said Thomas.

"Of course I'll come to cook for the wedding!! The restaurant is closed on Christmas Day and I limited the catering for Christmas Eve, so I won't have as much to do. Plus, I most certainly wouldn't miss the double wedding. I'm still quite shocked over it!"

"So am I!" said Michelle, reaching across the table to squeeze Thomas's hand. "Your brother quite swept me off my feet."

Robert looked at her. "I can certainly see why. If I'd seen you first, I would have tried to snatch you up for myself."

"But then you wouldn't have time for her with your restaurant as busy as it is," commented Carrie.

"True, true...I guess I just would have missed out then."

The conversation went on for several hours as Robert presented his special guests with course after course, paired with a different wine for each one. By the time they got to dessert and Robert brought the torch to use on the Crème Brulee, everyone was bursting at the seams.

When Michelle saw the Crème Brulee, she couldn't help but remark on it. "That's one of my mom's specialties. She's been making it ever since I can remember."

"Is it?" asked Robert. "Well then, you'll have to tell me how mine compares to hers." He fired up the torch and caramelized the sugar on top of the custard as he spoke. "I use only the finest ingredients, you know."

"So does my mom," said Michelle. "She's very picky about her Crème Brulee."

"I'm looking forward to meeting her then," said Robert. "Too bad she and Dad couldn't make it tonight."

Carrie dipped her spoon into the custard as Robert set it in front of her. "You'll love her! I'm so glad that Dad found love again. And, I think they're quite well suited."

"Well, we hope so," added Thomas. "You know how controlling Dad can be..."

"And my mom isn't one who likes to be bossed around" remarked Michelle.

"Should be interesting then," said Robert. "Maybe Dad could use someone who stands up to him now and again."

"I agree," chorused Thomas and Carrie together.

"Oh! I almost forgot to mention it," said Robert, re-filling everyone's coffee cups, "but I had a couple of strange diners show up last week. Some rich, old bloke and a young, painted up blonde woman. She was trying to pry information out of me as to where Dad was. I found it rather disconcerting."

Thomas, Michelle and Carrie all looked at each other, eyebrows raised.

"Is that so?" asked Michelle. "Did her name happen to be Hilary?"

Robert looked thoughtful. "I don't recall...let me think a moment...Yes, yes! That was her name! She said Thomas told her to come here and that Dad would be interested in her cause regarding animal welfare. She kept pressuring me for his phone number. I refused to give it to her and she was quite upset about it."

"Hmmm..." remarked Carrie. "Sounds like the same woman who was out badgering the aunties for information on Dad..."

"And the same one who tried to get information from us at the hotel in Brighton," added Michelle. "I don't like it. It's like she's hunting your dad down or something." She began to feel a sense of alarm when she thought of her mother and what she might do if ever confronted by the whore.

Just then, Robert was called away again regarding the risotto, and the other three decided it would be a good time to leave the restaurant. Thanking Robert profusely for the fabulous meal, they left, Thomas and Michelle going back to his flat and Carrie to hers.

James sent Susan off in the limo the next morning, exactly one week before the wedding, to pick up Michelle, Carrie and his female team member, Carla, to go shopping for wedding dresses and a new wardrobe for Susan. She didn't seem to be in a very happy mood when Michelle, the first one to be picked up from Thomas's flat, got in the car.

"Why the scowl, Mom?"

"Oh, just James being his normal, bossy self! I asked him if I could make breakfast for us this morning in that big kitchen of his, but he said, 'no,' that we'd be having it as usual, brought up on a tray to our rooms. You should see our rooms...they're like a small house upstairs all by itself. I keep getting lost in that damn house, but I'm too embarrassed to ask for directions when I see the household staff wandering around. I'm sure they know I'm lost and laugh about it behind my back."

"Now, Mom, you'll get used to the house and being waited on."

"Well, I don't like it...and then he had my personal maid, Lucy... can you believe I have a personal maid? ...take away all my clothes this morning except for what I'm wearing. He said it was to make sure I bought a whole new wardrobe and didn't keep any of my *rags*, is what he called them. He had no right to throw away my clothes!"

Michelle looked thoughtful. "You knew your life was going to change drastically if you stayed with him. You even said so. So, why get upset about it? Fighting it will get you nowhere...except maybe another black eye..."

Susan started. "How can you say or even think such a thing!? What happened at the cottage was an accident and..."

"Was it, Mom?"

When Susan bristled, she continued. "Okay, okay...It was an accident then. You said so, and I believe you."

Susan harrumphed. A moment later, they pulled up to Carrie's flat. She was waiting outside the building. The driver got out and opened the door for her.

"Morning!" she said cheerfully. "Ready to spend Dad's money?" She looked over at Susan, who pasted a smile on her face. It was obviously fake. Carrie turned to Michelle then back to Susan.

"What did Dad do now?"

"Threw her old clothes away so she'll be forced to buy new, nice ones."

Carrie laughed. "Looks like he let you keep the ones you've got on. You're lucky he didn't take those too and stick you in the car naked!"

Michelle and Carrie both laughed and a few seconds later, Susan laughed too.

After picking up Carla, one of James's female team members, at Cherry Studios, the limo headed to Harrod's, where the women were led to a private room and an army of sales women measured every inch of Susan's body then began parading models through the room wearing a variety of outfits from casual wear to evening gowns.

Susan felt overwhelmed, but was getting used to schooling her face to meet the situation, and after an exhausting two hours, she'd picked out a pale pink dress for the wedding that had long sleeves made of lace and came to just above her knees, as well as several pairs of jeans, a dozen or so tops and sweaters, several dresses and a few skirts.

From Harrod's, they went to Fenwick for shoes, House of Fraser for some enticing nightwear, ending up at Selfridges for undergarments. The ladies were treated like royalty at each store, Carla having arranged their shopping visits in advance.

At the last store, Carrie and Michelle left Susan in the private fitting room to find a loo, and as they were coming out, Michelle froze and grabbed Carrie's arm.

"Look! Over there by the perfume counter! It's that blonde floozy who's been trying to track down your dad!"

Carrie turned and looked towards where Michelle had nodded her head and saw a nicely endowed platinum blonde talking to a salesgirl on the other side of the perfume counter. The blonde was wearing a bright red pair of jeans that were so tight, she wondered how she could even manage to sit down, a green Christmas sweater with round ball ornaments embroidered on the front and red stiletto heels. One of her feet was tapping impatiently and she seemed to be arguing with the salesgirl about something.

Carrie's eyes opened wide. "Whoa! Other than those breasts, I can't see Dad looking at her twice!"

"Well, I certainly hope not! She looks like a piece of work for sure."

"I wonder what she does for a living."

"I'd be willing to guess, but don't want to say."

"Yeah, I don't think you need to say…"

Just then, the blonde, who so obviously was the Hilary woman, tossed her head and turned away from the counter. Her eyes met

Michelle's and an instant look of recognition spread across her face along with a menacing smile. She slowly sauntered over to the two women.

"Well, well, well…" she purred evilly, not taking her gaze from Michelle's face. "It's the little solicitor girlfriend of Thomas's, isn't it?"

Carrie looked from Hilary to Michelle.

"How did you know I was an attorney?" asked Michelle.

"Oh…I know a lot…in fact, you can't even imagine all I know about you…and…about your mother…"

Michelle's face paled. Hilary noticed, but not Carrie. Hilary continued.

"Might your mother be around? I'd actually like to have a word with her…"

"About what?"

"Something quite personal, actually. Something I know about her that I think James would be interested to know as well…"

Michelle tossed her head and grabbed Carrie's arm. She was shaking but doing her best to remain calm and aloof.

"Come on, Carrie. This is the bimbo Thomas and I told you about who faked tripping at the Claridon in Brighton then went to harass your aunties and Robert at his restaurant with a pile of lies. She's so obviously after your dad, that it's pathetic. She even has a phony cause she wants to shove down his throat…."

And, as Hilary wasn't very quick on her feet when it came to absorbing a conversation and thinking up a response, Michelle and Carrie were gone before she knew what happened.

Michelle was clearly shaken when she got back to the dressing room. Susan noticed at once.

"What's wrong? You look like you've seen a ghost or something."

"Worse than a ghost," responded Carrie. "It was some gaudy woman who's been trying to track down my dad to present some kind of crazy cause to him related to saving pigs. At least that's what I've been told."

"What woman?" asked Susan.

"Never mind, Mom," responded Michelle. "I can tell you about her later, if you really want to know. It's probably one of his crazy women fans who just wants money from him."

"And there are a *lot* of those!" added Carrie.

Susan finished picking out the last of the lingerie she wanted, and the women were soon on their way back, first to Cherry Studios to drop off Carla, then to Thomas's and Carrie's flats before Susan was headed home to James's house.

When Michelle got to Thomas's flat, she saw a note from him on the top of the piano, where they'd agreed to leave notes for each other if they were going out. It said that he had to meet with one of the conductors at the Philharmonic, but that he'd be back in time for dinner. He also asked if she could please make some of her knots.

She smiled before sitting down on the couch, her brow knitted. What had Hilary meant about knowing something about her mother that James would be interested to know? She couldn't think of anything off the top of her head. There was no way that evil piece of trash could know anything about her mom or about her, for that matter. They weren't even from this time period!

But, the feeling of unease wouldn't leave her, and she wondered what, if anything, Hilary was plotting.

Susan did *not* want to go jewelry shopping the next day, but didn't have a choice when James hunted her down in the library, her purse in his hand, and led her out the front door to the waiting limo.

He'd been quite happy with her purchases from the day before and enjoyed her trying on all the lingerie for his approval, even though she didn't get past the pink thongs and matching bra, garter belt and stockings before he tossed her on the bed and had his way with her.

"I really don't need any jewelry, James," she pleaded as the car pulled out of the gated estate and headed to downtown London. "I spent a fortune on clothes yesterday! Why, one stupid pair of shoes cost over three hundred of your pounds!"

"I have lots of pounds, so don't worry about it."

"But I *do* worry about it. It's a waste of money when I could go somewhere else and buy the same shoes for a tenth of the price!"

"But they wouldn't be the same shoes. They'd be cheap shoes and would probably fall apart after you wore them a few times."

"That's not true! There are a lot of high quality shoes that cost a lot less than three hundred pounds! Don't you have a Sears or JC Penney here somewhere?"

James gave an exasperated sigh. "Do you have to argue with me on everything, Susan? Why can't you just be agreeable? Do you know how many women would love to own a pair of three hundred pound shoes!?'

"Stupid women…"

"That's enough now. I'll be willing to bet that a couple of months from now, it won't matter to you anymore. Now, just be agreeable."

She gave in. "Oh, okay then…"

She didn't think it would be possible, but it was getting easier and easier to give in, most of her disagreeing with him on things being rather trivial, like arguing about the price of shoes. He was, after all, enormously wealthy, but spending a fortune on clothes or anything for herself just wasn't what she was used to doing. It just didn't feel right for some reason. She'd be more likely to buy something for the kitchen, like a new pair of oven mitts.

James scooted closer to her and draped his arm over her shoulder then leaned in to kiss her cheek. "Good girl…"

Oooooo…how she hated that phrase!

Forty five minutes later, they arrived in London. James directed the driver to Hatton Garden, and they were soon being ushered through the front door and into a private room at the back of the store.

Memories of being dragged into another jewelry store back in 1967 when James had also insisted on buying Susan an expensive wedding and engagement ring flew into her head and she cringed at the memory.

Moments later, three salesmen who looked like butlers, dressed in suit and tie, came into the room carrying trays of rings, bracelets, necklaces and earrings. Susan figured there must be a million dollars in jewelry if you counted up all the trays.

James stared at her and she stared back at him.

"Well?" he prompted. "How about if we get the rings out of the way first?"

She pursed her lips. "Fine."

He nudged her shoe with a warning look in his eyes. She smiled back at him sweetly then turned towards the salesmen, who were all looking at her in anticipation of a large sale.

"I'd like something simple for my wedding and engagement rings," she said. When she saw a frown cross James's face, she added, "but I'd like a few really nice cocktail rings for special occasions, maybe sapphires or rubies or emeralds."

"Emeralds to match your eyes…yes…" murmured James, squeezing her hand. "And a necklace, bracelet and pair of earrings to go with the ring."

"Why how generous of you, dear…" she simpered at him sarcastically.

"You'll be needing your ears pierced, though," he added, ignoring her tone of voice and looking at the salesmen. "Might you know where we can get that done?"

"Yes, Sir James," responded one of them. "We can actually have that done right here. We have a nurse on staff just for that purpose."

"Bring her in then," responded James without even looking at Susan. He felt her tense beside him, but didn't care. He wasn't happy with her attitude and would be saying something to her about it later.

"But…" she started to say.

"Pick out some other necklaces and bracelets, Susan…"

She pursed her lips and looked at him before looking back at the trays. "I like hearts and flowers…"

The salesmen jumped into action, lifting and displaying a variety of necklaces, bracelets and earrings, most of them matching. She pointed randomly at several before looking back at James. "Is that enough?"

Her lack of enthusiasm was obvious. Even the salesmen could feel tension building in the room between the couple that sat in the upholstered chairs in front of them. How odd! A woman who didn't "ooooo" and "awwww" over the fabulous gems that could all be hers if she wanted them.

The door opened and a nurse walked in carrying a box with the items needed to pierce Susan's ears. Susan sat stiff and unmoving in her chair, arms crossed, her eyes frosty, her mouth set in a straight line.

James stood up. "Would you all excuse us for just a moment, please?" he asked politely, looking at the crowd in the room.

"Certainly sir," replied one of the salesmen. "Just open the door when you're ready for us to come back."

The salesmen and nurse filed out, closing the door softly behind them. James came to stand in front of Susan, feet planted slightly apart on the carpeted floor, his own arms crossed and an angry look on his face. Susan uncrossed her arms, putting her hands in her lap and held them together, nervously twisting her fingers. She looked down at them as silence filled the room.

When she looked back up at him, he could see tears brimming in her eyes, and all the anger he felt washed out of him like water going down a drain. He crouched down in front of her, taking her hands in his.

"What's wrong, Susan? I just want to make you happy…I thought buying pretty things for you would make you happy…I want to see you in pretty things…show you off to the world…"

"It's *you* that makes me happy, James…not *things*…not diamonds or rubies or even emeralds…" Her voice turned to a whisper as a tear rolled down her cheek. "Just *you*…"

He sighed heavily before reaching up to brush the tear from her cheek with his forefinger. "Sometimes, I just don't know what to think about you…you're so different…and you surprise me and throw me at every turn… Okay then. How about just a few things, like the engagement and wedding rings, the emerald set…to match your eyes you know…" He winked at her. "And maybe a couple of other necklaces or bracelets."

"All right."

"I'll call everyone back in then…except…what about the nurse?"

"She can pierce my ears if that's what you'd like…"

He smiled at her tenderly and she smiled back at him as he opened the door and the salesmen and nurse came back in.

Chapter 32

A Scare in James's Library

The next few days seemed like a whirlwind to Susan, as she threw herself into decorating James's giant mansion of a house with Christmas festivity.

The household staff fell into the Christmas spirit along with her, helping to hang pine wreaths through the main rooms of the house and carrying in a 20-foot Christmas tree that Susan had placed to the left of the fireplace in the entry hall, right next to where the wedding ceremony would be held.

After a few uncomfortable days, even the chef warmed up to Susan, allowing her into his kitchen domain to make some of the yeast rolls James was so partial to. He was impressed with her ease and knowledge of preparation, and told her she was welcome to join him anytime or even to use the kitchen on her own.

Mrs. Bodkins urged the rest of the staff to be kinder to the American woman, who was so obviously in love with Sir James, and despite their dislike and mistrust of Americans, they quickly became fond of her due to her kindness. Unlike other houses they'd worked in, Susan always used the word "please" when making a request and made sure to proffer numerous "thank-you's." Only a few held to the belief that an American woman was inferior to an English one, but even they had to admit that Susan was making every effort possible to fit into their way of life and make James happy.

It was late Wednesday afternoon, just three days before the wedding, when James came out of the library after being closeted in with a few members of his team to discuss what would take place on Christmas Eve day. All Susan knew about it was that there would be an interview with the press about James's new album that he would start recording the first of the New Year when they got back from their honeymoon. He also wouldn't tell her where he planned on taking her for the honeymoon despite her begging and pleading.

When he came into the entry hall and saw her near the top of the ladder next to the Christmas tree, leaning with one foot off the ladder and reaching towards the tree to put an angel on top, he sucked in his breath. There was no one else about and she could easily fall and even break her neck.

He'd told her earlier in the day to stay off the ladder and to get help if she needed the tree decorated, but as usual, she obviously didn't listen to him. His heart thudded in his chest as he took in her precarious pose on the ladder, but he didn't want to yell and startle her. Instead, he advanced towards the ladder, where he firmly gripped the bottom and prepared to catch her if she fell.

She felt the movement at the bottom of the ladder right as she placed the angel on the top of the tree and looked down at him, seeing the worried expression on his face. Carefully, she put her feet on rung after rung and soon reached the bottom where he grabbed her off the last one before her feet hit the floor.

"And just what the hell do you think you were doing!? Didn't you hear me this morning when I told you to stay off the ladder? That you could fall and hurt yourself!?"

"Well, yes…but after the tree was all decorated, I thought it needed an angel on top, and when I found one in the boxes of decorations, I thought it would be no big deal to put it on top myself. As you can see, I managed it just fine."

"That's not the point! The point is that I told you *not* to do it, and you did it anyway! When are you going to learn to listen to me, Susan!?"

"Maybe when hell freezes over, James," she teased.

He looked at her a moment as her words sunk in, before shaking his head at her and sighing in exasperation.

"Oh, come on," she coaxed, wrapping her arms around him and looking up into his stern face. "Here I am all safe and sound and we have a beautiful angel on the top of our tree...doesn't it look pretty?"

He glanced up before looking back down into her face. "Yes, it looks very lovely...but I don't want you climbing up any more ladders, is that clear?"

"As clear as mud..." she said, giggling and moving her hands up around his neck, and before he could respond, she pressed her lips to his.

Michelle, also feeling as if she were being swept away in a whirlwind, went to rehearsals at the Philharmonic with Thomas during the day where he was preparing for a Christmas Eve concert, and then came back to his flat, where she cooked dinner and they watched movies. Sometimes they played the piano together.

It was Wednesday night just as they were finishing up dinner, when Michelle heard the intercom buzz from down in the building lobby. Thomas told her to stay at the table in the dining room where they were eating by candlelight, and went to answer the intercom.

Several minutes later, there was a knock at the door and Michelle heard Thomas speaking softly to someone before closing the door and coming back to the table. He had one hand behind his back and a smile on his face.

When she raised her eyebrows at him, he sat down and instructed her to put her hands on the table and close her eyes. She looked at him questioningly, but did as he asked. She felt him take her left hand in his and slip something onto her ring finger. Her eyes flew open, looking first down at her hand then at his face, her mouth open in surprise. A beautiful diamond glittered on her finger.

"Thomas!" she exclaimed, finally finding her voice. "Is this...is this what I think it is...an engagement ring!?"

"Well, what else would it be!? You did agree to marry me, didn't you? I thought it would be appropriate to buy you a ring."

"Yes, but..."

"And you do recall that we're getting married in just three days' time, don't you?"

"Well, yes...but I didn't think I really needed an engagement ring. A lot of people just have wedding bands, and..."

"Do you think I'm so shabby that I'd not want you to have an engagement ring?"

"No, I don't think you're shabby at all...in fact I think you're quite wonderful! Thank you, Thomas...thank you so much."

She sprang up from her chair at the same time Thomas stood up then came around the table, where he took her into his arms and kissed her. She drew away from him and looked down at her hand, tears in her eyes.

"It's so beautiful, so perfect..."

"Just like you are, Michelle... just like you are..."

Susan and James were able to go to Le Fonda that night for a gourmet, vegetarian dinner, personally prepared by Robert, and just like Thomas and Carrie, Robert thought Susan was the best thing that could have happened to his dad to move him out of his grief and back into happiness.

He and Susan hit it off immediately, talking about food, recipes, sauces, cookware and kitchen gadgets. James smiled at them fondly as they discussed the merits of European style butter over Irish or Danish butter. He was pleased that all three of his children loved Susan so much, and was actually looking forward to Christmas for the first time since his wife, Susan, had passed. And it wasn't just because he was getting married on that day; all three of his children would be celebrating the holiday with him as well as his two aunties. It would be a family Christmas just like old times.

When they got home, James told Susan to call Michelle to see if she and Thomas would be able to come over Friday, Christmas Eve morning at 9:00, for photos. He and his team had decided that afternoon that an engagement and wedding announcement would be made at 11:00 in the morning, four hours before James's press interview at Cherry Studios. The photos would be provided to the media along with a statement from both James and Thomas. Susan and Michelle would attend the press conference at 3:00 in the afternoon as well and would be coached in the morning as to what they would be allowed to say. After five minutes, Thomas, Michelle and Susan would be escorted into the studio and James would be interviewed for his new album.

It sounded to Susan as if James's team had everything planned down to the last detail, and when she mentioned it to him, he said that was the way it had to be; it was what he demanded and expected.

No wonder his bossiness seems to be worse, she thought as she went upstairs to call Michelle. James went back to the library to make some more phone calls, saying he'd join her as soon as he was done.

Susan sat down at the desk and picked up the phone to call Michelle then froze.

Oh my god! Her mobile phone! She suddenly thought about her mobile phone and remembered it was still out at Auntie Annabelle's cottage, wrapped up in towels in the cabinet under the bathroom sink. Crap!

Not that she really needed it, especially now that she was getting married and staying in the past. James would buy her a new phone if she wanted one. She shrugged her shoulders. Michelle still had her mobile phone, so if there were some reason either of them needed to communicate with the future, they could always use hers.

When Susan told Michelle about her mobile phone, Michelle agreed that it didn't matter. Neither of them would be needing their phones again anyway.

Susan confirmed with Michelle that she and Thomas would be at the house at 9:00 Friday morning before Michelle excitedly told her about the engagement ring Thomas had surprised her with.

"Oh, Mom! I don't think I've *ever* been so happy! I can't even believe so much has happened in just a few, short weeks! I have to keep pinching myself to believe it's for real! Thomas is so, so wonderful!!"

Susan smiled into the phone. It made her heart swell with happiness for her daughter, who up to this time had nothing but her career to bring her joy. And, it really couldn't be called "joy." Maybe a sense of accomplishment and self-satisfaction as she won legal case after case, but not the kind of joy that love and passion could bring.

"I'm thrilled for you, Michelle. I never really thought that dull and boring Thomas back in the future could make you happy."

"You're right, Mom! And, I guess I'm happy for you too. You finally get to keep your James! After all you've been through with him, he'll finally be yours. I originally thought it was a mistake to come back here, but now I realize it must have been fate…this must have been meant to be…"

"I believe that too. So, I guess I'll see you Friday morning then, and I have to warn you, that once word is out about us, it will be chaos. Be prepared."

"I will, Mom. I can handle it. Love you!"

"Love you too, sweetheart!"

As she placed the phone back on the cradle, she looked at the ring on her finger again…the *little sparkler*, and so many memories came flooding back into her brain. But, they were all good ones, and she knew in her heart that all her future ones would be good too.

James ended up in the library until almost 4:00 the following morning, and when he finally came to bed, he just cuddled up to Susan and fell instantly asleep. She wondered, now that he was going to be recording and out in the public again, if this might be a typical night where he either worked or had to talk to his team or others until the wee hours of the morning. If so, she would have a lot of adapting to do. She sighed before taking his warm hand in hers and falling back asleep, knowing she would have to.

It was raining the next morning when Susan crept out from under the covers around 8:00. James was still fast asleep, softly snoring with one hand tucked up under his cheek on the pillow. Her breath caught in her throat, as it always did, when she looked at him, and she told herself for the hundredth time how gorgeous he was even with the silver in his hair...maybe even more so now...

She wrapped a robe over her nightgown and went down to the kitchen for coffee. She could have called for Lucy to bring it up, but she still wasn't quite used to be waited on hand and foot and tried not to bother Lucy too much. James had a man who took care of his clothes and ran some personal errands for him, but he didn't depend too much on hired help either for his day-to-day personal needs. Susan was glad. She didn't like people fussing about all the time. It got on her nerves and felt like her privacy was being invaded.

When Susan got down to the kitchen, the chef was busy studying designs for the wedding cakes. Even though there would be only a handful of people at the ceremony, he felt that a proper wedding cake should be made for each couple. A baker would be coming in the next day to make and decorate the cakes while Robert, James's son, would be preparing the wedding dinner. The chef wasn't upset about Robert taking over his kitchen since he had been the one who first coaxed him into going to chef's school two years ago.

"Don't forget James's clover leaf rolls," Susan teased him, pouring herself a cup of coffee and settling into a chair at the large butcher block table that dominated the room.

"What!?" he looked up at her. "Oh...yes...of course...of course..."

When she saw that he was engrossed in wedding cake photos, she picked up her cup, left the kitchen and wandered down the hall to the library. There were floor to ceiling bookcases on three of the walls, with a fireplace tucked in-between on one wall. The fourth wall had floor to ceiling windows with French doors in the middle leading out onto a veranda. A large desk, piled with papers and mail was in front of the windows. It was a mess, and she was surprised, thinking that James would be more neat and tidy when it came to his paperwork. She figured maybe it was because he'd been gone for a few weeks.

Not meaning to snoop, but still feeling a bit curious about all the clutter, she wandered over to the desk and glanced down at the items on top. Everything seemed meaningless to her...until she got to something half covered with other papers and about ready to slide off the desk. When she saw what it was, she froze and her heart dropped down in to her stomach.

It was a large glossy photo of the woman, Hilary, who Susan knew had become James's second wife in 2001, two years from where Susan was now in time.

Sucking in her breath, she pulled the photo out along with a letter that was addressed to Sir James. The photo was a near nude, with Hilary's young, shapely body in full display. A seductive, come-hither smile was pasted on her face. On the upper left hand corner of the photo, "Dearest James" was penned in not very neat hand-writing. On the bottom right, it was signed, "Yours forever for the sake of our beloved animals," followed by a row of x's.

Susan felt sick to her stomach. She read the letter, which offered condolences for the loss of his dear and beautiful wife, praised him for continuing his quest to protect innocent animals and ended with a plea to meet with her to discuss her cause that was called, "Save the Pigs – Ban Bacon in Britain." She didn't find it funny or amusing; she just felt shivers go through her body from head to toe.

Feeling faint, she sat down in the large chair behind James's desk and took several deep breaths before looking down at the photo and letter in her shaking hand.

Had James seen and read the letter? Had he looked at the picture? For how long? Is this why he'd been in the library so late the night before? Had he called Hilary...talked to her about her pig cause? She had to slap her thoughts down before she made herself crazy.

What if he hadn't looked at the picture or the letter, or what if he'd just given both a glance? It wasn't like they were sitting on top of the piles. She looked over at the fireplace as an idea came into her head. Before she could stop herself, she walked over with the photo and letter in hand, crumpled them up, placed them on the grate in the fireplace and took a long match from a bucket sitting on the hearth. She lit it and watched as the picture and letter burned into ashes.

Taking a deep breath, she straightened up and looked into the fireplace. In current time, Hilary hadn't come into James's life until later. She wasn't sure exactly when, but he didn't marry her until 2001. And, now that Susan was staying in the past and marrying James in just two days' time, history would be changed and Hilary would never enter his life. In fact, she swore that conniving gold-digger would *never, ever* enter his life as long as she had breath in her body.

She turned and walked determinedly out of the room, clenching and unclenching her fists before remembering she'd left her coffee cup behind. Re-tracing her steps, she retrieved her cup, went to the kitchen for a re-fill and to make James a pot of tea, then carried the tray upstairs to their rooms.

It was almost 10:00 in the morning, but James was still asleep. Since he'd been up so late, she didn't want to wake him up, but she felt so unsettled by what she'd discovered in the library, that she decided to climb back in bed with him and feel his comforting warmth against her.

She removed her robe and nightgown, shivering at the chill in the air, then quickly climbed under the covers, reaching over to put her hand on his arm. His eyes blinked open and he smiled at her.

"Morning, sweetheart," he mumbled sleepily, giving a yawn. His eyes fluttered shut again but she knew he was awake. Taking her hand from his arm, he moved it down between them and placed it on his typical, rock hard, morning erection. Opening his eyes again, she could see little flecks of amber fire burning in the depths. She grinned back at him, wrapping her fingers around the shaft and squeezing gently. He moaned.

"I think I have something for you..."

"It appears that you do...will it be like this every morning even after we're married?"

"What if I promise you it will?"

"Then I'll tell you it will make me very happy…"

"I like making you happy…"

"I know you do…"

Before he could lean in to kiss her however, she ducked her head under the covers and moved her head down to his crotch, where she took him into her mouth and began swirling her tongue around his tip, dipping it now and again into the tiny slit at the top. His hands came down to grasp her head and he pushed himself deeper into her throat. She thought she might gag, but had schooled her brain to dwell on thoughts of pleasure when doing this to him, and was able to take him all the way in.

James moaned above her before pulling the bottom half of her body around and on top of him, positioning her most intimate part above his face, her legs spread on each side of his shoulders. Before pulling her down to his mouth, he pushed the bed covers off them both. He felt her quiver above him as he swirled his tongue on her, his hands firmly gripping her bottom so she couldn't move away. He loved the taste of her and it excited him as he heard her gasps and moans of pleasure from below. He increased his movements, swirling and licking her nub relentlessly, knowing he would soon throw her over the top.

Realizing she would quickly climax if he didn't slow down or let up, she increased the speed of her mouth on him, tightening her lips around his shaft to drive him more quickly to his own orgasm, and a moment later, as she felt her release shake her whole body, James spilled himself down her throat.

Susan rolled off of him and turned her body around where he gathered her in his arms, both of them on their sides facing each other, and kissed her. She could taste herself on his lips and sighed in satisfaction, her body still twitching from such a powerful release.

"That was good…but too quick," she complained as the kiss ended.

"Are you saying you didn't enjoy it?" He whispered, planting soft kisses on the side of her face.

"No...I always enjoy it...but you didn't come inside me..."

"I don't always have to, do I?" His lips moved down to the side of her neck.

"No...but I like it when you do..."

"Mmmmm...I know...so do I..." His mouth moved down to her shoulder, where he nipped at her with his teeth then he licked his way across her chest to the other shoulder.

"...I like it a lot."

"Do you then?" He cupped her breasts in both hands.

"Uh huh..." Her breath caught in her throat as he pinched her nipples that were still sensitive and hard.

"Would you like me to come inside you now?" His voice was soft and seductive, as he moved his mouth up to her ear and blew a puff of air into it.

Her eyes opened wide as he pushed his hips into hers and she could feel his stiffness poke into her belly.

"How can you do that!?" she panted, feeling a familiar sensation grow between her legs.

"Do what?" He nipped her earlobe before sucking his way back down her neck then suddenly rolling her onto her back.

"Get so big so fast...so soon..."

He captured her mouth with his before drawing back, climbing on top of her and kneeing her legs apart.

"Because I can..." He looked down at her and she could see from his eyes how much he wanted her...

Again.

Without waiting for her response, he slowly and torturously pushed into her a half inch at a time, watching her face intently as he did so. When she tried to wrap her legs around him and pull him in deeply and more quickly, he withdrew, pushing her legs off him and open wider before repeating the slow entry. He could feel her throbbing around him and knew it wouldn't take much to bring to her another climax, but he'd just spilled all of himself into her mouth and was now able to hold back and savor her slowly and deliberately.

She relaxed into his slow thrusts, rubbing her palms in circles on his chest, her eyes closed, mouth open. He leaned down to suckle each nipple one at a time then kissed her opened mouth softly and tenderly.

The moments passed as they unhurriedly melded their bodies together in an adagio of pleasure. Neither of them wanted the sensuality of their movements to end, and James prolonged it for them as long as he was able. But when Susan's sheath began to tighten around him, he knew her orgasm was approaching and increased the speed and urgency of his thrusts. Her release came first as she arched her back and screamed her gratification. James immediately followed her into bliss before collapsing on her and rolling them onto their sides again. They looked into each other's eyes, pupils large and smoky, and kissed again. Both were without words. Closing their eyes and pulling in tight to each other, they fell back asleep and didn't wake up again until early afternoon.

When they finally got up, both were near starving and ended up going down to the kitchen, where Susan made them grilled cheese sandwiches with sliced tomato and fresh basil. The chef didn't say anything about Susan invading his domain, being too occupied with table decorations for the wedding.

After eating, James went to the library. Susan tagged along, saying she wanted to look at what books he had, but what she really wanted to do was see if he looked through the things on his desk searching for Hilary's letter and photo.

The first thing he did, however, was to pick up his phone messages and write down names and numbers of people he needed to call back. He then began looking through the stack of papers on the right side of his desk, opposite to where Hilary's mail had been. Finding what he was looking for, he picked up the phone and made a call. Susan heard him talking to someone who must be on his team based on the conversation being about the upcoming press conference. After a few more calls, discussing the same thing, James sorted through the messy stacks of papers in the middle of the desk, taking a trash can out from under the desk and tossing the majority of the papers into it. The rest he sorted into one stack. Moving to the left of his desk, he picked up both stacks of papers that were lying there, and where Hilary's letter and photo had been, and shuffled them into one stack placing it on top of the other.

"Crazy people," he muttered to himself, but Susan heard him. "Always begging for money or wanting me to support some pet cause. I told my secretary to take all these to the office at the studio and sort through them all. I don't know why he brought them here in the first place. I don't have time for that sort of thing anymore…"

Susan sighed in relief before putting down the book she'd been pretending to read.

"But don't you like to support causes, especially those related to animals?"

He stood up. "Yes, of course, but I have people who look at the requests and check them out to see how legitimate they are. Then I might get involved or I might just give instructions on what I want done related to the cause. You can become involved in it if you want to. Carrie sometimes gets involved."

Susan felt even more relieved. If she became involved, Hilary would be stopped dead in her tracks. She could go wallow with her pigs for all she cared.

James and Susan spent a cozy evening together, asking for dinner to be served in their room, after which Susan played the piano and James his acoustic guitar. Trying to stay up late with James, Susan ordered up some coffee, feeling too lazy to go down to the kitchen to make it and get it herself. She felt guilty and apologized to Lucy when she brought up the tray, realizing it was past midnight and she probably got Lucy out of bed. Lucy insisted it was no problem, telling Susan it was a real pleasure to wait on such a kind lady.

Despite the coffee, Susan fell asleep watching the movie James put in the VCR, and he had to wake her up when it was over so they could go in to bed.

The next morning was somewhat of a repeat of the morning before, James keeping his promise to wake Susan with something hard and stiff poking at her.

She felt as if she'd died and gone to heaven. It was as if she could never get enough of him.

While she was in the shower, James ordered breakfast sent up along with a bottle of champagne.

"Champagne this early in the morning?" she commented, coming out of their room in a bathrobe, with her hair wrapped up in a towel.

"We have orange juice too," he responded, popping the cork on the bottle and pouring some champagne into a fluted glass before adding some orange juice. "Remember you told me about these the other day and thought we could serve them at the wedding. What are they called?"

"Mimosas."

"That's right! So, sit down...I want to propose a toast."

Susan sat down and James handed her a glass.

"To telling the world today of my love for you!" He bumped his glass against hers and they both took a sip.

"And to an HEA for us..." she responded.

"What's an HEA?"

"Why, a Happily Ever After, of course!"

He smiled at her before pulling a small box out of his trouser pocket and setting it on the table. He pushed it towards her and she opened it, already knowing what was inside. It was the engagement ring they'd bought at the jewelry store and she knew he was expecting her to wear it at the press interview for everyone to see. She looked down at it solemnly.

"You don't really want it, do you?" He asked her softly.

She shook her head, spreading the fingers of her left hand on the white table cloth. "I love my *little sparkler*. Please don't make me take it off."

He thought for a moment then they looked at each other. He reached forward, closed the box and moved it to the side of the table before taking her left hand in his. His thumb moved across the tiny diamond on top of the engagement ring he'd got for her all those years ago.

"I was going to tell you to just put the new one on with this one, but it would quite throw this one into the shade, wouldn't it? The stone in the other one is so much larger..."

She just nodded.

"You can wear just this one then," he said. "I don't really care what people think. I just know that I love you, and if this makes you happy, then all you need to wear is this one."

They both stood up and James moved around the table to take Susan in his arms. They were cheek to cheek.

"Tomorrow is Christmas and our wedding day," he whispered into her ear. "And you'll be making me the happiest man on earth."

"Oh James! You can't even know how much I love you...you're making my dream come true...to be with you always..."

"And forever..."

Chapter 33

Susan Exposed

Thomas and Michelle arrived at James's house shortly before 9:00, and they all went into the library together where two members of James's team were waiting for them along with a photographer.

Susan was wearing a green dress to match her eyes and had also agreed to wear the emerald necklace, bracelet and earrings James had insisted on buying for her. With her still golden locks swirling down over her arms and down to her waist in back, she was quite a stunning woman for her age. James looked at her almost hungrily and she winked at him.

Michelle was just as stunning in an aqua dress that also set off her eyes that were the color of the ocean. Thomas was enthralled. Her hair was tied back in a ribbon to match the dress.

Both James and Thomas were in full suit and tie.

Numerous photos were taken over the next hour then one of the members of James's team took Susan and Michelle aside and instructed them on what to do at the interview. They were not to answer personal questions about themselves, in fact, what they were allowed to say was quite limited. Mostly, they were just to smile and nod their heads.

As James had done thousands of interviews in the past, Susan was told to follow his lead. He would also be holding her hand, so would signal her with a squeeze if she was not to say something, in which case, he would answer the question for her. She was beginning to feel nervous, wondering just what kind of questions they would be asked.

Both Susan and Michelle were then queried by both team members, with James and Thomas sitting next to them. The information they gave about themselves, where they came from, how they met James and Thomas, how they felt about getting married, etc. would be edited and written up for the 11:00 press release.

At precisely 11:00, the release was sent to the media along with photos of the two couples, and they all went into one of the large downstairs drawing rooms to watch the reaction on t.v. It was on virtually every news channel.

They also saw that cameras were out in front of Cherry Studios, which was crowded with press and on-lookers waiting for the interview, which was still hours away.

After watching for about an hour and laughing at all the speculation by the news anchors as to who these American women were and how they had come to steal the hearts of one of the most famous musicians of all time along with his son, they all went to the dining room for luncheon. By the time they finished, it was time to leave for London as it would take forty five minutes to get there.

Susan and Michelle went up to Susan and James's rooms to freshen up, while father and son chatted over cups of tea.

"That's some ring you're wearing!" Susan exclaimed to Michelle, lifting her left hand and looking at the impressive diamond on the engagement ring Thomas had given her.

"It's beautiful, isn't it, Mom? Thomas is so generous and thoughtful...but I see you're still wearing that itty-bitty thing. I thought you told me James got you another one and was going to make you wear it."

"Well, he changed his mind. He knows how much this ring means to me, and I think it means a lot to him too. And, you know I'm not into jewelry anyway."

"Then why are you decked out in all those emeralds?"

"I wanted to make him happy. He wants to show me off and...how did he put it? He doesn't want people thinking he's a 'cheap bastard.' Pretty funny, huh?"

"Yeah, well, you look great in them. They match your eyes along with the dress."

Susan took a deep breath before pulling her daughter into her arms and hugging her tightly. "Are we doing the right thing, Michelle? Following our hearts like this?"

Michelle drew away and looked at her. "Yes, Mom. I think we are...I really and truly think we are..."

When the limo pulled up to the curb in front of Cherry Studios, the crowd had to be parted by police. There were well over a thousand people waiting that included fans of James, t.v. and newspaper reporters, magazine and tabloid reporters, cameramen and photographers.

As the doors to the limo were opened and James helped Susan out, she could feel butterflies pounding in her stomach and almost felt ill from it. James, sensing her unease, leaned in to kiss her cheek and gave a squeeze to her hand. Cameras flashed.

He'd talked softly to her on the drive, whispering words of love in her ear, ignoring the others in the back of the car. To him, only she existed. Thomas and Carrie were amused. And, Michelle had never seen her mother so happy.

Two microphones were set up at the top of the steps in front of the entrance to Cherry Studios. The engagement and wedding announcements would be made at the start of the interview, then Susan, Thomas and Michelle would go into to the studio to wait while James and his head team member would be interviewed regarding the new album. There would be a video monitor inside the studio so Susan, Thomas and Michelle could watch.

At precisely 3:00, James's stepped up to one of the microphones.

"As was announced earlier today, I've become engaged to be married as well as my son, Thomas here. Our two lovely ladies are mother and daughter who are American born. I'd like to introduce you to my new love, Susan, who I actually met many years ago at the Dusky Club in Brighton before our band became well known."

He wrapped an arm around Susan's waist and pulled her close for another kiss on the cheek. She smiled shyly as the crowd cheered and clapped.

He continued. "Our paths separated and our lives went in different directions. As you know, I married another woman named Susan and have three wonderful children from that union. This Susan also married and has two children, one of whom you see here today standing next to my son, Thomas. She has agreed to become his wife in a double wedding ceremony that will be held tomorrow on Christmas Day..."

Some of the crowd gasped, while others clapped and cheered again.

One of those who gasped was Hilary, who was impatiently and rudely worming her way through the crowd in an attempt to get to the front. What she had in her purse would certainly be a shock, not only to James and Thomas, but to the thousand people who were at the interview.

She smiled to herself thinking about what Marcus had been able to get for her from newspapers and public records back in California. This would put an end to Susan for sure and then it would only be a matter of cajoling and being tearfully sympathetic before James would fall into her bed and into her clutches.

Public records confirmed that Susan was married to a prominent attorney named Donald and that there was no record of any divorce, therefore Susan was still married and would be committing bigamy should she marry James.

But it was the newspaper clippings that were most damaging.

The first one, taken just a few weeks previous, showed Susan at a restaurant event, where she was demonstrating how to make a perfect Crème Brulee. The article included a comment regarding her husband, Donald, who was a prominent and well-known attorney.

The second article was from her wedding anniversary several months previous in August 1999, and was on the social page due to Donald's connection with his many wealthy clients. There was a picture of him and Susan in an intimate embrace with a quote from Donald saying how much he was in love with his beautiful wife even after twenty-nine years. There was another photo of the family, including Michelle and her brother, Steven, all smiling broadly.

Then there was another recent clipping from September 1999 of Donald and Susan at the airport where Susan was quoted as saying that Donald was the most thoughtful and romantic husband, taking her on a trip to Europe after winning an important case. She further stated that vacations with Donald were like honeymoons.

Although Marcus had dug up more information, Hilary figured this would be more than enough to destroy Susan and her snot-nosed daughter.

When she realized she wasn't having a lot of success pushing through the crowd, she turned to the man next to her, who she knew was a reporter for one of the most infamous tabloids in England. Flashing him a devastating smile and then showing him the articles and explaining she needed to get to the front quickly, he expertly pulled her through. But, just as she reached the front, James kissed Susan full on the lips and she, Thomas and Michelle disappeared through the doors of Cherry Studios. James's lead team member stepped up to the microphone to begin the interview for the new album.

Hilary, who was now standing directly in front of James, yelled, "Wait!!! How can you marry that woman when she's already married!!??"

The crowd around her was taken aback and quieted. James looked at her in disgust and his security people moved in to silence her. But, the reporter from the tabloid held onto her arm and shouted, "It's true!! It's true!!! The woman *is* married!! We have the proof!"

As word spread, everyone began to mumble and the sound was overwhelming, looks of shock on the faces of many. James face mottled in anger.

"Get that bitch out of here," he whispered to his closest security person.

Security moved in on both Hilary and the tabloid reporter.

"Wait!!!" they both screamed at the same time.

Hilary shoved the copies of public records and the newspaper clippings into the hands of the security person who was attempting to drag her away. "Just give these to him!!!" she pleaded. "I'm not lying!!!"

Reluctantly, James nodded his head and was handed the items. Looking down at the proof of Susan's marriage certificate didn't faze him. He knew she'd been married, but was now divorced.

It was the newspaper clippings, however, that made his face drain of all color. As he shuffled through them, looked at the photos and read parts of what they said, his hands tightened into fists, crumpling the papers between them. Without a word, he turned and stormed through the doors of the studio in pursuit of Susan.

While all this was taking place outside, Susan, Thomas and Michelle were ushered into an office off the main lobby of the studio where a t.v. was turned on so they could all listen to James's interview.

Both Susan and Michelle were glowing, knowing they'd made a favorable impression on the crowd, including all the t.v. people and reporters and they were basking in the love of their two men.

Until Michelle looked at the t.v. screen and saw Hilary at the front of the crowd, directly in front of James She was trying to hand him some papers and yelling "Wait!" as James's security people moved in on her.

Susan accepted a cup of tea from one of James's team members and settled herself on the sofa. When she noticed the startled expression on Michelle's face, she turned towards the t.v. screen and gasped, dropping the cup from her hand. The cup hit the coffee table in front of her and broke, the contents of the cup splashing all over the table and carpet. She stood back up, covering her mouth with her hand.

It was Hilary...Susan recognized her immediately. The woman who had sent the letter and photo to James...and the one who was destined to become James's second wife.

But...no, no, no!!! This couldn't be happening!!! James was going to marry *her*!!! She was going to change history! She and James were meant to be together! She would make him happy! If Hilary came into his life, it would be a disaster!

"Oh my god, Mom!!! It's that woman I kept meaning to tell you about! Thomas and I met her at the hotel in Brighton. She was trying to track down James!!"

Thomas's face paled too and he came over to grasp Michelle's hand as he heard Hilary scream that Susan was married.

They all watched as James took the papers Hilary had given to one of his security people and looked down at them. Then they saw him crush the papers in his hands before turning towards the door and pushing into the studio lobby. A moment later, the door to the office crashed open, James glaring at Susan with a look of rage and disbelief on his face.

As he advanced towards her, Michelle stepped in front of him. "It's not true!!" she shouted. "It's not true!!"

James wouldn't even look at her, shoving her to the side where she stumbled helplessly into Thomas.

He moved swiftly around the side of the couch, stopping only inches away from Susan and thrust the newspaper clippings and copy of her marriage license into her trembling hands. She looked down at them, swallowing as she looked through them before dropping them to the floor. When she looked back up at him, he could see the truth in her eyes and knew that, *unbelievably*, once again, she had lied to him and deceived him.

He started to grab her shoulders, but stopped himself, knowing he was too enraged and that he might do physical violence.

"Is it true or not, Susan?" he spit out between clenched teeth.

When she didn't respond, all color draining from her face, he tried to get a response from her again.

"Tell me, damn you!!!" he screamed. "Is it true!!!? Are you still married!!?"

His voice reverberated off the walls. Susan put her hands up over her face. How could things have been so wonderful one moment and turn into a nightmare the next!? She trembled in fear, waiting for James to take her by the throat and throttle her.

His eyes were on fire and his face was flushed; his voice turned low and cold. Her lack of response gave him her answer just as it had in the hotel room in London all those years ago.

"You need to get out of my life, Susan...get out of my sight and out of my life. Forever! You're nothing but lies and more lies. Why I believed you again, I don't know...I wanted to believe you...I wanted so badly to be with you again..."

And, suddenly, it was as if all the rage swept out of him. His face crumpled into a mask of pain and anguish and he began to sob, not taking his eyes from Susan's.

"How could you do this to me, Susan..." he choked out. "How *could* you?!!!"

Michelle and Thomas were struck numb, their feet frozen to the floor, until Michelle turned into Thomas's arms and began to cry. Not knowing what the papers were about or what they said, he held her tight, rubbing her back and whispering in her ear that everything was going to be okay...that there must be some kind of misunderstanding.

She pushed away from him, first looking down at the floor then back up at his face and took a deep breath.

"There's no misunderstanding, Thomas...My mom is still married to my dad...we've both lied to you...we thought...we thought we could change history...we..."

She looked back down at the floor, unable to say anything else and doing her best not to start crying again. Thomas's hands dropped limply to his sides, a stunned and confused expression on his face, but he said nothing. Both looked over towards James and Susan.

Susan's gaze turned away from James's penetrating one. She knew he wanted her to deny everything, to tell him the newspaper articles were all fake, that they'd been manufactured by one of his crazy fans... that she wasn't still married...

But he'd overheard Michelle's words to Thomas and as the words sunk into his brain, a despair like no other wrenched his heart.

Susan was too broken for tears. On the brink of happiness, she'd been defeated and all her hopes and dreams for the future had been destroyed.

She took several steps back from James then reached up behind her neck and unlatched the emerald necklace. She removed the matching bracelet next and set both of them on the coffee table next to pieces of the broken cup. She reached up to remove the earrings, but then saw the engagement ring on her finger...the *little sparkler*... and she thought she would perish right then and there from the pain she was feeling in her heart.

James's eyes followed hers as she slowly pulled it off her finger and looked up into his face. She held out her hand to him and he held out his, palm up. Carefully, with tears now running silently down her face, she placed it in his palm before closing his fingers around it.

She looked over at Michelle.

"We need to go now," she whispered in a shaking voice.

"No!" exclaimed Thomas, grabbing Michelle's arm as she started to walk towards her mother. "I don't want you to leave! I'm sure this can all be worked out somehow!"

But Michelle just shook her head at him, before breaking from his grip, walking over to the couch and picking up her purse. Susan came to stand next to her and Michelle nodded, removing her mobile phone from her purse.

Michelle looked back at Thomas, her heart over-flowing with love for him and felt a crushing pain in her chest. She didn't want to leave him. But, the only way her mom could now return to the present would be if she took her back with her mobile phone since Susan had left hers at the cottage. They would have to return together. Before she gave herself a chance to change her mind, she accessed the "Return" App on her phone.

"I love you, Thomas..." she whispered.

And, a moment later, before either James or Thomas could react, Susan and Michelle burst into thousands of fragments of light, just like sparkling confetti, and floated upward, outward and away.

Chapter 34

Return to the Future

Susan and Michelle came back together on the floor of Susan's library in her mountain home, the same place they'd left from three weeks previously. Susan, having time-travelled before, materialized first with Michelle following a minute later.

Thoughts of what had just occurred in the past swept over Susan and her face crumpled in anguish. She drew her knees up to her chest, tilting her head forward and began rocking back and forth as if she were a demented person.

Michelle came out of her daze, sat up and looked over at her mother before casting her eyes about the room. Realizing they were back in the future, a pained look came over her face too and she had to choke back a sob when she saw Thomas's engagement ring still on her finger.

She scooted over and wrapped her arms around her mom.

"Oh my God! Oh my God! What have we done!? What have we done!!?"

Her own tears came then, along with those of her mother. They stayed together for a full five minutes, each of them thinking their own tormented thoughts before Michelle finally released her hold, scooted back and stood up. She held her hand out to her mother, her head clearing and forced her attorney brain into focus. She knew if she didn't get her wits together, she'd end up a pile of mush, just like her mother. She also knew that her mother needed her more than ever now. After all, this had all been her idea...to take her mom into the past to give James back the engagement ring.

And, at least he *did* have the ring back now. Looking at her mom, however, she saw that she was still wearing the emerald earrings. Damn! What did that mean? Why did something else from the past have to come back with her to remind her of all that had happened there?

And, she thought, it was the same for her. She had come back with Thomas's engagement ring.

Were they both now doomed to never forget? To pine after the men they truly loved? Was it the price they would have to pay for daring to try and change history?

Just then, Michelle's mobile phone rang. When she looked at caller ID, she saw that it was her dad. She also saw that she'd missed over twenty calls from him.

"Hi, Dad!" she said as cheerfully as possible and as if nothing was untoward. "Mom and I just got back from our trip! Yes...we ended up going on a cruise...But before you start complaining about us not calling you, I have to tell you that Mom accidentally dropped her mobile phone overboard our first night out of port, and I forgot my battery charger...then the Internet Café lost its signal, and...yes, yes...I know you were worried, but we're back now, and...and, we had a great time. Only got off the ship once in Perth..."

Susan knew that Michelle was babbling away to give her time to collect herself. When she finally handed her the phone, she still felt shaken, but composed, steeling herself into a block of ice. In a stilting voice, she apologized to Donald for her past behavior and said she and Michelle had done a lot of talking on the cruise. Before she had a chance to change her mind, she asked if he might come home that night to talk and they could be together instead of him staying downtown at the condo. He agreed, telling her how much he missed her and how much he loved her. Waves of guilt washed over her at his words, but she knew deep inside that once again, no matter how badly she wished for it, that history could not be changed, and that she would have to get her life back on track and find happiness in what she had. Somehow, some way, she'd have to try and numb herself against thoughts and memories of James.

It would be hard, but she knew if she didn't make the effort, she would drown in grief and despair, and that it wouldn't be fair to the man she'd been married to for 45 years. Like it or not, this time, James was gone from her life forever.

When Susan looked over at Michelle, she saw her lips tremble as she removed Thomas's engagement ring from her finger and looked down at it. More guilt overcame her as she realized that her daughter was now feeling the same grief and torment that she herself had felt each time she had to come back to the future after being with James.

She sighed. Thomas and Michelle would have made such a marvelous couple. They complimented each other so well...and had been so deeply in love... She wondered if Michelle would ever find true love again as she had with James's handsome and talented son. She didn't think she would...

Susan walked down into the great room with Michelle following her. She was doing her best to be strong for her daughter, just as her daughter had been strong for her.

"Feel like a glass of wine?"

Michelle nodded. "Yeah, Mom...I could really use one right about now...maybe even a whole bottle..."

The sparks emitted as Susan and Michelle were transported back to the future blinded both James and Thomas, and just as it had been for James on previous occasions when Susan vanished, they were both left confused and disoriented.

James sat down on the couch and Thomas joined him. When there was a discreet knock on the door and James's lead team person asked if he'd be coming back out to resume the interview, he told him to cancel it and explain to the crowd that Susan had suddenly taken ill.

As the door closed, he lowered his face into his hands and began to sob again. Just saying the name, "Susan," wrenched his heart and he found it hard to breathe, let alone speak.

Thomas laid his hand on his dad's back.

"What just happened, Dad? I feel in shock..."

But James continued to sob, loud, painful sobs that shook his whole body. He picked up the crumpled newspaper clippings off the floor that were now stained with Susan's spilled tea and handed them to Thomas.

As Thomas read them, his eyes opened wide in disbelief. Looking over at his dad, he raised his eyebrows. "Is this all true? How could this be true!? Are you sure this isn't all fabricated? That woman...that blonde who gave you these...she's been trying to track you down... maybe she had these made up..."

"I heard Michelle tell you that her mother was still married to her dad."

Thomas thought for a moment. There had been such chaos going on at the time, it had virtually slipped his mind. Her words now struck him like a thunderbolt.

James looked over at his son. "If it weren't true, Susan would have denied it. She would have fought me on it...she would have tried to convince me, prove to me that it was all lies..." He hung his head.

"She didn't..."

He opened the palm of his hand, realizing he was still holding the engagement ring, the one he called the *little sparkler*. Fresh tears came into his eyes as he gazed at it.

"She lied to me and deceived me again...and she promised me... she *promised* me, Thomas!!! She swore she would *never* lie to me again!!!"

Thomas was at a loss for words. "I don't know what to say, Dad. This all seems too unbelievable. Where did Susan and Michelle go? What happened to them? It's as if they vanished into thin air!"

James didn't respond. He stood up and walked over to the window. When he peeked out, he could see the crowd disbursing. Turning around, he looked at Thomas.

"That's what Susan tends to do," he whispered miserably. "She breaks my heart and vanishes...it's what she's always done..."

Staring down at his open palm once more, he vowed that if he ever saw Susan again, she would pay dearly for what she'd done to him.

And, he meant it...

Epilogue

For all outward appearances, Michelle seemed to have recovered quickly after her journey into the past, returning to her job as an attorney for women's rights, discrimination and abuse, with an unrelenting zeal. She worked many twenty hour days and bought her dad's condo downtown near the office she shared with him.

Externally, she displayed a steel persona, but inwardly, she was something entirely different. When at work, and especially in the courtroom, she displayed a flair and determination that couldn't be matched by any of her contemporaries, and successfully won case after case. In public, she was aloof and businesslike, never sharing anything personal about herself.

Upon her return, she immediately contacted her fishy-eyed fiancé, Thomas, and informed him that the wedding was off, that she had no desire to marry him or anyone for that matter, that she preferred to stay single and concentrate on her career. Other than her mother, Susan, none of her friends or family could understand why she would choose such a lonely existence.

When she was alone, most often late at night in her condo after a grueling day at the office or in court, she would sit or stand quietly in front of the floor to ceiling windows of her living room on the fourteenth floor and look out onto the lights of the city. She could see planes coming in to land at the airport and as each one landed, she wondered where they had come from, often making up dreams like her mom used to do.

She imagined Thomas flying in from London, hunting her down, a look of love on his face as he found her again. He would take her in his arms and kiss her passionately and she would wrap her arms around his neck and pull him in closer.

She would take him home to her condo, where she would make yeast rolls shaped into knots for him, and then they would enjoy a candlelight dinner with wine...and they would toast to finding each other again.

Then he would look at her with those blue eyes of his, the gold in them turning into tiny flames as he led her into the bedroom for a night of love making.

But her thoughts of him were just dreams...and she discovered that it was painful to dream of what she would never have...

Michelle walked away from the window, a glass of wine in hand and set it on top of the baby grand piano she'd recently bought. She sat down on the bench and opened up the music on the stand above the piano keys. It was the *"Nature's Concerto"* that James had written for his son, Thomas.

She laid her hands on the keyboard and began to play, every now and then glancing tearfully at the diamond engagement ring that she kept on top of the piano in a glass dish...

It took time, but Susan resigned herself to fate, knowing she would never be with James again, that what she had done to him this time was the end. How it had happened made her angry, especially knowing what Hilary would end up doing to him, but she did her best to put him out of her mind, throwing herself into other activities, just like Michelle threw herself into her work.

She took daily walks, sometimes long hikes, in the mountains where she lived. She took ballet classes again, even though getting back up on pointe was a challenge. She took art classes and volunteered at a local school to help children read better. She even took cooking classes, anything and everything that would occupy her time and her mind.

She also took up writing again, which was something she had always wanted to do and which she'd started on a few weeks before going on the journey with Michelle into the past. Deciding to document her time-travel adventures, she eventually published four books, which were devoured by fans of James, thinking of course, they were very creative fiction. Susan, Michelle, and her friends who had gone back in time with her, however, knew the truth. Susan figured that James, as famous and out of reach as he was, would never find out about them. Writing them, however, was sometimes painful, but it also gave her a sense of peace to get it off her chest.

Susan reconciled with Donald, and three months later, he retired, finishing up the cases he'd been working on, to spend time with Susan and ensure that she would never be lonely or depressed again. She was grateful and appreciative, and kept telling herself repeatedly how fortunate and lucky she was.

But, despite her efforts to put James out of her mind, there was no forgetting him, and she knew that was the way it would always be...

Robert was stunned when he heard the news on t.v. about Susan and the cancelled wedding, and even more shocked when their dad began seeing Hilary. Having met her, he was disgusted and extremely disappointed that James would take up with someone so fake. There was no comparing her to Susan. He had really liked her and had a hard time believing what the newspapers, magazines and especially the tabloids were printing about her. He sincerely believed that the conniving slut who'd come into his restaurant with the old gent and demanding meat, was behind a conspiracy to discredit and get rid of Susan so she could move in for his dad's money. He asked that his dad not bring her to Le Fonda, and he refused to go to any family function when he knew she would be there.

Robert's one restaurant expanded into another the next year, and before long, there were a chain of gourmet, vegetarian restaurants all over England. He was even considering opening several in America. He ended up marrying Meredith, the girl who worked for him and who had also done cooking for Thomas before Michelle came along.

She later became a chef herself and they often traveled between their restaurants, adding new vegetarian items to the menus at each one.

When Carrie heard the news, she immediately called Thomas to find out what happened, and when he told her, she was in total disbelief. She tried to call and talk to her dad, but he asked to be left alone for a few days and she respected his wishes. When she finally did meet with him, it was at a new flat he decided to rent in London to be closer to Cherry Studios. She knew, however, that just as the Colorado retreat had become painful to him because her mother died there, his house outside of London had also become a raw memory of the short time he spent there with Susan. After ensuring that her dad would be okay, she left for another adventure, this time meeting her friend, David, in South America where they explored abandoned villages of ancient Inca and Aztec tribes.

Carrie never married, preferring the freedom of a being single woman. Over the years, she collected and donated numerous items of antiquity to museums around the world as well as creating her own works, which were much admired and made a name for her.

After the shock of having Michelle vanish on him, Thomas went into a decline, cancelling his performances with the Philharmonic for the next several months. Back at his flat, he paced and sat in despair at the piano, thinking of Michelle, not comprehending what had happened or *how* it could even have happened.

And as he paced, all he could see was her...in his kitchen, where there was still some green butter left in the fridge, in his living room sitting on the couch watching movies and playing "footsie" with him, at the dining table in the candlelight, but most painful of all, in his bed where he could still smell the scent of her on her pillow.

Feeling unsettled, he got up one morning a week after the interview disaster, got in his Audi and started driving. He didn't have plans to drive anywhere in particular, but several hours later, he found himself driving into Little Dippington then out to Auntie Annabelle's cottage. Knowing where the key was, he let himself in and shivered at the cold. He turned on the heating system and lit a fire in the fireplace before sitting down on the couch and staring into the flames.

All he could think about was Michelle, her aquamarine eyes, her tinkling laugh and sultry voice, her intelligence and wit...but most of all, the passion they had shared together. He winced at the painful memory.

Thomas stayed at the cottage for almost a week and on his last day there as he pulled the last clean towel out from under the bathroom sink, an object resembling a mobile phone fell out onto the floor. Picking it up, he stared at it curiously. It certainly looked like a phone, but he'd never seen anything like it before. When he touched the screen with his fingers, it lit up. There was a message on the bottom that said, "slide to unlock." When he slid his finger across the screen, a number pad appeared with words on the top that said, "Enter Passcode." Not knowing any passcode or even if the device really was a mobile phone, he just stared at it a minute before the screen went dark again. He took it out into the main room and set it on the end table, meaning to look at it after taking a shower, but then forgot about it until he was ready to leave the next morning. Spying the mysterious object again, he slipped it into his coat pocket, thinking to show it to his dad later, but he never did. He later packed it away in a box along with Michelle's personal items that she'd left behind and pushed the box to the back of his bedroom closet.

Two years later, Thomas married the daughter of one of the wealthy patrons of the London Philharmonic, but their marriage only lasted a year. Thomas was distracted with his music and career, and truth be told, he still hadn't forgotten Michelle.

In fact, whenever he performed the *"Nature's Concerto,"* that his dad had written for him, he thought of her. As he bowed to the audience at the beginning and end of each performance, it seemed as if her sultry, sea green eyes were looking at him, but no matter how many times he combed the audience, hoping for a glimpse of the American girl he had once loved so fiercely, he never saw her.

James was never able to forget Susan or put her out of his mind. For weeks after she left, he continued to yearn for her, despite what she'd done to him again. Although the sense of rage still overcame him from time to time, causing him to curse at people for no valid reason or throw objects at a wall, deep inside, the love he felt for her just wouldn't go away.

Hilary, however, determined to win him over and sooth the pain of his loss, was relentless in her pursuit, sending him letter after letter, in which she begged his forgiveness for exposing Susan and saying she would do *anything* to help him through *this most heart-breaking time.* She was eventually able to worm his mobile number from one of his team members, and then the daily phone calls began.

One night, after numerous glasses of wine, when James was drowning in thoughts of Susan, he called Hilary and begged her to come be with him, and when she arrived, he immediately took her into his bed without even saying "Hello" as she came through the door.

As he made love to her, he tried to pretend it was Susan, but it didn't work. Her touch wasn't as gentle; her kisses weren't as sweet. Her body, although fabulously proportioned and desirable, wasn't soft and welcoming like Susan's. As he took her, he almost felt as if he were in a brothel instead of his own bed, and even though she worked diligently on him, he was unable to perform a second time. He sent her home.

Hilary continued to pursue him, however, and James eventually gave in to her machinations. When she told him she was pregnant, he knew he had to marry her, which he did a few weeks later in a very elaborate and public way at a castle in France.

The marriage, however, didn't last long as Hilary's greed and obsession with living the high life began to disgust James. She was also rude and demanding to his household staff, most of them resigning not long after the marriage.

Hilary miscarried their first child, and truth be known, she was rather glad of it, not really knowing if it was James's or not, but she later gave birth to a girl that James insisted on naming "Sherry," after his mother. After the divorce, James filed for full custody of Sherry, and she became his new reason for going on.

He threw himself into his music once more, this time scheduling concert tours around the world where his popularity continued to grow to vast proportions. Millions of fans crowded into stadiums and arenas to see him, every performance sold out.

And, just like Thomas did at the end of a performance at the Philharmonic, James would look out at the sea of faces, wondering if Susan might be out there...still wanting him...and still needing him... as much as he still wanted and needed her.

Despite her deceit...

Despite everything...

Excerpt from "The Necklace V – Strawberries & Wine"

Part I – August 2016 – December 2016

Chapter 1 – The Mysterious Mobile Phone

It was August 2016, and Thomas, age 43, was clearing out boxes from his London flat in preparation for a move to Los Angeles, California. He'd been offered a position with the Los Angeles Symphony, where he would have the opportunity to share the role of conductor as well as maintain a position as concert pianist. It was a prospect he couldn't turn down and, to be honest, he was anxious to move to a sunnier climate.

Although he'd grown up in England and his father, sister and brother lived there, he was ready for a change in his life. His failed marriage haunted him. The London fog and rain depressed him, and the sameness of his position with the London Philharmonic bored him. He was given very little freedom to perform his own works and the politics had become intolerable.

There was one box left at the back of his closet when he heard his mobile phone ring out in the living room. He brushed the dust off his hands and went to answer it. It was his sister, Carrie.

"All packed up yet, Thomas? I'd offer to come help you, but I'm hands deep in clay. I'm almost done with the bust of Adonis...finally!"

"Haven't you been working on that for over a year now? And, no, I'm not all quite packed up yet. I had a few boxes left in my bedroom closet that I've been going through. Most of everything else, though, has been sent ahead to my flat in L.A."

"Won't you be sad to leave England? You know I'm going to miss you."

"Come on now, Carrie, you won't miss me. We hardly ever see each other with your gallivanting all about the globe."

"We see each other at Christmas when Dad's in town, and we had dinner at Robert's restaurant just last month. Plus, since my travelling companion, David, got married, I haven't been doing much exploring. No fun to go by myself."

"Still, I've only seen you two or three times in the past few months. No, I'm not sad to leave England. I'm ready for a change in my life. I need to brush all of the cobwebs off me, plus I'm ready for some California sunshine."

"Dad is going to miss you. I think he's rather enjoyed working with you on a few classical pieces for piano. It's diverted him from that awful marriage to Hilary. God, Robert! I'm so glad that woman is out of his life. What a disaster she was!"

"Not only a disaster but she took nearly half his fortune, especially when Dad insisted on having full custody of Sherry."

"Well, he *wanted* full custody of Sherry, but the witch only gave him 80%. I think he would have given his entire fortune to her if he could have got full custody."

"Probably, but it would have made her look bad...you know, a mother who gave up all contact with her child...and you remember how she loves the limelight."

"Yeah, horrible, hideous woman." Carrie shivered on the other end of the phone. "Dad said he's really enjoyed spending time with you when he's been in London. Like I just said, I know for sure he's going to miss you."

"Well, now that he's married again, he won't be missing me or any of us very much. He seems to be quite happy. I told him to bring Sherry on over to the states and stay with me in L.A. for a bit. He's talking about recording another new album before he goes back out on tour, and said he might even record it in L.A. You should come too. We could all take Sherry to Disneyland."

"Hmmmm...let me think on it, okay? Sounds like fun."

"Well, don't think too hard. Talk to Dad about it and let me know. I'll call you as soon as I'm settled in."

"Okay then, Tom-tom; I'll talk to you later." She giggled.

"Don't call me that!"

Carrie laughed again. "No promises, Thomas. Bye."

They disconnected, and Thomas went back to his closet for the one last box. It was way in the back and had been there for years. He knew what was in it, and for a few moments after pulling it out, he just stared at it, beginning to feel melancholy.

It was a box containing some clothing and personal items that had once belonged to a young woman named Michelle, the woman who had been his first true love, a love he'd never been able to forget. Just thinking about her and picturing her in his mind, brought sadness to his heart. He sighed heavily as he sat down on the floor next to the box, lifted the lid and looked inside.

The scent of a sweet perfume wafted up from the contents, and Thomas closed his eyes picturing a blonde girl with aquamarine eyes looking at him with a wistful look on her face. He blinked his eyes open and began lifting items from the box...a couple of dresses, blouses, jeans, intimate apparel, cosmetics, and a bottle of perfume that he'd bought for her. He wasn't sure what had made him pack her things away after she left, but here they were, and the longer he sifted them through his hands, the clearer the memories of the girl he'd once loved so passionately came flooding into his head.

Ahhh...lovely, feisty, intelligent and passionate Michelle...the woman he thought he would spend his life with...the one who was supposed to marry him in a double wedding ceremony with her mother and his dad on Christmas Day in 1999.

Was it really almost 17 years ago? It didn't seem that long. Seeing, smelling and touching her things made it seem just like yesterday.

He dug deeper into the box, removing a few more items of clothing before coming across another object at the bottom. It looked like a mobile phone, and as he examined it more closely, he realized that it must be the object he'd discovered out at Auntie Annabelle's cottage shortly after Michelle and her mum vanished into thin air on that disastrous Christmas Eve Day, the day before he would have made

Michelle his bride. At the time, he wasn't sure what it really was, never having seen a mobile phone of that type before.

He noticed that the phone had the image of an apple on the back of it and found that to be very curious, as Apple phones didn't exist back in 1999 when he'd found it at the cottage. Amazingly, it appeared to be an Apple iPhone, but it didn't quite resemble his own mobile phone, which was a Samsung.

He turned it over in his hands a few times and tapped on the screen, but nothing happened. He wondered how it had come to be in the cottage in the first place and who might have placed it in the bathroom cabinet wrapped in a towel. No answers came to mind, making him even more intrigued.

Deciding it was a mystery that needed to be solved, he stood up and put it in the backpack he planned on taking on the plane to Los Angeles. He had a techie friend who worked for Apple in L.A and thought he'd show it to him. Brett would certainly be able to tell him what it was.

He glanced back at the box of Michelle's things and sighed again as her vision passed through his head and heart. Sitting back down on the floor next to the box, he lifted one of her dresses up to his face and breathed in the scent.

Knowing she was from Southern California, would it be possible to find her once he moved there?

Dare he even try?

Readers…please send me your feedback either on my website or on my Facebook page or by sending me an e-mail.

https://www.LindaSRice.com

https://www.facebook.com/TheNecklaceLindaSice

LindainMtLaguna@aol.com

And…Please write an Amazon review and a Goodreads review! Please and thank you!